OXFORD WORLD'S CLAS

THE MONK ✎ P9-CQO-066

MATTHEW GREGORY LEWIS was born in London in 1775, the first of the four children of Frances Maria and Matthew Lewis. When he was 6 his mother left his father. Lewis was devoted to his mother, and later helped support her financially, writing his first plays for her benefit. In 1792 he spent six months in Weimar, learning German and reading and translating German literature, especially the works of the *Sturm-und-Drang* writers. This was to be an important influence on his later work.

Lewis's father, a high-ranking official in the War Office, hoped for a career in diplomacy for his son, but Matthew, plagued by ennui whilst working in the British Embassy in The Hague, started a prolific career as a writer by composing *The Monk* in ten weeks, at the age of 19. On publication in 1796 it became an extremely popular—and vilified—work, and Lewis, thereafter a literary celebrity, became known as 'Monk' Lewis. In 1798, after a law suit, he was forced to produce a censored version of the work.

Lewis wrote no more novels. The majority of his work between 1796 and 1812 consists of plays, mainly spectacular melodramas and comedies, many of which proved extremely successful. He also produced some volumes of poetry, and was well respected as a poet.

After his father's death in 1812, and his inheritance of a large fortune, Lewis produced no more plays. Instead he toured the Continent, staying with Byron and the Shelleys on the way, and visited the plantations in the West Indies that he had inherited, in order to improve the lot of the slaves.

Lewis is constantly referred to as a lovable man; 'a jewel of a man' even, though according to Byron, argumentative and 'a damned bore'. Likewise, Walter Scott musing on Lewis in 1825 wrote 'How few friends one has whose faults are only ridiculous'. In 1818, returning from the West Indies, Lewis died of yellow fever.

EMMA MCEVOY is a lecturer in the Department of English, Goldsmiths, University of London.

OXFORD WORLD'S CLASSICS

*For almost 100 years Oxford World's Classics have brought
readers closer to the world's great literature. Now with over 700
titles—from the 4,000-year-old myths of Mesopotamia to the
twentieth century's greatest novels—the series makes available
celebrated as well as lesser-known writing.*

*The pocket-sized hardbacks of the early years contained
introductions by Virginia Woolf, T. S. Eliot, Graham Greene,
and other literary figures that enriched the experience of reading.
Today the series is recognized for its fine scholarship and
reliability in texts that span world literature, drama and poetry,
religion, philosophy and politics. Each edition includes perceptive
commentary and essential background information to meet the
changing needs of readers.*

OXFORD WORLD'S CLASSICS

MATTHEW LEWIS

The Monk

Edited by
HOWARD ANDERSON

With an Introduction and Notes by
EMMA McEVOY

Oxford   New York
OXFORD UNIVERSITY PRESS

Oxford University Press, Great Clarendon Street, Oxford OX2 6DP

Oxford New York

Athens Auckland Bangkok Bogota Bombay Buenos Aires
Calcutta Cape Town Dar es Salaam Delhi Florence Hong Kong Istanbul
Karachi Kuala Lumpur Madras Madrid Melbourne Mexico City
Nairobi Paris Singapore Taipei Tokyo Toronto Warsaw

and associated companies in
Berlin Ibadan

Oxford is a trade mark of Oxford University Press

Introduction, Bibliography, Chronology,
Notes © Emma McEvoy 1995

First published as a World's Classics paperback 1980
Reissued as an Oxford World's Classics paperback 1998

British Library Cataloguing in Publication Data
Data available

Library of Congress Cataloging in Publication Data
Data available
ISBN 0-19-283394-4

1 3 5 7 9 10 8 6 4 2

Printed in Great Britain by
Caledonian International Book Manufacturing Ltd.
Glasgow

CONTENTS

ACKNOWLEDGEMENTS

To Mrs Anne Ehrenpries I owe the suggestion that first led me to the manuscript of *The Monk*. Mr W. L. Hanchant of the Wisbech and Fenland Museum was unfailingly generous in making the manuscript available for my study in Wisbech and in allowing me to obtain a copy for use in preparing this edition. Aid from Indiana University and from Michigan State University helped to make my work possible. I am indebted to the Librarian of Harvard University, to Mr William Cagle of the Lilly Library at Indiana University, and to Professor William Todd for providing copies of the early editions of the novel. Professor Ronald Gottesman gave me advice on every aspect of the preparation of my text, and Mrs Susan Gaylord, Miss Lorraine Hart, Mr Robert Ouellette, Mr Robert Reno, and Mr David Wright are all to be thanked for their help in carrying it out. Finally I want to acknowledge the initial encouragement of the late Professor Herbert Davis, to whose memory I dedicate the work I have done on this volume.

HOWARD ANDERSON

I should like to thank Julie Cooper, Robert Lee, and my father for many interesting conversations on *The Monk*, which produced some useful ideas and suggestions. I am indebted to Karen Tiedtke, Robert Lee, my father, and Malcolm Upham for their help in researching the notes, to Robert, Julie, my mother, Dan, Ayesha, Rusty, and Ted for proof-reading, and to Richard Haslam for information on surrealism and *The Monk*. I should also particularly like to thank Karen Tiedtke for the translations from Lewis's German sources in the Explanatory Notes.

EMMA McEVOY

INTRODUCTION

WHEN Matthew Lewis's *The Monk: A Romance* appeared in 1796, it was greeted by a variety of critical opinions. 'Lust, murder, incest, and every atrocity that can disgrace human nature, brought together, without the apology of probability, or even possibility, for their introduction',[1] read the review in *The British Critic*, in a manner which unfortunately resembled the lurid advertising found at the beginning of the extra-salacious abridged editions of the work in circulating libraries. Coleridge, writing for the *Critical Review*, declared it to be 'a romance, which if a parent saw in the hands of a son or daughter, he might reasonably turn pale'.[2] He also called it blasphemous—a charge which signalled the start of much trouble for Lewis. On the other hand, the *Monthly Mirror* reckoned not to remember 'to have read a more interesting production'[3]—praise which it was to increase in an attempt to defend the novel two years later.

The battleground on which most of the controversy about *The Monk* arose was the issue of its morality. A novel had not only to please, but also to instruct, and it should instruct in the ways of virtue rather than vice. An issue of a journal entitled *The Flapper* provides a nice illustration of these more conservative demands. The novel form was still young and not highly respected, and its latest development in what we now call the Gothic novel was the cause of much alarm for more serious educationalists and moralists within the tradition of rationalism. It takes the form of a letter from a newly reformed, anonymous (or rather pseudonymous, for he calls himself 'Aurelius') novel-addict who

---

[1] *The British Critic*, 7 (1796), 677.
[2] *Critical Review*, 19 (1796), 194–200: 197.
[3] *Monthly Mirror*, 2 (1796), 98.

had been reduced to 'inert imbecility'[4] by his habit. Aurelius now, however, is able to partake of the occasional novel without fear and has set out to perform an act of public duty to the novel-readers of Ireland by warning them about *The Monk*. He refers to its 'scenes of the most wanton and immodest nature, described in terms scarcely decent' (p. 4) and declares that, as the temptations Ambrosio faces are practically irresistible, the novel may have no moral, an opinion which redounds unfortunately upon Aurelius.

Most of the adverse criticism was aimed at the novel's lewdness and blasphemy. Exception was taken to a certain passage in volume ii, chapter IV, where we are told of Elvira's censoring of her daughter's Bible; she omits the 'improper' passages lest they encourage the wrong ideas in Antonia's breast (p. 259). The 'lewd exploits' and 'lascivious jokes' of various romances, it is declared, are less provocative than the Bible. What might seem strangest to a modern reader is that the tongue-in-cheek tone of this passage is overlooked. It pokes fun at sacred cows, and makes deliberately outrageous comparisons which mock the pious tones of Elvira, and the pomposities of overseers of education, prurient matrons, and critics who express horror at the decadence of romances. However, in the eyes of many, the passage was a statement from an irreligious Lewis, a serious case of blasphemy.

The more conservative critics increased their cries against Lewis. For them, *The Monk* threatened to corrupt youth because of its supposed irreligion, which they associated with a dangerous revolutionary spirit. Thus, the *European Magazine* of 1797 suggests that it was Lewis's intention to attack religious orders and religion itself, comparing *The Monk* to the anti-religious publications which appeared in France before the Revolution, and declaring it to have

[4] *The Flapper*, 1/4 (17 Sept. 1796), 3–4: 3.

'neither *originality, morals* nor *probability* to recommend it'.[5] In the revised fifth edition of *The Pursuits of Literature,* a well-known satirical work remarkable for its sustained spleen, the alarmist author, T. J. Mathias, appealed to fears of growing irreligion and democratic tendencies raised by the French Revolution, asking, 'Is this a time to poison the water of our land in their springs and fountains?'[6] It is strange how easily the supposed assault against traditional morality is declared to have been inspired by the French Revolution. But, for Mathias, literature is capable of overthrowing the state.[7] One of the main grievances expressed by Coleridge in his piece for the *Critical Review* is that Lewis signed the second edition (the first appeared anonymously) 'M. G. LEWIS, Esq. M.P.'. He announces that we must 'stare and tremble'[8] at the fact that a 'LEGISLATOR' has brought forward such a work. For his part, Mathias suggests that the Bible passage is '*indictable* at Common Law' (p. 239), and calls for the prosecution of Lewis. Although contemporary accounts do not make clear how far the proceedings went, it is known that Lewis was taken to court, with the result that he had to pledge to recall existing copies of the third edition and alter and delete certain passages for the fourth. In the censored edition there are no mentions of sexual activity, no 'on-stage' seductions or murder attempts, and gone are the descriptions of unclothed female bodies. All the musings on physical pleasure and the physical differences between the sexes have disappeared, and the climactic crypt scene is omitted, as are all mentions of such provocative words as 'lust', 'incontinence', and 'enjoyment'.

So much for the critics, whose behaviour Lewis had already predicted in volume ii, chapter II, when Raymond discusses the attempts 'made by partial and ill-humoured

---

[5] *European Magazine,* 31 (1797), 111–15: 111.
[6] T. J. Mathias, *The Pursuits of Literature,* 5th edn. (London: T. Becket, 1798).
[7] *Ibid.* 194.   [8] *Critical Review,* 198.

Criticism' at 'stigmatizing the Author' (p. 199). It is not that the 1790s was a homogeneously conservative decade, but rather that the frightened conservatives of the time reacted strongly to the work. One of the main causes of the more hysterical reactions was that no critic denied, and nearly all affirmed, that Lewis had 'genius', and it must be borne in mind that these adverse reactions do not reflect majority opinion. Some critics championed the cause of *The Monk*, but their insistence on its moral purity seems just the reverse side of their colleagues' criteria for criticism. The *Monthly Mirror*, in its 'Apology for the Monk' of 1797, declares that the work preaches the danger of being over-confident in virtue and of straying even once from the path of strict moral rectitude. It insists that this 'beautiful romance is well-calculated to support the cause of virtue',[9] although this defence seems more ludicrous than the charges of immorality. Other papers avoid the issue of moral purity altogether and treat the novel merely as a good read. *The Monthly Magazine* only mentions its lack of regard for decorum.[10] The *Analytical Review* adopts a more glib tone, and declares, of Ambrosio's temptations and fall, 'a man would deserve to be d[amn]ed who could resist even devilish spells conducted with such address, and assuming such a heavenly form'.[11]

The public reacted very differently from the critics. The novel went through two issues of a first edition, and a second edition six months later, in September 1796. A third edition appeared in 1797 and the fourth in 1798. The censored fourth edition was received with so much disappointment that by 1800 the few remaining copies of the unexpurgated third edition were selling for a guinea. The adverse reaction of some of the critics was very good publicity for Lewis, and illustrates well the fine, if existent,

---

[9] 'An Apology for the Monk', *Monthly Mirror*, 3 (1797), 210–15: 211.

[10] *The Monthly Magazine*, 4 (1798), 121.

[11] *Analytical Review*, 24 (1796), 403–4: 403.

line between horror and fascination, and the attractiveness of condemnation; as does the following anecdote told by Montague Summers in *The Gothic Quest*. The obliging owner of a circulating library in Dublin '*underscored* all the naughty passages'[12] so that her young female readers would know which parts to avoid. Whether this was intended to be an anti-Irish anecdote or not, it certainly shows the benefits of lip-service. The work was adapted into play form many times, the ballad in volume iii, chapter 11—of Alonzo the Brave and Fair Imogine—was shown as a pantomime ballet, and Lewis became a celebrity—'Monk' Lewis. As a play it made for popular adaptations, although a censored version in 1798, where Matilda is a virtuous woman and all ends happily, outraged its audiences so much that they hissed, causing one of the actresses who was carrying a wooden baby to exit too quickly, bump into a door, and knock the baby's head off.

On 27 July 1792, at the age of 17, Matthew Gregory Lewis arrived at Weimar in Germany, where he was to stay until February 1793. Whilst there, he kept the company of people with titles (he was fonder of them than he ought to have been, reported Walter Scott[13]) and studied German intensively. By the end of this period he was a fluent speaker and reader, and had started to translate some of the literature he found around him.

The most horrifying literature available to Lewis in the English tradition would have comprised Jacobean tragedies (Shakespeare provides much inspiration for Gothic novelists), Milton's *Paradise Lost* (compare Milton's Satan to some of the descriptions of Ambrosio), and the productions of the 'graveyard school'—an example of which Lewis includes in *The Monk*: Blair's *The Grave*, a poem which, after 368 lines

[12] Montague Summers, *The Gothic Quest* (London: Fortune Press, 1938), 219.
[13] MS note on Byron's *Detached Thoughts*, quoted in Louis F. Peck, *A Life of Matthew G. Lewis* (Cambridge, Mass.: Harvard University Press, 1961), 45.

of descriptions of mouldering corpses and death agonies, has the stunningly placed exclamation 'Sure, 'tis a Serious Thing *to die!*'[14] The German literary scene, however, was specializing in a whole new horror aesthetic in the works of the *Sturm-und-Drang* writers. *Sturm und Drang* translates roughly as 'Storm and Stress', and the writers involved placed great emphasis on revolt, strong feeling, and the passionate power of genius.

Lewis was much taken with this shocking and often violent German writing and, later, he introduced much German Romantic writing to Britain. He met Goethe and translated some of his poetry, and brought translations of German plays to the English stage. We know from Byron's letters and journals that Lewis translated Goethe's *Faust* aloud for him at Coligny in 1816.[15] Struck by the folk ballads he encountered, Lewis translated some originals and composed poetry in this style for *The Monk* (see 'The Water King' and the 'Ballad of Alonzo the Brave and Fair Imogine'). The latter takes its central theme from Bürger's 'Lenore' (1773) and was much admired by critics and public when it first appeared. Coleridge was struck by Lewis's power of rendering ballads in easy modern language and declared it a great success.[16]

However, the *Schauer-Romantik*—horror-Romantic—tradition proved the most important inspiration for Lewis. This writing features ghosts, murders, rapes, secret societies, devils, and tortures, and Lewis assimilated a variety of incidents, plots, and themes which he was to rework a couple of years later in *The Monk*. He used the works of *Schauer-Romantik* writers both indirectly and directly. Not

---

[14] Robert Blair, *The Grave: A Poem* (London: M. Cooper, 1743), line 369.

[15] See letter to John Murray, 4 Apr. 1817.

[16] S. T. Coleridge, Letter to William Wordsworth, Jan. 1798: 'The simplicity and naturalness is his own, and not imitated; for it is made to subsist in congruity with a language perfectly modern, the language of his own times . . . This, I think, a rare merit.' Quoted in André Parreaux, *The Publication of* The Monk: *A Literary Event* 1796–1798 (Paris: Librairie Marcel Didier, 1960), 50 n.

only did he contribute to the English Gothic novel the
pleasures of grisly descriptions and real devils, he also used
some of the plots and characters he found in the German
writing. Lewis mentions finding the legend of the Bleeding
Nun in German folklore. The character of the Wandering
Jew appears both in a poem by Schubart, 'Der Ewige Jude',
which supplies many of the details for Lewis, and in a story
by Schiller—*Der Geisterseher*—a work which also gave him
the idea of a picture of the Madonna being used to inspire
love for a living woman. Flammenberg's *Der Geisterbanner*,
translated for English audiences in 1794 as *The Necromancer*,
provides a source for the banditti episode in the Black
Forest and details for Elvira's ghost. Many more sources
have been suggested, but it is important to note that the
Gothic thrives so much on convention that to cite direct
sources is often impossible when so many works share the
same stock episodes, characters, and even phrases. However, his most blatant 'borrowing' is the almost exact copy
of the description of Ambrosio's fate from a story by Veit
Weber, 'Die Teufelsbeschwörung' (1791). Further details may
be found in the explanatory notes, together with translations
of some of the more relevant passages from the German.

Ann Radcliffe, in an essay 'On the Super-natural in Poetry',
first published in 1826, declares that whereas terror 'expands the soul, and awakens the faculties to a high degree
of life', horror 'contracts, freezes, and nearly annihilates
them'.[17] When Radcliffe made this terror–horror distinction
she probably had *The Monk* in mind. Lewis had been
reading *The Mysteries of Udolpho* just prior to writing *The Monk*,
and declared it to be 'one of the most interesting Books that
ever have been published'.[18] Radcliffe read *The Monk* and

---

[17] 'On the Supernatural in Poetry', *New Monthly Magazine and Literary Journal*,
16, 145–52.

[18] Letter to his mother, The Hague, Sunday, 18 May 1794, quoted in Peck,
A Life of Matthew G. Lewis, 208–9.

was so horrified that in 1797 she produced *The Italian*, which in many respects is a reworking of material from *The Monk*, as well as a review of her own works in the light of Lewis's novel.

Radcliffe was the most famous writer of romances of her time. She was commonly thought of as a 'poetess' and often compared to Shakespeare. Her works are informed by the terror—rather than the horror—aesthetic, and are a constant stream of suspense and mystery, of vaguely glimpsed objects behind veils and strange voices singing outside prison windows. The supernatural terrors she conjures up have their source in a mixture of fear and anticipation which demands a curious kind of reader-response technique. What the heroine fears, awaits, and often faints before is what the reader also encounters, enduring all the agonies of suspense, and remaining as ignorant of the reality as the heroine. The structure in Radcliffe's works of long-drawn-out, interlacing mysteries whose secrets are suspended over hundreds of pages gives way to a more episodic form in Lewis's book, a work which enjoys short climaxes, rather than long anticipation.

Radcliffe's supernatural terrors are always finally explained away. In contrast, Lewis's supernatural incidents, which are not hidden or awaited, partake of the horror aesthetic in that they are displayed in all their gory and ghastly totality. What is threatened and usually avoided in Radcliffe is completed and handed out for the reader's disgusted delectation in Lewis. The empathetic reading—the heroine-reader sympathy—demanded by Radcliffe's text, gives way to the presenter-spectator relationship of Lewis's. Lewis's *Monk* belongs to a branch of literature that has not traditionally been honoured with a distinguished place in the literary canon. Throughout the eighteenth century the novel as an art form never enjoyed a reputation as serious literature, and Gothic novels remained classified as minor works or as literary rubbish into this century.

Recently, however, there have been attempts to write a literary history in which Gothic is recognized as the workings of Romantic imaginations, in prose—though often it is merely treated as a prosaic Romanticism. Lewis's Romantic credentials are especially convincing: his poetry was appreciated by Coleridge; he inspired and advised Walter Scott; he was acquainted with German Romanticism; and he met the Shelleys and was a friend of Byron.

The first connections between Romanticism and the Gothic were made earlier this century, with the suggestion that the Gothic is a kind of pre-Romanticism that enacts a literalization of Romantic metaphor. Thus what is internalized in Romantic poetry is externalized in the Gothic, so that the castles and storms of the Gothic act as crude symbols of the passions more subtly treated in the poetry. However, this approach seems to deny the *content*, effect, and sensationalism of the Gothic, as well as the specificity of its own symbolic systems. *The Monk*, for example, features some strange slippages between the metaphorical and the literal. The precipices and abysses which appear in Lorenzo's and Elvira's dreams, and in much clichéd imagery throughout the novel, become literal reality at the end of the work.

There have been many different accounts of the significance of the Gothic. Some critics have seen it as an expression of the spiritual or the irrational side of the human psyche that had been too long repressed by the prevailing rationalist ethos of the eighteenth century. Such accounts of the Gothic dwell on the descent into crypts and prisons as images of the unconscious or of the numinous. However, as will be discussed below, more recently the Gothic has been analysed in the light of the challenge that it poses through what many critics have called its superficiality.

The Gothic has often been linked to the outbreak of the French Revolution, and declared to be revolutionary in politics itself. The Marquis de Sade, jotting down his ideas about novels, declared the Gothic to be the 'necessary fruit of the Revolutionary terrors felt by the whole of Europe'. Of these shocking novels—these *romans noirs* or black novels—the crown goes to Lewis's *Monk*, superior even 'to the bizarre flashes of the brilliant imagination of Radcliffe'.[19] As a glance at the criticism surrounding *The Monk* shows, some eighteenth-century readers did perceive it in this way, though this tends to be the opinion of a conservative minority. Much recent criticism has challenged the revolutionary credentials of the Gothic, showing how its tendency is to annul the threats of terror posed by unruly elements.

Ronald Paulson, in *Representations of Revolution*, takes up this idea when he studies the peculiar figure of Ambrosio as victim and aggressor.[20] He gives a convincing explanation of the pattern of revolutionary activity imaged through Ambrosio's career, as the progression from repression, through revolution, to the Terror, where the repressed son assumes the same aspect as the tyrannical father. Ambrosio's victimization under the old regime of Catholicism, and his seizure of liberty, quickly become a new tyranny as he turns to murder and rape.

However, there is also a side of *The Monk* which is more concerned with a supposedly benevolent paternalism, in which kind uncles, fathers, dukes, and cardinals step in and right wrongs. More particularly they seem to have to step in to right the wrongs caused by the seizure of power by unruly elements—mobs and women. The Abbess's power must be curbed by the Cardinal-Duke. The Duke de Medina must try and prevent the mob from destroying all

---

[19] Extracts from 'Idée sur les romans', in *Les Crimes de l'amour*, quoted in Victor Sage (ed.), *The Gothick Novel: A Casebook* (Basingstoke: Macmillan, 1990), 48–9.

[20] Ronald Paulson, *Representations of Revolution* 1789–1820 (New Haven, Conn.: Yale University Press, 1983), 219–22.

that lies in its path, though not until all the previously
suppressed anger of the mob, displaced from Ambrosio,
Raymond, and Lorenzo, has torn the Abbess to pieces. It is
no accident that the worst excesses of the Church are
represented by a female figure—or that the satanic comes
in the figure of Matilda.

The Gothic tradition, for those used to reading realist novels,
can prove strange and inaccessible. In contrast to the realist
novel, set in modern society, amongst ordinary folk in small
towns or cities, the Gothic novel is most often set in a foreign
country (usually Italy or Spain), in a barbarous medieval past
(though it has a pragmatic blitheness as far as anachronism
is concerned), populated by virtuous heroes and heroines
and unspeakably evil villains. The typical Gothic is ultimate-
ly conventional—in the sense that a thousand versions have
been spawned from a limited set of elements. Its plots are
proscribed and prescribed beforehand, and characteristically
involve evil (Catholic) ecclesiastics, beautiful heroines, handsome heroes, separation, imprisonment in dungeons and
convents, mazes of passages, the evil (sexual) older woman,
wild scenery, castles, and ruins.

Eve Kosofsky Sedgwick, in *The Coherence of Gothic Conventions* [21], declares that it would be possible to write a Gothic
novel using such a description as a formula, in a way that
would be impossible with a realist novel. Whereas much
past criticism has concentrated on metaphors of depth in
the Gothic, Sedgwick and other critics more recently have
concentrated on the tendency of the Gothic to write in
terms of surfaces—its speciality is its superficiality.

Sedgwick points out several Gothic conventions that are
particularly relevant to *The Monk*: stories within stories,
multiple plots, and flights from imprisonment to reimprison-
ment, where there is no sense of progression or of descent

[21] Eve Kosofsky Sedgwick, *The Coherence of Gothic Conventions* (London:
Methuen, 1986), ch. 1.

to the depths that the reader might like to think of as the heart of the novel. One Gothic convention that seems to fly in the face of the habits of the reading of character that we expect in the realist novel is the technique of paralleling or doubling, where character is conveyed through the use of doubles and correspondences. In *The Monk* character traits have a habit of turning up again and again. Innumerable parallels are drawn, as if the points of comparison are deliberately limited, so that the fewer details there are, the greater the similarities. The Bleeding Nun occupies a pivotal role in this respect; she acts as both a cypher for Rodolpha's sexuality and as a foreshadowing of Agnes's. Raymond and Agnes's elopement repeats an ancestral pattern, and Antonia finds herself shrouded and murdered like her mother.

There is an aspect of contagion to a Gothic text. The fates of the characters seem to spread over and through them, as if they are communicated from one to another, and characters repeat patterns set up by their ancestors. Thus, Agnes's victimization by the Church may be compared to Ambrosio's, and Ambrosio's victimization of Antonia is similar to that of Agnes by the Abbess. Agnes and Antonia swallow the same poison and share the same living death in the crypt.

Characters are very easily interchangeable, so that Antonia seems to become Virginia de Villa-Franca. The vanished modesty and chastity of Matilda is quickly replaced by that of Antonia. The story told in the Ballad of Alonzo and Imogine exemplifies another pattern which spreads through the text: that of the demon lover killing his (or her) partner. The embrace of the Bleeding Nun almost makes a ghost of Raymond, as does Raymond's embrace of Agnes. Likewise, the embraces of Matilda and Ambrosio prove fatal to their respective partners.

Lewis, however, is also a determined saboteur of convention and of the more conventional sensibilities of his readers. Before him, sex in the Gothic novel had taken place in the lascivious prehistory of the individual work, when the evil characters would have indulged in real sex and orgies of emotion. For the heroine and hero sex would wait until after the finale, and virtuous marriage. But in *The Monk* it is about to take place at the end of the first volume. Where a kerchief on a bosom might suffer disarray in a more demure earlier Gothic novel, Matilda's 'beauteous Orb' (p. 65) suffers full exposure in a very co-operative moonlight in chapter 11. Where previously the pursuit of Gothic heroines by avid lechers had been doomed to failure, the rape in *The Monk* proves devastatingly successful. Lewis has followed all the conventions up to this point: we are given the heroine's screams and the usual band of men led by the lover-hero—yet they are too late. For *The Monk*'s first readers, this flouting of convention must have been almost as shocking as the rape itself. The sex featured in *The Monk* throws a disturbing, retrospective light on the excitement of earlier Gothic novels, and reveals their prurience. 'This is the way it was all tending,' Lewis seems to say, 'only you didn't dare say it.'

However, it is not only the Gothic's supposed sexual innocence that is called into question in *The Monk*, but the innocence of the characters themselves. It seems as if Lewis is determined to wreak vengeance on the unbelievably virtuous characters of other novelists. Radcliffe's heroines, never guilty of impropriety, would refuse to elope with the hero whether or not on the point of being abducted or murdered, but Agnes, mischievous and willing to elope, and Antonia, naïve and chattering, have slipped from the pitch of perfection to which other Gothic heroines are wound. As soon as Antonia appears at the beginning of the book, she is doubled by the grotesque Leonella, who takes on the attributes of Antonia's virgin modesty, and wantonly and self-consciously abuses them in a parade that becomes parody. Where Antonia would blush, Leonella writes in red ink. That which is attractive in feminine modesty can be manipulated by the female. Leonella is the crudest version of this, but an eminently subtler and more perplexing example is presented in Virginia de Villa-Franca. Though supposedly the virginal, virtuous heroine, Virginia displays a self-consciousness which would never occur in a Radcliffean heroine. Where the latter might be glimpsed musing in a glade by an enamoured hero (who, unfortunately for the exigencies of such female purity, must be cast in the role of voyeur), Virginia de Villa-Franca *makes sure* that she is seen nursing the unfortunate Agnes; she is aware of the attraction of female demureness, compassion, and modesty, and displays it to Lorenzo. Modesty displayed is not modesty, yet Virginia continues her illustrious career as heroine. We might read this as worldly cynicism, as a realization of the problems of the feminine condition, or as latent misogyny.

Stereotyping of characters is compulsory in the Gothic novel, but the character-coding is different to that employed in the realist novel. Though the use of a metonymic shorthand is familiar to readers of the realist novel, so that we instantly decode the significance of Uriah Heep's sweaty palms or Maggie Tulliver's wild hair, metonymy (or more accurately, synecdoche) in the Gothic, and especially in *The Monk*, comes close to usurping the experience of the authenticity of character altogether. The disguises characters wear too easily become their fates. Agnes's disguise as the Bleeding Nun leads to Raymond becoming the consort of the Bleeding Nun, and to Agnes becoming a nun herself. In a strangely misleading way, clothes are constantly proffered as an index of a character's essence. Compared with a fairytale, where a witch's dress merely represents her essential witchiness, the clothing in *The Monk* more often conveys the lack of essential qualities. Thus, the narrative presents Rosario-Matilda through the clothes worn or the hair that escapes. As the clothing is modified, so, it seems, is the character. Rosario-Matilda is subject to constant metamorphosis, from monk to noblewoman to devil. Ambrosio's habit proves at first a sign of, then merely a substitution for, his holiness. The Agnes of 'graceful simplicity of . . . dress and manner' (p. 130) is a very different character from the later, more tragic version of Agnes clothed as a nun. Does the change of clothes signify the change in character, or does the constant change of covering actually lead the character into another stereotype, and act as a veil for a lack of essential character?

Another strange technique of character shorthand used in Gothic writing, which appears to great effect in *The Monk*, is the equation of character with what is inscribed on the flesh. The Wandering Jew with the burning cross on his forehead is the most extreme case of this, but all the characters who have horror writ on their faces are examples. It seems to be an extension of the belief, indebted to sentimental philosophy, that the body signifies character, but in a strange and almost parodic fashion.

In such novels as Henry Mackenzie's *The Man of Feeling* or Samuel Richardson's *Clarissa* set postures and bodily reactions act as evidence of the character's proclivities. Tears constantly well up in the eyes of Mackenzie's man of feeling, and Richardson's Mrs Jewkes betrays her corrupt nature through her evil countenance. This is continued into the terror tradition, which has strong links with the sentimental. Thus, Radcliffe's heroines constantly find themselves at the mercy of their bodies, and this often proves to be very useful. Being too modest to avow their love, heroines can always find it admitted by blushes and by the quickened movement of their bosoms. On being abducted, their bodies display proper ladylike temerity, they faint, and then, just in time for the hero to get a glimpse, their incredibly white bosoms get a little exposure, and their curling ringlets tumble down in sweet disorder.

Lewis's relationship to the sentimental tradition of character inscription seems rather different, though he often uses its shorthand effectively. Sentimentalism bequeaths a deceptive form of notation at many points in the novel. The only time Agnes is betrayed by her body she ends up pregnant. In the episode in the Black Forest, Marguerite's and Baptiste's characters prove to be the opposite of what their countentances promise. And the body language of Rosario-Matilda proves to be in constant need of reinterpretation. Often even bodies themselves deceive, or the guarantee of truth presented by the body is undercut when it turns out to be the wrong body: as in the case of Rosario, or Agnes and the Bleeding Nun. A well-known shorthand is being used—yet it proves false: bodies lie, clothes lie, and identity either seems to be constantly shifting, or reveals itself as inessential. In the same way as clothes maketh the man— and woman—but are subsequently proved to have been deceptive, and the reader is left with nothing to fix the character, bodies become interchangeable, or the body itself is treated merely as that which is to be marked with character.

There is a good faith in Radcliffe's use of the superficial—of veil or clothes or body—as an index, which is absent from Lewis. In many ways *The Monk* is a novel of bad faith—and parody. Compared to Radcliffe's *œuvre*, where ultra-feminine heroines are the centre of an ultra-feminine atmosphere, where male aggression never triumphs finally over female passivity, and where comfort is to be found in a feminized nature, Lewis's novel reeks of irreverence. There is a kind of desperate sincerity about Radcliffe's work, for the author, sympathetic to the plight of her heroines, ensures that their propriety, naïvety, and unconsciousness survive intact. Lewis's work is much more self-conscious about these elements and smacks of wicked exposure. Whereas, the sentimental self was based on innate virtue, the unrestrained self according to Lewis turns to riot, and the nature which leads it is seen to be essentially unruly and all-devouring.

The 'feminine' aesthetic, which, though problematic, is certainly pervasive in Radcliffe, is constantly scrutinized in Lewis's work. Much of the previous Gothic aesthetic is imputed with insincerity: the feminine modesty, the freedom from sex, and the sentimental reliance on truth as guaranteed by the body. The nature of the passive, sentimental mode and the possibly scurrilous end-points of its vicarious experiences are played out dangerously in Lewis's text.

In 1813, having been to the theatre with Lewis a couple of nights before, Byron decided to reread *The Monk*. Referring to the supposedly indecent passages in the novel, he noted in his journal, 'These descriptions ought to have been written by Tiberius at Caprea—they are forced—the *philtered* ideas of a jaded voluptuary.'[22]

One of the most contradictory aspects of *The Monk* is that though it acquired a reputation for salaciousness, the further the sex descends into the realm of necrophiliac and incestuous fantasy, the more distant it becomes. It tends, as Byron commented, to leave the reader cold. This is characteristic of the lust and rapaciousness in the book. The warmest, most intriguing moments occur, perhaps, at the points of Ambrosio's first encounter with Rosario, where the as yet unrevealed transvestism suggests homoeroticism. The tension drops when Matilda's 'beauteous Orb' is revealed. The sex in the book is curiously static and concentrates on the importance of the visual. Ambrosio first sees an image of Antonia in Venus de Medici pose, in a magic mirror. The whole scene is uncomfortably poised and staged. Furthermore, it is possibly an illusion, strategically placed by Matilda.

To an extent, the rhythm of the work could be said to be that of Ambrosio's psychopathology. Ambrosio is driven

[22] Byron's Journal, Monday, 6 Dec. 1813.

from atrocity to atrocity, by satiety of Matilda, then Antonia. Constantly sickened, satiated, or disgusted, he continues
sexwards. Just as insistent are the rhythms of volume I,
which depend on a constant delaying of gratification.
Ambrosio and the reader are granted a slow strip-tease of
Rosario-Matilda. First, the hair, then the 'beauteous Orb',
then the face and rest of the body, as the virtue which will
not allow Ambrosio to be more than friend falls away.

It was Coleridge who first pointed out that one of the
most perverse aspects of *The Monk* is that it makes both
'shameless harlotry' (Matilda) and 'trembling innocence'
(Antonia) 'vehicles of the most voluptuous images'.[23] The
deliberate eroticization of modesty in the work is disturbing.
Ambrosio rejects a Matilda who enjoys their sex—and goes
for a virtue which will not. Antonia provokes him with her
modesty and naïvety, and her very innocence renders her
powerless and contributes to her downfall. Through Ambrosio's experience we are taken from the standard language of modesty's beauties to the translation of its terms
into sex, which necessitates rape.

There is a sense in which the imperative to rape, imposed
on Ambrosio by his author's perverse aesthetic of modesty,
is encoded in the work itself. After the rape, it is only
Ambrosio's perspective which is recorded by the narrative.
From 'the violence of his lustful delirium' (p. 383) we reach
the accomplishment of his 'design', then his characteristic
post-coital depression and a realization of his guilt: 'She,
who so lately had been the object of his adoration, now
raised no other sentiment in his heart than aversion and
rage. He turned away from her; or if his eyes rested upon
her figure involuntarily, it was only to dart upon her looks
of hate' (p. 384). The narrative is completely enfolded by
Ambrosio's perspective. We are told of Antonia's 'dishonour', as she becomes what his crime has made her. There

[23] *Critical Review*, 19 (1796), 194–200: 197.

is no sense that she, later described as a 'serpent' and an object of disgust and pity, is other than that.

Lewis always hits a style of convincing realism when describing death or torture, and the text seems to have a Sadean fixation on female mortality, and the idea of the pure woman. Agnes, fallen from virginal purity, becomes spectral and is rewarded with the livid corruption of her babe. Beautiful Antonia is eroticized through her modesty—but is defiled and dies. Marguerite, who succumbed to lust and eloped with the man of her choice, is raped by her enforced husband, Baptiste. There is an insistent harping on mortality and sex. Ambrosio might find the sepulchre to be a bower of love—though Antonia remains unconvinced—but more often bowers of love, and the female body, are associated with the sepulchre. There is a close correspondence between Agnes and the Bleeding Nun, who foreshadows Agnes's near-fatal sexuality. The lovers go to embrace, but the first embrace wins Raymond a ghost, and the second renders Agnes a replica of the Bleeding Nun as she starves in her cell.

Ambrosio is satiated and disgusted by the avid Matilda, and starts away from her to Antonia, from whom he all too quickly recoils as if she were a serpent: a movement which echoes his initiation into sex when the rose he finds for Matilda conceals the serpent which poisons him, parodying Genesis. A recurrent and dominant gesture shared by all the male characters is this movement away from a woman whom they find to be an object of disgust and pity. Even Lorenzo encountering his sister, Agnes, fails to recognize her and signals only his recognition of mortality. The reaction is the same whether it is that of Ambrosio to Antonia, or to Elvira. It is only the female bodies which suffer mutilation and corruption.

Fleshliness is curiously absent from *The Monk*, and one of the main causes seems to be the conflation of art and eroticism, and the constant interchange of image and flesh in the work. It is permeated by what Alan Watts called Western 'sex in the head'.[24] Ambrosio's first sexual experiences involve using a portrait of the Madonna as pornographic material. To entrap his sex the devil leads him through art. This association of art and sex—a kind of cultural masturbation—is well understood by Matilda. Ambrosio's sexuality is culturally determined and very intellectualized. He responds to a mirror image of the naked Antonia, posed coyly like the Venus de Medici with one hand over her private parts. The image, and the veneer of the allure which modesty provides, provoke Ambrosio. The real turn-on is the knowledge that modesty itself is imbued with sex because it so rigorously excludes it. Hence his surfeit of the violated Antonia whereby she becomes an object of disgust.

It is not only Ambrosio's sex that is presented in this way: what Ambrosio sees is presented as delectation for the reader, in a manner that is equally theatrical. The description of Matilda with the dagger at her chest is a tableau. Matilda is presented as a picture, in theatrical pose, a static image, rendered to the devouring eye. Unfortunately the image is so static that it seems almost impossible to imagine Matilda with more than one 'beauteous Orb'. Lewis's eroticism is that of barely glimpsed flesh; it is tantalizing because it is poised on the borderline between the clothed and the naked. So much for lust. Sex inheres within image, theatricality, downright negation. It lies in the fascination with what is denied, or proved impossible, and it flirts round the boundaries of definition of man and woman, chaste and whore, and even living and dead, when Ambrosio enjoys the body of a living woman, disguised as a corpse, laid in a crypt.

The difficulty in distinguishing the tone of *The Monk* is one of its most interesting features. *The Monk* seems to be always

---

[24] Alan Watts, *The Wisdom of Insecurity* (London: Rider, 1974).

actively transforming itself. It seems constantly to recur to certain literary styles and allude to other genres only to transgress their limits. It veers dangerously between the Gothic and the grotesque, the moralizing and the burlesque—just as Rosario becomes Matilda becomes devil. Like other Gothic novelists Lewis sets his work in a Latin country of superstition and Catholic foreignness, and he includes the Wandering Jew, a Bleeding Nun, and a Promethean ending. Yet his reader is assailed not only by Gothic horror, but also by the tones of mocking rationality, and, most elusively, of comedy.

The Monk employs a peculiar texture where two-dimensional representations—of, for example, the ideas conjured up by Ambrosio's impassioned oratory or the spurious reality of the mirror image of Antonia—are overlaid on to the continuous 'reality' of the text, in a way in which neither seems finally to exert a more convincing presence. Pictures, speeches, and projections seem as real as the 'real' of the text. And rhetoric—Ambrosio's or Matilda's—constantly dictates and shapes the future of the characters, who seem stuck in a world of surfaces.

Lewis is a glutton of literary styles, and has an incredible capacity for having his cake and eating it. The work constantly changes direction. The opening, with its anti-Spanish, anti-Catholic social comedy, and its cynicism about the religious impulses of the congregation at the Cathedral—with the hint that sex is what lies behind religious enthusiasm, both the attraction of Ambrosio and the sexual power of rhetoric—is a strange opening for a Gothic novel. The tone is disconcertingly light. It is an impressive feat that this style, continued through the portrait of the good Catholic Jacintha, exists alongside painful depictions in the style of German horror. Lewis has a sense of heightened realism when it comes to the depiction of loathsome reptiles and mouldering corpses. The more turbulent *Sturm-und-Drang* utterances of Agnes's anguished plea to Ambrosio, or the Gothic dream scenes of Lorenzo's and Elvira's, exist alongside the more optimistic tones of the traditional English Gothic where order is restored (in the sub-plot) and the excesses of the passions are modified by rational happiness.

Moreover, the Gothic tones easily give way to comedy. Its bizarre sense of humour is one of *The Monk*'s most surprising aspects and must have disturbed many of its early readers. Certainly many of his contemporaries complained that Lewis always though he was funnier than he was. There is a dangerous sense of parody in the work which has annoyed the worshipful as well as the hostile. After the terrors of the incident in which Raymond's six-liner 'Agnes! Agnes! Thou art mine!' has such drastic effect, Raymond jokes to Theodore about his lack of success in writing verse. And, to the chagrin of the critics who had been defending the genius and purity of his work for the last two years, Lewis included his own parody of 'The Ballad of Alonzo the Brave and Fair Imogine' ('Giles Jollup the Grave and Brown Sally Green') in the fourth and fifth editions of *The Monk*.

More daring still is the parody of the older Gothic tradition, where in a style not unlike the ponderous clumsiness of Walpole's *The Castle of Otranto* Agnes delivers the story of the Bleeding Nun. But here Gothic parody gives way to Gothic reality. However, in the face of all this, what seems most disturbing is the suggestion, made twice, that the riotousness of the passions gives way not to calm but to ennui—so that passion seems not a necessity but a debauched form of entertainment.

It is as if the narrator of *The Monk* is a sorcerer—carelessly bringing into being a variety of conflicting styles and happenings. Nowhere is this more apparent than in the constant harping on superstition. The word 'supersitition' asks to be understood in a variety of ways in the novel, and one of the most important is as a near-synonym for

Catholicism. Superstition and Catholicism have a long association in the English Protestant lexicon. The Church of Rome was supposed to prey upon the fear and irrationality of its devotees (which is the reason for Ambrosio's 'cowardice' when we are told that by nature he was suited to be a hero). It was supposed to thrive on idolatory, and its spirituality was thus debased and materialistic. The use of the picture of the Madonna to corrupt Ambrosio is a perfect example of the supposed dangers of the Catholicism. The materialistic and sensual nature of his religion leads to the friar's fall, as the image which is supposedly for prayer instead proves to be the way in for luxuriance, sexuality, and the devil. Catholic superstition is connected—in the easy steps of a Protestant thought progression—with devil-worship.

The Catholics in *The Monk*—supposedly all the characters, but everyone who is more tolerant and possesses powers of rationality is really a closet Anglican—are constantly starting at ghosts. The little clique of heroes and heroines, Raymond, Lorenzo, and Agnes, criticize superstition as the fall of weak minds. So far, so good. At the end of the novels of Clara Reeve, Charlotte Smith, and Ann Radcliffe supernatural terrors are (supposedly) exorcized, and superstition is revealed to be built on fear. But *The Monk* finds itself on difficult ground, in that superstition is more calumniated than disproved: Agnes exclaims against the Bleeding Nun—and lo! she appears; Raymond laughs at superstition and finds himself chilled by the spectre till he is released by the Wandering Jew; and Lewis's incredibly conventional Satan gives the lie rather to Lutheran optimism. What is more, Lewis is so nonchalant as to have Agnes accept the story with no surprise.

The crux of the matter is that *The Monk*, like many Gothic novels, feeds off a 'Catholic' aesthetic, though it takes its morality from its Protestantism. Thus, though the convent's procession, with the glittering carriage, impish devils, and beautiful nuns, is shown to us as an example of Catholic substitution of glamour and wealth for religion, it is also that which Lewis's art thrives on. Virtuous Anglicanism does not make for a good story. Spectacle—violent, showy, abrupt, and glittering—is the dominant aesthetic of this work.

With its constant offering of short plot climaxes, tableaux, and scenes within scenes, *The Monk* illustrates Lewis's strong sense of theatricality. After this, his only novel, Lewis's continued celebrity was mainly owing to his success as a playwright.

Walter Scott declared that '*The Monk* was so highly popular that it seemed to create an epoch in our literature.'[25] Although Lewis's plays are now hardly ever read, and never performed, *The Monk* has proved popular in the twentieth century. Taking their cue from the Marquis de Sade, the French surrealists canonized it. Breton, a novel-hater, loved the work for its appeal to the marvellous, its leaping of the boundaries of time and space—and probably also for its deliberate bad taste.[26] Antonin Artaud made an adaptation-translation of it, and the film director Buñuel, in his memoirs (*My Last Breath*), mentions writing a script for it some time between 1964 and 1966, which he did not direct, though it was turned into a film directed by Ado Kyrou in 1972.

Another film version of *The Monk*, directed by Paco Lara, with Paul McGann as Ambrosio, was released in 1990. Strangely enough, it resembles the censored versions of the eighteenth century in that Ambrosio is a sensitive character, and there are no real devils in it.

[25] Walter Scott, 'Essay on Imitations of the Ancient Ballad', in *Minstrelsy of the Scottish Border*, iv (Edinburgh: Blackwood, 1902), 33.
[26] André Breton, *Manifestos of Surrealism*, trans. Richard Seaver and Helen R. Lane (Ann Arbor, Mich.: University of Michigan Press, 1972), 14–15 and 300.

NOTE ON THE TEXT

This edition of *The Monk* is the only one since the first
edition (1796) to be set from the manuscript which M. G.
Lewis prepared for his printer. The manuscript, in the
collection of the Wisbech and Fenland Museum in Wisbech, Cambridgeshire, first came to light in recent years in
the *Romantic Movement* Exhibition in London, 1959. It has
been the property of the Museum since 1868, when they
received it as part of the bequest of the Reverend Chauncey
Hare Townshend, along with a part of his valuable collection of autograph letters and the manuscript of *Great
Expectations*. The last had been a gift from Dickens to his
friend; Townshend acquired *The Monk* when it came up as
lot 541 at T. and C. Evans's auction, 93 Pall Mall, on 7 July
1849. The manuscript is unsigned, but comparison of the
handwriting with that of letters by Lewis and with the notes
which he made in his copy of the third edition (now in the
British Museum) shows that the body of it is unquestionably
autograph. The condition of the manuscript is briefly
described in the draft catalogue of the collection:

Townshend MS, ix: Complete except for the preliminaries and the
beginning of the first and the conclusion of the last chapters. On
206 [actually 205] loose sheets (approx. 8 by 6 $\frac{3}{4}$ ins.), written on
both sides (except for 129 and 130, the unnumbered reverses of
which are entirely blank), numbered 5–412. The missing portions
of the original have been supplied on slightly larger sheets (approx.
8$\frac{7}{8}$ BY 7$\frac{3}{8}$ ins.), the pages being numbered 1–7 (the reverse of
the title being unnumbered) and 413–416. The MS is contained in
a black morocco-covered box case, with clasp, lettered: MANU-
SCRIPT./THE MONK./LEWIS.

As this description reveals, the first and last pages of the
original (presumably worn out) have been replaced; these
sheets are written in a different hand and the textual

variants show that they were made from the fourth or a
subsequent edition. The holograph begins at page 11, l. 8 of
the present edition, and ends after the word 'still' on page
439, l. 13. Evidence that it is the fair copy from which the
compositors in the firm of Joseph Bell set the first edition of
the novel is provided, not only by the fact that the
manuscript's readings are closer to those of the first edition
than to any of the later ones, but also by the appearance of
page numbers corresponding to the same point in the first
edition, inked into the manuscript at intervals. The beginning of a new signed gathering in the first edition is nearly
always signalled by the appropriate letter written in the
margins of the manuscript in a hand presumably belonging
to a compositor, and names—also presumably compositors'—appear in the margins, with lines drawn to indicate
precisely a new type-setting stint.

The paper of the manuscript is Dutch, the watermark
'Pieter De Vries' clearly visible in many of the sheets. Since
Dutch paper was imported into England, no certain conclusions can be drawn from this fact, but it suggests that Lewis
may have finished not only a draft but also this fair copy of
the novel before returning from The Hague, where he had
been attached to the British Embassy, in later November or
December of 1794. Its complete readiness for printing at
that time would support the tradition that the book was first
published in 1795, though distributed with new title pages
on 12 March 1796. The discovery during the 1950s of two
copies with the original 1795 title pages provides further
evidence for such a conclusion.[1]

The early publishing history of *The Monk* is complex.
Lewis was apparently attacked for the salacious and blasphemous elements of his narrative, which were judged

[1] For further description of the manuscript, see Howard Anderson, 'The
Manuscript of M. G. Lewis's *The Monk*: Some Preliminary Notes', *Publications
of the Bibliographical Society of America*, 62, 3 (1968), 427–34.

particularly unsuitable from a Member of Parliament. The attacks apparently resulted in a thorough expurgation for the fourth edition, and in various subterfuges on the part of the publisher to enable him to get rid of remaining copies of earlier editions. The resultant complications were brilliantly disentangled by William Todd in 1949.[2] Because the variations that enter the five editions issued by Lewis's original publisher, Joseph Bell, between 1796 and 1800 are very considerable, I have collated the manuscript with each of those editions. The copies consulted are those belonging to the Harvard University Library (for the first, fourth, and fifth editions), the Lilly Library at Indiana University (for the third), and to Professor Todd (for the second). The results of the collation are recorded in my Oxford English Novels edition (1973).

I have also recorded in those notes the textual changes Lewis made within the manuscript itself. The text as it is here printed is substantially that of the manuscript in both substantives and accidentals. While some of the changes between the manuscript and the first edition, and between the first and second editions, may constitute the author's preference, the cases are so rare and problematic that it has seemed better simply to record the differences. I have taken the readings for those portions of the manuscript not in Lewis's hand from the first edition, and have revised the accidentals there according to his usage in the manuscript. Beyond that, I have regularized Lewis's capitalization and punctuation where his dominant practice is discernible: *he* and *she* have been regularly capitalized; *you*, *we*, *they*, and *his* have been made to begin with small letters; Lewis's concluding dashes before quotation marks have been replaced with periods; words that he customarily hyphenates have been consistently hyphenated; with a few

[2] 'The Early Editions and Issues of *The Monk*, with a Bibliography', *Studies in Bibliography*, II, 1949–50, 3–24.

exceptions the second word in hyphenated words has been
made to begin with a small letter; and adjectives occasionally capitalized in error have been made to start with small
letters instead.

H. A.

SELECT BIBLIOGRAPHY

Significant Early Editions of *The Monk*

The Monk: A Romance, 3 vols. (London: J. Bell, 1796).

Ambrosio; or, The Monk: A Romance, 3 vols. 4th edn. With considerable Additions and Alterations (London: J. Bell, 1798).

Early Criticism of *The Monk*

Analytical Review, review, 24 (1796), 403–4.

'An Apology for the Monk', *Monthly Mirror*, 3 (1797), 210–15.

The British Critic, review, 7 (1796), 677.

Coleridge, S. T., review in *Critical Review*, 19 (1796), 194–200.

European Magazine, review, 31 (1797), 111–15.

The Flapper, review, 14, (17 Sept. 1796), 3–4.

The Monthly Magazine, review, 4 (1798), 121.

Mathias, T. J., *The Pursuits of Literature*, 5th edn. (London: T. Becket, 1798).

Monthly Mirror, review, 2 (1796), 98.

Scott, Walter, 'Essay on Imitations of the Ancient Ballad', in *Minstrelsy of the Scottish Border*, iv (Edinburgh: Blackwood, 1902).

Works Specifically on Lewis and *The Monk*

Conger, Syndy M., *Matthew G. Lewis, Charles Robert Maturin and the Germans: An Interpretative Study of the Influence of German Literature on Two Gothic Novels* (Salzburg: Institüt für Englisch Sprache und Literatur, Universität Salzburg, 1977).

Parreaux, André, *The Publication of* The Monk: *A Literary Event* 1796–1798 (Paris: Libraire Marcel Didier, 1960).

Peck, Louis F., *A Life of Matthew G. Lewis* (Cambridge, Mass. Harvard University Press, 1961).

Works on the Gothic which Contain Reference to *The Monk*

Day, William Patrick, *In the Circles of Fear and Desire: A Study of Gothic Fantasy* (Chicago: University of Chicago Press, 1985).

Hogle, Jerrold E., 'The Restless Labyrinth: Cryptonomy in the Gothic Novel', *Arizona Quarterly*, 36 (1980), 330–58.

Kiely, Robert, *The Romantic Novel in England* (Cambridge, Mass. Harvard University Press, 1972).

Miles, Robert, *Gothic Writing 1750–1820: A Genealogy* (London: Routledge, 1993).

Napier, Elizabeth R., *The Failure of Gothic: Problems of Disjunction in an Eighteenth-Century Literary Form* (Oxford: Clarendon Press, 1987).

Paulson, Ronald, *Representations of Revolution 1789–1820* (New Haven, Conn.: Yale University Press, 1983).

Punter, David, *The Literature of Terror: A History of Gothic Fictions from 1765 to the Present Day* (London: Longman, 1980).

Sage, Victor (ed.), *The Gothick Novel: A Casebook* (Basingstoke: Macmillan, 1990).

Sedgwick, Eve Kosofsky, *The Coherence of Gothic Conventions* (London: Methuen, 1986).

Summers, Montague, *The Gothic Quest: A History of the Gothic Novel* (London: Fortune Press, 1938).

Other Relevant Works

Bredvold, Louis, I., *The Natural History of Sensibility* (Detroit: Wayne State University Press, 1962).

Cox, Jeffrey N. (ed.), *Seven Gothic Dramas: 1789–1825* (containing two of Matthew Lewis's dramatic works, *The Castle Spectre* and *The Captive*) (Athens, Ohio: Ohio University Press, 1992).

Radcliffe, Ann, *The Mysteries of Udolpho*, ed. Bonamy Dobrée (Oxford: Oxford University Press, 1986).

——, *The Italian; or, The Confessional of the Black Penitents*, ed. Frederick Garber (Oxford: Oxford University Press, 1986).

Todd, Janet, *Sensibility: An Introduction* (London: Methuen, 1986).

A CHRONOLOGY OF
MATTHEW GREGORY LEWIS

1775 Born 9 July to Frances Maria and Matthew Lewis, in London. He is to be the oldest of four children.

1781 His mother, to whom he is devoted throughout his life, leaves his father. In later years he adds his own financial support to the allowance his father gives her.

1783 Finishes at Marylebone Seminary and goes on to Westminster School.

1790 Enters Christ Church, Oxford.

1791 Spends the summer in Paris.

1792 Writes *The East Indian* whilst still 16. It is performed at Drury Lane seven years later. Goes to Weimar, learns German, and starts translating works of literature. Meets Goethe and Weiland.

1794 Receives his bachelor's degree from Oxford. Spends May to December at The Hague, Holland, on diplomatic service. He is plagued with 'ennui', and writes *The Monk* in ten weeks, which he has completed by 23 September.

1795 Possible date of publication of a small number of copies of *The Monk*. Walter Scott refers to this as the date of publication, and two copies bearing this date have been found.

1796 12 March: definite date of publication of *The Monk: A Romance*. Becomes an MP, taking up the seat for Hindon, Wiltshire, recently vacated by William Beckford (author of *Vathek*). The second edition of *The Monk* bears Lewis's name and the initials 'MP'. Published *Village Virtues: A Dramatic Satire* anonymously, a limited edition quickly forgotten.

1797 Receives his master's degree from Oxford. Publishes a translation of Schiller's *Kabale und Liebe* entitled *The Minister*.

1798 After much adverse criticism and a prosecution, publishes the censored fourth edition of *Ambrosio; or, The Monk*. Writes

The Castle Spectre: A Drama in Five Acts. It is his first play to be produced, and proves to be enormously successful. Meets Walter Scott.

1799 *The Love of Gain: A Poem. The Twins; or, Is it He, or His Brother? A Farce in Two Acts*, a translation-adaptation of Régnard's *Les Ménechmes*, performed at Drury Lane, but unpublished. Published *Rolla; or, The Peruvian Hero*, a translation of Kotzebue's *Die Spanier in Peru oder Rollas Tod*, unperformed.

1800 *The East Indian: A Comedy in Five Acts*, written when he was 16, finally published and performed with success.

1801 *Tales of Wonder*, a collection of poetry with contributions by Scott and Southey amongst others; however, it contained so much material previously published elsewhere it became known as 'Tales of Plunder'. *Adelmorn the Outlaw: A Romantic Drama in Three Acts*, performed relatively unsuccessfully and received damning reviews. Lewis from now until 1806 writes for Drury Lane rather than Covent Garden.

1802 *Alfonso, King of Castile: A Tragedy in Five Acts*, in blank verse, considered by many of his contemporaries to be the finest tragedy of the day.

1803 Lewis quarrels with his father and they are not reconciled until his father is on his deathbed, nine years later. He writes *The Captive: A Scene in a Private Mad-House*, a dramatic monologue which only survived one performance as, according to contemporary accounts, it threw ten members of the audience into hysterical fits; it was not separately published. *The Harper's Daughter; or, Love and Ambition: A Tragedy in Five Acts* is performed for a benefit night but not published; it is an abridged version of *The Minister*.

1805 He produces *The Bravo of Venice: A Romance*, a translation of Zschokke's *Aballino der Grosse Bandit*, which he also converts into a play entitled *Rugantino; or, The Bravo of Venice: A Grand Romantic Melodrama in Two Acts*, which proves very successful.

1806 He writes *Adelgitha; or, The Fruit of a Single Error: A Tragedy in Five Acts*, which is performed in 1807. Publication of *Feudal Tyrants; or, The Counts of Carlsheim and Sargans: A Romance*, a four-volume romance translated from Christiane Naubert's *Elisabeth, Erbin von Toggenburg*.

1807 *The Wood Daemon; or, The Clock has Struck: A Grand Romantic Melo-Drama in Two Acts* is performed; it is a play remarkable for its elaborate stage effects, and is very well received by the public if not by the critics; it was not published.

1808 Publication of *He Loves and He Rides Away: A Favourite Ballad* and *Twelve Ballads, the Words and Music by M. G. Lewis*. He also produces a work in four volumes entitled *Romantic Tales*, which contains one long poem, seven ballads, and five prose stories; much of this collection is translated from Spanish and German originals. Performance of *Venoni; or, The Novice of St Mark's: A Drama in Three Acts*, an adaptation of Monvel's *Les Victimes cloîtrées*

1809 Performance of *Monody on the Death of Sir John Moore*, a theatrical recitation in praise of the dead Lieutenant-General. Performances at the Lyceum of *Temper; or, The Domestic Tyrant: A Farce in Two Acts*, an adaptation of a play, *The Grumbler*, translated from a French original, *Le Grondeur*, by Sir Charles Sedley.

1811 Performance of the spectacular *Timour the Tartar: A Grand Romantic Melo-Drama in Two Acts*, a popular piece, largely owing to a performance by a talented white horse. Production at the Lyceum of *One O'Clock! or, The Knight and the Wood Daemon: A Grand Musical Romance in Three Acts*, a successful musical version of *The Wood Daemon*.

1812 Lewis is supposed to have written a romantic drama called *Zoroaster*, but no manuscript has been found. *Rich and Poor: A Comic Opera in Three Acts*, a reworking of *The East Indian*, with music, is successfully performed. He publishes a small volume of *Poems*, the majority of which are not 'Gothic' but neoclassical odes and lyrics; they were well thought-of. His father dies 17 May and Lewis inherits a large fortune and his father's two slave plantations in the West Indies.

1813 Meets Byron.

1815 Journeys to Jamaica; tries to improve the life of the slaves on his plantations. Lewis is against slavery, but believes that emancipation of the existing slaves on the island would result in a blood-bath. He returns for England May 1816.

1816 Meets the anti-slavery campaigner William Wilberforce to discuss ways in which he can improve the lot of his slaves. Starts a year and a half tour of the Continent. Meets Mary and Percy Bysshe Shelley, and Polidori. Translates Goethe's *Faust* aloud for Byron.

1817 Returns to England. Goes to Jamaica again on 5 November. Institutes more slave reforms.

1818 Leaves for England 4 May. Dies of yellow fever at sea, 16 May. His coffin refuses to sink, and floats away from the ship.

1834 His *Journal of a West India Proprietor*, kept from 1815 to 1817, is finally published, to favourable reviews.

THE MONK

A ROMANCE

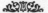

Somnia, terrores magicos, miracula, fagas,
Nocturnos lemures, portentaque.
                              Horat.*

Dreams, magic terrors, spells of mighty power,
Witches, and ghosts who rove at midnight hour.

PREFACE

IMITATION OF HORACE

Ep. 20.—B. 1.

METHINKS, Oh! vain ill-judging Book,
I see thee cast a wishful look,
Where reputations won and lost are
In famous row called Paternoster.*
Incensed to find your precious olio
Buried in unexplored port-folio,
You scorn the prudent lock and key,
And pant well bound and gilt to see
Your Volume in the window set
Of Stockdale, Hookham, or Debrett.*

Go then, and pass that dangerous bourn
Whence never Book can back return:
And when you find, condemned, despised,
Neglected, blamed, and criticised,
Abuse from All who read you fall,
(If haply you be read at all)
Sorely will you your folly sigh at,
And wish for me, and home, and quiet.

  Assuming now a conjuror's office, I
Thus on your future Fortune prophesy:—
Soon as your novelty is o'er,
And you are young and new no more,
In some dark dirty corner thrown,
Mouldy with damps, with cobwebs strown,
Your leaves shall be the Book-worm's prey;

Or sent to Chandler-Shop away,
And doomed to suffer public scandal,
Shall line the trunk, or wrap the candle!

But should you meet with approbation,
And some one find an inclination
To ask, by natural transition,
Respecting me and my condition;
That I am one, the enquirer teach,
Nor very poor, nor very rich;
Of passions strong, of hasty nature,
Of graceless form and dwarfish stature;*
By few approved, and few approving;
Extreme in hating and in loving;

Abhorring all whom I dislike,
Adoring who my fancy strike;
In forming judgements never long,
And for the most part judging wrong;
In friendship firm, but still believing
Others are treacherous and deceiving,
And thinking in the present æra
That Friendship is a pure chimæra:
More passionate no creature living,
Proud, obstinate, and unforgiving,
But yet for those who kindness show,
Ready through fire and smoke to go.

Again, should it be asked your page,
'Pray, what may be the author's age?'
Your faults, no doubt, will make it clear,
I scarce have seen my twentieth year,
Which passed, kind Reader, on my word,
While England's Throne held George the Third.

Now then your venturous course pursue;
Go, my delight! Dear Book, adieu!

Hague,
Oct. 28, 1794.   M. G. L.

TABLE OF THE POETRY

ADVERTISEMENT

THE first idea of this Romance was suggested by the story of the *Santon Barsisa*,* related in The Guardian. —The *Bleeding Nun* is a tradition still credited in many parts of Germany; and I have been told, that the ruins of the Castle of *Lauenstein*,* which She is supposed to haunt, may yet be seen upon the borders of *Thuringia*.*—The *Water-King*, from the third to the twelfth stanza, is the fragment of an original Danish Ballad—And *Belerma and Durandarte* is translated from some stanzas to be found in a collection of old Spanish poetry, which contains also the popular song of *Gayferos and Melesindra*, mentioned in Don Quixote.—I have now made a full avowal of all the plagiarisms of which I am aware myself; but I doubt not, many more may be found, of which I am at present totally unconscious.

VOLUME I

CHAPTER I

——Lord Angelo is precise;
Stands at a guard with envy; Scarce confesses
That his blood flows, or that his appetite
Is more to bread than stone.

*Measure for Measure.**

SCARCELY HAD THE Abbey-Bell tolled for five minutes, and already was the Church of the Capuchins* thronged with Auditors. Do not encourage the idea that the Crowd was assembled either from motives of piety or thirst of information. But very few were influenced by those reasons; and in a city where superstition reigns with such despotic sway as in Madrid, to seek for true devotion would be a fruitless attempt. The Audience now assembled in the Capuchin Church was collected by various causes, but all of them were foreign to the ostensible motive. The Women came to show themselves, the Men to see the Women: Some were attracted by curiosity to hear an Orator so celebrated; Some came because they had no better means of employing their time till the play began; Some, from being assured that it would be impossible to find places in the Church; and one half of Madrid was brought thither by expecting to meet the other half. The only persons truly anxious to hear the Preacher were a few antiquated devotees, and half a dozen rival Orators, determined to find fault with and ridicule the discourse. As to the remainder of the Audience, the Sermon might have been omitted altogether, certainly without their being disappointed, and very probably without their perceiving the omission.

Whatever was the occasion, it is at least certain that

the Capuchin Church had never witnessed a more numerous assembly. Every corner was filled, every seat was occupied. The very Statues which ornamented the long aisles were pressed into the service. Boys suspended themselves upon the wings of Cherubims; St. Francis and St. Mark bore each a spectator on his shoulders; and St. Agatha found herself under the necessity of carrying double. The consequence was, that in spite of all their hurry and expedition, our two newcomers, on entering the Church, looked round in vain for places.

However, the old Woman continued to move forwards. In vain were exclamations of displeasure vented against her from all sides: In vain was She addressed with—'I assure you, Segnora, there are no places here.'— 'I beg, Segnora, that you will not crowd me so intolerably!'—'Segnora, you cannot pass this way. Bless me! How can people be so troublesome!'—The old Woman was obstinate, and on She went. By dint of perseverance and two brawny arms She made a passage through the Crowd, and managed to bustle herself into the very body of the Church, at no great distance from the Pulpit. Her companion had followed her with timidity and in silence, profiting by the exertions of her conductress.

'Holy Virgin!' exclaimed the old Woman in a tone of disappointment, while She threw a glance of enquiry round her; 'Holy Virgin! What heat! What a Crowd! I wonder what can be the meaning of all this. I believe we must return: There is no such thing as a seat to be had, and nobody seems kind enough to accommodate us with theirs.'

This broad hint attracted the notice of two Cavaliers, who occupied stools on the right hand, and were leaning their backs against the seventh column from the Pulpit. Both were young, and richly habited. Hearing this appeal to their politeness pronounced in a female voice,

they interrupted their conversation to look at the speaker.
She had thrown up her veil in order to take a clearer
look round the Cathedral. Her hair was 'red, and She
squinted. The Cavaliers turned round, and renewed
their conversation.

'By all means,' replied the old Woman's companion;
'By all means, Leonella, let us return home immediately;
The heat is excessive, and I am terrified at such a
crowd.'

These words were pronounced in a tone of unexampled
sweetness. The Cavaliers again broke off their discourse,
but for this time they were not contented with looking
up: Both started involuntarily from their seats, and
turned themselves towards the Speaker.

The voice came from a female, the delicacy and
elegance of whose figure inspired the Youths with the
most lively curiosity to view the face to which it belonged. This satisfaction was denied them. Her features
were hidden by a thick veil; But struggling through the
crowd had deranged it sufficiently to discover a neck
which for symmetry and beauty might have vied with
the Medicean Venus.* It was of the most dazzling whiteness, and received additional charms from being shaded
by the tresses of her long fair hair, which descended in
ringlets to her waist. Her figure was rather below than
above the middle size: It was light and airy as that of an
Hamadryad.* Her bosom was carefully veiled. Her dress
was white; it was fastened by a blue sash, and just permitted to peep out from under it a little foot of the most
delicate proportions. A chaplet of large grains hung upon
her arm, and her face was covered with a veil of thick
black gauze. Such was the female, to whom the youngest
of the Cavaliers now offered his seat, while the other
thought it necessary to pay the same attention to her
companion.

The old Lady with many expressions of gratitude, but

without much difficulty, accepted the offer, and seated herself: The young one followed her example, but made no other compliment than a simple and graceful reverence. Don Lorenzo (such was the Cavalier's name, whose seat She had accepted) placed himself near her; But first He whispered a few words in his Friend's ear, who immediately took the hint, and endeavoured to draw off the old Woman's attention from her lovely charge.

'You are doubtless lately arrived at Madrid,' said Lorenzo to his fair Neighbour; 'It is impossible that such charms should have long remained unobserved; and had not this been your first public appearance, the envy of the Women and adoration of the Men would have rendered you already sufficiently remarkable.'

He paused, in expectation of an answer. As his speech did not absolutely require one, the Lady did not open her lips: After a few moments He resumed his discourse:

'Am I wrong in supposing you to be a Stranger to Madrid?'

The Lady hesitated; and at last, in so low a voice as to be scarcely intelligible, She made shift to answer,— 'No, Segnor.'

'Do you intend making a stay of any length?'

'Yes, Segnor.'

'I should esteem myself fortunate, were it in my power to contribute to making your abode agreeable. I am well known at Madrid, and my Family has some interest at Court. If I can be of any service, you cannot honour or oblige me more than by permitting me to be of use to you.'—'Surely,' said He to himself, 'She cannot answer that by a monosyllable; now She must say something to me.'

Lorenzo was deceived, for the Lady answered only by a bow.

By this time He had discovered that his Neighbour

was not very conversible; But whether her silence proceeded from pride, discretion, timidity, or idiotism, He was still unable to decide.

After a pause of some minutes—'It is certainly from your being a Stranger,' said He, 'and as yet unacquainted with our customs, that you continue to wear your veil. Permit me to remove it.'

At the same time He advanced his hand towards the Gauze: The Lady raised hers to prevent him.

'I never unveil in public, Segnor.'

'And where is the harm, I pray you?' interrupted her Companion somewhat sharply; 'Do not you see, that the other Ladies have all laid their veils aside, to do honour no doubt to the holy place in which we are? I have taken off mine already; and surely if I expose my features to general observation, you have no cause to put yourself in such a wonderful alarm! Blessed Maria! Here is a fuss and a bustle about a chit's face! Come, come, Child! Uncover it; I warrant you that nobody will run away with it from you—'

'Dear aunt, it is not the custom in Murcia.'*

'Murcia, indeed! Holy St. Barbara,* what does that signify? You are always putting me in mind of that villainous Province. If it is the custom in Madrid, that is all that we ought to mind, and therefore I desire you to take off your veil immediately. Obey me this moment Antonia, for you know that I cannot bear contradiction—'

Her niece was silent, but made no further opposition to Don Lorenzo's efforts, who armed with the Aunt's sanction hastened to remove the Gauze. What a Seraph's head presented itself to his admiration! Yet it was rather bewitching than beautiful; It was not so lovely from regularity of features, as from sweetness and sensibility of Countenance. The several parts of her face considered separately, many of them were far from handsome; but when examined together, the whole was adorable. Her skin though fair was not entirely without freckles; Her eyes were not very large, nor their lashes particularly long. But then her lips were of the most rosy freshness; Her fair and undulating hair, confined by a simple ribband, poured itself below her waist in a profusion of ringlets; Her throat was full and beautiful in the extreme; Her hand and arm were formed with the most perfect symmetry; Her mild blue eyes seemed an heaven of sweetness, and the crystal in which they moved, sparkled with all the brilliance of Diamonds: She appeared to be scarcely fifteen; An arch smile, playing round her mouth, declared her to be possessed of liveliness, which excess of timidity at present represt; She looked round her with a bashful glance; and whenever her eyes accidentally met Lorenzo's, She dropt them hastily upon her Rosary; Her cheek was immediately suffused with blushes, and She began to tell her beads; though her manner evidently showed that She knew not what She was about.

Lorenzo gazed upon her with mingled surprise and admiration; but the Aunt thought it necessary to apologize for Antonia's *mauvaise honte.*

' 'Tis a young Creature,' said She, 'who is totally ignorant of the world. She has been brought up in an old Castle in Murcia; with no other Society than her Mother's, who, God help her! has no more sense, good Soul, than is necessary to carry her Soup to her mouth. Yet She is my own Sister, both by Father and Mother.'

'And has so little sense?' said Don Christoval with feigned astonishment; 'How very Extraordinary!'

'Very true, Segnor; Is it not strange? However, such is the fact; and yet only to see the luck of some people! A young Nobleman, of the very first quality, took it into his head that Elvira had some pretensions to Beauty —As to pretensions, in truth, She had always enough of

them; But as to Beauty. . . .! If I had only taken half the
pains to set myself off which She did. . . .! But this is
neither here nor there. As I was saying, Segnor, a young
Nobleman fell in love with her, and married her unknown to his Father. Their union remained a secret near
three years, But at last it came to the ears of the old
Marquis, who, as you may well suppose, was not much
pleased with the intelligence. Away He posted in all
haste to Cordova,* determined to seize Elvira, and send
her away to some place or other, where She would never
be heard of more. Holy St. Paul! How He stormed on
finding that She had escaped him, had joined her
Husband, and that they had embarked together for the
Indies. He swore at us all, as if the Evil Spirit had
possessed him; He threw my Father into prison, as
honest a pains-taking Shoe-maker as any in Cordova;
and when He went away, He had the cruelty to take
from us my Sister's little Boy, then scarcely two years old,
and whom in the abruptness of her flight, She had been
obliged to leave behind her. I suppose, that the poor little
Wretch met with bitter bad treatment from him, for in
a few months after, we received intelligence of his death.'
   'Why, this was a most terrible old Fellow, Segnora!'
   'Oh! shocking! and a Man so totally devoid of taste!
Why, would you believe it, Segnor? When I attempted
to pacify him, He cursed me for a Witch, and wished
that to punish the Count, my Sister might become as
ugly as myself! Ugly indeed! I like him for that.'
   'Ridiculous', cried Don Christoval; 'Doubtless the
Count would have thought himself fortunate, had he
been permitted to exchange the one Sister for the other.'
   'Oh! Christ! Segnor, you are really too polite. However, I am heartily glad that the Condé*was of a different
way of thinking. A mighty pretty piece of business, to be
sure, Elvira has made of it! After broiling and stewing
in the Indies for thirteen long years, her Husband dies,

and She returns to Spain, without an House to hide her head, or money to procure her one! This Antonia was then but an Infant, and her only remaining Child. She found that her Father-in-Law had married again, that he was irreconcileable to the Condé, and that his second Wife had produced him a Son, who is reported to be a very fine young Man. The old Marquis refused to see my Sister or her Child; But sent her word that on condition of never hearing any more of her, He would assign her a small pension, and She might live in an old Castle which He possessed in Murcia; This had been the favourite habitation of his eldest Son; But since his flight from Spain, the old Marquis could not bear the place, but let it fall to ruin and confusion—My Sister accepted the proposal; She retired to Murcia, and has remained there till within the last Month.'

'And what brings her now to Madrid?' enquired Don Lorenzo, whom admiration of the young Antonia compelled to take a lively interest in the talkative old Woman's narration.

'Alas! Segnor, her Father-in-Law being lately dead, the Steward of his Murcian Estates has refused to pay her pension any longer. With the design of supplicating his Son to renew it, She is now come to Madrid; But I doubt, that She might have saved herself the trouble! You young Noblemen have always enough to do with your money, and are not very often disposed to throw it away upon old Women. I advised my Sister to send Antonia with her petition; But She would not hear of such a thing. She is so obstinate! Well! She will find herself the worse for not following my counsels: the Girl has a good pretty face, and possibly might have done much.'

'Ah! Segnora,' interrupted Don Christoval, counterfeiting a passionate air; 'If a pretty face will do the business, why has not you Sister recourse to you?'

'Oh! Jesus! my Lord, I swear you quite over-power me with your gallantry! But I promise you that I am too well aware of the danger of such Expeditions to trust myself in a young Nobleman's power! No, no; I have as yet preserved my reputation without blemish or reproach, and I always knew how to keep the Men at a proper distance.'

'Of that, Segnora, I have not the least doubt. But permit me to ask you; Have you then any aversion to Matrimony?'

'That is an home question. I cannot but confess, that if an amiable Cavalier was to present himself. . . .'

Here She intended to throw a tender and significant look upon Don Christoval; But, as She unluckily happened to squint most abominably, the glance fell directly upon his Companion: Lorenzo took the compliment to himself, and answered it by a profound bow.

'May I enquire,' said He, 'the name of the Marquis?'

'The Marquis de las Cisternas.'

'I know him intimately well. He is not at present in Madrid, but is expected here daily. He is one of the best of Men; and if the lovely Antonia will permit me to be her Advocate with him, I doubt not my being able to make a favourable report of her cause.'

Antonia raised her blue eyes, and silently thanked him for the offer by a smile of inexpressible sweetness. Leonella's satisfaction was much more loud and audible: Indeed, as her Niece was generally silent in her company, She thought it incumbent upon her to talk enough for both: This She managed without difficulty, for She very seldom found herself deficient in words.

'Oh! Segnor!' She cried; 'You will lay our whole family under the most signal obligations! I accept your offer with all possible gratitude, and return you a thousand thanks for the generosity of your proposal. Antonia, why do not you speak, Child? While the

Cavalier says all sorts of civil things to you, you sit like a Statue, and never utter a syllable of thanks, either bad, good, or indifferent!'

'My dear Aunt, I am very sensible that. . . .'

'Fye, Niece! How often have I told you, that you never should interrupt a Person who is speaking!? When did you ever know me do such a thing? Are these your Murcian manners? Mercy on me! I shall never be able to make this Girl any thing like a Person of good-breeding. But pray, Segnor,' She continued, addressing herself to Don Christoval, 'inform me, why such a Crowd is assembled to-day in this Cathedral?'

'Can you possibly be ignorant, that Ambrosio, Abbot of this Monastery, pronounces a Sermon in this Church every Thursday? All Madrid rings with his praises. As yet He has preached but thrice; But all who have heard him are so delighted with his eloquence, that it is as difficult to obtain a place at Church, as at the first representation of a new Comedy. His fame certainly must have reached your ears—'

'Alas! Segnor, till yesterday I never had the good fortune to see Madrid; and at Cordova we are so little informed of what is passing in the rest of the world, that the name of Ambrosio has never been mentioned in its precincts.'

'You will find it in every one's mouth at Madrid. He seems to have fascinated the Inhabitants; and not having attended his Sermons myself, I am astonished at the Enthusiasm which He has excited. The adoration paid him both by Young and Old, by Man and Woman is unexampled. The Grandees load him with presents; Their Wives refuse to have any other Confessor, and he is known through all the city by the name of the "Man of Holiness".'

'Undoubtedly, Segnor, He is of noble origin—'

'That point still remains undecided. The late Superior

of the Capuchins found him while yet an Infant at the
Abbey-door. All attempts to discover who had left him
there were vain, and the Child himself could give no
account of his Parents. He was educated in the Monastery, where He has remained ever since. He early
showed a strong inclination for study and retirement,
and as soon as He was of a proper age, He pronounced
his vows. No one has ever appeared to claim him, or
clear up the mystery which conceals his birth; and the
Monks, who find their account in the favour which is
shewn to their establishment from respect to him, have
not hesitated to publish, that He is a present to them
from the Virgin. In truth the singular austerity of his
life gives some countenance to the report. He is now
thirty years old, every hour of which period has been
passed in study, total seclusion from the world, and
mortification of the flesh. Till these last three weeks,
when He was chosen superior of the Society to which He
belongs, He had never been on the outside of the Abbey-
walls: Even now He never quits them except on Thurs-
days, when He delivers a discourse in this Cathedral
which all Madrid assembles to hear. His knowledge is
said to be the most profound, his eloquence the most
persuasive. In the whole course of his life He has never
been known to transgress a single rule of his order; The
smallest stain is not to be discovered upon his character;
and He is reported to be so strict an observer of Chastity,
that He knows not in what consists the difference of Man
and Woman. The common People therefore esteem him
to be a Saint.'

'Does that make a Saint?' enquired Antonia; 'Bless
me! Then am I one?'

'Holy St. Barbara!' exclaimed Leonella; 'What a
question! Fye, Child, Fye! These are not fit subjects for
young Women to handle. You should not seem to
remember, that there is such a thing as a Man in the

world, and you ought to imagine every body to be of the same sex with yourself. I should like to see you give people to understand, that you know that a Man has no breasts, and no hips, and no . . .'.

Luckily for Antonia's ignorance which her Aunt's lecture would soon have dispelled, an universal murmur through the Church announced the Preacher's arrival. Donna Leonella rose from her seat to take a better view of him, and Antonia followed her example.

He was a Man of noble port and commanding presence. His stature was lofty, and his features uncommonly handsome. His Nose was aquiline, his eyes large black and sparkling, and his dark brows almost joined together. His complexion was of a deep but clear Brown; Study and watching had entirely deprived his cheek of colour. Tranquillity reigned upon his smooth unwrinkled forehead; and Content, expressed upon every feature, seemed to announce the Man equally unacquainted with cares and crimes. He bowed himself with humility to the audience: Still there was a certain severity in his look and manner that inspired universal awe, and few could sustain the glance of his eye at once fiery and penetrating. Such was Ambrosio, Abbot of the Capuchins, and surnamed, 'The Man of Holiness'.

Antonia, while She gazed upon him eagerly, felt a pleasure fluttering in her bosom which till then had been unknown to her, and for which She in vain endeavoured to account. She waited with impatience till the Sermon should begin; and when at length the Friar spoke, the sound of his voice seemed to penetrate into her very soul. Though no other of the Spectators felt such violent sensations as did the young Antonia, yet every one listened with interest and emotion. They who were insensible to Religion's merits, were still enchanted with Ambrosio's oratory. All found their attention irresistibly attracted while He spoke, and the most profound silence reigned through the crowded Aisles. Even Lorenzo could not resist the charm: He forgot that Antonia was seated near him, and listened to the Preacher with undivided attention.

In language nervous, clear, and simple, the Monk expatiated on the beauties of Religion. He explained some abstruse parts of the sacred writings in a style that carried with it universal conviction. His voice at once distinct and deep was fraught with all the terrors of the Tempest, while He inveighed against the vices of humanity, and described the punishments reserved for them in a future state. Every Hearer looked back upon his past offences, and trembled: The Thunder seemed to roll, whose bolt was destined to crush him, and the abyss of eternal destruction to open before his feet. But when Ambrosio changing his theme spoke of the excellence of an unsullied conscience, of the glorious prospect which Eternity presented to the Soul untainted with reproach, and of the recompense which awaited it in the regions of everlasting glory, His Auditors felt their scattered spirits insensibly return. They threw themselves with confidence upon the mercy of their Judge; They hung with delight upon the consoling words of the Preacher; and while his full voice swelled into melody, They were transported to those happy regions which He painted to their imaginations in colours so brilliant and glowing.

The discourse was of considerable length; Yet when it concluded, the Audience grieved that it had not lasted longer. Though the Monk had ceased to speak, enthusiastic silence* still prevailed through the Church: At length the charm gradually dissolving, the general admiration was expressed in audible terms. As Ambrosio descended from the Pulpit, His Auditors crowded round him, loaded him with blessings, threw themselves at his feet, and kissed the hem of his Garment. He passed on slowly with his hands crossed devoutly upon his bosom, to the door opening into the Abbey-Chapel, at which his Monks waited to receive him. He ascended the Steps, and then turning towards his Followers, addressed to them a few words of gratitude, and exhortation. While He spoke, his Rosary, composed of large grains of amber, fell from his hand, and dropped among the surrounding multitude. It was seized eagerly, and immediately divided amidst the Spectators. Whoever became possessor of a Bead, preserved it as a sacred relique;* and had it been the Chaplet* of thrice-blessed St. Francis himself,* it could not have been disputed with greater vivacity. The Abbot, smiling at their eagerness, pronounced his benediction, and quitted the Church, while humility dwelt upon every feature. Dwelt She also in his heart?

Antonia's eyes followed him with anxiety. As the Door closed after him, it seemed to her as had she lost some one essential to her happiness. A tear stole in silence down her cheek.

'He is separated from the world!' said She to herself; 'Perhaps, I shall never see him more!'

As she wiped away the tear, Lorenzo observed her action.

'Are you satisfied with our Orator?' said He; 'Or do you think that Madrid over-rates his talents?'

Antonia's heart was so filled with admiration for the Monk, that She eagerly seized the opportunity of speaking of him: Besides, as She now no longer considered Lorenzo as an absolute Stranger, She was less embarrassed by her excessive timidity.

'Oh! He far exceeds all my expectations,' answered She; 'Till this moment I had no idea of the powers of eloquence. But when He spoke, his voice inspired me with such interest, such esteem, I might almost say such affection for him, that I am myself astonished at the acuteness of my feelings.'

Lorenzo smiled at the strength of her expressions.

'You are young and just entering into life,' said He; 'Your heart new to the world, and full of warmth and sensibility, receives its first impressions with eagerness. Artless yourself, you suspect not others of deceit; and viewing the world through the medium of your own truth and innocence, you fancy all who surround you to deserve your confidence and esteem. What pity, that these gay visions must soon be dissipated! What pity, that you must soon discover the baseness of mankind, and guard against your fellow-creatures, as against your Foes!'

'Alas! Segnor,' replied Antonia; 'The misfortunes of my Parents have already placed before me but too many sad examples of the perfidy of the world! Yet surely in the present instance the warmth of sympathy cannot have deceived me.'

'In the present instance, I allow that it has not. Ambrosio's character is perfectly without reproach; and a Man who has passed the whole of his life within the walls of a Convent, cannot have found the opportunity to be guilty, even were He possessed of the inclination. But now, when, obliged by the duties of his situation, He must enter occasionally into the world, and be thrown into the way of temptation, it is now that it behoves him to show the brilliance of his virtue. The trial is dangerous; He is just at that period of life when the passions are most vigorous, unbridled, and despotic; His established reputation will mark him out to Seduction as an illustrious Victim; Novelty will give additional charms to the allurements of pleasure; and even the Talents with which Nature has endowed him will contribute to his ruin, by facilitating the means of obtaining his object. Very few would return victorious from a contest so severe.'

'Ah! surely Ambrosio will be one of those few.'

'Of that I have myself no doubt: By all accounts He is an exception to mankind in general, and Envy would seek in vain for a blot upon his character.'

'Segnor, you delight me by this assurance! It encourages me to indulge my prepossession in his favour; and you know not with what pain I should have repressed the sentiment! Ah! dearest Aunt, entreat my Mother to choose him for our Confessor.'

'I entreat her?' replied Leonella; 'I promise you that I shall do no such thing. I do not like this same Ambrosio in the least; He has a look of severity about him that made me tremble from head to foot: Were He my Confessor, I should never have the courage to avow one half of my peccadilloes, and then I should be in a rare condition! I never saw such a stern-looking Mortal, and hope that I never shall see such another. His description of the Devil, God bless us! almost terrified me out of my wits, and when He spoke about Sinners He seemed as if He was ready to eat them.'

'You are right, Segnora,' answered Don Christoval; 'Too great severity is said to be Ambrosio's only fault. Exempted himself from human failings, He is not sufficiently indulgent to those of others; and though strictly just and disinterested in his decisions, his government of the Monks has already shown some proofs of his inflexibility. But the crowd is nearly dissipated: Will you permit us to attend you home?'

'Oh! Christ! Segnor,' exclaimed Leonella affecting to blush; 'I would not suffer such a thing for the Universe! If I came home attended by so gallant a Cavalier, My Sister is so scrupulous that She would read me an hour's lecture, and I should never hear the last of it. Besides, I rather wish you not to make your proposals just at present.'

'My proposals? I assure you, Segnora. . . .'

'Oh! Segnor, I believe that your assurances of impatience are all very true; But really I must desire a little respite. It would not be quite so delicate in me to accept your hand at first sight.'

'Accept my hand? As I hope to live and breathe. . . .'

'Oh! dear Segnor, press me no further, if you love me! I shall consider your obedience as a proof of your affection; You shall hear from me to-morrow, and so farewell. But pray, Cavaliers, may I not enquire your names?'

'My Friend's,' replied Lorenzo, 'is the Condé d'Ossorio, and mine Lorenzo de Medina.'

' 'Tis sufficient. Well, Don Lorenzo, I shall acquaint my Sister with your obliging offer, and let you know the result with all expedition. Where may I send to you?'

'I am always to be found at the Medina Palace.'

'You may depend upon hearing from me. Farewell, Cavaliers. Segnor Condé, let me entreat you to moderate the excessive ardour of your passion: However, to prove to you that I am not displeased with you, and prevent your abandoning yourself to despair, receive this mark of my affection, and sometimes bestow a thought upon the absent Leonella.'

As She said this, She extended a lean and wrinkled hand; which her supposed Admirer kissed with such sorry grace and constraint so evident, that Lorenzo with difficulty repressed his inclination to laugh. Leonella then hastened to quit the Church; The lovely Antonia followed her in silence; but when She reached the Porch, She turned involuntarily, and cast back her eyes towards Lorenzo. He bowed to her, as bidding her farewell; She returned the compliment, and hastily with-drew.

'So, Lorenzo!' said Don Christoval as soon as they were alone, 'You have procured me an agreeable Intrigue! To favour your designs upon Antonia, I obligingly make a few civil speeches which mean nothing, to the Aunt, and at the end of an hour I find myself upon the brink of Matrimony! How will you reward me for having suffered so grievously for your sake? What can repay me for having kissed the leathern paw of that confounded old Witch? Diavolo! She has left such a scent upon my lips, that I shall smell of garlick for this month to come! As I pass along the Prado, I shall be taken for a walking Omelet, or some large Onion running to seed!'

'I confess, my poor Count,' replied Lorenzo, 'that your service has been attended with danger; Yet am I so far from supposing it be past all endurance, that I shall probably solicit you to carry on your amours still further.'

'From that petition I conclude, that the little Antonia has made some impression upon you.'

'I cannot express to you how much I am charmed with her. Since my Father's death, My Uncle the Duke de Medina, has signified to me his wishes to see me married; I have till now eluded his hints, and refused to understand them; But what I have seen this Evening. . . .'

'Well? What have you seen this Evening? Why surely, Don Lorenzo, You cannot be mad enough to think of making a Wife out of this Grand-daughter of "as honest a pains-taking Shoe-maker as any in Cordova"?'

'You forget, that She is also the Grand-daughter of the late Marquis de las Cisternas; But without disputing about birth and titles, I must assure you, that I never beheld a Woman so interesting as Antonia.'

'Very possibly; But you cannot mean to marry her?'

'Why not, my dear Condé? I shall have wealth enough for both of us, and you know that my Uncle thinks liberally upon the subject. From what I have seen of Raymond de las Cisternas, I am certain that he will readily acknowledge Antonia for his Niece. Her birth therefore will be no objection to my offering her my hand. I should be a Villain, could I think of her on any other terms than marriage; and in truth She seems possessed of every quality requisite to make me happy in a Wife. Young, lovely, gentle, sensible. . . .'

'Sensible? Why, She said nothing but "Yes," and "No".'

'She did not say much more, I must confess—But then She always said "Yes," or "No," in the right place.'

'Did She so? Oh! your most obedient! That is using a right Lover's argument, and I dare dispute no longer with so profound a Casuist.* Suppose we adjourn to the Comedy?'

'It is out of my power. I only arrived last night at Madrid, and have not yet had an opportunity of seeing my Sister; You know that her Convent is in this Street, and I was going thither, when the Crowd which I saw thronging into this Church excited my curiosity to know what was the matter. I shall now pursue my first intention, and probably pass the Evening with my Sister at the Parlour-grate.'

'Your Sister in a Convent, say you? Oh! very true, I had forgotten. And how does Donna Agnes? I am amazed, Don Lorenzo, how you could possibly think of immuring so charming a Girl within the walls of a Cloister!'

'I think of it, Don Christoval? How can you suspect me of such barbarity? You are conscious that She took the veil by her own desire, and that particular circumstances made her wish for a seclusion from the World. I used every means in my power to induce her to change her resolution; The endeavour was fruitless, and I lost a Sister!'

'The luckier fellow you; I think, Lorenzo, you were a considerable gainer by that loss: If I remember right, Donna Agnes had a portion of ten thousand pistoles,* half of which reverted to your Lordship. By St. Jago!* I wish that I had fifty Sisters in the same predicament.

I should consent to losing them every soul without much heart-burning—'

'How, Condé?' said Lorenzo in an angry voice; 'Do you suppose me base enough to have influenced my Sister's retirement? Do you suppose that the despicable wish to make myself Master of her fortune could. . . .'

'Admirable! Courage, Don Lorenzo! Now the Man is all in a blaze. God grant, that Antonia may soften that fiery temper, or we shall certainly cut each other's throat before the Month is over! However, to prevent such a tragical Catastrophe for the present, I shall make a retreat, and leave you Master of the field. Farewell, my Knight of Mount Ætna!* Moderate that inflammable disposition, and remember that whenever it is necessary to make love to yonder Harridan, you may reckon upon my services.'

He said, and darted out of the Cathedral.

'How wild-brained!' said Lorenzo; 'With so excellent an heart, what pity that He possesses so little solidity of judgment!'

The night was now fast advancing. The Lamps were not yet lighted. The faint beams of the rising Moon scarcely could pierce through the gothic obscurity of the Church. Lorenzo found himself unable to quit the Spot. The void left in his bosom by Antonia's absence, and his Sister's sacrifice which Don Christoval had just recalled to his imagination, created that melancholy of mind, which accorded but too well with the religious gloom surrounding him. He was still leaning against the seventh column from the Pulpit. A soft and cooling air breathed along the solitary Aisles: The Moon-beams darting into the Church through painted windows, tinged the fretted roofs and massy pillars with a thousand various tints of light and colours: Universal silence prevailed around, only interrupted by the occasional closing of Doors in the adjoining Abbey.

The calm of the hour and solitude of the place contributed to nourish Lorenzo's disposition to melancholy. He threw himself upon a seat which stood near him, and abandoned himself to the delusions of his fancy. He thought of his union with Antonia; He thought of the obstacles which might oppose his wishes; and a thousand changing visions floated before his fancy, sad 'tis true, but not unpleasing. Sleep insensibly stole over him, and the tranquil solemnity of his mind when awake, for a while continued to influence his slumbers.

He still fancied himself to be in the Church of the Capuchins; but it was no longer dark and solitary. Multitudes of silver Lamps shed splendour from the vaulted Roof; Accompanied by the captivating chaunt of distant choristers, the Organ's melody swelled through the Church; The Altar seemed decorated as for some distinguished feast; It was surrounded by a brilliant Company; and near it stood Antonia arrayed in bridal white, and blushing with all the charms of Virgin Modesty.

Half hoping, half fearing, Lorenzo gazed upon the scene before him. Sudden the door leading to the Abbey unclosed, and He saw, attended by a long train of Monks, the Preacher advance to whom He had just listened with so much admiration. He drew near Antonia.

'And where is the Bridegroom?' said the imaginary Friar.

Antonia seemed to look round the Church with anxiety. Involuntarily the Youth advanced a few steps from his concealment. She saw him; The blush of pleasure glowed upon her cheek; With a graceful motion of her hand She beckoned to him to advance. He disobeyed not the command; He flew towards her, and threw himself at her feet.

She retreated for a moment; Then gazing upon him

with unutterable delight;—'Yes!' She exclaimed, 'My
Bridegroom! My destined Bridegroom!'

She said, and hastened to throw herself into his arms;
But before He had time to receive her, an Unknown
rushed between them. His form was gigantic; His
complexion was swarthy, His eyes fierce and terrible;
his Mouth breathed out volumes of fire; and on his
forehead was written in legible characters—'Pride!
Lust! Inhumanity!'

Antonia shrieked. The Monster clasped her in his
arms, and springing with her upon the Altar, tortured
her with his odious caresses. She endeavoured in vain to
escape from his embrace. Lorenzo flew to her succour,
but ere He had time to reach her, a loud burst of thunder
was heard. Instantly the Cathedral seemed crumbling
into pieces; The Monks betook themselves to flight,
shrieking fearfully; The Lamps were extinguished, the
Altar sank down, and in its place appeared an abyss
vomiting forth clouds of flame. Uttering a loud and
terrible cry the Monster plunged into the Gulph, and
in his fall attempted to drag Antonia with him. He strove
in vain. Animated by supernatural powers She disengaged herself from his embrace; But her white Robe was
left in his possession. Instantly a wing of brilliant splendour
spread itself from either of Antonia's arms. She darted
upwards, and while ascending cried to Lorenzo,

'Friend! we shall meet above!'

At the same moment the Roof of the Cathedral
opened; Harmonious voices pealed along the Vaults;
and the glory into which Antonia was received, was
composed of rays of such dazzling brightness, that
Lorenzo was unable to sustain the gaze. His sight failed,
and He sank upon the ground.

When He woke, He found himself extended upon the
pavement of the Church: It was Illuminated, and the
chaunt of Hymns sounded from a distance. For a while

Lorenzo could not persuade himself that what He had just witnessed had been a dream, so strong an impression had it made upon his fancy. A little recollection convinced him of its fallacy: The Lamps had been lighted during his sleep, and the music which he heard, was occasioned by the Monks, who were celebrating their Vespers in the Abbey-Chapel.

Lorenzo rose, and prepared to bend his steps towards his Sister's Convent. His mind fully occupied by the singularity of his dream, He already drew near the Porch, when his attention was attracted by perceiving a Shadow moving upon the opposite wall. He looked curiously round, and soon descried a Man wrapped up in his Cloak, who seemed carefully examining whether his actions were observed. Very few people are exempt from the influence of curiosity. The Unknown seemed anxious to conceal his business in the Cathedral, and it was this very circumstance, which made Lorenzo wish to discover what He was about.

Our Hero was conscious that He had no right to pry into the secrets of this unknown Cavalier.

'I will go,' said Lorenzo. And Lorenzo stayed, where He was.

The shadow thrown by the Column, effectually concealed him from the Stranger, who continued to advance with caution. At length He drew a letter from beneath his cloak, and hastily placed it beneath a Colossal Statue of St. Francis. Then retiring with precipitation, He concealed himself in a part of the Church at a considerable distance from that in which the Image stood.

'So!' said Lorenzo to himself; 'This is only some foolish love affair. I believe, I may as well be gone, for I can do no good in it.'

In truth till that moment it never came into his head, that He could do any good in it; But He thought it necessary to make some little excuse to himself for having indulged his curiosity. He now made a second attempt to retire from the Church: For this time He gained the Porch without meeting with any impediment; But it was destined that He should pay it another visit that night. As He descended the steps leading into the Street, a Cavalier rushed against him with such violence, that Both were nearly overturned by the concussion. Lorenzo put his hand to his sword.

'How now, Segnor?' said He; 'What mean you by this rudeness?'

'Ha! Is it you, Medina?' replied the New-comer, whom Lorenzo by his voice now recognized for Don Christoval; 'You are the luckiest Fellow in the Universe, not to have left the Church before my return. In, in! my dear Lad! They will be here immediately!'

'Who will be here?'

'The old Hen and all her pretty little Chickens! In, I say, and then you shall know the whole History.'

Lorenzo followed him into the Cathedral, and they concealed themselves behind the Statue of St. Francis.

'And now,' said our Hero, 'may I take the liberty of asking, what is the meaning of all this haste and rapture?'

'Oh! Lorenzo, we shall see such a glorious sight! The Prioress of St. Clare* and her whole train of Nuns are coming hither. You are to know, that the pious Father Ambrosio [The Lord reward him for it!] will upon no account move out of his own precincts: It being absolutely necessary for every fashionable Convent to have him for its Confessor, the Nuns are in consequence obliged to visit him at the Abbey; since when the Mountain will not come to Mahomet, Mahomet must needs go to the Mountain. Now the Prioress of St. Clare, the better to escape the gaze of such impure eyes as belong to yourself and your humble Servant, thinks proper to bring her holy flock to confession in the Dusk: She is to be admitted into the Abbey-Chapel by yon private door. The Porteress of St. Clare, who is a worthy old Soul and a particular Friend of mine, has just assured me of their being here in a few moments. There is news for you, you Rogue! We shall see some of the prettiest faces in Madrid!'

'In truth, Christoval, we shall do no such thing. The Nuns are always veiled.'

'No! No! I know better. On entering a place of worship, they ever take off their veils from respect to the Saint to whom 'tis dedicated. But Hark! They are coming! Silence, silence! Observe, and be convinced.'

'Good!' said Lorenzo to himself; 'I may possibly discover to whom the vows are addressed of this mysterious Stranger.'

Scarcely had Don Christoval ceased to speak, when the Domina* of St. Clare appeared, followed by a long procession of Nuns. Each upon entering the Church took off her veil. The Prioress crossèd her hands upon her bosom, and made a profound reverence as She passed the Statue of St. Francis, the Patron of this Cathedral. The Nuns followed her example, and several moved onwards without having satisfied Lorenzo's curiosity. He almost began to despair of seeing the mystery cleared up, when in paying her respects to St. Francis, one of the Nuns happened to drop her Rosary. As She stooped to pick it up, the light flashed full upon her face. At the same moment She dexterously removed the letter from beneath the Image, placed it in her bosom, and hastened to resume her rank in the procession.

'Ha!' said Christoval in a low voice; 'Here we have some little Intrigue, no doubt.'

'Agnes, by heaven!' cried Lorenzo.

'What, your Sister? Diavolo!* Then somebody, I suppose, will have to pay for our peeping.'

'And shall pay for it without delay,' replied the incensed Brother.

The pious procession had now entered the Abbey; The Door was already closed upon it. The Unknown immediately quitted his concealment, and hastened to leave the Church: Ere He could effect his intention, He descried Medina stationed in his passage. The Stranger hastily retreated, and drew his Hat over his eyes.

'Attempt not to fly me!' exclaimed Lorenzo; 'I will know who you are, and what were the contents of that Letter.'

'Of that Letter?' repeated the Unknown. 'And by what title do you ask the question?'

'By a title of which I am now ashamed; But it becomes not you to question me. Either reply circumstantially to my demands, or answer me with your Sword.'

'The latter method will be the shortest,' rejoined the Other, drawing his Rapier; 'Come on, Segnor Bravo!* I am ready!'

Burning with rage, Lorenzo hastened to the attack: The Antagonists had already exchanged several passes, before Christoval, who at that moment had more sense than either of them, could throw himself between their weapons.

'Hold! Hold! Medina!' He exclaimed; 'Remember the consequences of shedding blood on consecrated ground!'*

The Stranger immediately dropped his Sword.

'Medina?' He cried; 'Great God, is it possible! Lorenzo, have you quite forgotten Raymond de las Cisternas?'

Lorenzo's astonishment increased with every succeeding moment. Raymond advanced towards him, but with a look of suspicion He drew back his hand, which the Other was preparing to take.

'You here, Marquis? What is the meaning of all this? You engaged in a clandestine correspondence with my Sister, whose affections . . .'.

'Have ever been, and still are mine. But this is no fit place for an explanation. Accompany me to my Hotel, and you shall know every thing. Who is that with you?'

'One whom I believe you to have seen before,' replied Don Christoval, 'though probably not at Church.'

'The Condé d'Ossorio?'

'Exactly so, Marquis.'

'I have no objection to entrusting you with my secret, for I am sure, that I may depend upon your silence.'

'Then your opinion of me is better than my own, and therefore I must beg leave to decline your confidence. Do you go your own way, and I shall go mine. Marquis, where are you to be found?'

'As usual, at the Hotel de las Cisternas; But remember, that I am incognito, and that if you wish to see me, you must ask for Alphonso d'Alvarada.'

'Good! Good! Farewell, Cavaliers!' said Don Christoval, and instantly departed.

'You, Marquis,' said Lorenzo in the accent of surprise; 'You, Alphonso d'Alvarada?'

'Even so, Lorenzo: But unless you have already heard my story from your Sister, I have much to relate that will astonish you. Follow me, therefore, to my Hotel without delay.'

At this moment the Porter of the Capuchins entered the Cathedral to lock up the doors for the night. The two Noblemen instantly withdrew, and hastened with all speed to the Palace de las Cisternas.

'Well, Antonia!' said the Aunt, as soon as She had quitted the Church; 'What think you of our Gallants? Don Lorenzo really seems a very obliging good sort of young Man: He paid you some attention, and nobody knows what may come of it. But as to Don Christoval, I protest to you, He is the very Phœnix of politeness. So

gallant! so well-bred! So sensible, and so pathetic! Well!
If ever Man can prevail upon me to break my vow never
to marry, it will be that Don Christoval. You see, Niece,
that every thing turns out exactly as I told you: The
very moment that I produced myself in Madrid, I knew
that I should be surrounded by Admirers. When I took
off my veil, did you see, Antonia, what an effect the
action had upon the Condé? And when I presented him
my hand, did you observe the air of passion with which
He kissed it? If ever I witnessed real love, I then saw it
impressed upon Don Christoval's countenance!'

Now Antonia had observed the air, with which Don
Christoval had kissed this same hand; But as She drew
conclusions from it somewhat different from her Aunt's,
She was wise enough to hold her tongue. As this is the
only instance known of a Woman's ever having done so,
it was judged worthy to be recorded here.

The old Lady continued her discourse to Antonia in
the same strain, till they gained the Street in which was
their Lodging. Here a Crowd collected before their door
permitted them not to approach it; and placing themselves on the opposite side of the Street, they endeavoured to make out, what had drawn all these people
together. After some minutes the Crowd formed itself
into a Circle; And now Antonia perceived in the midst
of it a Woman of extraordinary height, who whirled
herself repeatedly round and round, using all sorts of
.extravagant gestures. Her dress was composed of shreds
of various-coloured silks and Linens fantastically arranged, yet not entirely without taste. Her head was
covered with a kind of Turban, ornamented with vine-
leaves and wild flowers. She seemed much sun-burnt,
and her complexion was of a deep olive: Her eyes looked
fiery and strange; and in her hand She bore a long black
Rod, with which She at intervals traced a variety of
singular figures upon the ground, round about which

She danced in all the eccentric attitudes of folly and delirium. Suddenly She broke off her dance, whirled herself round thrice with rapidity, and after a moment's pause She sang the following Ballad.

THE GYPSY'S SONG

Come, cross my hand! My art surpasses
    All that did ever Mortal know;
Come, Maidens, come! My magic glasses
    Your future Husband's form can show:

For 'tis to me the power is given
    Unclosed the book of Fate to see;
To read the fixed resolves of heaven,
    And dive into futurity.

I guide the pale Moon's silver waggon;
    The winds in magic bonds I hold;
I charm to sleep the crimson Dragon,
    Who loves to watch o'er buried gold:

Fenced round with spells, unhurt I venture
    Their sabbath strange where Witches keep;
Fearless the Sorcerer's circle enter,
    And woundless tread on snakes asleep.

Lo! Here are charms of mighty power!
    This makes secure an Husband's truth;
And this composed at midnight hour
    Will force to love the coldest Youth:

If any Maid too much has granted,
    Her loss this Philtre* will repair;
This blooms a cheek where red is wanted,
    And this will make a brown girl fair!

Then silent hear, while I discover
    What I in Fortune's mirror view;
And each, when many a year is over,
    Shall own the Gypsy's sayings true.

'Dear Aunt!' said Antonia when the Stranger had finished, 'Is She not mad?'

'Mad? Not She, Child; She is only wicked. She is a Gypsy, a sort of Vagabond, whose sole occupation is to run about the country telling lyes, and pilfering from those who come by their money honestly. Out upon such Vermin! If I were King of Spain, every one of them should be burnt alive, who was found in my dominions after the next three weeks.'

These words were pronounced so audibly, that they reached the Gypsy's ears. She immediately pierced through the Crowd, and made towards the Ladies. She saluted them thrice in the Eastern fashion, and then addressed herself to Antonia.

THE GYPSY

'Lady! gentle Lady! Know,
I your future fate can show;
Give your hand, and do not fear;
Lady! gentle Lady! hear!'

'Dearest Aunt!' said Antonia, 'Indulge me this once! Let me have my fortune told me!'

'Nonsense, Child! She will tell you nothing but falsehoods.'

'No matter; Let me at least hear what She has to say. Do, my dear Aunt! Oblige me, I beseech you!'

'Well, well! Antonia, since you are so bent upon the thing, . . . Here, good Woman, you shall see the hands of both of us. There is money for you, and now let me hear my fortune.'

As She said this, She drew off her glove, and presented her hand; The Gypsy looked at it for a moment, and then made this reply.

THE GYPSY

'Your fortune? You are now so old,
Good Dame, that 'tis already told:
Yet for your money, in a trice
I will repay you in advice.
Astonished at your childish vanity,
Your Friends all tax you with insanity,
And grieve to see you use your art
To catch some youthful Lover's heart.
Believe me, Dame, when all is done,
Your age will still be fifty one;
And Men will rarely take an hint
Of love, from two grey eyes that squint.
Take then my counsels; Lay aside
Your paint and patches, lust and pride,
And on the Poor those sums bestow,
Which now are spent on useless show.
Think on your Maker, not a Suitor;
Think on your past faults, not on future;
And think Time's Scythe will quickly mow
The few red hairs, which deck your brow.

The audience rang with laughter during the Gypsy's address; and—'fifty one,'—'squinting eyes,'—'red hair,' —'paint and patches,'—&c. were bandied from mouth to mouth. Leonella was almost choaked with passion, and loaded her malicious Adviser with the bitterest reproaches. The swarthy Prophetess for some time listened to her with a contemptuous smile: at length She made her a short answer, and then turned to Antonia.

THE GYPSY

'Peace, Lady! What I said was true;
And now, my lovely Maid, to you;
Give me your hand, and let me see
Your future doom, and heaven's decree.'

In imitation of Leonella, Antonia drew off her glove, and presented her white hand to the Gypsy, who having gazed upon it for some time with a mingled expression of pity and astonishment, pronounced her Oracle in the following words.

THE GYPSY

'Jesus! what a palm is there!
Chaste, and gentle, young and fair,
Perfect mind and form possessing,
You would be some good Man's blessing:
But Alas! This line discovers,
That destruction o'er you hovers;
Lustful Man and crafty Devil
Will combine to work your evil;
And from earth by sorrows driven,
Soon your Soul must speed to heaven.
Yet your sufferings to delay,
Well remember what I say.
When you One more virtuous see
Than belongs to Man to be,
One, whose self no crimes assailing,
Pities not his Neighbour's Failing,
Call the Gypsy's words to mind:
Though He seem so good and kind,
Fair Exteriors oft will hide
Hearts, that swell with lust and pride!
 Lovely Maid, with tears I leave you!
Let not my prediction grieve you;
Rather with submission bending
Calmly wait distress impending,
And expect eternal bliss
In a better world than this.

Having said this, the Gypsy again whirled herself round thrice, and then hastened out of the Street with frantic gesture. The Crowd followed her; and Elvira's

door being now unembarrassed Leonella entered the
House out of honour with the Gypsy, with her Niece, and
with the People; In short with every body, but herself
and her charming Cavalier. The Gypsy's predictions had
also considerably affected Antonia; But the impression
soon wore off, and in a few hours She had forgotten the
adventure, as totally as had it never taken place.

CHAPTER II

Fòrse sé tu gustassi una sòl volta
La millésima parte délle giòje,
Ché gusta un còr amato riamando,
Diresti ripentita sospirando,
Perduto è tutto il tempo
Ché in amar non si spènde.

                         Tasso.*

Hadst Thou but tasted once the thousandth part
Of joys, which bless the loved and loving heart,
Your words repentant and your sighs would prove,
Lost is the time which is not past in love.

THE MONKS HAVING attended their Abbot to the door
of his Cell, He dismissed them with an air of conscious
superiority, in which Humility's semblance combated
with the reality of pride.

He was no sooner alone, than He gave free loose to the
indulgence of his vanity. When He remembered the
Enthusiasm which his discourse had excited, his heart
swelled with rapture, and his imagination presented him
with splendid visions of aggrandizement. He looked
round him with exultation, and Pride told him loudly,

that He was superior to the rest of his fellow-Creatures.

'Who,' thought He; 'Who but myself has passed the ordeal of Youth, yet sees no single stain upon his conscience? Who else has subdued the violence of strong passions and an impetuous temperament, and submitted even from the dawn of life to voluntary retirement? I seek for such a Man in vain. I see no one but myself possessed of such resolution. Religion cannot boast Ambrosio's equal! How powerful an effect did my discourse produce upon its Auditors! How they crowded round me! How they loaded me with benedictions, and pronounced me the sole uncorrupted Pillar of the Church! What then now is left for me to do? Nothing, but to watch as carefully over the conduct of my Brothers, as I have hitherto watched over my own. Yet hold! May I not be tempted from those paths, which till now I have pursued without one moment's wandering? Am I not a Man, whose nature is frail, and prone to error? I must now abandon the solitude of my retreat; The fairest and noblest Dames of Madrid continually present themselves at the Abbey, and will use no other Confessor. I must accustom my eyes to Objects of temptation, and expose myself to the seduction of luxury and desire. Should I meet in that world which I am constrained to enter some lovely Female, lovely . . . as you Madona. . . .!'

As He said this, He fixed his eyes upon a picture of the Virgin, which was suspended opposite to him: This for two years had been the Object of his increasing wonder and adoration. He paused, and gazed upon it with delight.

'What Beauty in that countenance!' He continued after a silence of some minutes; 'How graceful is the turn of that head! What sweetness, yet what majesty in her divine eyes! How softly her cheek reclines upon her hand! Can the Rose vie with the blush of that cheek? Can the Lily rival the whiteness of that hand?

Oh! if such a Creature existed, and existed but for me! Were I permitted to twine round my fingers those golden ringlets, and press with my lips the treasures of that snowy bosom! Gracious God, should I then resist the temptation? Should I not barter for a single embrace the reward of my sufferings for thirty years? Should I not abandon. . . . Fool that I am! Whither do I suffer my admiration of this picture to hurry me? Away, impure ideas! Let me remember, that Woman is for ever lost to me. Never was Mortal formed so perfect as this picture. But even did such exist, the trial might be too mighty for a common virtue, but Ambrosio's is proof against temptation. Temptation, did I say? To me it would be none. What charms me, when ideal and considered as a superior Being, would disgust me, become Woman and tainted with all the failings of Mortality. It is not the Woman's beauty that fills me with such enthusiasm; It is the Painter's skill that I admire, it is the Divinity that I adore! Are not the passions dead in my bosom? Have I not freed myself from the frailty of Mankind? Fear not, Ambrosio! Take confidence in the strength of your virtue. Enter boldly into a world, to whose failings you are superior; Reflect that you are now exempted from Humanity's defects, and defy all the arts of the Spirits of Darkness. They shall know you for what you are!'

Here his Reverie was interrupted by three soft knocks at the door of his Cell. With difficulty did the Abbot awake from his delirium. The knocking was repeated.

'Who is there?' said Ambrosio at length.

'It is only Rosario,' replied a gentle voice.

'Enter! Enter, my Son!'

The Door was immediately opened, and Rosario appeared with a small basket in his hand.

Rosario was a young Novice* belonging to the Monastery, who in three Months intended to make his profession. A sort of mystery enveloped this Youth which rendered him at once an object of interest and curiosity. His hatred of society, his profound melancholy, his rigid observation of the duties of his order, and his voluntary seclusion from the world at his age so unusual, attracted the notice of the whole fraternity. He seemed fearful of being recognised, and no one had ever seen his face. His head was continually muffled up in his Cowl; Yet such of his features as accident discovered, appeared the most beautiful and noble. Rosario was the only name by which He was known in the Monastery. No one knew from whence He came, and when questioned in the subject He preserved a profound silence. A Stranger, whose rich habit and magnificent equipage declared him to be of distinguished rank, had engaged the Monks to receive a Novice, and had deposited the necessary sums. The next day He returned with Rosario, and from that time no more had been heard of him.

The Youth had carefully avoided the company of the Monks: He answered their civilities with sweetness, but reserve, and evidently showed that his inclination led him to solitude. To this general rule the Superior was the only exception. To him He looked up with a respect approaching idolatry: He sought his company with the most attentive assiduity, and eagerly seized every means to ingratiate himself in his favour. In the Abbot's society his Heart seemed to be at ease, and an air of gaiety pervaded his whole manners and discourse. Ambrosio on his side did not feel less attracted towards the Youth; With him alone did He lay aside his habitual severity. When He spoke to him, He insensibly assumed a tone milder than was usual to him; and no voice sounded so sweet to him as did Rosario's. He repayed the Youth's attentions by instructing him in various sciences; The Novice received his lessons with docility; Ambrosio was every day more charmed with the vivacity of his Genius, the simplicity of his manners, and the rectitude of his heart: In short He loved him will all the affection of a Father. He could not help sometimes indulging a desire secretly to see the face of his Pupil; But his rule of self-denial extended even to curiosity, and prevented him from communicating his wishes to the Youth.

'Pardon my intrusion, Father,' said Rosario, while He placed his basket upon the Table; 'I come to you a Suppliant. Hearing that a dear Friend is dangerously ill, I entreat your prayers for his recovery. If supplications can prevail upon heaven to spare him, surely yours must be efficacious.'

'Whatever depends upon me, my Son, you know that you may command. What is your Friend's name?'

'Vincentio della Ronda.'

' 'Tis sufficient. I will not forget him in my prayers, and may our thrice-blessed St. Francis deign to listen to my intercession!—What have you in your basket, Rosario?'

'A few of those flowers, reverend Father, which I have observed to be most acceptable to you. Will you permit my arranging them in your chamber?'

'Your attentions charm me, my Son.'

While Rosario dispersed the contents of his Basket in small Vases, placed for that purpose in various parts of the room, the Abbot thus continued the conversation.

'I saw you not in the Church this evening, Rosario.'

'Yet I was present, Father. I am too grateful for your protection to lose an opportunity of witnessing your Triumph.'

'Alas! Rosario, I have but little cause to triumph: The Saint spoke by my mouth; To him belongs all the merit. It seems then you were contented with my discourse?'

'Contented, say you? Oh! you surpassed yourself! Never did I hear such eloquence . . . save once!'

Here the Novice heaved an involuntary sigh.

'When was that once?' demanded the Abbot.

'When you preached upon the sudden indisposition of our late Superior.'

'I remember it: That is more than two years ago. And were you present? I knew you not at that time, Rosario.'

' 'Tis true, Father; and would to God! I had expired, ere I beheld that day! What sufferings, what sorrows should I have escaped!'

'Sufferings at your age, Rosario?'

'Aye, Father; Sufferings, which if known to you, would equally raise your anger and compassion! Sufferings, which form at once the torment and pleasure of my existence! Yet in this retreat my bosom would feel tranquil, were it not for the tortures of apprehension. Oh God! Oh God! how cruel is a life of fear!—Father! I have given up all; I have abandoned the world and its delights for ever: Nothing now remains, Nothing now has charms for me, but your friendship, but your affection. If I lose that, Father! Oh! if I lose that, tremble at the effects of my despair!'

'You apprehend the loss of my friendship? How has my conduct justified this fear? Know me better, Rosario, and think me worthy of your confidence. What are your sufferings? Reveal them to me, and believe that if 'tis in my power to relieve them. . . .'

'Ah! 'tis in no one's power but yours. Yet I must not let you know them. You would hate me for my avowal! You would drive me from your presence with scorn and ignominy!'

'My Son, I conjure you! I entreat you!'

'For pity's sake, enquire no further! I must not . . . I dare not . . . Hark! The Bell rings for Vespers! Father, your benediction, and I leave you!'

As He said this, He threw himself upon his knees, and received the blessing which He demanded. Then pressing the Abbot's hand to his lips, He started from the ground, and hastily quitted the apartment. Soon after Ambrosio descended to Vespers, [which were celebrated in a small chapel belonging to the Abbey] filled with surprise at the singularity of the Youth's behaviour.

Vespers being over, the Monks retired to their respective Cells. The Abbot alone remained in the Chapel to receive the Nuns of St. Clare. He had not been long seated in the confessional chair, before the Prioress made her appearance. Each of the Nuns was heard in her turn, while the Others waited with the Domina in the adjoining Vestry. Ambrosio listened to the confessions with attention, made many exhortations, enjoined penance proportioned to each offence, and for some time every thing went on as usual: till at last one of the Nuns, conspicuous from the nobleness of her air and elegance of her figure carelessly permitted a letter to fall from her bosom. She was retiring, unconscious of her loss. Ambrosio supposed it to have been written by some one of her Relations, and picked it up intending to restore it to her.

'Stay, Daughter,' said He; 'You have let fall. . . .'

At this moment, the paper being already open, his eye involuntarily read the first words. He started back with surprise! The Nun had turned round on hearing his voice: She perceived her letter in his hand, and uttering a shriek of terror, flew hastily to regain it.

'Hold!' said the Friar in a tone of severity; 'Daughter, I must read this letter.'

'Then I am lost!' She exclaimed clasping her hands together wildly.

All colour instantly faded from her face; she trembled with agitation, and was obliged to fold her arms round a Pillar of the Chapel to save herself from sinking upon the floor. In the mean while the Abbot read the following lines.

'All is ready for your escape, my dearest Agnes. At

twelve tomorrow night I shall expect to find you at the Garden-door: I have obtained the Key, and a few hours will suffice to place you in a secure asylum. Let no mistaken scruples induce you to reject the certain means of preserving yourself and the innocent Creature whom you nourish in your bosom. Remember that you had promised to be mine, long ere you engaged yourself to the church; that your situation will soon be evident to the prying eyes of your Companions; and that flight is the only means of avoiding the effects of their malevolent resentment. Farewell, my Agnes! my dear and destined Wife! Fail not to be at the Garden-door at twelve!'

As soon as He had finished, Ambrosio bent an eye stern and angry upon the imprudent Nun.

'This letter must to the Prioress!' said He, and passed her.

His words sounded like thunder to her ears: She awoke from her torpidity only to be sensible of the dangers of her situation. She followed him hastily, and detained him by his garment.

'Stay! Oh! stay!' She cried in the accents of despair, while She threw herself at the Friar's feet, and bathed them with her tears. 'Father, compassionate my youth! Look with indulgence on a Woman's weakness, and deign to conceal my frailty! The remainder of my life shall be employed in expiating this single fault, and your lenity will bring back a soul to heaven!'

'Amazing confidence! What! Shall St. Clare's Convent become the retreat of Prostitutes? Shall I suffer the Church of Christ to cherish in its bosom debauchery and shame? Unworthy Wretch! such lenity would make me your accomplice. Mercy would here be criminal. You have abandoned yourself to a Seducer's lust; You have defiled the sacred habit by your impurity; and still dare you think yourself deserving my compassion? Hence, nor detain me longer! Where is the Lady Prioress?' He added, raising his voice.

'Hold! Father, Hold! Hear me but for one moment! Tax me not with impurity, nor think that I have erred from the warmth of temperament. Long before I took the veil, Raymond was Master of my heart: He inspired me with the purest, the most irreproachable passion, and was on the point of becoming my lawful husband. An horrible adventure, and the treachery of a Relation, separated us from each other: I believed him for ever lost to me, and threw myself into a Convent from motives of despair. Accident again united us; I could not refuse myself the melancholy pleasure of mingling my tears with his: We met nightly in the Gardens of St. Clare, and in an unguarded moment I violated my vows of Chastity. I shall soon become a Mother: Reverend Ambrosio, take compassion on me; take compassion on the innocent Being, whose existence is attached to mine. If you discover my imprudence to the Domina, both of us are lost: The punishment, which the laws of St. Clare assign to Unfortunates like myself, is most severe and cruel. Worthy, worthy Father! Let not your own un-tainted conscience render you unfeeling towards those less able to withstand temptation! Let not mercy be the only virtue of which your heart is unsusceptible! Pity me, most reverend! Restore my letter, nor doom me to inevitable destruction!'

'Your boldness confounds me! Shall I conceal your crime, I whom you have deceived by your feigned confession? No, Daughter, no! I will render you a more essential service. I will rescue you from perdition in spite of yourself; Penance and mortification shall expiate your offence, and Severity force you back to the paths of holiness. What; Ho! Mother St. Agatha!'

'Father! By all that is sacred, by all that is most dear to you, I supplicate, I entreat. . . .'

'Release me! I will not hear you. Where is the Domina? Mother St. Agatha, where are you?'

The door of the Vestry opened, and the Prioress entered the Chapel, followed by her Nuns.

'Cruel! Cruel!' exclaimed Agnes, relinquishing her hold.

Wild and desperate, She threw herself upon the ground, beating her bosom, and rending her veil in all the delirium of despair. The Nuns gazed with astonishment upon the scene before them. The Friar now presented the fatal paper to the Prioress, informed her of the manner in which he had found it, and added, that it was her business to decide, what penance the delinquent merited.

While She perused the letter, the Domina's countenance grew inflamed with passion. What! Such a crime committed in her Convent, and made known to Ambrosio, to the Idol of Madrid, to the Man whom She was most anxious to impress with the opinion of the strictness and regularity of her House! Words were inadequate to express her fury. She was silent, and darted upon the prostrate Nun looks of menace and malignity.

'Away with her to the Convent!' said She at length to some of her Attendants.

Two of the oldest Nuns now approaching Agnes, raised her forcibly from the ground, and prepared to conduct her from the Chapel.

'What!' She exclaimed suddenly shaking off their hold with distracted gestures; 'Is all hope then lost? Already do you drag me to punishment? Where are you, Raymond? Oh! save me! save me!' Then casting upon the Abbot a frantic look, 'Hear me!' She continued; 'Man of an hard heart! Hear me, Proud, Stern, and Cruel! You could have saved me; you could have restored me to happiness and virtue, but would not! You are the destroyer of my Soul; You are my Murderer, and on you fall the curse of my death and my unborn Infant's! Insolent in your yet-unshaken virtue, you disdained the prayers of a Penitent; But God will show mercy, though you show none. And where is the merit of your boasted virtue? What temptations have you vanquished? Coward! you have fled from it, not opposed seduction. But the day of Trial will arrive! Oh! then when you yield to impetuous passions! when you feel that Man is weak, and born to err; When shuddering you look back upon your crimes, and solicit with terror the mercy of your God, Oh! in that fearful moment think upon me! Think upon your Cruelty! Think upon Agnes, and despair of pardon!'

As She uttered these last words, her strength was exhausted, and She sank inanimate upon the bosom of a Nun who stood near her. She was immediately conveyed from the Chapel, and her Companions followed her.

Ambrosio had not listened to her reproaches without emotion. A secret pang at his heart made him feel, that He had treated this Unfortunate with too great severity. He therefore detained the Prioress, and ventured to pronounce some words in favour of the Delinquent.

'The violence of her despair,' said He, 'proves, that at least Vice is not become familiar to her. Perhaps by treating her with somewhat less rigour than is generally practised, and mitigating in some degree the accustomed penance. . . .'

'Mitigate it, Father?' interrupted the Lady Prioress; 'Not I, believe me. The laws of our order are strict and severe; they have fallen into disuse of late, But the crime of Agnes shows me the necessity of their revival. I go to signify my intention to the Convent, and Agnes shall be the first to feel the rigour of those laws, which shall be obeyed to the very letter. Father, Farewell.'

Thus saying, She hastened out of the Chapel.

'I have done my duty,' said Ambrosio to himself.

Still did He not feel perfectly satisfied by this reflection. To dissipate the unpleasant ideas which this scene had excited in him, upon quitting the Chapel He descended into the Abbey-Garden.* In all Madrid there was no spot more beautiful or better regulated. It was laid out with the most exquisite taste; The choicest flowers adorned it in the height of luxuriance, and though artfully arranged, seemed only planted by the hand of Nature: Fountains, springing from basons of white Marble, cooled the air with perpetual showers; and the Walls were entirely covered by Jessamine,* vines, and Honeysuckles. The hour now added to the beauty of the scene. The full Moon ranging through a blue and cloudless sky, shed upon the trees a trembling lustre, and the waters of the fountains sparkled in the silver beam: A gentle breeze breathed the fragrance of Orange-blossoms along the Alleys; and the Nightingale poured forth her melodious murmur from the shelter of an artificial wilderness. Thither the Abbot bent his steps.

In the bosom of this little Grove stood a rustic Grotto, formed in imitation of an Hermitage. The walls were constructed of roots of trees, and the interstices filled up with Moss and Ivy. Seats of Turf were placed on either side, and a natural Cascade fell from the Rock above. Buried in himself the Monk approached the spot. The universal calm had communicated itself to his bosom, and a voluptuous tranquillity spread languor through his soul.

He reached the Hermitage, and was entering to repose himself, when He stopped on perceiving it to be already occupied. Extended upon one of the Banks lay a man in a melancholy posture. His head was supported upon his arm, and He seemed lost in mediation. The Monk drew nearer, and recognised Rosario: He watched him in silence, and entered not the Hermitage. After some minutes the Youth raised his eyes, and fixed them mournfully upon the opposite Wall.

'Yes!' said He with a deep and plaintive sigh; 'I feel all the happiness of thy situation, all the misery of my own! Happy were I, could I think like Thee! Could I look like Thee with disgust upon Mankind, could bury myself for ever in some impenetrable solitude, and forget that the world holds Beings deserving to be loved! Oh God! What a blessing would Misanthropy be to me!'

'That is a singular thought, Rosario,' said the Abbot, entering the Grotto.

'You here, reverend Father?' cried the Novice.

At the same time starting from his place in confusion, He drew his Cowl hastily over his face. Ambrosio seated himself upon the Bank, and obliged the Youth to place himself by him.

'You must not indulge this disposition to melancholy,' said He; 'What can possibly have made you view in so desirable a light, Misanthropy, of all sentiments the most hateful?'

'The perusal of these Verses, Father, which till now had escaped my observation. The Brightness of the Moon-beams permitted my reading them; and Oh! how I envy the feelings of the Writer!'

As He said this, He pointed to a marble Tablet fixed against the opposite Wall: On it were engraved the following lines.

INSCRIPTION IN AN HERMITAGE

Who-e'er Thou art these lines now reading,
Think not, though from the world receding
I joy my lonely days to lead in
      This Desart*drear,
That with remorse a conscience bleeding
      Hath led me here.

No thought of guilt my bosom sowrs:
Free-willed I fled from courtly bowers;

For well I saw in Halls and Towers
    That Lust and Pride,
The Arch-Fiend's dearest darkest Powers,
    In state preside.

I saw Mankind with vice incrusted;
I saw that Honour's sword was rusted;
That few for aught but folly lusted;
That He was still deceiv'd, who trusted
    In Love or Friend;
And hither came with Men disgusted
    My life to end.

In this lone Cave, in garments lowly,
Alike a Foe to noisy folly,
And brow-bent gloomy melancholy
    I wear away
My life, and in my office holy
    Consume the day.

Content and comfort bless me more in
This Grot, than e'er I felt before in
A Palace; and with thoughts still soaring
    To God on high,
Each night and morn with voice imploring
    This wish I sigh.

'Let me, Oh! Lord! from life retire,
Unknown each guilty worldly fire,
Remorseful throb, or loose desire;
    And when I die,
Let me in this belief expire,
    "To God I fly"!'

Stranger, if full of youth and riot
As yet no grief has marred thy quiet,
Thou haply throw'st a scornful eye at
    The Hermit's prayer:
But if Thou hast a cause to sigh at
    Thy fault, or care;

> If Thou hast known false Love's vexation,
>> Or hast been exil'd from thy Nation,
>>> Or guilt affrights thy contemplation,
>>>>   And makes thee pine,
>> Oh! how must Thou lament *thy* station,
>>>>   And envy mine!

'Were it possible' said the Friar, 'for Man to be so totally wrapped up in himself as to live in absolute seclusion from human nature, and could yet feel the contented tranquillity which these lines express, I allow that the situation would be more desirable, than to live in a world so pregnant with every vice and every folly. But this never can be the case. This inscription was merely placed here for the ornament of the Grotto, and the sentiments and the Hermit are equally imaginary. Man was born for society. However little He may be attached to the World, He never can wholly forget it, or bear to be wholly forgotten by it. Disgusted at the guilt or absurdity of Mankind, the Misanthrope flies from it: He resolves to become an Hermit, and buries himself in the Cavern of some gloomy Rock. While Hate inflames his bosom, possibly He may feel contented with his situation: But when his passions begin to cool; when Time has mellowed his sorrows, and healed those wounds which He bore with him to his solitude, think you that Content becomes his Companion? Ah! no, Rosario. No longer sustained by the violence of his passions, He feels all the monotony of his way of living, and his heart becomes the prey of Ennui* and weariness. He looks round, and finds himself alone in the Universe: The love of society revives in his bosom, and He pants to return to that world which He has abandoned. Nature loses all her charms in his eyes: No one is near him to point out her beauties, or share in his admiration of her excellence and variety. Propped upon the fragment of some Rock,

He gazes upon the tumbling water-fall with a vacant eye, He views without emotion the glory of the setting Sun. Slowly He returns to his Cell at Evening, for no one there is anxious for his arrival; He has no comfort in his solitary unsavoury meal: He throws himself upon his couch of Moss despondent and dissatisfied, and wakes only to pass a day as joyless, as monotonous as the former.'

'You amaze me, Father! Suppose that circumstances condemned you to solitude; Would not the duties of Religion and the consciousness of a life well spent communicate to your heart that calm which. . . .'

'I should deceive myself, did I fancy that they could. I am convinced of the contrary, and that all my fortitude would not prevent me from yielding to melancholy and disgust. After consuming the day in study, if you knew my pleasure at meeting my Brethren in the Evening! After passing many a long hour in solitude, if I could express to you the joy which I feel at once more beholding a fellow-Creature! 'Tis in this particular that I place the principal merit of a Monastic Institution. It secludes Man from the temptations of Vice; It procures that leisure necessary for the proper service of the Supreme; It spares him the mortification of witnessing the crimes of the worldly, and yet permits him to enjoy the blessings of society. And do you, Rosario, do *You* envy an Hermit's life? Can you be thus blind to the happiness of your situation? Reflect upon it for a moment. This Abbey is become your Asylum: Your regularity, your gentleness, your talents have rendered you the object of universal esteem: You are secluded from the world which you profess to hate; yet you remain in possession of the benefits of society, and that a society composed of the most estimable of Mankind.'

'Father! Father! 'tis that which causes my Torment! Happy had it been for me, had my life been passed among the vicious and abandoned! Had I never heard pronounced the name of Virtue! 'Tis my unbounded adoration of religion; 'Tis my soul's exquisite sensibility of the beauty of fair and good, that loads me with shame! that hurries me to perdition! Oh! that I had never seen these Abbey-walls!'

'How, Rosario? When we last conversed, you spoke in a different tone. Is my friendship then become of such little consequence? Had you never seen these Abbey-walls, you never had seen me: Can that really be your wish?'

'Had never seen you?' repeated the Novice, starting from the Bank, and grasping the Friar's hand with a frantic air; 'You? You? Would to God, that lightning had blasted them, before you ever met my eyes! Would to God! that I were never to see you more, and could forget that I had ever seen you!'

With these words He flew hastily from the Grotto. Ambrosio remained in his former attitude, reflecting on the Youth's unaccountable behaviour. He was inclined to suspect the derangement of his senses: yet the general tenor of his conduct, the connexion of his ideas, and calmness of his demeanour till the moment of his quitting the Grotto, seemed to discountenance this conjecture. After a few minutes Rosario returned. He again seated himself upon the Bank: He reclined his cheek upon one hand, and with the other wiped away the tears which trickled from his eyes at intervals.

The Monk looked upon him with compassion, and forbore to interrupt his meditations. Both observed for some time a profound silence. The Nightingale had now taken her station upon an Orange Tree fronting the Hermitage, and poured forth a strain the most melancholy and melodious. Rosario raised his head, and listened to her with attention.

'It was thus,' said He, with a deep-drawn sigh; 'It

was thus, that during the last month of her unhappy life, my Sister used to sit listening to the Nightingale. Poor Matilda! She sleeps in the Grave, and her broken heart throbs no more with passion.'

'You had a Sister?'

'You say right, that I *had*; Alas! I have one no longer. She sunk beneath the weight of her sorrows in the very spring of life.'

'What were those sorrows?'

'They will not excite *your* pity: *You* know not the power of those irresistible, those fatal sentiments, to which her Heart was a prey. Father, She loved unfortunately. A passion for One endowed with every virtue, for a Man, Oh! rather let me say, for a divinity, proved the bane of her existence. His noble form, his spotless character, his various talents, his wisdom solid, wonderful, and glorious, might have warmed the bosom of the most insensible. My Sister saw him, and dared to love though She never dared to hope.'

'If her love was so well bestowed, what forbad her to hope the obtaining of its object?'

'Father, before He knew her, Julian had already plighted his vows to a Bride most fair, most heavenly! Yet still my Sister loved, and for the Husband's sake She doted upon the Wife. One morning She found means to escape from our Father's House: Arrayed in humble weeds She offered herself as a Domestic to the Consort of her Beloved, and was accepted. She was now continually in his presence: She strove to ingratiate herself into his favour: She succeeded. Her attentions attracted Julian's notice; The virtuous are ever grateful, and He distinguished Matilda above the rest of her Companions.'

'And did not your Parents seek for her? Did they submit tamely to their loss, nor attempt to recover their wandering Daughter?'

'Ere they could find her, She discovered herself. Her

love grew too violent for concealment; Yet She wished
not for Julian's person, She ambitioned but a share of his
heart. In an unguarded moment She confessed her
affection. What was the return? Doting upon his Wife,
and believing that a look of pity bestowed upon another,
was a theft from what He owed to her, He drove Matilda
from his presence. He forbad her ever again appearing
before him. His severity broke her heart: She returned
to her Father's, and in a few Months after was carried to
her Grave.'

'Unhappy Girl! Surely her fate was too severe, and
Julian was too cruel.'

'Do you think so, Father?' cried the Novice with
vivacity; 'Do you think that He was cruel?'

'Doubtless I do, and pity her most sincerely.'

'You pity her? You pity her? Oh! Father! Father!
Then pity me!'

The Friar started; when after a moment's pause
Rosario added with a faltering voice,—'for my sufferings
are still greater. My Sister had a Friend, a real Friend,
who pitied the acuteness of her feelings, nor reproached
her with her inability to repress them. I . . . .! I have no
Friend! The whole wide world cannot furnish an heart,
that is willing to participate in the sorrows of mine!'

As He uttered these words, He sobbed audibly. The
Friar was affected. He took Rosario's hand, and pressed
it with tenderness.

'You have no Friend, say you? What then am I? Why
will you not confide in me, and what can you fear? My
severity? Have I ever used it with you? The dignity of
my habit? Rosario, I lay aside the Monk, and bid
you consider me as no other than your Friend, your
Father. Well may I assume that title, for never did
Parent watch over a Child more fondly than I have
watched over you. From the moment in which I first
beheld you, I perceived sensations in my bosom, till then

unknown to me; I found a delight in your society which no one's else could afford; and when I witnessed the extent of your genius and information, I rejoiced as does a Father in the perfections of his Son. Then lay aside your fears; Speak to me with openness: Speak to me, Rosario, and say that you will confide in me. If my aid or my pity can alleviate your distress. . . .'

'Yours can! Yours only can! Ah! Father, how willingly would I unveil to you my heart! How willingly would I declare the secret, which bows me down with its weight! But Oh! I fear! I fear!'

'What, my Son?'

'That you should abhor me for my weakness; That the reward of my confidence should be the loss of your esteem.'

'How shall I reassure you? Reflect upon the whole of my past conduct, upon the paternal tenderness which I have ever shown you. Abhor you, Rosario? It is no longer in my power. To give up your society would be to deprive myself of the greatest pleasure of my life. Then reveal to me what afflicts you, and believe me while I solemnly swear. . . .'

'Hold!' interrupted the Novice; 'Swear, that whatever be my secret, you will not oblige me to quit the Monastery till my Noviciate shall expire.'

'I promise it faithfully, and as I keep my vows to you, may Christ keep his to Mankind. Now then explain this mystery, and rely upon my indulgence.'

'I obey you. Know then. . . . Oh! how I tremble to name the word! Listen to me with pity, revered Ambrosio! Call up every latent spark of human weakness that may teach you compassion for mine! Father!' continued He throwing himself at the Friar's feet, and pressing his hand to his lips with eagerness, while agitation for a moment choaked his voice; 'Father!' continued He in faltering accents, 'I am a Woman!'

The Abbot started at this unexpected avowal. Prostrate on the ground lay the feigned Rosario, as if waiting in silence the decision of his Judge. Astonishment on the one part, apprehension on the other, for some minutes chained them in the same attitudes, as had they been touched by the Rod of some Magician. At length recovering from his confusion, the Monk quitted the Grotto, and sped with precipitation towards the Abbey. His action did not escape the Suppliant. She sprang from the ground; She hastened to follow him, over-took him, threw herself in his passage, and embraced his knees. Ambrosio strove in vain to disengage himself from her grasp.

'Do not fly me!' She cried; 'Leave me not abandoned to the impulse of despair! Listen, while I excuse my imprudence; while I acknowledge my Sister's story to be my own! I am Matilda; You are her Beloved.'

If Ambrosio's surprise was great at her first avowal, upon hearing her second it exceeded all bounds. Amazed, embarrassed, and irresolute He found himself incapable of pronouncing a syllable, and remained in silence gazing upon Matilda: This gave her opportunity to continue her explanation as follows.

'Think not, Ambrosio, that I come to rob your Bride of your affections. No, believe me: Religion alone deserves you; and far is it from Matilda's wish to draw you from the paths of virtue. What I feel for you is love, not licentiousness; I sigh to be possessor of your heart, not lust for the enjoyment of your person. Deign to listen to my vindication: A few moments will convince you, that this holy retreat is not polluted by my presence, and that you may grant me your compassion without trespassing against your vows.'—She seated herself: Ambrosio, scarcely conscious of what He did, followed her example, and She proceeded in her discourse.

'I spring from a distinguished family: My Father was

Chief of the noble House of Villanegas. He died, while I was still an Infant, and left me sole Heiress of his immense possessions. Young and wealthy, I was sought in marriage by the noblest Youths of Madrid; But no one succeeded in gaining my affections. I had been brought up under the care of an Uncle, possessed of the most solid judgment and extensive erudition. He took pleasure in communicating to me some portion of his knowledge. Under his instructions my understanding acquired more strength and justness, than generally falls to the lot of my sex: The ability of my Preceptor being aided by natural curiosity, I not only made a considerable progress in sciences universally studied, but in others, revealed but to few, and lying under censure from the blindness of superstition.* But while my Guardian laboured to enlarge the sphere of my knowledge, He carefully inculcated every moral precept: He relieved me from the shackles of vulgar prejudice; He pointed out the beauty of Religion; He taught me to look with adoration upon the pure and virtuous, and, woe is me! I have obeyed him but too well!

'With such dispositions, Judge whether I could observe with any other sentiment than disgust the vice, dissipation, and ignorance, which disgrace our Spanish Youth. I rejected every offer with disdain. My heart remained without a Master, till chance conducted me to the Cathedral of the Capuchins. Oh! surely on that day my Guardian-Angel slumbered neglectful of his charge! Then was it that I first beheld you: You supplied the Superior's place, absent from illness. You cannot but remember the lively enthusiasm which your discourse created. Oh! how I drank your words! How your eloquence seemed to steal me from myself! I scarcely dared to breathe, fearing to lose a syllable; and while you spoke, Methought a radiant glory beamed round your head, and your countenance shone with the majesty of a God. I retired from the Church, glowing with admiration. From that moment you became the idol of my heart, the never-changing object of my Meditations. I enquired respecting you. The reports which were made me of your mode of life, of your knowledge, piety, and self-denial riveted the chains imposed on me by your eloquence. I was conscious that there was no longer a void in my heart; That I had found the Man whom I had sought till then in vain. In expectation of hearing you again every day I visited your Cathedral: You remained secluded within the Abbey-walls, and I always withdrew, wretched and disappointed. The Night was more propitious to me, for then you stood before me in my dreams; You vowed to me eternal friendship; You led me through the paths of virtue, and assisted me to support the vexations of life. The Morning dispelled these pleasing visions; I woke, and found myself separated from you by Barriers, which appeared insurmountable. Time seemed only to increase the strength of my passion: I grew melancholy and despondent; I fled from society, and my health declined daily. At length no longer able to exist in this state of torture, I resolved to assume the disguise in which you see me. My artifice was fortunate: I was received into the Monastery, and succeeded in gaining your esteem.

'Now then I should have felt compleatly happy, had not my quiet been disturbed by the fear of detection. The pleasure, which I received from your society, was embittered by the idea, that perhaps I should soon be deprived of it: and my heart throbbed so rapturously at obtaining the marks of your friendship, as to convince me that I never should survive its loss. I resolved, therefore, not to leave the discovery of my sex to chance, to confess the whole to you, and throw myself entirely on your mercy and indulgence. Ah! Ambrosio, can I have been deceived? Can you be less generous than I thought you? I will not suspect it. You will not drive a Wretch to despair; I shall still be permitted to see you, to converse with you, to adore you! Your virtues shall be my example through life; and when we expire, our bodies shall rest in the same Grave.'

She ceased. While She spoke, a thousand opposing sentiments combated in Ambrosio's bosom. Surprise at the singularity of this adventure, Confusion at her abrupt declaration, Resentment at her boldness in entering the Monastery, and Consciousness of the austerity with which it behoved him to reply, such were the sentiments of which He was aware; But there were others also which did not obtain his notice. He perceived not, that his vanity was flattered by the praises bestowed upon his eloquence and virtue; that He felt a secret pleasure in reflecting that a young and seemingly lovely Woman had for his sake abandoned the world, and sacrificed every other passion to that which He had inspired: Still less did He perceive that his heart throbbed with desire, while his hand was pressed gently by Matilda's ivory fingers.

By degrees He recovered from his confusion. His ideas became less bewildered: He was immediately sensible of the extreme impropriety, should Matilda be permitted to remain in the Abbey, after this avowal of her sex. He assumed an air of severity, and drew away his hand.

'How, Lady!' said He; 'Can you really hope for my permission to remain amongst us? Even were I to grant your request, what good could you derive from it? Think you, that I ever can reply to an affection, which . . .'.

'No, Father, No! I expect not to inspire you with a love like mine. I only wish for the liberty to be near you, to pass some hours of the day in your society; to obtain your compassion, your friendship and esteem. Surely my request is not unreasonable.'

'But reflect, Lady! Reflect only for a moment on the impropriety of my harbouring a Woman in the Abbey; and that too a Woman, who confesses that She loves me. It must not be. The risque of your being discovered is too great, and I will not expose myself to so dangerous a temptation.'

'Temptation, say you? Forget, that I am a Woman, and it no longer exists: Consider me only as a Friend, as an Unfortunate, whose happiness, whose life depends upon your protection. Fear not, lest I should ever call to your remembrance, that love the most impetuous, the most unbounded, has induced me to disguise my sex; or that instigated by desires, offensive to *your* vows and my own honour, I should endeavour to seduce you from the path of rectitude. No, Ambrosio, learn to know me better. I love you for your virtues: Lose them, and with them you lose my affections. I look upon you as a Saint; Prove to me that you are no more than Man, and I quit you with disgust. Is it then from me that you fear temptation? From me, in whom the world's dazzling pleasures created no other sentiment than contempt? From me, whose attachment is grounded on your exemption from human frailty? Oh! dismiss such injurious apprehensions! Think nobler of me, think nobler of yourself. I am incapable of seducing you to error; and surely your Virtue is established on a basis too firm to be shaken by unwarranted desires. Ambrosio, dearest Ambrosio! drive me not from your presence; Remember your promise, and authorize my stay!'

'Impossible, Matilda; *Your* interest commands me to refuse your prayer, since I tremble for you, not for myself. After vanquishing the impetuous ebullitions of Youth; After passing thirty years in mortification and penance, I might safely permit your stay, nor fear your inspiring me with warmer sentiments than pity. But to yourself, remaining in the Abbey can produce none but fatal consequences. You will misconstrue my every word and action; You will seize every circumstance with avidity, which encourages you to hope the return of your affection; Insensibly your passions will gain a superiority over your reason; and far from these being repressed by my presence, every moment which we pass together, will only serve to irritate and excite them. Believe me, unhappy Woman! you possess my sincere compassion. I am convinced that you have hitherto acted upon the purest motives; But though you are blind to the imprudence of your conduct, in me it would be culpable not to open your eyes. I feel that Duty obliges my treating you with harshness: I must reject your prayer, and remove every shadow of hope, which may aid to nourish sentiments so pernicious to your repose. Matilda, you must from hence to-morrow.'

'To-morrow, Ambrosio? To-morrow? Oh! surely you cannot mean it! You cannot resolve on driving me to despair! You cannot have the cruelty. . . .'

'You have heard my decision, and it must be obeyed. The Laws of our Order forbid your stay: It would be perjury to conceal that a Woman is within these Walls, and my vows will oblige me to declare your story to the Community. You must from hence!—I pity you, but can do no more!'

He pronounced these words in a faint and trembling voice: Then rising from his seat, He would have hastened towards the Monastery. Uttering a loud shriek, Matilda followed, and detained him.

'Stay yet one moment, Ambrosio! Hear me yet speak one word!'

'I dare not listen! Release me! You know my resolution!'

'But one word! But one last word, and I have done!'

'Leave me! Your entreaties are in vain! You must from hence to-morrow!'

'Go then, Barbarian! But this resource is still left me.'

As She said this, She suddenly drew a poignard: She rent open her garment, and placed the weapon's point against her bosom.

'Father, I will never quit these Walls alive!'

'Hold! Hold, Matilda! What would you do?'

'You are determined, so am I: The Moment that you leave me, I plunge this Steel in my heart.'

'Holy St. Francis! Matilda, have you your senses? Do you know the consequences of your action? That Suicide is the greatest of crimes? That you destroy your Soul? That you lose your claim to salvation? That you prepare for yourself everlasting torments?'

'I care not! I care not!' She replied passionately; 'Either your hand guides me to Paradise, or my own dooms me to perdition! Speak to me, Ambrosio! Tell me that you will conceal my story, that I shall remain your Friend and your Companion, or this poignard drinks my blood!'

As She uttered these last words, She lifted her arm, and made a motion as if to stab herself. The Friar's eyes followed with dread the course of the dagger. She had torn open her habit, and her bosom was half exposed. The weapon's point rested upon her left breast: And Oh! that was such a breast! The Moon-beams darting full upon it, enabled the Monk to observe its dazzling whiteness. His eye dwelt with insatiable avidity upon the beauteous Orb. A sensation till then unknown filled his heart with a mixture of anxiety and delight: A raging fire shot through every limb; The blood boiled in his veins, and a thousand wild wishes bewildered his imagination.

'Hold!' He cried in an hurried faultering voice; 'I can resist no longer! Stay, then, Enchantress; Stay for my destruction!'

He said, and rushing from the place, hastened towards

the Monastery: He regained his Cell, and threw himself upon his Couch, distracted irresolute and confused.

He found it impossible for some time to arrange his ideas. The scene in which He had been engaged, had excited such a variety of sentiments in his bosom, that He was incapable of deciding which was predominant. He was irresolute, what conduct He ought to hold with the disturber of his repose, He was conscious that prudence, religion, and propriety necessitated his obliging her to quit the Abbey: But on the other hand such powerful reasons authorized her stay, that He was but too much inclined to consent to her remaining. He could not avoid being flattered by Matilda's declaration, and at reflecting that He had unconsciously vanquished an heart, which had resisted the attacks of Spain's noblest Cavaliers: The manner in which He had gained her affections was also the most satisfactory to his vanity: He remembered, the many happy hours which He had passed in Rosario's society, and dreaded that void in his heart which parting with him would occasion. Besides all this, He considered, that as Matilda was wealthy, her favour might be of essential benefit to the Abbey.

'And what do I risque,' said He to himself, 'by authorizing her stay? May I not safely credit her assertions? Will it not be easy for me to forget her sex, and still consider her as my Friend and my disciple? Surely her love is as pure as She describes. Had it been the offspring of mere licentiousness, would She so long have concealed it in her own bosom? Would She not have employed some means to procure its gratification? She has done quite the contrary: She strove to keep me in ignorance of her sex; and nothing but the fear of detection, and my instances, would have compelled her to reveal the secret. She has observed the duties of religion not less strictly than myself. She has made no attempts to rouze my slumbering passions, nor has She ever conversed with me till this night on the subject of Love. Had She been desirous to gain my affections, not my esteem, She would not have concealed from me her charms so carefully: At this very moment I have never seen her face: Yet certainly that face must be lovely, and her person beautiful, to judge by her . . . by what I have seen.'

As this last idea passed through his imagination, a blush spread itself over his cheek. Alarmed at the sentiments which He was indulging, He betook himself to prayer; He started from his Couch, knelt before the beautiful Madona, and entreated her assistance in stifling such culpable emotions. He then returned to his Bed, and resigned himself to slumber.

He awoke, heated and unrefreshed. During his sleep his inflamed imagination had presented him with none but the most voluptuous objects. Matilda stood before him in his dreams, and his eyes again dwelt upon her naked breast. She repeated her protestations of eternal love, threw her arms round his neck, and loaded him with kisses: He returned them; He clasped her passionately to his bosom, and . . . the vision was dissolved. Sometimes his dreams presented the image of his favourite Madona, and He fancied that He was kneeling before her: As He offered up his vows to her, the eyes of the Figure seemed to beam on him with inexpressible sweetness. He pressed his lips to hers, and found them warm: The animated form started from the Canvas, embraced him affectionately, and his senses were unable to support delight so exquisite. Such were the scenes, on which his thoughts were employed while sleeping: His unsatisfied Desires placed before him the most lustful and provoking Images, and he rioted in joys till then unknown to him.

He started from his Couch, filled with confusion at the remembrance of his dreams. Scarcely was He less ashamed, when He reflected on his reasons of the former night, which induced him to authorize Matilda's stay. The cloud was now dissipated which had obscured his judgment: He shuddered, when He beheld his arguments blazoned in their proper colours, and found that He had been a slave to flattery, to avarice, and self-love. If in one hour's conversation Matilda had produced a change so remarkable in his sentiments, what had He not to dread from her remaining in the Abbey? Become sensible of his danger, awakened from his dream of confidence, He resolved to insist on her departing without delay. He began to feel that He was not proof against temptation; and that however Matilda might restrain herself within the bounds of modesty, He was unable to contend with those passions, from which He falsely thought himself exempted.

'Agnes! Agnes!' He exclaimed, while reflecting on his embarrassments, 'I already feel thy curse!'

He quitted his Cell, determined upon dismissing the feigned Rosario. He appeared at Matins; But his thoughts were absent, and He paid them but little attention. His heart and brain were both of them filled with worldly objects, and He prayed without devotion. The service over, He descended into the Garden. He bent his steps towards the same spot, where on the preceding night He had made this embarrassing dis-covery. He doubted not but that Matilda would seek him there: He was not deceived. She soon entered the Hermitage, and approached the Monk with a timid air. After a few minutes during which both were silent, She appeared as if on the point of speaking; But the Abbot, who during this time had been summoning up all his resolution, hastily interrupted her. Though still un-conscious how extensive was its influence, He dreaded the melodious seduction of her voice.

'Seat yourself by my side, Matilda,' said He, assuming

a look of firmness, though carefully avoiding the least mixture of severity; 'Listen to me patiently, and believe, that in what I shall say, I am not more influenced by my own interest, than by yours: Believe, that I feel for you the warmest friendship, the truest compassion, and that you cannot feel more grieved than I do, when I declare to you that we must never meet again.'

'Ambrosio!' She cried, in a voice at once expressive of surprise and sorrow.

'Be calm, my Friend! My Rosario! Still let me call you by that name so dear to me! Our separation is unavoidable; I blush to own, how sensibly it affects me.— But yet it must be so. I feel myself incapable of treating you with indifference, and that very conviction obliges me to insist upon your departure. Matilda, you must stay here no longer.'

'Oh! where shall I now seek for probity? Disgusted with a perfidious world, in what happy region does Truth conceal herself? Father, I hoped that She resided here; I thought that your bosom had been her favourite shrine. And you too prove false? Oh God! And you too can betray me?'

'Matilda!'

'Yes, Father, Yes! 'Tis with justice that I reproach you. Oh! where are your promises? My Noviciate is not expired, and yet will you compel me to quit the Monastery? Can you have the heart to drive me from you? And have I not received your solemn oath to the contrary?'

'I will not compel you to quit the Monastery: You have received my solemn oath to the contrary. But yet when I throw myself upon your generosity, when I declare to you the embarrassments in which your presence involves me, will you not release me from that oath? Reflect upon the danger of a discovery, upon the opprobrium in which such an event would plunge me:

Reflect, that my honour and reputation are at stake, and that my peace of mind depends on your compliance. As yet my heart is free; I shall separate from you with regret, but not with despair. Stay here, and a few weeks will sacrifice my happiness on the altar of your charms. You are but too interesting, too amiable! I should love you, I should doat on you! My bosom would become the prey of desires, which Honour and my profession forbid me to gratify. If I resisted them, the impetuosity of my wishes unsatisfied would drive me to madness: If I yielded to the temptation, I should sacrifice to one moment of guilty pleasure my reputation in this world, my salvation in the next. To you then I fly for defence against myself. Preserve me from losing the reward of thirty years of sufferings! Preserve me from becoming the Victim of Remorse! *Your* heart has already felt the anguish of hopeless love; Oh! then if you really value me, spare mine that anguish! Give me back my promise; Fly from these walls. Go, and you bear with you my warmest prayers for your happiness, my friendship, my esteem and admiration: Stay, and you become to me the source of danger, of sufferings, of despair! Answer me, Matilda; What is your resolve?'—She was silent—'Will you not speak, Matilda? Will you not name your choice?'

'Cruel! Cruel!' She exclaimed, wringing her hands in agony; 'You know too well that you offer me no choice! You know too well that I can have no will but yours!'

'I was not then deceived! Matilda's generosity equals my expectations.'

'Yes; I will prove the truth of my affection by submitting to a decree which cuts me to the very heart. Take back your promise. I will quit the Monastery this very day. I have a Relation, Abbess of a Covent in Estramadura:* To her will I bend my steps, and shut myself from the world for ever. Yet tell me, Father; Shall

I bear your good wishes with me to my solitude? Will you sometimes abstract your attention from heavenly objects to bestow a thought upon me?'

'Ah! Matilda, I fear that I shall think on you but too often for my repose!'

'Then I have nothing more to wish for, save that we may meet in heaven. Farewell, my Friend! my Ambrosio!—And yet methinks, I would fain bear with me some token of your regard!'

'What shall I give you?'

'Something.—Any thing.—One of those flowers will be sufficient.' [Here She pointed to a bush of Roses, planted at the door of the Grotto.] 'I will hide it in my bosom, and when I am dead, the Nuns shall find it withered upon my heart.'

The Friar was unable to reply: With slow steps, and a soul heavy with affliction, He quitted the Hermitage. He approached the Bush, and stooped to pluck one of the Roses. Suddenly He uttered a piercing cry, started back hastily, and let the flower, which He already held, fall from his hand. Matilda heard the shriek, and flew anxiously towards him.

'What is the matter?' She cried; 'Answer me, for God's sake! What has happened?'

'I have received my death!' He replied in a faint voice; 'Concealed among the Roses . . . A Serpent. . . .'

Here the pain of his wound became so exquisite, that Nature was unable to bear it: His senses abandoned him, and He sank inanimate into Matilda's arms.

Her distress was beyond the power of description. She rent her hair, beat her bosom, and not daring to quit Ambrosio, endeavoured by loud cries to summon the Monks to her assistance. She at length succeeded. Alarmed by her shrieks Several of the Brothers hastened to the spot, and the Superior was conveyed back to the Abbey. He was immediately put to bed, and the Monk, who officiated as Surgeon to the Fraternity, prepared to examine the wound. By this time Ambrosio's hand had swelled to an extraordinary size; The remedies which had been administered to him, 'tis true, restored him to life, but not to his senses; He raved in all the horrors of delirium, foamed at the mouth, and four of the strongest Monks were scarcely able to hold him in his bed.

Father Pablos, such was the Surgeon's name, hastened to examine the wounded hand. The Monks surrounded the Bed, anxiously waiting for the decision: Among these the feigned Rosario appeared not the most insensible to the Friar's calamity. He gazed upon the Sufferer with inexpressible anguish; and the groans, which every moment escaped from his bosom, sufficiently betrayed the violence of his affliction.

Father Pablos probed the wound. As He drew out his Lancet, its point was tinged with a greenish hue. He shook his head mournfully, and quitted the bed-side.

' 'Tis as I feared!' said He; 'There is no hope.'

'No hope?' exclaimed the Monks with one voice; 'Say you, no hope?'

'From the sudden effects, I suspected that the Abbot was stung by a Cientipedoro:[1] The venom which you see upon my Lancet confirms my idea: He cannot live three days.'

'And can no possible remedy be found?' enquired Rosario.

'Without extracting the poison, He cannot recover; and how to extract it is to me still a secret. All that I can do is to apply such herbs to the wound, as will relieve the anguish: The Patient will be restored to his senses; But the venom will corrupt the whole mass of his blood, and in three days He will exist no longer.'

---

[1] The Cientipedoro is supposed to be a Native of Cuba, and to have been brought into Spain from that Island in the Vessel of Columbus.

Excessive was the universal grief, at hearing this decision. Pablos, as He had promised, dressed the wound, and then retired, followed by his Companions: Rosario alone remained in the Cell, the Abbot at his urgent entreaty having been committed to his care. Ambrosio's strength worn out by the violence of his exertions, He had by this time fallen into a profound sleep. So totally was He overcome by weariness, that He scarcely gave any signs of life; He was still in this situation, when the Monks returned to enquire, whether any change had taken place. Pablos loosened the bandage which concealed the wound, more from a principle of curiosity, than from indulging the hope of discovering any favourable symptoms. What was his astonishment at finding, that the inflammation had totally subsided! He probed the hand; His Lancet came out pure and unsullied; No traces of the venom were perceptible; and had not the orifice still been visible, Pablos might have doubted that there had ever been a wound.

He communicated this intelligence to his Brethren; their delight was only equalled by their surprize. From the latter sentiment, however, they were soon released by explaining the circumstance according to their own ideas: They were perfectly convinced that their Superior was a Saint, and thought, that nothing could be more natural than for St. Francis to have operated a miracle in his favour. This opinion was adopted unanimously: They declared it so loudly, and vociferated,—'A miracle! a miracle!'—with such fervour, that they soon interrupted Ambrosio's slumbers.

The Monks immediately crowded round his Bed, and expressed their satisfaction at his wonderful recovery. He was perfectly in his senses, and free from every complaint except feeling weak and languid. Pablos gave him a strengthening medicine, and advised his keeping his bed for the two succeeding days: He then retired, having desired his Patient not to exhaust himself by conversation, but rather to endeavour at taking some repose. The other Monks followed his example, and the Abbot and Rosario were left without Observers.

For some minutes Ambrosio regarded his Attendant with a look of mingled pleasure and apprehension. She was seated upon the side of the Bed, her head bending down, and as usual enveloped in the Cowl of her Habit.

'And you are still here, Matilda?' said the Friar at length. 'Are you not satisfied with having so nearly effected my destruction, that nothing but a miracle could have saved me from the Grave? Ah! surely Heaven sent that Serpent to punish. . . .'

Matilda interrupted him by putting her hand before his lips with an air of gaiety.

'Hush! Father, Hush! You must not talk!'

'He who imposed that order, knew not how interesting are the subjects on which I wish to speak.'

'But I know it, and yet issue the same positive command. I am appointed your Nurse, and you must not disobey my orders.'

'You are in spirits, Matilda!'

'Well may I be so: I have just received a pleasure unexampled through my whole life.'

'What was that pleasure?'

'What I must conceal from all, but most from you.'

'But most from me? Nay then, I entreat you, Matilda. . . .'

'Hush, Father! Hush! You must not talk. But as you do not seem inclined to sleep, shall I endeavour to amuse you with my Harp?'

'How? I knew not that you understood Music.'

'Oh! I am a sorry Performer! Yet as silence is prescribed you for eight and forty hours, I may possibly entertain you, when wearied of your own reflections. I go to fetch my Harp.'

She soon returned with it.

'Now, Father; What shall I sing? Will you hear the Ballad which treats of the gallant Durandarte, who died in the famous battle of Roncevalles?'*

'What you please, Matilda.'

'Oh! call me not Matilda! Call me Rosario, call me your Friend! Those are the names, which I love to hear from your lips. Now listen!'

She then tuned her harp, and afterwards preluded for some moments with such exquisite taste, as to prove her a perfect Mistress of the Instrument. The air which She played was soft and plaintive: Ambrosio, while He listened, felt his uneasiness subside, and a pleasing melancholy spread itself into his bosom. Suddenly Matilda changed the strain: With an hand bold and rapid She struck a few loud martial chords, and then chaunted the following Ballad to an air at once simple and melodious.

DURANDARTE AND BELERMA

Sad and fearful is the story
Of the Roncevalles fight;
On those fatal plains of glory
Perished many a gallant Knight.

There fell Durandarte; Never
Verse a nobler Chieftain named:
He, before his lips for ever
Closed in silence thus exclaimed.

'Oh! Belerma! Oh! my dear-one!
For my pain and pleasure born!
Seven long years I served thee, fair-one,
Seven long years my fee was scorn:

'And when now thy heart replying
To my wishes, burns like mine,
Cruel Fate my bliss denying
Bids me every hope resign.

'Ah! Though young I fall, believe me,
Death would never claim a sigh;
'Tis to lose thee, 'tis to leave thee,
Makes me think it hard to die!

'Oh! my Cousin Montesinos,
By that friendship firm and dear
Which from Youth has lived between us,
Now my last petition hear!

'When my Soul these limbs forsaking
Eager seeks a purer air,
From my breast the cold heart taking,
Give it to Belerma's care.

'Say, I of my lands Possessor
Named her with my dying breath:
Say, my lips I op'd to bless her,
Ere they closed for aye in death:

'Twice a week too how sincerely
I adored her, Cousin, say;
Twice a week for one who dearly
Loved her, Cousin, bid her pray.

'Montesinos, now the hour
Marked by fate is near at hand:
Lo! my arm has lost its power!
Lo! I drop my trusty brand!

'Eyes, which forth beheld me going,
Homewards ne'er shall see me hie!
Cousin, stop those tears o'er-flowing,
Let me on thy bosom die!

'Thy kind hand my eye-lids closing,
  Yet one favour I implore:
Pray Thou for my Soul's reposing,
  When my heart shall throb no more;

'So shall Jesus, still attending
  Gracious to a Christian's vow,
Pleased accept my Ghost ascending,
  And a seat in heaven allow.'

Thus spoke gallant Durandarte;
  Soon his brave heart broke in twain.
Greatly joyed the Moorish party,
  That the gallant Knight was slain.

Bitter weeping Montesinos
  Took from him his helm and glaive;
Bitter weeping Montesinos
  Dug his gallant Cousin's grave.

To perform his promise made, He
  Cut the heart from out the breast,
That Belerma, wretched Lady!
  Might receive the last bequest.

Sad was Montesinos' heart, He
  Felt distress his bosom rend.
'Oh! my Cousin Durandarte,
  Woe is me to view thy end!

'Sweet in manners, fair in favour,
  Mild in temper, fierce in fight,
Warrior, nobler, gentler, braver,
  Never shall behold the light!

'Cousin, Lo! my tears bedew thee!
  How shall I thy loss survive!
Durandarte, He who slew thee,
  Wherefore left He me alive!'

While She sung, Ambrosio listened with delight:
Never had He heard a voice more harmonious; and He
wondered, how such heavenly sounds could be produced
by any but Angels. But though He indulged the sense of
hearing; a single look convinced him, that He must not
trust to that of sight. The Songstress sat at a little distance
from his Bed. The attitude in which She bent over her
harp, was easy and graceful: Her Cowl had fallen back-
warder than usual: Two coral lips were visible, ripe,
fresh, and melting, and a Chin in whose dimples seemed
to lurk a thousand Cupids. Her Habit's long sleeve would
have swept along the Chords of the Instrument: To
prevent this inconvenience She had drawn it above her
elbow, and by this means an arm was discovered formed
in the most perfect symmetry, the delicacy of whose skin
might have contended with snow in whiteness. Ambrosio
dared to look on her but once: That glance sufficed to
convince him, how dangerous was the presence of this
seducing Object. He closed his eyes, but strove in vain
to banish her from his thoughts. There She still moved
before him, adorned with all those charms which his
heated imagination could supply: Every beauty which
He had seen, appeared embellished, and those still concealed Fancy represented to him in glowing colours. Still,
however, his vows and the necessity of keeping to them
were present to his memory. He struggled with desire,
and shuddered when He beheld, how deep was the
precipice before him.

Matilda ceased to sing. Dreading the influence of her
charms, Ambrosio remained with his eyes closed, and
offered up his prayers to St. Francis to assist him in this
dangerous trial! Matilda believed that He was sleeping.
She rose from her seat, approached the Bed softly, and
for some minutes gazed upon him attentively.

'He sleeps!' said She at length in a low voice, but
whose accents the Abbot distinguished perfectly; 'Now

then I may gaze upon him without offence! I may mix
my breath with his; I may doat upon his features, and
He cannot suspect me of impurity and deceit!—He fears
my seducing him to the violation of his vows! Oh! the
Unjust! Were it my wish to excite desire, should I conceal my features from him so carefully? Those features,
of which I daily hear him. . . .'

She stopped, and was lost in her reflections.

'It was but yesterday!' She continued; 'But a few
short hours have past, since I was dear to him! He
esteemed me, and my heart was satisfied! Now! . . . . Oh!
now how cruelly is my situation changed! He looks on
me with suspicion! He bids me leave him, leave him for
ever! Oh! You, my Saint! my Idol! You, holding the
next place to God in my breast! Yet two days, and my
heart will be unveiled to you.—Could you know my
feelings, when I beheld your agony! Could you know,
how much your sufferings have endeared you to me!
But the time will come, when you will be convinced that
my passion is pure and disinterested. Then you will pity
me, and feel the whole weight of these sorrows!'

As She said this, her voice was choaked by weeping.
While She bent over Ambrosio, a tear fell upon his cheek.
'Ah! I have disturbed him!' cried Matilda, and
retreated hastily.

Her alarm was ungrounded. None sleep so profoundly,
as those who are determined not to wake. The Friar was
in this predicament: He still seemed buried in a repose,
which every succeeding minute rendered him less
capable of enjoying. The burning tear had communicated its warmth to his heart.

'What affection! What purity!' said He internally;
'Ah! since my bosom is thus sensible of pity, what would
it be if agitated by love?'

Matilda again quitted her seat, and retired to some
distance from the Bed. Ambrosio ventured to open his

eyes, and to cast them upon her fearfully. Her face was turned from him. She rested her head in a melancholy posture upon her Harp, and gazed on the picture which hung opposite to the Bed.

'Happy, happy Image!' Thus did She address the beautiful Madona; ' 'Tis to you that He offers his prayers! 'Tis on you that He gazes with admiration! I thought, you would have lightened my sorrows; You have only served to increase their weight: You have made me feel that had I known him ere his vows were pronounced, Ambrosio and happiness might have been mine. With what pleasure He views this picture! With what fervour He addresses his prayers to the insensible Image! Ah! may not his sentiments be inspired by some kind and secret Genius, Friend to my affection? May it not be Man's natural instinct which informs him. . . Be silent, idle hopes! Let me not encourage an idea, which takes from the brilliance of Ambrosio's virtue. 'Tis Religion, not Beauty which attracts his admiration; 'Tis not to the Woman, but the Divinity that He kneels. Would He but address to me the least tender expression, which He pours forth to this Madona! Would He but say, that were He not already affianced to the Church, He would not have despised Matilda! Oh! let me nourish that fond idea! Perhaps, He may yet acknowledge that He feels for me more than pity, and that affection like mine might well have deserved a return; Perhaps, He may own thus much when I lye on my death-bed! He then need not fear to infringe his vows, and the confession of his regard will soften the pangs of dying. Would I were sure of this! Oh! how earnestly should I sigh for the moment of dissolution!'

Of this discourse the Abbot lost not a syllable; and the tone in which She pronounced these last words pierced to his heart. Involuntarily He raised himself from his pillow.

'Matilda!' He said in a troubled voice; 'Oh! my Matilda!'

She started at the sound, and turned towards him hastily. The suddenness of her movement made her Cowl fall back from her head; Her features became visible to the Monk's enquiring eye. What was his amazement at beholding the exact resemblance of his admired Madona? The same exquisite proportion of features, the same profusion of golden hair, the same rosy lips, heavenly eyes, and majesty of countenance adorned Matilda! Uttering an exclamation of surprize, Ambrosio sank back upon his pillow, and doubted whether the Object before him was mortal or divine.

Matilda seemed penetrated with confusion. She remained motionless in her place, and supported herself upon her Instrument. Her eyes were bent upon the earth, and her fair cheeks over-spread with blushes. On recovering herself, her first action was to conceal her features. She then in an unsteady and troubled voice ventured to address these words to the Friar.

'Accident has made you Master of a secret, which I never would have revealed but on the Bed of death. Yes, Ambrosio; In Matilda de Villanegas you see the original of your beloved Madona. Soon after I conceived my unfortunate passion, I formed the project of conveying to you my Picture: Crowds of Admirers had persuaded me that I possessed some beauty, and I was anxious to know, what effect it would produce upon you. I caused my Portrait to be drawn by Martin Galuppi,* a celebrated Venetian at that time resident in Madrid. The resemblance was striking: I sent it to the Capuchin-Abbey as if for sale, and the Jew from whom you bought it, was one of my Emissaries. You purchased it. Judge of my rapture, when informed, that you had gazed upon it with delight., or rather with adoration; that you had suspended it in your Cell, and that you addressed your supplications to no other Saint. Will this discovery make me still more regarded as an object of suspicion? Rather should it convince you how pure is my affection, and engage you to suffer me in your society and esteem. I heard you daily extol the praises of my Portrait: I was an eye-witness of the transports, which its beauty excited in you: Yet I forbore to use against your virtue those arms, with which yourself had furnished me. I concealed those features from your sight, which you loved unconsciously. I strove not to excite desire by displaying my charms, or to make myself Mistress of your heart through the medium of your senses. To attract your notice by studiously attending to religious duties, to endear myself to you by convincing you that my mind was virtuous and my attachment sincere, such was my only aim. I suc-ceeded; I became your companion and your Friend. I concealed my sex from your knowledge; and had you not pressed me to reveal my secret, had I not been tor-mented by the fear of a discovery, never had you known me for any other than Rosario. And still are you resolved to drive me from you? The few hours of life which yet remain for me, may I not pass them in your presence? Oh! speak, Ambrosio, and tell me that I may stay!'

This speech gave the Abbot an opportunity of re-collecting himself. He was conscious that in the present disposition of his mind, avoiding her society was his only refuge from the power of this enchanting Woman.

'You declaration has so much astonished me,' said He, 'that I am at present incapable of answering you. Do not insist upon a reply, Matilda; Leave me to myself; I have need to be alone.'

'I obey you—But before I go, promise not to insist upon my quitting the Abbey immediately.'

'Matilda, reflect upon your situation; Reflect upon the consequences of your stay. Our separation is in-dispensable, and we must part.'

'But not to-day, Father! Oh! in pity not to-day!'

'You press me too hard, but I cannot resist that tone of supplication. Since you insist upon it, I yield to your prayer: I consent to your remaining here a sufficient time to prepare in some measure the Brethren for your departure. Stay yet two days; But on the third,' . . . [He sighed involuntarily.]—'Remember, that on the third we must part for ever!'

She caught his hand eagerly, and pressed it to her lips.

'On the third?' She exclaimed with an air of wild solemnity; 'You are right, Father! You are right! On the third we must part for ever!'

There was a dreadful expression in her eye as She uttered these words, which penetrated the Friar's soul with horror: Again She kissed his hand, and then fled with rapidity from the chamber.

Anxious to authorise the presence of his dangerous Guest, yet conscious that her stay was infringing the laws of his order, Ambrosio's bosom became the Theatre of a thousand contending passions. At length his attachment to the feigned Rosario, aided by the natural warmth of his temperament, seemed likely to obtain the victory: The success was assured, when that presumption which formed the ground-work of his character, came to Matilda's assistance. The Monk reflected, that to vanquish temptation was an infinitely greater merit than to avoid it: He thought, that He ought rather to rejoice in the opportunity given him of proving the firmness of his virtue. St. Anthony had withstood all seductions to lust;* Then why should not He? Besides, St. Anthony was tempted by the Devil, who put every art into practice to excite his passions: Whereas, Ambrosio's danger proceeded from a mere mortal Woman, fearful and modest, whose apprehensions of his yielding were not less violent than his own.

'Yes,' said He; 'The Unfortunate shall stay; I have

nothing to fear from her presence. Even should my own prove too weak to resist the temptation, I am secured from danger by the innocence of Matilda.'

Ambrosio was yet to learn, that to an heart unacquainted with her, Vice is ever most dangerous when lurking behind the Mask of Virtue.

He found himself so perfectly recovered, that when Father Pablos visited him again at night, He entreated permission to quit his chamber on the day following. His request was granted. Matilda appeared no more that evening, except in company with the Monks when they came in a body to enquire after the Abbot's health. She seemed fearful of conversing with him in private, and stayed but a few minutes in his room. The Friar slept well; But the dreams of the former night were repeated, and his sensations of voluptuousness were yet more keen and exquisite. The same lust-exciting visions floated before his eyes: Matilda, in all the pomp of beauty, warm, tender, and luxurious, clasped him to her bosom, and lavished upon him the most ardent caresses. He returned them as eagerly, and already was on the point of satisfying his desires, when the faithless form disappeared, and left him to all the horrors of shame and disappointment.

The Morning dawned. Fatigued, harassed, and exhausted by his provoking dreams, He was not disposed to quit his Bed. He excused himself from appearing at Matins: It was the first morning in his life that He had ever missed them. He rose late. During the whole of the day He had no opportunity of speaking to Matilda without witnesses. His Cell was thronged by the Monks, anxious to express their concern at his illness; And He was still occupied in receiving their compliments on his recovery, when the Bell summoned them to the Refectory.

After dinner the Monks separated, and dispersed themselves in various parts of the Garden, where the shade of trees or retirement of some Grotto presented the most agreeable means of enjoying the Siesta. The Abbot bent his steps towards the Hermitage: A glance of his eye invited Matilda to accompany him. She obeyed, and followed him thither in silence. They entered the Grotto, and seated themselves. Both seemed unwilling to begin the conversation, and to labour under the influence of mutual embarrassment. At length the Abbot spoke: He conversed only on indifferent topics, and Matilda answered him in the same tone. She seemed anxious to make him forget, that the Person who sat by him was any other than Rosario. Neither of them dared, or indeed wished to make an allusion, to the subject which was most at the hearts of both.

Matilda's efforts to appear gay were evidently forced: Her spirits were oppressed by the weight of anxiety, and when She spoke her voice was low and feeble. She seemed desirous of finishing a conversation which embarrassed her; and complaining that She was unwell, She requested Ambrosio's permission to return to the Abbey. He accompanied her to the door of her cell; and when arrived there, He stopped her to declare his consent to her continuing the Partner of his solitude so long as should be agreeable to herself.

She discovered no marks of pleasure at receiving this intelligence, though on the preceding day She had been so anxious to obtain the permission.

'Alas! Father,' She said, waving her head mournfully; 'Your kindness comes too late! My doom is fixed. We must separate for ever. Yet believe, that I am grateful for your generosity, for your compassion of an Unfortunate who is but too little deserving of it!'

She put her hand-kerchief to her eyes. Her Cowl was only half drawn over her face. Ambrosio observed that She was pale, and her eyes sunk and heavy.

'Good God!' He cried; 'You are very ill, Matilda! I shall send Father Pablos to you instantly.'

'No; Do not. I am ill, 'tis true; But He cannot cure my malady. Farewell, Father! Remember me in your prayers to-morrow, while I shall remember you in heaven!'

She entered her cell, and closed the door.

The Abbot dispatched to her the Physician without losing a moment, and waited his report impatiently. But Father Pablos soon returned, and declared that his errand had been fruitless. Rosario refused to admit him, and had positively rejected his offers of assistance. The uneasiness, which this account gave Ambrosio was not trifling: Yet He determined that Matilda should have her own way for that night: But that if her situation did not mend by the morning, he would insist upon her taking the advice of Father Pablos.

He did not find himself inclined to sleep. He opened his casement, and gazed upon the moon-beams as they played upon the small stream whose waters bathed the walls of the Monastery. The coolness of the night-breeze and tranquillity of the hour inspired the Friar's mind with sadness. He thought upon Matilda's beauty and affection; Upon the pleasures which He might have shared with her; had He not been restrained by monastic-fetters. He reflected, that unsustained by hope her love for him could not long exist; That doubtless She would succeed in extinguishing her passion, and seek for happiness in the arms of One more fortunate. He shuddered at the void which her absence would leave in his bosom. He looked with disgust on the monotony of a Convent, and breathed a sigh towards that world, from which He was for ever separated. Such were the reflections, which a loud knocking at his door interrupted. The Bell of the Church had already struck Two. The Abbot hastened to enquire the cause of this disturbance. He opened the door of his Cell, and a Lay-Brother entered, whose looks declared his hurry and confusion.

'Hasten, reverend Father!' said He; 'Hasten to the

young Rosario. He earnestly requests to see you; He lies at the point of death.'

'Gracious God! Where is Father Pablos? Why is He not with him? Oh! I fear! I fear!'

'Father Pablos has seen him, but his art can do nothing. He says, that He suspects the Youth to be poisoned.'

'Poisoned? Oh! The Unfortunate! It is then as I suspected! But let me not lose a moment; Perhaps it may yet be time to save her!'

He said, and flew towards the Cell of the Novice. Several Monks were already in the chamber. Father Pablos was one of them, and held a medicine in his hand, which He was endeavouring to persuade Rosario to swallow. The Others were employed in admiring the Patient's divine countenance, which They now saw for the first time. She looked lovelier than ever. She was no longer pale or languid; A bright glow had spread itself over her cheeks; her eyes sparkled with a serene delight, and her countenance was expressive of confidence and resignation.

'Oh! torment me no more!' was She saying to Pablos, when the terrified Abbot rushed hastily into the Cell; 'My disease is far beyond the reach of your skill, and I wish not to be cured of it'—Then perceiving Ambrosio,— 'Ah! 'tis He!' She cried; 'I see him once again, before we part for ever! Leave me, my Brethren; Much have I to tell this holy Man in private.'

The Monks retired immediately, and Matilda and the Abbot remained together.

'What have you done, imprudent Woman!' exclaimed the Latter, as soon as they were left alone; 'Tell me; Are my suspicions just? Am I indeed to lose you? Has your own hand been the instrument of your destruction?'

She smiled, and grasped his hand.

'In what have I been imprudent, Father? I have

sacrificed a pebble, and saved a diamond: My death preserves a life valuable to the world, and more dear to me than my own. Yes, Father; I am poisoned; But know, that the poison once circulated in your veins.'

'Matilda!'

'What I tell you I resolved never to discover to you, but on the bed of death: That moment is now arrived. You cannot have forgotten the day already, when your life was endangered by the bite of a Cientipedoro. The Physician gave you over, declaring himself ignorant how to extract the venom: I knew but of one means, and hesitated not a moment to employ it. I was left alone with you: You slept; I loosened the bandage from your hand; I kissed the wound, and drew out the poison with my lips. The effect has been more sudden than I expected. I feel death at my heart; Yet an hour, and I shall be in a better world.'

'Almighty God!' exclaimed the Abbot, and sank almost lifeless upon the Bed.

After a few minutes He again raised himself up suddenly, and gazed upon Matilda with all the wildness of despair.

'And you have sacrificed yourself for me! You die, and die to preserve Ambrosio! And is there indeed no remedy, Matilda? And is there indeed no hope? Speak to me, Oh! speak to me! Tell me, that you have still the means of life!'

'Be comforted, my only Friend! Yes, I have still the means of life in my power: But 'tis a means which I dare not employ. It is dangerous! It is dreadful! Life would be purchased at too dear a rate, . . . unless it were permitted me to live for you.'

'Then live for me, Matilda, for me and gratitude!'— [He caught her hand, and pressed it rapturously to his lips.]—'Remember our late conversations; I now consent to every thing: Remember in what lively colours you described the union of souls; Be it ours to realize those ideas. Let us forget the distinctions of sex, despise the world's prejudices, and only consider each other as Brother and Friend. Live then, Matilda! Oh! live for me!'

'Ambrosio, it must not be. When I thought thus, I deceived both you and myself. Either I must die at present, or expire by the lingering torments of unsatisfied desire. Oh! since we last conversed together, a dreadful veil has been rent from before my eyes. I love you no longer with the devotion which is paid to a Saint: I prize you no more for the virtues of your soul; I lust for the enjoyment of your person. The Woman reigns in my bosom, and I am become a prey to the wildest of passions. Away with friendship! 'tis a cold unfeeling word. My bosom burns with love, with unutterable love, and love must be its return. Tremble then, Ambrosio, tremble to succeed in your prayers. If I live, your truth, your reputation, your reward of a life past in sufferings, all that you value is irretrievably lost. I shall no longer be able to combat my passions, shall seize every opportunity to excite your desires, and labour to effect your dishonour and my own. No, no, Ambrosio; I must not live! I am convinced with every moment, that I have but one alternative; I feel with every heart-throb, that I must enjoy you, or die.'

'Amazement!—Matilda!—Can it be you who speak to me?'

He made a movement as if to quit his seat. She uttered a loud shriek, and raising herself half out of the Bed, threw her arms round the Friar to detain him.

'Oh! do not leave me! Listen to my errors with compassion! In a few hours I shall be no more; Yet a little, and I am free from this disgraceful passion.'

'Wretched Woman, what can I say to you! I cannot . . . I must not . . . But live, Matilda! Oh! live!'

'You do not reflect on what you ask. What? Live to plunge myself in infamy? To become the Agent of Hell? To work the destruction both of you and of Myself? Feel this heart, Father!'

She took his hand: Confused, embarrassed, and fascinated, He withdrew it not, and felt her heart throb under it.

'Feel this heart, Father! It is yet the seat of honour, truth, and chastity: If it beats to-morrow, it must fall a prey to the blackest crimes. Oh! let me then die to-day! Let me die, while I yet deserve the tears of the virtuous! Thus will I expire!'—[She reclined her head upon his shoulder; Her golden Hair poured itself over his Chest.]—'Folded in your arms, I shall sink to sleep; Your hand shall close my eyes for ever, and your lips receive my dying breath. And will you not sometimes think of me? Will you not sometimes shed a tear upon my Tomb? Oh! Yes! Yes! Yes! That kiss is my assurance!'

The hour was night. All was silence around. The faint beams of a solitary Lamp darted upon Matilda's figure, and shed through the chamber a dim mysterious light. No prying eye, or curious ear was near the Lovers: Nothing was heard but Matilda's melodious accents. Ambrosio was in the full vigour of Manhood. He saw before him a young and beautiful Woman, the preserver of his life, the Adorer of his person, and whom affection for him had reduced to the brink of the Grave. He sat upon her Bed; His hand rested upon her bosom; Her head reclined voluptuously upon his breast. Who then can wonder, if He yielded to the temptation? Drunk with desire, He pressed his lips to those which sought them: His kisses vied with Matilda's in warmth and passion. He clasped her rapturously in his arms; He forgot his vows, his sanctity, and his fame: He remembered nothing but the pleasure and opportunity.

'Ambrosio! Oh! my Ambrosio!' sighed Matilda.

'Thine, ever thine!' murmured the Friar, and sank upon her bosom.

CHAPTER III

⸙⸙⸙⸙⸙⸙⸙⸙⸙

——These are the Villains
Whom all the Travellers do fear so much.
——Some of them are Gentlemen,
Such as the fury of ungoverned Youth
Thrust from the company of awful Men.
Two Gentlemen of Verona.*

THE MARQUIS AND Lorenzo proceeded to the Hotel in silence. The Former employed himself in calling every circumstance to his mind, which related might give Lorenzo's the most favourable idea of his connexion with Agnes. The Latter, justly alarmed for the honour of his family, felt embarrassed by the presence of the Marquis: The adventure which He had just witnessed, forbad his treating him as a Friend; and Antonia's interests being entrusted to his mediation, He saw the impolicy of treating him as a Foe. He concluded from these reflections, that profound silence would be the wisest plan, and waited with impatience for Don Raymond's explanation.

They arrived at the Hotel de las Cisternas. The Marquis immediately conducted him to his apartment, and began to express his satisfaction at finding him at Madrid. Lorenzo interrupted him.

'Excuse me. my Lord,' said He with a distant air,

'if I reply somewhat coldly to your expressions of regard. A Sister's honour is involved in this affair: Till that is established, and the purport of your correspondence with Agnes cleared up, I cannot consider you as my Friend. I am anxious to hear the meaning of your conduct, and hope, that you will not delay the promised explanation.'

'First give me your word, that you will listen with patience and indulgence.'

'I love my Sister too well to judge her harshly; and till this moment I possessed no Friend so dear to me as yourself. I will also confess, that your having it in your power to oblige me in a business which I have much at heart, makes me very anxious to find you still deserving my esteem.'

'Lorenzo, you transport me! No greater pleasure can be given me, than an opportunity of serving the Brother of Agnes.'

'Convince me that I can accept your favours without dishonour, and there is no Man in the world, to whom I am more willing to be obliged.'

'Probably, you have already heard your Sister mention the name of Alphonso d'Alvarada?'

'Never. Though I feel for Agnes an affection truly fraternal, circumstances have prevented us from being much together. While yet a Child She was consigned to the care of her Aunt, who had married a German Nobleman. At his Castle She remained till two years since, when She returned to Spain, determined upon secluding herself from the world.'

'Good God! Lorenzo, you knew of her intention, and yet strove not to make her change it?'

'Marquis, you wrong me. The intelligence, which I received at Naples, shocked me extremely, and I hastened my return to Madrid for the express purpose of preventing the sacrifice. The moment that I arrived, I flew to the Convent of St. Clare, in which Agnes had

chosen to perform her Noviciate. I requested to see my
Sister. Conceive my surprise, when She sent me a
refusal; She declared positively, that apprehending my
influence over her mind, She would not trust herself in
my society, till the day before that on which She was to
receive the Veil. I supplicated the Nuns; I insisted upon
seeing Agnes, and hesitated not to avow my suspicions,
that her being kept from me was against her own inclinations. To free herself from the imputation of violence, the
Prioress brought me a few lines written in my Sister's
well-known hand, repeating the message already delivered. All future attempts to obtain a moment's
conversation with her were as fruitless as the first. She
was inflexible, and I was not permitted to see her till the
day preceding that on which She entered the Cloister
never to quit it more. This interview took place in the
presence of our principal Relations. It was for the first
time since her childhood that I saw her, and the scene
was most affecting. She threw herself upon my bosom,
kissed me, and wept bitterly. By every possible argument,
by tears, by prayers, by kneeling, I strove to make her
abandon her intention. I represented to her all the
hardships of a religious life; I painted to her imagination
all the pleasures which She was going to quit, and besought her to disclose to me, what occasioned her disgust
to the world. At this last question She turned pale, and
her tears flowed yet faster. She entreated me not to press
her on that subject; That it sufficed me to know that her
resolution was taken, and that a Convent was the only
place where She could now hope for tranquillity. She
persevered in her design, and made her profession. I
visited her frequently at the Grate, and every moment
that I passed with her, made me feel more affliction at her
loss. I was shortly after obliged to quit Madrid; I returned but yesterday evening, and since then have not
had time to call at St. Clare's Convent.'

'Then till I mentioned it, you never heard the name of Alphonso d'Alvarada?'

'Pardon me: my Aunt wrote me word, that an Adventurer so called had found means to get introduced into the Castle of Lindenberg; That He had insinuated himself into my Sister's good graces, and that She had even consented to elope with him. However, before the plan could be executed, the Cavalier discovered, that the estates which He believed Agnes to possess in Hispaniola,* in reality belonged to me. This intelligence made him change his intention; He disappeared on the day that the elopement was to have taken place, and Agnes in despair at his perfidy and meanness had resolved upon seclusion in a Convent. She added, that as this adventurer had given himself out to be a Friend of mine, She wished to know whether I had any knowledge of him. I replied in the negative. I had then very little idea, that Alphonso d'Alvarada and the Marquis de las Cisternas were one and the same person: The description given me of the first by no means tallied with what I knew of the latter.'

'In this I easily recognize Donna Rodolpha's perfidious character. Every word of this account is stamped with marks of her malice, of her falsehood, of her talents for misrepresenting those whom She wishes to injure. Forgive me, Medina, for speaking so freely of your Relation. The mischief which She has done me, authorises my resentment, and when you have heard my story, you will be convinced that my expressions have not been too severe.'

He then began his narrative in the following manner.

HISTORY OF DON RAYMOND,
MARQUIS DE LAS CISTERNAS

Long experience, my dear Lorenzo, has convinced me, how generous is your nature: I waited not for your declaration of ignorance respecting your Sister's adventures, to suppose that they had been purposely concealed from you. Had they reached your knowledge, from what misfortunes should both Agnes and myself have escaped! Fate had ordained it otherwise! You were on your Travels, when I first became acquainted with your Sister; and as our Enemies took care to conceal from her your direction, it was impossible for her to implore by letter your protection and advice.

On leaving Salamanca,* at which University as I have since heard, you remained a year after I quitted it, I immediately set out upon my Travels. My Father supplied me liberally with money; But He insisted upon my concealing my rank, and presenting myself as no more than a private Gentleman. This command was issued by the counsels of his Friend, the Duke of Villa Hermosa,* a Nobleman for whose abilities and knowledge of the world I have ever entertained the most profound veneration.

'Believe me,' said He, 'my dear Raymond, you will hereafter feel the benefits of this temporary degradation. 'Tis true, that as the Condé de las Cisternas you would have been received with open arms; and your youthful vanity might have felt gratified by the attentions showered upon you from all sides. At present, much will depend upon yourself: You have excellent recommendations, but it must be your own business to make them of use to you. You must lay yourself out to please; You must labour to gain the approbation of those, to whom you are presented: They who would have courted the friendship of the Condé de las Cisternas, will have no interest in finding out the merits, or bearing patiently with the faults of Alphonso d'Alvarada. Consequently, when you find yourself really liked, you may safely ascribe it to your good qualities, not your rank, and the distinction shown you will be infinitely more flattering. Besides, your exalted birth would not permit your mixing with the lower classes of society, which will now be in your power, and from which, in my opinion, you will derive considerable benefit. Do not confine yourself to the Illustrious of those Countries through which you pass. Examine the manners and customs of the multitude: Enter into the Cottages; and by observing how the Vassals of Foreigners are treated, learn to diminish the burthens, and augment the comforts of your own. According to my ideas, of those advantages, which a Youth destined to the possession of power and wealth may reap from travel, He should not consider as the least essential, the opportunity of mixing with the classes below him, and becoming an eye-witness of the sufferings of the People."

Forgive me, Lorenzo, if I seem tedious in my narration. The close connexion which now exists between us, makes me anxious that you should know every particular respecting me; and in my fear of omitting the least circumstance which may induce you to think favourably of your Sister and myself, I may possibly relate many which you may think uninteresting.

I followed the Duke's advice; I was soon convinced of its wisdom. I quitted Spain, calling myself by the assumed title of Don Alphonso d'Alvarada, and attended by a single Domestic of approved fidelity. Paris was my first station. For some time I was enchanted with it, as indeed must be every Man, who is young, rich, and fond of pleasure. Yet among all its gaieties, I felt that something was wanting to my heart. I grew sick of dissipation:

I discovered, that the People among whom I lived, and whose exterior was so polished and seducing, were at bottom frivolous, unfeeling and insincere. I turned from the Inhabitants of Paris with disgust,* and quitted that Theatre of Luxury without heaving one sigh of regret.

I now bent my course towards Germany, intending to visit most of the principal courts: Prior to this expedition, I meant to make some little stay at Strasbourg.* On quitting my Chaise at Luneville* to take some refreshment, I observed a splendid Equipage, attended by four Domestics in rich liveries, waiting at the door of the Silver Lion. Soon after as I looked out of the window, I saw a Lady of noble presence, followed by two female Attendants, step into the Carriage, which drove off immediately.

I enquired of the Host, who the Lady was, that had just departed.

'A German Baroness, Monsieur, of great rank and fortune. She has been upon a visit to the Duchess of Longueville,* as her Servants informed me; She is going to Strasbourg, where She will find her Husband, and then both return to their Castle in Germany.'

I resumed my journey, intending to reach Strasbourg that night. My hopes, however were frustrated by the breaking down of my Chaise. The accident happened in the middle of a thick Forest, and I was not a little embarrassed as to the means of proceeding. It was the depth of winter: The night was already closing round us; and Strasbourg, which was the nearest Town, was still distant from us several leagues. It seemed to me, that my only alternative to passing the night in the Forest, was to take my Servant's Horse, and ride on to Strasbourg, an undertaking at that season very far from agreeable. However, seeing no other resource, I was obliged to make up my mind to it. Accordingly I communicated my design to the Postillion, telling him that

I would send People to assist him as soon as I reached
Strasbourg. I had not much confidence in his honesty;
But Stephano being well-armed, and the Driver to all
appearance considerably advanced in years, I believed
I ran no danger of losing my Baggage.

Luckily, as I then thought, an opportunity presented
itself of passing the night more agreeably than I expected.
On mentioning my design of proceeding by myself to
Strasbourg, the Postillion shook his head in disapprobation.

'It is a long way,' said He; 'You will find it a difficult
matter to arrive there without a Guide. Besides, Monsieur seems unaccustomed to the season's severity, and
'tis possible that unable to sustain the excessive cold. . . .'

'What use is there to present me with all these objections?' said I, impatiently interrupting him; 'I have no
other resource: I run still greater risque of perishing with
cold by passing the night in the Forest.'

'Passing the night in the Forest?' He replied; 'Oh! by
St. Denis!*We are not in quite so bad a plight as that
comes to yet. If I am not mistaken, we are scarcely five
minutes walk from the Cottage of my old Friend,
Baptiste. He is a Wood-cutter, and a very honest Fellow.
I doubt not, but He will shelter you for the night with
pleasure. In the mean time I can take the saddle-Horse,
ride to Strasbourg, and be back with proper people to
mend your Carriage by break of day.'

'And in the name of God,' said I, 'How could you
leave me so long in suspense? Why did you not tell me
of this Cottage sooner? What excessive stupidity!'

'I thought, that perhaps Monsieur would not deign
to accept. . . .'

'Absurd! Come, come! Say no more, but conduct us
without delay to the Wood-man's Cottage.'

He obeyed, and we moved onwards: The Horses
contrived with some difficulty to drag the shattered

vehicle after us. My Servant was become almost speechless, and I began to feel the effects of the cold myself,
before we reached the wished-for Cottage. It was a small
but neat Building: As we drew near it, I rejoiced at
observing through the window the blaze of a comfortable
fire. Our Conductor knocked at the door: It was some
time before any one answered; The People within
seemed in doubt whether we should be admitted.

'Come! Come, Friend Baptiste!' cried the Driver with
impatience; 'What are you about? Are you asleep? Or
will you refuse a night's lodging to a Gentleman, whose
Chaise has just broken down in the Forest?'

'Ah! is it you, honest Claude?' replied a Man's voice
from within; 'Wait a moment, and the door shall be
opened.'

Soon after the bolts were drawn back. The door was
unclosed, and a Man presented himself to us with a
Lamp in his hand. He gave the Guide an hearty reception,
and then addressed himself to me.

'Walk in, Monsieur; Walk in, and welcome! Excuse
me for not admitting you at first: But there are so many
Rogues about this place, that saving your presence, I
suspected you to be one.'

Thus saying, He ushered me into the room, where I
had observed the fire: I was immediately placed in an
Easy Chair, which stood close to the Hearth. A Female,
whom I supposed to be the Wife of my Host, rose from
her seat upon my entrance, and received me with a slight
and distant reverence. She made no answer to my
compliment, but immediately re-seating herself, continued the work on which She had been employed. Her
Husband's manners were as friendly, as hers were harsh
and repulsive.

'I wish, I could lodge you more conveniently, Monsieur,' said He; 'But we cannot boast of much spare room
in this hovel. However, a chamber for yourself, and

another for your Servant, I think, we can make shift to supply. You must content yourself with sorry fare; But to what we have, believe me, you are heartily welcome.' ——Then turning to his wife—'Why, how you sit there, Marguerite, with as much tranquillity as if you had nothing better to do! Stir about, Dame! Stir about! Get some supper; Look out some sheets; Here, here; throw some logs upon the fire, for the Gentleman seems perished with cold.'

The Wife threw her work hastily upon the Table, and proceeded to execute his commands with every mark of unwillingness. Her countenance had displeased me on the first moment of my examining it. Yet upon the whole her features were handsome unquestionably; But her skin was sallow, and her person thin and meagre; A louring gloom over-spread her countenance; and it bore such visible marks of rancour and ill-will, as could not escape being noticed by the most inattentive Observer. Her every look and action expressed discontent and impatience, and the answers which She gave Baptiste, when He reproached her good-humouredly for her dissatisfied air, were tart, short, and cutting. In fine, I conceived at first sight equal disgust for her, and prepossession in favour of her Husband, whose appearance was calculated to inspire esteem and confidence. His countenance was open, sincere, and friendly; his manners had all the Peasant's honesty unaccompanied by his rudeness; His cheeks were broad, full, and ruddy; and in the solidity of his person He seemed to offer an ample apology for the leanness of his Wife's. From the wrinkles on his brow I judged him to be turned of sixty; But He bore his years well, and seemed still hearty and strong: The Wife could not be more than thirty, but in spirits and vivacity She was infinitely older than the Husband.

However, in spite of her unwillingness, Marguerite began to prepare the supper, while the Wood-man conversed gaily on different subjects. The Postillion who had been furnished with a bottle of spirits, was now ready to set out for Strasbourg, and enquired, whether I had any further commands.

'For Strasbourg?' interrupted Baptiste; 'You are not going thither to-night?'

'I beg your pardon: If I do not fetch Workmen to mend the Chaise, How is Monsieur to proceed tomorrow?'

'That is true, as you say; I had forgotten the Chaise. Well but Claude; You may at least eat your supper here? That can make you lose very little time, and Monsieur looks too kind-hearted to send you out with an empty stomach on such a bitter cold night as this is.'

To this I readily assented, telling the Postillion, that my reaching Strasbourg the next day an hour or two later would be perfectly immaterial. He thanked me, and then leaving the Cottage with Stephano, put up his Horses in the Wood-man's Stable. Baptiste followed them to the door, and looked out with anxiety.

' 'Tis a sharp biting wind!' said He; 'I wonder, what detains my Boys so long! Monsieur, I shall show you two of the finest Lads, that ever stept in shoe of leather. The eldest is three and twenty, the second a year younger: Their Equals for sense, courage, and activity, are not to be found within fifty miles of Strasbourg. Would They were back again! I begin to feel uneasy about them.'

Marguerite was at this time employed in laying the cloth.

'And are you equally anxious for the return of your Sons?' said I to her.

'Not I!' She replied peevishly; 'They are no children of mine.'

'Come! Come, Marguerite!' said the Husband; 'Do not be out of humour with the Gentleman for asking a simple question. Had you not looked so cross, He would never have thought you old enough to have a Son of three and twenty: But you see how many years illtemper adds to you!—Excuse my Wife's rudeness, Monsieur. A little thing puts her out, and She is somewhat displeased, at your not thinking her to be under thirty. That is the truth, is it not, Marguerite? You know, Monsieur, that Age is always a ticklish subject with a Woman. Come! come! Marguerite, clear up a little. If you have not Sons as old, you will some twenty years hence, and I hope, that we shall live to see them just such Lads as Jacques and Robert.'

Marguerite clasped her hands together passionately.

'God forbid!' said She; 'God forbid! If I thought it, I would strangle them with my own hands!'

She quitted the room hastily, and went up stairs.

I could not help expressing to the Wood-man, how much I pitied him for being chained for life to a Partner of such ill-humour.

'Ah! Lord! Monsieur, Every one has his share of grievances, and Marguerite has fallen to mine. Besides, after all She is only cross, and not malicious. The worst is, that her affection for two children by a former Husband makes her play the Step-mother with my two Sons. She cannot bear the sight of them, and by her good-will they would never set a foot within my door. But on this point I always stand firm, and never will consent to abandon the poor Lads to the world's mercy, as She has often solicited me to do. In every thing else I let her have her own way; and truly She manages a family rarely, that I must say for her.'

We were conversing in this manner, when our discourse was interrupted by a loud halloo, which rang through the Forest.

'My Sons, I hope!' exclaimed the Wood-man, and ran to open the door.

The halloo was repeated: We now distinguished the

trampling of Horses, and soon after a Carriage, attended
by several Cavaliers stopped at the Cottage door. One
of the Horse-men enquired how far they were still from
Strasbourg. As He addressed himself to me, I answered
in the number of miles which Claude had told me; Upon
which a volley of curses was vented against the Drivers
for having lost their way. The Persons in the Coach were
now informed of the distance of Strasbourg, and also
that the Horses were so fatigued as to be incapable of
proceeding further. A Lady, who appeared to be the
principal, expressed much chagrin at this intelligence;
But as there was no remedy, one of the Attendants asked
the Wood-man, whether He could furnish them with
lodging for the night.

He seemed much embarrassed, and replied in the
negative; Adding that a Spanish Gentleman and his
Servant were already in possession of the only spare
apartments in his House. On hearing this, the gallantry
of my nation would not permit me to retain those
accommodations, of which a Female was in want. I
instantly signified to the Wood-man, that I transferred
my right to the Lady; He made some objections; But I
over-ruled them, and hastening to the Carriage, opened
the door, and assisted the Lady to descend. I immediately recognized her for the same person, whom I had
seen at the Inn at Luneville. I took an opportunity of
asking one of her Attendants, what was her name?

'The Baroness Lindenberg,' was the answer.

I could not but remark how different a reception our
Host had given these new-comers and myself. His
reluctance to admit them was visibly expressed on his
countenance, and He prevailed on himself with difficulty
to tell the Lady, that She was welcome. I conducted her
into the House, and placed her in the armed-chair, which
I had just quitted. She thanked me very graciously; and
made a thousand apologies for putting me to an in-

convenience. Suddenly the Wood-man's countenance cleared up.

'At last I have arranged it!' said He, interrupting her excuses; 'I can lodge you and your suite, Madam, and you will not be under the necessity of making this Gentleman suffer for his politeness. We have two spare chambers, one for the Lady, the other, Monsieur, for you: My Wife shall give up hers to the two Waiting-women; As for the Men-servants, they must content themselves with passing the night in a large Barn, which stands at a few yards distance from the House. There they shall have a blazing fire, and as good a supper as we can make shift to give them.'

After several expressions of gratitude on the Lady's part, and opposition on mine to Marguerite's giving up her bed, this arrangement was agreed to. As the Room was small, the Baroness immediately dismissed her Male Domestics: Baptiste was on the point of conducting them to the Barn which He had mentioned, when two young Men appeared at the door of the Cottage.

'Hell and Furies!' exclaimed the first starting back; 'Robert, the House is filled with Strangers!'

'Ha! There are my Sons!' cried our Host. 'Why, Jacques! Robert! whither are you running, Boys? There is room enough still for you.'

Upon this assurance the Youths returned. The Father presented them to the Baroness and myself: After which He withdrew with our Domestics, while at the request of the two Waiting-women, Marguerite conducted them to the room designed for their Mistress.

The two new-comers were tall, stout, well-made young Men, hard-featured, and very much sun-burnt. They paid their compliments to us in few words, and acknowledged Claude, who now entered the room, as an old acquaintance. They then threw aside their cloaks in which they were wrapped up, took off a leathern belt

to which a large Cutlass was suspended, and each drawing a brace of pistols from his girdle laid them upon a
shelf.

'You travel well-armed,' said I.

'True, Monsieur;' replied Robert. 'We left Strasbourg late this Evening, and 'tis necessary to take precautions at passing through this Forest after dark. It
does not bear a good repute, I promise you.'

'How?' said the Baroness; 'Are there Robbers here-
about?'

'So it is said, Madame; For my own part, I have
travelled through the wood at all hours, and never met
with one of them.'

Here Marguerite returned. Her Step-sons drew her to
the other end of the room, and whispered her for some
minutes. By the looks which they cast towards us at
intervals, I conjectured them to be enquiring our
business in the Cottage.

In the mean while the Baroness expressed her apprehensions, that her Husband would be suffering much
anxiety upon her account. She had intended to send on
one of her Servants to inform the Baron of her delay;
But the account which the young Men gave of the
Forest, rendered this plan impracticable. Claude relieved
her from her embarrassment. He informed her, that
He was under the necessity of reaching Strasbourg that
night, and that would She trust him with a letter, She
might depend upon its being safely delivered.

'And how comes it,' said I, 'that you are under no
apprehension of meeting these Robbers?'

'Alas! Monsieur, a poor Man with a large family must
not lose certain profit, because 'tis attended with a little
danger, and perhaps my Lord the Baron may give me a
trifle for my pains. Besides, I have nothing to lose except
my life, and that will not be worth the Robbers taking.'

I thought his arguments bad, and advised his waiting

till the Morning; But as the Baroness did not second me, I was obliged to give up the point. The Baroness Lindenberg, as I found afterwards, had long been accustomed to sacrifice the interests of others to her own, and her wish to send Claude to Strasbourg blinded her to the danger of the undertaking. Accordingly, it was resolved, that He should set out without delay. The Baroness wrote her letter to her Husband, and I sent a few lines to my Banker, apprising him that I should not be at Strasbourg till the next day. Claude took our letters, and left the Cottage.

The Lady declared herself much fatigued by her journey: Besides having come from some distance, the Drivers had contrived to lose their way in the Forest. She now addressed herself to Marguerite, desiring to be shown to her chamber, and permitted to take half an hour's repose. One of the Waiting-women was immediately summoned; She appeared with a light, and the Baroness followed her up stairs. The cloth was spreading in the chamber where I was, and Marguerite soon gave me to understand, that I was in her way. Her hints were too broad to be easily mistaken; I therefore desired one of the young Men to conduct me to the chamber where I was to sleep, and where I could remain till supper was ready.

'Which chamber is it, Mother?' said Robert.

'The One with green hangings,' She replied; 'I have just been at the trouble of getting it ready, and have put fresh sheets upon the Bed; If the Gentleman chooses to lollop and lounge upon it, He may make it again himself for me.'

'You are out of humour, Mother, but that is no novelty. Have the goodness to follow me, Monsieur.'

He opened the door, and advanced towards a narrow stair-case.

'You have got no light!' said Marguerite; 'Is it your

own neck or the Gentleman's that you have a mind to break?'

She crossed by me, and put a candle into Robert's hand, having received which, He began to ascend the stair-case. Jacques was employed in laying the cloth, and his back was turned towards me. Marguerite seized the moment, when we were unobserved. She caught my hand, and pressed it strongly.

'Look at the Sheets!' said She as She passed me, and immediately resumed her former occupation.

Startled by the abruptness of her action, I remained as if petrified. Robert's voice, desiring me to follow him, recalled me to myself. I ascended the stair-case. My conductor ushered me into a chamber, where an excellent wood-fire was blazing upon the hearth. He placed the light upon the Table, enquired whether I had any further commands, and on my replying in the negative, He left me to myself. You may be certain, that the moment when I found myself alone, was that on which I complied with Marguerite's injunction. I took the candle, hastily approached the Bed, and turned down the Coverture. What was my astonishment, my horror, at finding the sheets crimsoned with blood!

At that moment a thousand confused ideas passed before my imagination. The Robbers who infested the Wood, Marguerite's exclamation respecting her Children, the arms and appearance of the two young Men, and the various Anecdotes which I had heard related, respecting the secret correspondence which frequently exists between Banditti*and Postillions, all these circumstances flashed upon my mind, and inspired me with doubt and apprehension. I ruminated on the most probable means of ascertaining the truth of my conjectures. Suddenly I was aware of Some-one below pacing hastily backwards and forwards. Every thing now appeared to me an object of suspicion. With precaution

I drew near the window, which, as the room had been long shut up, was left open in spite of the cold. I ventured to look out. The beams of the Moon permitted me to distinguish a Man, whom I had no difficulty to recognize for my Host. I watched his movements. He walked swiftly, then stopped, and seemed to listen: He stamped upon the ground, and beat his stomach with his arms as if to guard himself from the inclemency of the season. At the least noise, if a voice was heard in the lower part of the House, if a Bat flitted past him, or the wind rattled amidst the leafless boughs, He started, and looked round with anxiety.

'Plague take him!' said He at length with impatience; 'What can He be about!'

He spoke in a low voice; but as He was just below my window, I had no difficulty to distinguish his words.

I now heard the steps of one approaching. Baptiste went towards the sound; He joined a man, whom his low stature and the Horn suspended from his neck, declared to be no other than my faithful Claude, whom I had supposed to be already on his way to Strasbourg. Expecting their discourse to throw some light upon my situation, I hastened to put myself in a condition to hear it with safety. For this purpose I extinguished the candle, which stood upon a table near the Bed: The flame of the fire was not strong enough to betray me, and I immediately resumed my place at the window.

The objects of my curiosity had stationed themselves directly under it. I suppose, that during my momentary absence the Wood-man had been blaming Claude for tardiness, since when I returned to the window, the latter was endeavouring to excuse his fault.

'However,' added He, 'my diligence at present shall make up for my past delay.'

'On that condition,' answered Baptiste, 'I shall readily forgive you. But in truth as you share equally with us in our prizes, your own interest will make you use all possible diligence. 'Twould be a shame to let such a noble booty escape us! You say, that this Spaniard is rich?'

'His Servant boasted at the Inn, that the effects in his Chaise were worth above two thousand Pistoles.'

Oh! how I cursed Stephano's imprudent vanity!

'And I have been told,' continued the Postillion, 'that this Baroness carries about her a casket of jewels of immense value.'

'May be so, but I had rather She had stayed away. The Spaniard was a secure prey. The Boys and myself could easily have mastered him and his Servant, and then the two thousand Pistoles would have been shared between us four. Now we must let in the Band for a share, and perhaps the whole Covey may escape us. Should our Friends have betaken themselves to their different posts before you reach the Cavern, all will be lost. The Lady's Attendants are too numerous for us to over-power them: Unless our Associates arrive in time, we must needs let these Travellers set out to-morrow without damage or hurt.'

' 'Tis plaguy unlucky, that my Comrades, who drove the Coach, should be those unacquainted with our Confederacy! But never fear, Friend Baptiste. An hour will bring me to the Cavern; It is now but ten o'clock, and by twelve you may expect the arrival of the Band. By the bye, take care of your Wife: You know how strong is her repugnance to our mode of life, and She may find means to give information to the Lady's Servants of our design.'

'Oh! I am secure of her silence; She is too much afraid of me, and fond of her children, to dare to betray my secret. Besides, Jacques and Robert keep a strict eye over her, and She is not permitted to set a foot out of the Cottage. The Servants are safely lodged in the Barn;

I shall endeavour to keep all quiet till the arrival of our Friends. Were I assured of your finding them, the Strangers should be dispatched this instant; But as it is possible for you to miss the Banditti, I am fearful of being summoned to produce them by their Domestics in the Morning.'

'And suppose either of the Travellers should discover your design?'

'Then we must poignard those in our power, and take our chance about mastering the rest. However, to avoid running such a risque, hasten to the Cavern: The Banditti never leave it before eleven, and if you use diligence, you may reach it in time to stop them.'

'Tell Robert, that I have taken his Horse: My own has broken his bridle, and escaped into the Wood. What is the watch-word?'

'The reward of Courage.'

' 'Tis sufficient. I hasten to the Cavern.'

'And I to rejoin my Guests, lest my absence should create suspicion. Farewell, and be diligent.'

These worthy Associates now separated: The One bent his course towards the Stable, while the Other returned to the House.

You may judge, what must have been my feelings during this conversation, of which I lost not a single syllable. I dared not trust myself to my reflections, nor did any means present itself to escape the dangers which threatened me. Resistance, I knew to be vain; I was unarmed, and a single Man against Three: However, I resolved at least to sell my life as dearly as I could. Dreading lest Baptiste should perceive my absence, and suspect me to have overheard the message with which Claude was dispatched, I hastily relighted my candle and quitted the chamber. On descending, I found the Table spread for six Persons. The Baroness sat by the fire-side: Marguerite was employed in dressing a sallad, and her

Step-sons were whispering together at the further end of
the room. Baptiste having the round of the Garden
to make, ere He could reach the Cottage-door, was not
yet arrived. I seated myself quietly opposite to the
Baroness.

A glance upon Marguerite told her, that her hint had
not been thrown away upon me. How different did She
now appear to me! What before seemed gloom and
sullenness, I now found to be disgust at her Associates,
and compassion for my danger. I looked up to her as to
my only resource; Yet knowing her to be watched by
her Husband with a suspicious eye, I could place but
little reliance on the exertions of her good-will.

In spite of all my endeavours to conceal it, my agitation was but too visibly expressed upon my countenance.
I was pale, and both my words and actions were disordered and embarrassed. The young Men observed this,
and enquired the cause. I attributed it to excess of
fatigue, and the violent effect produced on me by the
severity of the season. Whether they believed me or not,
I will not pretend to say: They at least ceased to embarrass me with their questions. I strove to divert my
attention from the perils which surrounded me, by
conversing on different subjects with the Baroness. I
talked of Germany, declaring my intention of visiting it
immediately: God knows, that I little thought at that
moment of ever seeing it! She replied to me with great
ease and politeness, professed that the pleasure of making
my acquaintance amply compensated for the delay in
her journey, and gave me a pressing invitation to make
some stay at the Castle of Lindenberg. As She spoke thus,
the Youths exchanged a malicious smile, which declared
that She would be fortunate if She ever reached that
Castle herself. This action did not escape me; But I
concealed the emotion which it excited in my breast.
I continued to converse with the Lady; But my dis-

course was so frequently incoherent, that as She has since informed me, She began to doubt whether I was in my right senses. The fact was, that while my conversation turned upon one subject, my thoughts were entirely occupied by another. I meditated upon the means of quitting the Cottage, finding my way to the Barn, and giving the Domestics information of our Host's designs. I was soon convinced, how impracticable was the attempt. Jacques and Robert watched my every movement with an attentive eye, and I was obliged to abandon the idea. All my hopes now rested upon Claude's not finding the Banditti: In that case, according to what I had over-heard, we should be permitted to depart unhurt.

I shuddered involuntarily, as Baptiste entered the room. He made many apologies for his long absence, but 'He had been detained by affairs impossible to be delayed.' He then entreated permission for his family to sup at the same table with us, without which, respect would not authorize his taking such a liberty. Oh! how in my heart I cursed the Hypocrite! How I loathed his presence, who was on the point of depriving me of an existence, at that time infinitely dear! I had every reason to be satisfied with life; I had youth, wealth, rank, and education; and the fairest prospects presented themselves before me. I saw those prospects on the point of closing in the most horrible manner: Yet was I obliged to dissimulate, and to receive with a semblance of gratitude the false civilities of him, who held the dagger to my bosom.

The permission which our Host demanded, was easily obtained. We seated ourselves at the Table. The Baroness and myself occupied one side: The Sons were opposite to us with their backs to the door. Baptiste took his seat by the Baroness at the upper end, and the place next to him was left for his Wife. She soon entered the room, and placed before us a plain but comfortable Peasant's repast. Our Host thought it necessary to apologize for the poorness of the supper: 'He had not been apprized of our coming; He could only offer us such fare as had been intended for his own family:'

'But,' added He, 'should any accident detain my noble Guests longer than they at present intend, I hope to give them a better treatment.'

The Villain! I well knew the accident to which He alluded; I shuddered at the treatment which He taught us to expect!

My Companion in danger seemed entirely to have got rid of her chagrin at being delayed. She laughed, and conversed with the family with infinite gaiety. I strove but in vain to follow her example. My spirits were evidently forced, and the constraint which I put upon myself, escaped not Baptiste's observation.

'Come, come, Monsieur, cheer up!' said He; 'You seem not quite recovered from your fatigue. To raise your spirits, what say you to a glass of excellent old wine which was left me by my Father? God rest his soul, He is in a better world! I seldom produce this wine; But as I am not honoured with such Guests every day, this is an occasion which deserves a Bottle.'

He then gave his Wife a Key, and instructed her where to find the wine of which He spoke. She seemed by no means pleased with the commission; She took the Key with an embarrassed air, and hesitated to quit the Table.

'Did you hear me?' said Baptiste in an angry tone.

Marguerite darted upon him a look of mingled anger and fear, and left the chamber. His eyes followed her suspiciously, till She had closed the door.

She soon returned with a bottle sealed with yellow wax. She placed it upon the table, and gave the Key back to her Husband. I suspected that this liquor was not presented to us without design, and I watched Marguerite's movements with inquietude. She was employed in rinsing some small horn Goblets. As She placed them before Baptiste, She saw that my eye was fixed upon her; and at the moment when She thought herself unobserved by the Banditti, She motioned to me with her head not to taste the liquor, She then resumed her place.

In the mean while our Host had drawn the Cork, and filling two of the Goblets offered them to the Lady and myself. She at first made some objections, but the instances of Baptiste were so urgent, that She was obliged to comply. Fearing to excite suspicion, I hesitated not to take the Goblet presented to me. By its smell and colour I guessed it to be Champagne; But some grains of powder floating upon the top, convinced me that it was not unadulterated. However, I dared not to express my repugnance to drinking it; I lifted it to my lips, and seemed to be swallowing it: Suddenly starting from my chair, I made the best of my way towards a Vase of water at some distance, in which Marguerite had been rinsing the Goblets. I pretended to spit out the wine with disgust, and took an opportunity unperceived of emptying the liquor into the Vase.

The Banditti seemed alarmed at my action. Jacques half rose from his chair, put his hand into his bosom, and I discovered the haft of a dagger. I returned to my seat with tranquillity, and affected not to have observed their confusion.

'You have not suited my taste, honest Friend,' said I, addressing myself to Baptiste. 'I never can drink Champagne without its producing a violent illness. I swallowed a few mouthfuls ere I was aware of its quality, and fear that I shall suffer for my imprudence.'

Baptiste and Jacques exchanged looks of distrust.

'Perhaps,' said Robert, 'the smell may be disagreeable to you.'

He quitted his chair, and removed the Goblet. I observed, that He examined, whether it was nearly empty.

'He must have drank sufficient,' said He to his Brother in a low voice, while He reseated himself.

Marguerite looked apprehensive, that I had tasted the liquor: A glance from my eye re-assured her.

I waited with anxiety for the effects which the Beverage would produce upon the Lady. I doubted not but the grains which I had observed, were poisonous, and lamented, that it had been impossible for me to warn her of the danger. But a few minutes had elapsed, before I perceived her eyes grow heavy; Her head sank upon her shoulder, and She fell into a deep sleep. I affected not to attend to this circumstance, and continued my conversation with Baptiste, with all the outward gaiety in my power to assume. But He no longer answered me without constraint. He eyed me with distrust and astonishment, and I saw that the Banditti were frequently whispering among themselves. My situation became every moment more painful; I sustained the character of confidence with a worse grace than ever. Equally afraid of the arrival of their Accomplices, and of their suspecting my knowledge of their designs, I knew not how to dissipate the distrust, which the Banditti evidently entertained for me. In this new dilemma the friendly Marguerite again assisted me. She passed behind the Chairs of her Step-sons, stopped for a moment opposite to me, closed her eyes, and reclined her head upon her shoulder. This hint immediately dispelled my incertitude. It told me, that I ought to imitate the Baroness, and pretend that the liquor had taken its full effect upon me. I did so, and in a few minutes seemed perfectly overcome with slumber.

'So!' cried Baptiste, as I fell back in my chair; 'At last He sleeps! I began to think that He had scented our design, and that we should have been forced to dispatch him at all events.'

'And why not dispatch him at all events?' enquired the ferocious Jacques. 'Why leave him the possibility of betraying our secret? Marguerite, give me one of my Pistols: A single touch of the trigger will finish him at once.'

'And supposing,' rejoined the Father, 'Supposing that our Friends should not arrive to-night, a pretty figure we should make when the Servants enquire for him in the Morning! No, no, Jacques; We must wait for our Associates. If they join us, we are strong enough to dispatch the Domestics as well as their Masters, and the booty is our own; If Claude does not find the Troop, we must take patience, and suffer the prey to slip through our fingers. Ah! Boys, Boys, had you arrived but five minutes sooner, the Spaniard would have been done for, and two thousand Pistoles our own. But you are always out of the way when you are most wanted. You are the most unlucky Rogues!'

'Well, well, Father!' answered Jacques; 'Had you been of my mind, all would have been over by this time. You, Robert, Claude, and myself, why the Strangers were but double the number, and I warrant you we might have mastered them. However, Claude is gone; 'Tis too late to think of it now. We must wait patiently for the arrival of the Gang; and if the Travellers escape us to-night, we must take care to way-lay them to-morrow.'

'True! True!' said Baptiste; 'Marguerite, have you given the sleeping-draught to the Waiting-women?'

She replied in the affirmative.

'All then is safe. Come, come, Boys; Whatever falls out, we have no reason to complain of this adventure. We run no danger, may gain much, and can lose nothing.'

At this moment I heard a trampling of Horses. Oh! how dreadful was the sound to my ears. A cold sweat flowed down my forehead, and I felt all the terrors of impending death. I was by no means re-assured by hearing the compassionate Marguerite exclaim in the accents of despair,

'Almighty God! They are lost!'

Luckily the Wood-man and his Sons were too much occupied by the arrival of their Associates to attend to me, or the violence of my agitation would have convinced them, that my sleep was feigned.

'Open! Open!' exclaimed several voices on the outside of the Cottage.

'Yes! Yes!' cried Baptiste joyfully; 'They are our Friends sure enough! Now then our booty is certain. Away! Lads, Away! Lead them to the Barn; You know, what is to be done there.'

Robert hastened to open the door of the Cottage.

'But first,' said Jacques, taking up his arms; 'first let me dispatch these Sleepers.'

'No, no, no!' replied his Father; 'Go you to the Barn, where your presence is wanted. Leave me to take care of these and the Women above.'

Jacques obeyed, and followed his Brother. They seemed to converse with the New-Comers for a few minutes: After which I heard the Robbers dismount, and as I conjectured, bend their course towards the Barn.

'So! That is wisely done!' muttered Baptiste; 'They have quitted their Horses, that They may fall upon the Strangers by surprise. Good! Good! and now to business.'

I heard him approach a small Cup-board which was fixed up in a distant part of the room, and unlock it. At this moment I felt myself shaken gently.

'Now! Now!' whispered Marguerite.

I opened my eyes. Baptiste stood with his back towards

me. No one else was in the room save Marguerite and the sleeping Lady. The Villain had taken a dagger from the Cup-board, and seemed examining whether it was sufficiently sharp. I had neglected to furnish myself with arms; But I perceived this to be my only chance of escaping, and resolved not to lose the opportunity. I sprang from my seat, darted suddenly upon Baptiste, and clasping my hands round his throat, pressed it so forcibly as to prevent his uttering a single cry. You may remember, that I was remarkable at Salamanca for the power of my arm: It now rendered me an essential service. Surprised, terrified, and breathless, the Villain was by no means an equal Antagonist. I threw him upon the ground; I grasped him still tighter; and while I fixed him without motion upon the floor, Marguerite wresting the dagger from his hand, plunged it repeatedly in his heart till He expired.

No sooner was this horrible but necessary act perpetrated, than Marguerite called on me to follow her.

'Flight is our only refuge!' said She; 'Quick! Quick! Away!'

I hesitated not to obey her: but unwilling to leave the Baroness a victim to the vengeance of the Robbers, I raised her in my arms still sleeping, and hastened after Marguerite. The Horses of the Banditti were fastened near the door: My Conductress sprang upon one of them. I followed her example, placed the Baroness before me, and spurred on my Horse. Our only hope was to reach Strasbourg, which was much nearer than the perfidious Claude had assured me. Marguerite was well acquainted with the road, and galloped on before me. We were obliged to pass by the Barn, where the Robbers were slaughtering our Domestics. The door was open: We distinguished the shrieks of the dying and imprecations of the Murderers! What I felt at that moment language is unable to describe!

Jacques heard the trampling of our Horses, as we rushed by the Barn. He flew to the Door with a burning Torch in his hand, and easily recognised the Fugitives.

'Betrayed! Betrayed!' He shouted to his Companions.

Instantly they left their bloody work, and hastened to regain their Horses. We heard no more. I buried my spurs in the sides of my Courser, and Marguerite goaded on hers with the poignard, which had already rendered us such good service. We flew like lightning, and gained the open plains. Already was Strasbourg's Steeple in sight, when we heard the Robbers pursuing us. Marguerite looked back, and distinguished our followers descending a small Hill at no great distance. It was in vain that we urged on our Horses; The noise approached nearer with every moment.

'We are lost!' She exclaimed; 'The Villains gain upon us!'

'On! On!' replied I; 'I hear the trampling of Horses coming from the Town.'

We redoubled our exertions, and were soon aware of a numerous band of Cavaliers, who came towards us at full speed. They were on the point of passing us.

'Stay! Stay!' shrieked Marguerite; 'Save us! For God's sake, save us!'

The Foremost, who seemed to act as Guide, immediately reined in his Steed.

' 'Tis She! 'Tis She!' exclaimed He, springing upon the ground; 'Stop, my Lord, stop! They are safe! 'Tis my Mother!'

At the same moment Marguerite threw herself from her Horse, clasped him in her arms, and covered him with Kisses. The other Cavaliers stopped at the exclamation.

'The Baroness Lindenberg?' cried another of the Strangers eagerly; 'Where is She? Is She not with you?'

He stopped on beholding her lying senseless in my

arms. Hastily He caught her from me. The profound sleep in which She was plunged, made him at first tremble for her life; but the beating of her heart soon re-assured him.

'God be thanked!' said He; 'She has escaped unhurt.'

I interrupted his joy by pointing out the Brigands, who continued to approach. No sooner had I mentioned them, than the greatest part of the Company, which appeared to be chiefly composed of soldiers, hastened forward to meet them. The Villains stayed not to receive their attack: Perceiving their danger they turned the heads of their Horses, and fled into the wood, whither they were followed by our Preservers. In the mean while the Stranger, whom I guessed to be the Baron Lindenberg, after thanking me for my care of his Lady, proposed our returning with all speed to the Town. The Baroness, on whom the effects of the opiate had not ceased to operate, was placed before him; Marguerite and her Son remounted their Horses; the Baron's Domestics followed, and we soon arrived at the Inn, where He had taken his apartments.

This was at the Austrian Eagle, where my Banker, whom before my quitting Paris I had apprised of my intention to visit Strasbourg, had prepared Lodgings for me. I rejoiced at this circumstance. It gave me an opportunity of cultivating the Baron's acquaintance, which I foresaw would be of use to me in Germany. Immediately upon our arrival the Lady was conveyed to bed; A Physician was sent for, who prescribed a medicine likely to counteract the effects of the sleepy potion, and after it had been poured down her throat, She was committed to the care of the Hostess. The Baron then addressed himself to me, and entreated me to recount the particulars of this adventure. I complied with his request instantaneously; for in pain respecting Stephano's fate, whom I had been compelled to abandon to the cruelty of the Banditti, I found it impossible for me to repose, till I had some news of him. I received but too soon the intelligence, that my trusty Servant had perished. The Soldiers who had pursued the Brigands, returned while I was employed in relating my adventure to the Baron. By their account I found, that the Robbers had been overtaken: Guilt and true courage are incompatible; They had thrown themselves at the feet of their Pursuers, had surrendered themselves without striking a blow, had discovered their secret retreat, made known their signals by which the rest of the Gang might be seized, and in short had betrayed every mark of cowardice and baseness. By this means the whole of the Band, consisting of near sixty persons, had been made Prisoners, bound, and conducted to Strasbourg. Some of the Soldiers hastened to the Cottage, One of the Banditti serving them as Guide. Their first visit was to the fatal Barn, where they were fortunate enough to find two of the Baron's Servants still alive, though desperately wounded. The rest had expired beneath the swords of the Robbers, and of these my unhappy Stephano was one.

Alarmed at our escape, the Robbers in their haste to over-take us, had neglected to visit the Cottage. In consequence, the Soldiers found the two Waiting-women unhurt, and buried in the same death-like slumber which had overpowered their Mistress. There was nobody else found in the Cottage, except a child not above four years old, which the Soldiers brought away with them. We were busying ourselves with conjectures respecting the birth of this little unfortunate, when Marguerite rushed into the room with the Baby in her arms. She fell at the feet of the Officer who was making us this report, and blessed him a thousand times for the preservation of her Child.

When the first burst of maternal tenderness was over, I besought her to declare, by what means She had been united to a Man whose principles seemed so totally discordant with her own. She bent her eyes down-wards, and wiped a few tears from her cheek.

'Gentlemen,' said She after a silence of some minutes, 'I would request a favour of you: You have a right to know, on whom you confer an obligation. I will not therefore stifle a confession which covers me with shame; But permit me to comprise it in as few words as possible.

'I was born in Strasbourg of respectable Parents; Their names I must at present conceal: My Father still lives, and deserves not to be involved in my infamy; If you grant my request, you shall be informed of my family name. A Villain made himself Master of my affections, and to follow him I quitted my Father's House. Yet though my passions over-powered my virtue, I sank not into that degeneracy of vice, but too commonly the lot of Women who make the first false step. I loved my Seducer; dearly loved him! I was true to his Bed; this Baby, and the Youth who warned you, my Lord Baron, of your Lady's danger, are the pledges of our affection. Even at this moment I lament his loss, though 'tis to him that I owe all the miseries of my existence.

'He was of noble birth, but He had squandered away his paternal inheritance. His Relations considered him as a disgrace to their name, and utterly discarded him. His excesses drew upon him the indignation of the Police. He was obliged to fly from Strasbourg, and saw no other resource from beggary, than an union with the Banditti, who infested the neighbouring Forest, and whose Troop was chiefly composed of Young Men of family in the same predicament with himself. I was determined not to forsake him. I followed him to the Cavern of the Brigands, and shared with him the misery inseparable from a life of pillage. But though I was aware that our existence was supported by plunder, I knew not all the horrible circumstances attached to my Lover's profession. These He concealed from me with the utmost care; He was conscious, that my sentiments were not sufficiently depraved to look without horror upon assassination: He supposed, and with justice, that I should fly with detestation from the embraces of a Murderer. Eight years of possession had not abated his love for me; and He cautiously removed from my knowledge every circumstance, which might lead me to suspect the crimes in which He but too often participated. He succeeded perfectly: It was not till after my Seducer's death, that I discovered his hands to have been stained with the blood of innocence.

'One fatal night He was brought back to the Cavern, covered with wounds: He received them in attacking an English Traveller, whom his Companions immediately sacrificed to their resentment. He had only time to entreat my pardon for all the sorrows which He had caused me: He pressed my hand to his lips, and expired. My grief was inexpressible. As soon as its violence abated, I resolved to return to Strasbourg, to throw myself with my two Children at my Father's feet, and implore his forgiveness, though I little hoped to obtain it. What was my consternation when informed, that no one entrusted with the secret of their retreat, was ever permitted to quit the troop of the Banditti; That I must give up all hopes of ever rejoining society, and consent instantly to accepting one of their Band for my Husband! My prayers and remonstrances were vain. They cast lots to decide to whose possession I should fall; I became the property of the infamous Baptiste. A Robber, who had once been a Monk, pronounced over us a burlesque rather than a religious Ceremony: I and my Children were delivered into the hands of my new Husband, and He conveyéd us immediately to his home.

'He assured me that He had long entertained for me the most ardent regard; But that Friendship for my deceased Lover had obliged him to stifle his desires. He endeavoured to reconcile me to my fate, and for some time treated me with respect and gentleness: At length finding that my aversion rather increased than diminished, He obtained those favours by violence, which I persisted to refuse him. No resource remained for me but to bear my sorrows with patience; I was conscious, that I deserved them but too well. Flight was forbidden: My Children were in the power of Baptiste, and He had sworn that if I attempted to escape, their lives should pay for it. I had had too many opportunities of witnessing the barbarity of his nature, to doubt his fulfilling his oath to the very letter. Sad experience had convinced me of the horrors of my situation: My first Lover had carefully concealed them from me; Baptiste rather rejoiced in opening my eyes to the cruelties of his profession, and strove to familiarise me with blood and slaughter.

'My nature was licentious and warm, but not cruel: My conduct had been imprudent, but my heart was not unprincipled. Judge then what I must have felt at being a continual witness of crimes the most horrible and revolting! Judge how I must have grieved at being united to a Man, who received the unsuspecting Guest with an air of openness and hospitality, at the very moment that He meditated his destruction. Chagrin and discontent preyed upon my constitution: The few charms bestowed on me by nature withered away, and the dejection of my countenance denoted the sufferings of my heart. I was tempted a thousand times to put an end to my existence; But the remembrance of my Children held my hand. I trembled to leave my dear Boys in my Tyrant's power, and trembled yet more for their virtue than their lives. The Second was still too young to benefit by my instructions; But in the heart of my Eldest I laboured unceasingly to plant those principles, which might enable him to avoid the crimes of his Parents. He listened to me with docility, or rather with eagerness. Even at his early age, He showed that He was not calculated for the society of Villains; and the only comfort which I enjoyed among my sorrows, was to witness the dawning virtues of my Theodore.

'Such was my situation, when the perfidy of Don Alphonso's postillion conducted him to the Cottage. His youth, air, and manners interested me most forcibly in his behalf. The absence of my Husband's Sons gave me an opportunity which I had long wished to find, and I resolved to risque every thing to preserve the Stranger. The vigilance of Baptiste prevented me from warning Don Alphonso of his danger: I knew that my betraying the secret would be immediately punished with death; and however embittered was my life by calamities, I wanted courage to sacrifice it for the sake of preserving that of another Person. My only hope rested upon procuring succour from Strasbourg: At this I resolved to try; and should an opportunity offer of warning Don Alphonso of his danger unobserved, I was determined to seize it with avidity. By Baptiste's orders I went up stairs to make the Stranger's Bed: I spread upon it Sheets in which a Traveller had been murdered but a few nights before, and which still were stained with blood. I hoped that these marks would not escape the vigilance of our Guest, and that He would collect from them the designs of my perfidious Husband. Neither was this the only step, which I took to preserve the Stranger. Theodore was confined to his bed by illness. I stole into his room unobserved by my Tyrant, communicated to him my project, and He entered into it with eagerness. He rose in spite of his malady, and dressed himself with all speed. I fastened one of the Sheets round his arms, and lowered him from the Window. He flew to the Stable, took Claude's Horse, and hastened to Strasbourg. Had He been accosted by the Banditti, He was to have declared

himself sent upon a message by Baptiste, but fortunately
He reached the Town without meeting any obstacle.
Immediately upon his arrival at Strasbourg, He entreated assistance from the Magistrature: His Story passed
from mouth to mouth, and at length came to the
knowledge of my Lord the Baron. Anxious for the safety
of his Lady, whom He knew would be upon the road
that Evening, it struck him that She might have fallen
into the power of the Robbers. He accompanied Theodore who guided the Soldiers towards the Cottage, and
arrived just in time to save us from falling once more into
the hands of our Enemies.'

Here I interrupted Marguerite to enquire, why the
sleepy potion had been presented to me. She said, that
Baptiste supposed me to have arms about me, and
wished to incapacitate me from making resistance: It
was a precaution which He always took, since as the
Travellers had no hopes of escaping, Despair would have
incited them to sell their lives dearly.

The Baron then desired Marguerite to inform him,
what were her present plans. I joined him in declaring
my readiness to show my gratitude to her for the
preservation of my life.

'Disgusted with a world,' She replied, 'in which I have
met with nothing but misfortunes, my only wish is to
retire into a Convent. But first I must provide for my
Children. I find that my Mother is no more, probably
driven to an untimely grave by my desertion! My
Father is still living; He is not an hard Man; Perhaps,
Gentlemen, in spite of my ingratitude and imprudence,
your intercessions may induce him to forgive me, and to
take charge of his unfortunate Grand-sons. If you obtain
this boon for me, you will repay my services a thousand-
fold!'

Both the Baron and myself assured Marguerite, that
we would spare no pains to obtain her pardon: and that

even should her Father be inflexible, She need be under no apprehensions respecting the fate of her Children. I engaged myself to provide for Theodore, and the Baron promised to take the youngest under his protection. The grateful Mother thanked us with tears for what She called generosity, but which in fact was no more than a proper sense of our obligations to her. She then left the room to put her little Boy to bed, whom fatigue and sleep had compleatly overpowered.

The Baroness, on recovering and being informed from what dangers I had rescued her, set no bounds to the expressions of her gratitude. She was joined so warmly by her Husband in pressing me to accompany them to their Castle in Bavaria, that I found it impossible to resist their entreaties. During a week which we passed at Strasbourg, the interests of Marguerite were not forgotten: In our application to her Father we succeeded as amply as we could wish. The good old Man had lost his Wife: He had no Children but this unfortunate Daughter, of whom He had received no news for almost fourteen years. He was surrounded by distant Relations, who waited with impatience for his decease in order to get possession of his money. When therefore Marguerite appeared again so unexpectedly, He considered her as a gift from heaven: He received her and her Children with open arms, and insisted upon their establishing themselves in his House without delay. The disappointed Cousins were obliged to give place. The old Man would not hear of his Daughter's retiring into a Convent: He said, that She was too necessary to his happiness, and She was easily persuaded to relinquish her design. But no persuasions could induce Theodore to give up the plan, which I had at first marked out for him. He had attached himself to me most sincerely, during my stay at Strasbourg; and when I was on the point of leaving it, He besought me with tears to take him into my service:

He set forth all his little talents in the most favourable
colours, and tried to convince me that I should find him
of infinite use to me upon the road. I was unwilling to
charge myself with a Lad but scarcely turned of thirteen,
whom I knew, could only be a burthen to me: However,
I could not resist the entreaties of this affectionate
Youth, who in fact possessed a thousand estimable
qualities. With some difficulty He persuaded his relations to let him follow me, and that permission once
obtained, He was dubbed with the title of my Page.
Having passed a week at Strasbourg, Theodore and
myself set out for Bavaria* in company with the Baron
and his Lady. These Latter as well as myself had forced
Marguerite to accept several presents of value, both for
herself, and her youngest Son: On leaving her, I promised
his Mother faithfully, that I would restore Theodore to
her within the year.

I have related this adventure at length, Lorenzo, that
you might understand the means, by which 'The
Adventurer, Alphonso d'Alvarada got introduced into
the Castle of Lindenberg.' Judge from this specimen,
how much faith should be given to your Aunt's assertions!

END OF THE FIRST VOLUME

VOLUME II

CHAPTER I

Avaunt! and quit my sight! Let the Earth hide thee!
Thy bones are marrowless; thy blood is cold;
Thou hast no speculation in those eyes
Which Thou dost glare with! Hence, horrible shadow!
Unreal mockery hence!

Macbeth.*

Continuation of the History of Don Raymond.

MY JOURNEY WAS uncommonly agreeable: I found
the Baron a Man of some sense, but little knowledge of
the world. He had past a great part of his life without
stirring beyond the precincts of his own domains, and
consequently his manners were far from being the most
polished: But He was hearty, good-humoured, and
friendly. His attention to me was all that I could wish,
and I had every reason to be satisfied with his behaviour.
His ruling passion was Hunting, which He had brought
himself to consider as a serious occupation; and when
talking over some remarkable chace, He treated the
subject with as much gravity, as it had been a Battle on
which the fate of two kingdoms was depending. I
happened to be a tolerable Sportsman: Soon after my
arrival at Lindenberg*I gave some proofs of my dexterity.
The Baron immediately marked me down for a Man of
Genius, and vowed to me an eternal friendship.

That friendship was become to me by no means
indifferent. At the Castle of Lindenberg I beheld for the
first time your Sister, the lovely Agnes. For me whose

heart was unoccupied, and who grieved at the void, to see her and to love her were the same. I found in Agnes all that was requisite to secure my affection. She was then scarcely sixteen; Her person light and elegant was already formed; She possessed several talents in perfection, particularly those of Music and drawing: Her character was gay, open, and good-humoured; and the graceful simplicity of her dress and manners formed an advantageous contrast to the art and studied Coquetry of the Parisian Dames, whom I had just quitted. From the moment that I beheld her, I felt the most lively interest in her fate. I made many enquiries respecting her of the Baroness.

'She is my Niece,' replied that Lady; 'You are still ignorant, Don Alphonso, that I am your Countrywoman. I am Sister to the Duke of Medina Celi: Agnes is the Daughter of my second Brother, Don Gaston: She has been destined to the Convent from her cradle, and will soon make her profession at Madrid.'

[Here Lorenzo interrupted the Marquis by an exclamation of surprise.

'Intended for the Convent from her cradle?' said He; 'By heaven, this is the first word that I ever heard of such a design!'

'I believe it, my dear Lorenzo,' answered Don Raymond; 'But you must listen to me with patience. You will not be less surprised, when I relate some particulars of your family still unknown to you, and which I have learnt from the mouth of Agnes herself.'

He then resumed his narrative as follows.]

You cannot but be aware, that your Parents were unfortunately Slaves to the grossest superstition: When this foible was called into play, their every other sentiment, their every other passion yielded to its irresistible strength. While She was big with Agnes, your Mother was seized by a dangerous illness, and given over by her

Physicians. In this situation, Donna Inesilla vowed, that if She recovered from her malady, the Child then living in her bosom if a Girl should be dedicated to St. Clare, if a Boy to St. Benedict. Her prayers were heard; She got rid of her complaint; Agnes entered the world alive, and was immediately destined to the service of St. Clare.

Don Gaston readily chimed in with his Lady's wishes: But knowing the sentiments of the Duke, his Brother, respecting a Monastic life, it was determined that your Sister's destination should be carefully concealed from him. The better to guard the secret, it was resolved that Agnes should accompany her Aunt, Donna Rodolpha into Germany, whither that Lady was on the point of following her new-married Husband, Baron Lindenberg. On her arrival at that Estate, the young Agnes was put into a Convent, situated but a few miles from the Castle. The Nuns, to whom her education was confided, performed their charge with exactitude: They made her a perfect Mistress of many talents, and strove to infuse into her mind a taste for the retirement and tranquil pleasures of a Convent. But a secret instinct made the young Recluse sensible that She was not born for solitude: In all the freedom of youth and gaiety She scrupled not to treat as ridiculous many ceremonies, which the Nuns regarded with awe; and She was never more happy than when her lively imagination inspired her with some scheme to plague the stiff Lady Abbess, or the ugly illtempered old Porteress. She looked with disgust upon the prospect before her: However no alternative was offered to her, and She submitted to the decree of her Parents, though not without secret repining.

That repugnance She had not art enough to conceal long: Don Gaston was informed of it. Alarmed, Lorenzo, lest your affection for her should oppose itself to his projects, and lest you should positively object to your

Sister's misery, He resolved to keep the whole affair from *your* knowledge as well as the Duke's, till the sacrifice should be consummated. The season of her taking the veil was fixed for the time when you should be upon your travels: In the mean while no hint was dropped of Donna Inesilla's fatal vow. Your Sister was never permitted to know your direction. All your letters were read before She received them, and those parts effaced, which were likely to nourish her inclination for the world: Her answers were dictated either by her Aunt, or by Dame Cunegonda,° her Governess. These particulars I learnt partly from Agnes, partly from the Baroness herself.

I immediately determined upon rescuing this lovely Girl from a fate so contrary to her inclinations, and ill-suited to her merit. I endeavoured to ingratiate myself into her favour: I boasted of my friendship and intimacy with you. She listened to me with avidity; She seemed to devour my words while I spoke in your praise, and her eyes thanked me for my affection to her Brother. My constant and unremitted attention at length gained me her heart, and with difficulty I obliged her to confess that She loved me. When however, I proposed her quitting the Castle of Lindenberg, She rejected the idea in positive terms.

'Be generous, Alphonso,' She said; 'You possess my heart, but use not the gift ignobly. Employ not your ascendancy over me in persuading me to take a step, at which I should here-after have to blush. I am young and deserted: My Brother, my only Friend, is separated from me, and my other Relations act with me as my Enemies. Take pity on my unprotected situation. Instead of seducing me to an action which would cover me with shame, strive rather to gain the affections of those who govern me. The Baron esteems you. My Aunt, to others ever harsh proud and contemptuous, remembers that you rescued her from the hands of Murderers, and wears with you alone the appearance of kindness and benignity. Try then your influence over my Guardians. If they consent to our union my hand is yours: From your account of my Brother, I cannot doubt your obtaining his approbation: And when they find the impossibility of executing their design, I trust that my Parents will excuse my disobedience, and expiate by some other sacrifice my Mother's fatal vow.'

From the first moment that I beheld Agnes, I had endeavoured to conciliate the favour of her Relations. Authorised by the confession of her regard, I redoubled my exertions. My principal Battery was directed against the Baroness; It was easy to discover, that her word was law in the Castle: Her Husband paid her the most absolute submission, and considered her as a superior Being. She was about forty: In her youth She had been a Beauty; But her charms had been upon that large scale which can but ill sustain the shock of years: However She still possessed some remains of them. Her understanding was strong and excellent when not obscured by prejudice, which unluckily was but seldom the case. Her passions were violent: She spared no pains to gratify them, and pursued with unremitting vengeance those who opposed themselves to her wishes. The warmest of Friends, the most inveterate of Enemies, such was the Baroness Lindenberg.

I laboured incessantly to please her: Unluckily I succeeded but too well. She seemed gratified by my attention, and treated me with a distinction accorded by her to no one else. One of my daily occupations was reading to her for several hours: Those hours I should much rather have past with Agnes; But as I was conscious, that complaisance for her Aunt would advance our union, I submitted with a good grace to the penance imposed upon me. Donna Rodolpha's Library was principally composed of old Spanish Romances: These were her favourite studies, and once a day one of these unmerciful Volumes was put regularly into my hands. I read the wearisome adventures of '*Perceforest*,' '*Tirante the White*,' '*Palmerin of England*,' and '*the Knight of the Sun*,' till the Book was on the point of falling from my hands through Ennui. However, the increasing pleasure which the Baroness seemed to take in my society, encouraged me to persevere; and latterly She showed for me a partiality so marked, that Agnes advised me to seize the first opportunity of declaring our mutual passion to her Aunt.

One Evening, I was alone with Donna Rodolpha in her own apartment. As our readings generally treated of love, Agnes was never permitted to assist at them. I was just congratulating myself on having finished '*the Loves of Tristan and the Queen Iseult*——*'

'Ah! The Unfortunates!' cried the Baroness; 'How say you, Segnor? Do you think it possible for Man to feel an attachment so disinterested and sincere?'

'I cannot doubt it,' replied I; 'My own heart furnishes me with the certainty. Ah! Donna Rodolpha, might I but hope for your approbation of my love! Might I but confess the name of my Mistress without incurring your resentment!'

She interrupted me.

'Suppose, I were to spare you that confession? Suppose, I were to acknowledge, that the object of your desires is not unknown to me? Suppose, I were to say that She returns your affection, and laments not less sincerely than yourself, the unhappy vows which separate her from you?'

'Ah! Donna Rodolpha!' I exclaimed, throwing myself upon my knees before her, and pressing her hand to my lips, 'You have discovered my secret! What is your decision? Must I despair, or may I reckon upon your favour?'

She withdrew not the hand which I held; But She turned from me, and covered her face with the other.

'How can I refuse it you?' She replied; 'Ah! Don Alphonso, I have long perceived to whom your attentions were directed, but till now I perceived not the impression which they made upon my heart. At length I can no longer hide my weakness either from myself or from you. I yield to the violence of my passion, and own, that I adore you! For three long months I stifled my desires; But grown stronger by resistance, I submit to their impetuosity. Pride, fear, and honour, respect for myself, and my engagements to the Baron, all are vanquished. I sacrifice them to my love for you, and it still seems to me that I pay too mean a price for your possession.'

She paused for an answer.—Judge, my Lorenzo, what must have been my confusion at this discovery. I at once saw all the magnitude of this obstacle, which I had raised myself to my happiness. The Baroness had placed those attentions to her own account, which I had merely paid her for the sake of Agnes: And the strength of her expressions, the looks which accompanied them, and my knowledge of her revengeful disposition made me tremble for myself and my Beloved. I was silent for some minutes. I knew not how to reply to her declaration: I could only resolve to clear up the mistake without delay, and for the present to conceal from her knowledge the name of my Mistress. No sooner had She avowed her passion, than the transports which before were evident in my features, gave place to consternation and constraint. I dropped her hand, and rose from my knees. The change in my countenance did not escape her observation.

'What means this silence?' said She in a trembling voice; 'Where is that joy which you led me to expect?'

'Forgive me, Segnora,' I answered, 'if what necessity forces from me should seem harsh and ungrateful: To

encourage you in an error, which, however it may
flatter myself, must prove to you the source of disappointment, would make me appear criminal in every
eye. Honour obliges me to inform you, that you have
mistaken for the solicitude of Love what was only the
attention of Friendship. The latter sentiment is that
which I wished to excite in your bosom: To entertain
a warmer, respect for you forbids me, and gratitude for
the Baron's generous treatment. Perhaps these reasons
would not be sufficient to shield me from your attractions, were it not that my affections are already bestowed upon another. You have charms, Segnora, which
might captivate the most insensible; No heart unoccupied could resist them. Happy is it for me that mine
is no longer in my possession; or I should have to
reproach myself for ever with having violated the Laws
of Hospitality. Recollect yourself, noble Lady; Recollect
what is owed by you to honour, by me to the Baron, and
replace by esteem and friendship those sentiments which
I never can return.'

The Baroness turned pale at this unexpected and
positive declaration: She doubted whether She slept or
woke. At length recovering from her surprise, consternation gave place to rage, and the blood rushed back into
her cheeks with violence.

'Villain!' She cried; 'Monster of deceit! Thus is the
avowal of my love received? Is it thus that. . . . But no,
no! It cannot, it shall not be! Alphonso, behold me at
your feet! Be witness of my despair! Look with pity on a
Woman who loves you with sincere affection! She who
possesses your heart, how has She merited such a
treasure? What sacrifice has She made to you? What
raises her above Rodolpha?'

I endeavoured to lift her from her Knees.

'For God's sake, Segnora, restrain these transports:
They disgrace yourself and me. Your exclamations may be

heard, and your secret divulged to your Attendants. I see, that my presence only irritates you: permit me to retire.'

I prepared to quit the apartment: The Baroness caught me suddenly by the arm.

'And who is this happy Rival?' said She in a menacing tone; 'I will know her name, and *when* I know it. . . .! She is some one in my power; You entreated my favour, my protection! Let me but find her, let me but know who dares to rob me of your heart, and She shall suffer every torment, which jealousy and disappointment can inflict! Who is She? Answer me this moment. Hope not to conceal her from my vengeance! Spies shall be set over you; every step, every look shall be watched; Your eyes will discover my Rival; I shall know her, and when She is found, tremble, Alphonso for her and for yourself!'

As She uttered these last words her fury mounted to such a pitch as to stop her powers of respiration. She panted, groaned, and at length fainted away. As She was falling I caught her in my arms, and placed her upon a Sopha. Then hastening to the door, I summoned her Women to her assistance; I committed her to their care, and seized the opportunity of escaping.

Agitated and confused beyond expression I bent my steps towards the Garden. The benignity with which the Baroness had listened to me at first raised my hopes to the highest pitch: I imagined her to have perceived my attachment for her Niece, and to approve of it. Extreme was my disappointment at understanding the true purport of her discourse. I knew not what course to take: The superstition of the Parents of Agnes, aided by her Aunt's unfortunate passion, seemed to oppose such obstacles to our union as were almost insurmountable.

As I past by a low parlour, whose windows looked into the Garden, through the door which stood half open I observed Agnes seated at a Table. She was occupied in drawing, and several unfinished sketches were scattered round her. I entered, still undetermined whether I should acquaint her with the declaration of the Baroness.

'Oh! is it only you?' said She, raising her head; 'You are no Stranger, and I shall continue my occupation without ceremony. Take a Chair, and seat yourself by me.'

I obeyed, and placed myself near the Table. Unconscious what I was doing, and totally occupied by the scene which had just passed, I took up some of the drawings, and cast my eye over them. One of the subjects struck me from its singularity. It represented the great Hall of the Castle of Lindenberg. A door conducting to a narrow stair-case stood half open. In the fore-ground appeared a Groupe of figures, placed in the most grotesque attitudes; Terror was expressed upon every countenance. Here was One upon his knees with his eyes cast up to heaven, and praying most devoutly; There Another was creeping away upon all fours. Some hid their faces in their cloaks or the laps of their Companions; Some had concealed themselves beneath a Table, on which the remnants of a feast were visible; While Others with gaping mouths and eyes wide-stretched pointed to a Figure, supposed to have created this disturbance. It represented a Female of more than human stature, clothed in the habit of some religious order. Her face was veiled; On her arm hung a chaplet of beads; Her dress was in several places stained with the blood which trickled from a wound upon her bosom. In one hand She held a Lamp, in the other a large Knife, and She seemed advancing towards the iron gates of the Hall.

'What does this mean, Agnes?' said I; 'Is this some invention of your own?'

She cast her eye upon the drawing.

'Oh! no,' She replied; ' 'Tis the invention of much

wiser heads than mine. But can you possibly have lived at Lindenberg for three whole Months without hearing of the Bleeding Nun?'

'You are the first, who ever mentioned the name to me. Pray, who may the Lady be?'

'That is more than I can pretend to tell you. All my knowledge of her History comes from an old tradition in this family, which has been handed down from Father to Son, and is firmly credited throughout the Baron's domains. Nay, the Baron believes it himself; and as for my Aunt who has a natural turn for the marvellous, She would sooner doubt the veracity of the Bible, than of the Bleeding Nun. Shall I tell you this History?'

I answered that She would oblige me much by relating it: She resumed her drawing, and then proceeded as follows in a tone of burlesqued gravity.

'It is surprising that in all the Chronicles of past times, this remarkable Personage is never once mentioned. Fain would I recount to you her life; But unluckily till after her death She was never known to have existed. Then first did She think it necessary to make some noise in the world, and with that intention She made bold to seize upon the Castle of Lindenberg. Having a good taste, She took up her abode in the best room of the House: and once established there, She began to amuse herself by knocking about the tables and chairs in the middle of the night. Perhaps, She was a bad Sleeper, but this I have never been able to ascertain. According to the tradition, this entertainment commenced about a Century ago. It was accompanied with shrieking, howling, groaning, swearing, and many other agreeable noises of the same kind. But though one particular room was more especially honoured with her visits, She did not entirely confine herself to it. She occasionally ventured into the old Galleries, paced up and down the spacious Halls, or sometimes stopping at the doors of the

Chambers, She wept and wailed there to the universal terror of the Inhabitants. In these nocturnal excursions She was seen by different People, who all describe her appearance as you behold it here, traced by the hand of her unworthy Historian.'

The singularity of this account insensibly engaged my attention.

'Did She never speak to those who met her?' said I.

'Not She. The specimens indeed which She gave nightly of her talents for conversation, were by no means inviting. Sometimes the Castle rung with oaths and execrations: A Moment after She repeated her Paternoster.* Now She howled out the most horrible blasphemies, and then chaunted De Profundis,* as orderly as if still in the Choir. In short She seemed a mighty capricious Being: But whether She prayed or cursed, whether She was impious or devout, She always contrived to terrify her Auditors out of their senses. The Castle became scarcely habitable; and its Lord was so frightened by these midnight Revels, that one fine morning He was found dead in his bed. This success seemed to please the Nun mightily, for now She made more noise than ever. But the next Baron proved too cunning for her. He made his appearance with a celebrated Exorciser in his hand, who feared not to shut himself up for a night in the haunted Chamber. There it seems, that He had an hard battle with the Ghost, before She would promise to be quiet. She was obstinate, but He was more so, and at length She consented to let the Inhabitants of the Castle take a good night's rest. For some time after no news was heard of her. But at the end of five years the Exorciser died, and then the Nun ventured to peep abroad again. However, She was now grown much more tractable and well-behaved. She walked about in silence, and never made her appearance above once in five years. This custom, if you will believe

the Baron, She still continues. He is fully persuaded, that
on the fifth of May of every fifth year, as soon as the
Clock strikes One the Door of the haunted Chamber
opens. [Observe, that this room has been shut up for near
a Century.] Then out walks the Ghostly Nun with her
Lamp and dagger: She descends the stair-case of the
Eastern Tower; and crosses the great Hall! On that night
the Porter always leaves the Gates of the Castle open, out
of respect to the Apparition: Not that this is thought by
any means necessary, since She could easily whip through
the Key-hole if She chose it; But merely out of politeness,
and to prevent her from making her exit in a way so
derogatory to the dignity of her Ghost-ship.'

'And whither does She go on quitting the Castle?'

'To Heaven, I hope; But if She does, the place certainly is not to her taste, for She always returns after an
hour's absence. The Lady then retires to her chamber,
and is quiet for another five years.'

'And you believe this, Agnes?'

'How can you ask such a question? No, no, Alphonso!
I have too much reason to lament superstition's influence
to be its Victim myself. However I must not avow my
incredulity to the Baroness: She entertains not a doubt
of the truth of this History. As to Dame Cunegonda, my
Governess, She protests that fifteen years ago She saw
the Spectre with her own eyes. She related to me one
evening, how She and several other Domestics had been
terrified while at Supper by the appearance of the
Bleeding Nun, as the Ghost is called in the Castle: 'Tis
from her account that I drew this sketch, and you may
be certain that Cunegonda was not omitted. There She
is! I shall never forget what a passion She was in, and
how ugly She looked while She scolded me for having
made her picture so like herself!'

Here She pointed to a burlesque figure of an old
Woman in an attitude of terror.

In spite of the melancholy which oppressed me, I could not help smiling at the playful imagination of Agnes: She had perfectly preserved Dame Cunegonda's resemblance, but had so much exaggerated every fault, and rendered every feature so irresistibly laughable, that I could easily conceive the Duenna's* anger.

'The figure is admirable, my dear Agnes! I knew not that you possessed such talents for the ridiculous.'

'Stay a moment,' She replied; 'I will show you a figure still more ridiculous than Dame Cunegonda's. If it pleases you, you may dispose of it as seems best to yourself.'

She rose, and went to a Cabinet at some little distance. Unlocking a drawer, She took out a small case, which She opened, and presented to me.

'Do you know the resemblance?' said She smiling.

It was her own.

Transported at the gift, I pressed the portrait to my lips with passion: I threw myself at her feet, and declared my gratitude in the warmest and most affectionate terms. She listened to me with complaisance, and assured me that She shared my sentiments: When suddenly She uttered a loud shriek, disengaged the hand which I held, and flew from the room by a door which opened to the Garden. Amazed at this abrupt departure, I rose hastily from my knees. I beheld with confusion the Baroness standing near me glowing with jealousy, and almost choaked with rage. On recovering from her swoon, She had tortured her imagination to discover her concealed Rival. No one appeared to deserve her suspicions more than Agnes. She immediately hastened to find her Niece, tax her with encouraging my addresses, and assure herself whether her conjectures were well-grounded. Unfortunately She had already seen enough to need no other confirmation. She arrived at the door of the room at the precise moment, when Agnes gave

me her Portrait. She heard me profess an everlasting
attachment to her Rival, and saw me kneeling at her feet.
She advanced to separate us; We were too much occupied by each other to perceive her approach, and were not
aware of it, till Agnes beheld her standing by my side.

Rage on the part of Donna Rodolpha, embarrassment
on mine, for some time kept us both silent. The Lady
recovered herself first.

'My suspicions then were just,' said She; 'The
Coquetry of my Niece has triumphed, and 'tis to her
that I am sacrificed. In one respect however I am
fortunate: I shall not be the only one who laments a
disappointed passion. You too shall know, what it is to
love without hope! I daily expect orders for restoring
Agnes to her Parents. Immediately upon her arrival in
Spain, She will take the veil, and place an insuperable
barrier to your union. You may spare your supplications.' She continued, perceiving me on the point of
speaking; 'My resolution is fixed and immoveable. Your
Mistress shall remain a close Prisoner in her chamber,
till She exchanges this Castle for the Cloister. Solitude
will perhaps recall her to a sense of her duty: But to
prevent your opposing that wished event, I must inform
you, Don Alphonso, that your presence here is no longer
agreeable either to the Baron or Myself. It was not to
talk nonsense to my Niece, that your Relations sent you
to Germany: Your business was to travel, and I should
be sorry to impede any longer so excellent a design.
Farewell, Segnor; Remember, that to-morrow morning
we meet for the last time.'

Having said this, She darted upon me a look of pride,
contempt, and malice, and quitted the apartment. I also
retired to mine, and consumed the night in planning the
means of rescuing Agnes from the power of her tyrannical
Aunt.

After the positive declaration of its Mistress, it was

impossible for me to make a longer stay at the Castle of Lindenberg. Accordingly I the next day announced my immediate departure. The Baron declared that it gave him sincere pain; and He expressed himself in my favour so warmly, that I endeavoured to win him over to my interest. Scarcely had I mentioned the name of Agnes when He stopped me short, and said, that it was totally out of his power to interfere in the business. I saw that it was in vain to argue; The Baroness governed her Husband with despotic sway, and I easily perceived, that She had prejudiced him against the match. Agnes did not appear: I entreated permission to take leave of her, but my prayer was rejected. I was obliged to depart without seeing her.

At quitting him the Baron shook my hand affectionately, and assured me that as soon as his Niece was gone, I might consider his House as my own.

'Farewell, Don Alphonso!' said the Baroness, and stretched out her hand to me.

I took it, and offered to carry it to my lips. She prevented me. Her Husband was at the other end of the room, and out of hearing.

'Take care of yourself,' She continued; 'My love is become hatred, and my wounded pride shall not be un-atoned. Go where you will, my vengeance shall follow you!'

She accompanied these words with a look sufficient to make me tremble. I answered not, but hastened to quit the Castle.

As my Chaise drove out of the Court, I looked up to the windows of your Sister's chamber. Nobody was to be seen there: I threw myself back despondent in my Carriage. I was attended by no other servants than a French-man whom I had hired at Strasbourg in Stephano's room, and my little Page whom I before mentioned to you. The fidelity, intelligence, and good

temper of Theodore had already made him dear to me;
But He now prepared to lay an obligation on me, which
made me look upon him as a Guardian Genius. Scarcely
had we proceeded half a mile from the Castle, when He
rode up to the Chaise-door.

'Take courage, Segnor!' said He in Spanish, which He
had already learnt to speak with fluency and correctness.
'While you were with the Baron, I watched the moment
when Dame Cunegonda was below stairs, and mounted
into the chamber over that of Donna Agnes. I sang as
loud as I could a little German air well-known to her,
hoping that She would recollect my voice. I was not
disappointed, for I soon heard her window open. I
hastened to let down a string with which I had provided
myself: Upon hearing the casement closed again, I drew
up the string, and fastened to it I found this scrap of
paper.'

He then presented me with a small note addressed to
me. I opened it with impatience: It contained the
following words written in pencil:

Conceal yourself for the next fortnight in some
neighbouring Village. My Aunt will believe you to have
quitted Lindenberg, and I shall be restored to liberty. I
will be in the West Pavilion at twelve on the night of the
thirtieth. Fail not to be there, and we shall have an
opportunity of concerting our future plans. Adieu.

Agnes.

At perusing these lines my transports exceeded all
bounds; Neither did I set any to the expressions of
gratitude which I heaped upon Theodore. In fact his
address and attention merited my warmest praise. You
will readily believe, that I had not entrusted him with
my passion for Agnes; But the arch Youth had too much
discernment not to discover my secret, and too much
discretion not to conceal his knowledge of it. He observed

in silence what was going on, nor strove to make himself an Agent in the business till my interests required his interference. I equally admired his judgment, his penetration, his address, and his fidelity. This was not the first occasion in which I had found him of infinite use, and I was every day more convinced of his quickness and capacity. During my short stay at Strasbourg, He had applied himself diligently to learning the rudiments of Spanish: He continued to study it, and with so much success that He spoke it with the same facility as his native language. He past the greatest part of his time in reading; He had acquired much information for his Age; and united the advantages of a lively countenance and prepossessing figure to an excellent understanding, and the very best of hearts. He is now fifteen; He is still in my service, and when you see him, I am sure that He will please you. But excuse this digression: I return to the subject which I quitted.

I obeyed the instructions of Agnes. I proceeded to Munich. There I left my Chaise under the care of Lucas my French Servant, and then returned on Horse-back to a small Village about four miles distant from the Castle of Lindenberg. Upon arriving there a story was related to the Host at whose Inn I descended, which prevented his wondering at my making so long a stay in his House. The old Man fortunately was credulous and incurious: He believed all I said, and sought to know no more than what I thought proper to tell him. Nobody was with me but Theodore; Both were disguised, and as we kept ourselves close, we were not suspected to be other than what we seemed. In this manner the fortnight passed away. During that time I had the pleasing conviction that Agnes was once more at liberty. She past through the Village with Dame Cunegonda: She seemed in health and spirits, and talked to her Companion without any appearance of constraint.

'Who are those Ladies?' said I to my Host, as the Carriage past.

'Baron Lindenberg's Niece with her Governess,' He replied; 'She goes regularly every Friday to the Convent of St. Catharine, in which She was brought up, and which is situated about a mile from hence.'

You may be certain that I waited with impatience for the ensuing Friday. I again beheld my lovely Mistress. She cast her eyes upon me, as She passed the Inn-door. A blush which overspread her cheek, told me that in spite of my disguise I had been recognised. I bowed profoundly. She returned the compliment by a slight inclination of the head as if made to one inferior, and looked another way till the Carriage was out of sight.

The long-expected, long-wished for night arrived. It was calm, and the Moon was at the full. As soon as the Clock struck eleven I hastened to my appointment, determined not to be too late. Theodore had provided a Ladder; I ascended the Garden-wall without difficulty; The Page followed me, and drew the Ladder after us. I posted myself in the West Pavilion, and waited impatiently for the approach of Agnes. Every breeze that whispered, every leaf that fell, I believed to be her footstep, and hastened to meet her. Thus was I obliged to pass a full hour, every minute of which appeared to me an age. The Castle-Bell at length tolled twelve, and scarcely could I believe the night to be no further advanced. Another quarter of an hour elapsed, and I heard the light foot of my Mistress approaching the Pavilion with precaution. I flew to receive her, and conducted her to a seat. I threw myself at her feet, and was expressing my joy at seeing her, when She thus interrupted me.

'We have no time to lose, Alphonso: The moments are precious, for though no more a Prisoner, Cunegonda watches my every step. An express is arrived from my

Father; I must depart immediately for Madrid, and 'tis with difficulty that I have obtained a week's delay. The superstition of my Parents, supported by the representations of my cruel Aunt, leaves me no hope of softening them to compassion. In this dilemma I have resolved to commit myself to your honour: God grant, that you may never give me cause to repent my resolution! Flight is my only resource from the horrors of a Convent, and my imprudence must be excused by the urgency of the danger. Now listen to the plan, by which I hope to effect my escape.

'We are now at the thirtieth of April. On the fifth day from this the Visionary Nun is expected to appear. In my last visit to the Convent I provided myself with a dress proper for the character: A Friend, whom I have left there and to whom I made no scruple to confide my secret, readily consented to supply me with a religious habit. Provide a carriage, and be with it at a little distance from the great Gate of the Castle. As soon as the Clock strikes 'one,' I shall quit my chamber, drest in the same apparel as the Ghost is supposed to wear. Whoever meets me will be too much terrified to oppose my escape. I shall easily reach the door, and throw myself under your protection. Thus far success is certain: But Oh! Alphonso, should you deceive me! Should you despise my imprudence and reward it with ingratitude, the World will not hold a Being more wretched than myself! I feel all the dangers to which I shall be exposed. I feel, that I am giving you a right to treat me with levity: But I rely upon your love, upon your honour! The step, which I am on the point of taking, will incense my Relations against me: Should you desert me, should you betray the trust reposed in you, I shall have no friend to punish your insult, or support my cause. On yourself alone rests all my hope, and if your own heart does not plead in my behalf, I am undone for ever!'

The tone in which She pronounced these words was so touching, that in spite of my joy at receiving her promise to follow me, I could not help being affected. I also repined in secret, at not having taken the precaution to provide a Carriage at the Village, in which case I might have carried off Agnes that very night. Such an attempt was now impracticable: Neither Carriage or Horses were to be procured nearer than Munich, which was distant from Lindenberg two good days journey. I was therefore obliged to chime in with her plan, which in truth seemed well arranged: Her disguise would secure her from being stopped in quitting the Castle, and would enable her to step into the Carriage at the very Gate without difficulty or losing time.

Agnes reclined her head mournfully upon my shoulder, and by the light of the Moon I saw tears flowing down her cheek. I strove to dissipate her melancholy, and encouraged her to look forward to the prospect of happiness. I protested in the most solemn terms that her virtue and innocence would be safe in my keeping, and that till the church had made her my lawful Wife, her honour should be held by me as sacred as a Sister's. I told her, that my first care should be to find you out, Lorenzo, and reconcile you to our union; and I was continuing to speak in the same strain, when a noise without alarmed me. Suddenly the door of the Pavilion was thrown open, and Cunegonda stood before us. She had heard Agnes steal out of her chamber, followed her into the Garden, and perceived her entering the Pavilion. Favoured by the Trees, which shaded it, and unperceived by Theodore who waited at a little distance, She had approached in silence, and over-heard our whole conversation.

'Admirable!' cried Cunegonda in a voice shrill with passion, while Agnes uttered a loud shriek; 'By St. Barbara, young Lady, you have an excellent invention!

You must personate the Bleeding Nun, truly? What impiety! What incredulity! Marry, I have a good mind to let you pursue your plan: When the real Ghost met you, I warrant, you would be in a pretty condition! Don Alphonso, you ought to be ashamed of yourself for seducing a young ignorant Creature to leave her family and Friends: However, for this time at least I shall mar your wicked designs. The noble Lady shall be informed of the whole affair, and Agnes must defer playing the Spectre till a better opportunity. Farewell, Segnor—Donna Agnes, let me have the honour of conducting your Ghost-ship back to your apartment.'

She approached the Sopha on which her trembling Pupil was seated, took her by the hand, and prepared to lead her from the Pavilion.

I detained her, and strove by entreaties, soothing, promises, and flattery to win her to my party: But finding all that I could say of no avail, I abandoned the vain attempt.

'Your obstinacy must be its own punishment,' said I; 'But one resource remains to save Agnes and myself, and I shall not hesitate to employ it.'

Terrified at this menace, She again endeavoured to quit the Pavilion; But I seized her by the wrist, and detained her forcibly. At the same moment Theodore, who had followed her into the room, closed the door, and prevented her escape. I took the veil of Agnes: I threw it round the Duenna's head, who uttered such piercing shrieks that in spite of our distance from the Castle, I dreaded their being heard. At length I succeeded in gagging her so compleatly, that She could not produce a single sound. Theodore and myself with some difficulty next contrived to bind her hands and feet with our hand-kerchiefs; And I advised Agnes to regain her chamber with all diligence. I promised that no harm should happen to Cunegonda, bad her remember that on the fifth of May I should be in waiting at the Great Gate of the Castle, and took of her an affectionate farewell. Trembling and uneasy She had scarce power enough to signify her consent to my plans, and fled back to her apartment in disorder and confusion.

In the mean-while Theodore assisted me in carrying off my antiquated Prize. She was hoisted over the wall, placed before me upon my Horse like a Portmanteau, and I galloped away with her from the Castle of Lindenberg. The unlucky Duenna never had made a more disagreeable journey in her life: She was jolted and shaken till She was become little more than an animated Mummy; not to mention her fright, when we waded through a small River, through which it was necessary to pass in order to regain the Village. Before we reached the Inn, I had already determined how to dispose of the troublesome Cunegonda. We entered the Street in which the Inn stood, and while the page knocked, I waited at a little distance. The Landlord opened the door with a Lamp in his hand.

'Give me the light!' said Theodore; 'My Master is coming.'

He snatched the Lamp hastily, and purposely let it fall upon the ground: The Landlord returned to the Kitchen to re-light the Lamp, leaving the door open. I profited by the obscurity, sprang from my Horse with Cunegonda in my arms, darted up stairs, reached my chamber unperceived, and unlocking the door of a spacious Closet, stowed her within it, and then turned the Key. The Landlord and Theodore soon after appeared with lights: The Former expressed himself a little surprised at my returning so late, but asked no impertinent questions. He soon quitted the room, and left me to exult in the success of my undertaking.

I immediately paid a visit to my Prisoner. I strove to persuade her submitting with patience to her temporary confinement. My attempt was unsuccessful. Unable to speak or move, She expressed her fury by her looks, and except at meals I never dared to unbind her, or release her from the Gag. At such times I stood over her with a drawn sword, and protested, that if She uttered a single cry, I would plunge it in her bosom. As soon as She had done eating, the Gag was replaced. I was conscious, that this proceeding was cruel, and could only be justified by the urgency of circumstances: As to Theodore, He had no scruples upon the subject. Cunegonda's captivity entertained him beyond measure. During his abode in the Castle, a continual warfare had been carried on between him and the Duenna; and now that He found his Enemy so absolutely in his power, He triumphed without mercy. He seemed to think of nothing but how to find out new means of plaguing her: Sometimes He affected to pity her misfortune, then laughed at, abused, and mimicked her; He played her a thousand tricks, each more provoking than the other, and amused himself by telling her, that her elopement must have occasioned much surprise at the Baron's. This was in fact the case. No one except Agnes could imagine what was become of Dame Cunegonda: Every hole and corner was searched for her; The Ponds were dragged, and the Woods underwent a thorough examination. Still no Dame Cunegonda made her appearance. Agnes kept the secret, and I kept the Duenna: The Baroness, therefore, remained in total ignorance respecting the old Woman's fate, but suspected her to have perished by suicide. Thus past away five days, during which I had prepared every thing necessary for my enterprise. On quitting Agnes, I had made it my first business to dispatch a Peasant with a letter to Lucas at Munich, ordering him to take care that a Coach and four should arrive about ten o'clock on the fifth of May at the Village of Rosenwald. He obeyed my instructions punctually

The Equipage arrived at the time appointed. As the period of her Lady's elopement drew nearer, Cunegonda's rage increased. I verily believe that spight and passion would have killed her, had I not luckily discovered her prepossession in favour of Cherry-Brandy. With this favourite liquor She was plentifully supplied, and Theodore always remaining to guard her, the Gag was occasionally removed. The liquor seemed to have a wonderful effect in softening the acrimony of her nature; and her confinement not admitting of any other amusement, She got drunk regularly once a day just by way of passing the time.

The fifth of May arrived, a period by me never to be forgotten! Before the Clock struck twelve, I betook myself to the scene of action. Theodore followed me on horse-back. I concealed the Carriage in a spacious Cavern of the Hill, on whose brow the Castle was situated: This Cavern was of considerable depth, and among the peasants was known by the name of Lindenberg Hole. The night was calm and beautiful: The Moonbeams fell upon the antient Towers of the Castle, and shed upon their summits a silver light. All was still around me: Nothing was to be heard except the nightbreeze sighing among the leaves, the distant barking of Village Dogs, or the Owl who had established herself in a nook of the deserted Eastern Turret. I heard her melancholy shriek, and looked upwards. She sat upon the ride of a window, which I recognized to be that of the haunted Room. This brought to my remembrance the story of the Bleeding Nun, and I sighed while I reflected on the influence of superstition and weakness of human reason. Suddenly I heard a faint chorus steal upon the silence of the night.

'What can occasion that noise, Theodore?'

'A Stranger of distinction,' replied He, 'passed through the Village to-day in his way to the Castle: He is reported to be the Father of Donna Agnes. Doubtless, the Baron has given an entertainment to celebrate his arrival.'

The Castle-Bell announced the hour of midnight: This was the usual signal for the family to retire to Bed. Soon after I perceived lights in the Castle moving backwards and forwards in different directions. I conjectured the company to be separating. I could hear the heavy doors grate as they opened with difficulty, and as they closed again the rotten Casements rattled in their frames. The chamber of Agnes was on the other side of the Castle. I trembled, lest She should have failed in obtaining the Key of the haunted Room: Through this it was necessary for her to pass, in order to reach the narrow Stair-case by which the Ghost was supposed to descend into the great Hall. Agitated by this apprehension, I kept my eyes constantly fixed upon the window, where I hoped to perceive the friendly glare of a Lamp borne by Agnes. I now heard the massy Gates unbarred. By the candle in his hand I distinguished old Conrad, the Porter. He set the Portal-doors wide open, and retired. The lights in the Castle gradually disappeared, and at length the whole Building was wrapt in darkness.

While I sat upon a broken ridge of the Hill, the stillness of the scene inspired me with melancholy ideas not altogether unpleasing. The Castle which stood full in my sight, formed an object equally awful and picturesque. Its ponderous Walls tinged by the moon with solemn brightness, its old and partly-ruined Towers lifting themselves into the clouds and seeming to frown on the plains around them, its lofty battlements oër-grown with ivy, and folding Gates expanding in honour of the Visionary Inhabitant, made me sensible of a sad and reverential horror. Yet did not these sensations occupy me so fully, as to prevent me from witnessing with

impatience the slow progress of time. I approached the
Castle, and ventured to walk round it. A few rays of
light still glimmered in the chamber of Agnes. I observed
them with joy. I was still gazing upon them, when I
perceived a figure draw near the window, and the
Curtain was carefully closed to conceal the Lamp which
burned there. Convinced by this observation that Agnes
had not abandoned our plan, I returned with a light
heart to my former station.

The half-hour struck! The three-quarters struck!
My bosom beat high with hope and expectation. At
length the wished-for sound was heard. The Bell tolled
'One,' and the Mansion echoed with the noise loud and
solemn. I looked up to the Casement of the haunted
Chamber. Scarcely had five minutes elapsed, when the
expected light appeared. I was now close to the Tower.
The window was not so far from the Ground, but that
I fancied I perceived a female figure with a Lamp in her
hand moving slowly along the Apartment. The light
soon faded away, and all was again dark and gloomy.

Occasional gleams of brightness darted from the Stair-
case windows, as the lovely Ghost past by them. I
traced the light through the Hall: It reached the Portal,
and at length I beheld Agnes pass through the folding-
gates. She was habited exactly as She had described the
Spectre. A chaplet of Beads hung upon her arm; her
head was enveloped in a long white veil; Her Nun's
dress was stained with blood, and She had taken care to
provide herself with a Lamp and dagger. She advanced
towards the spot where I stood. I flew to meet her, and
clasped her in my arms.

'Agnes!' said I while I pressed her to my bosom,

Agnes! Agnes! Thou art mine!
Agnes! Agnes! I am thine!
In my veins while blood shall roll,

Thou art mine!
I am thine!
Thine my body! Thine my soul!*

Terrified and breathless She was unable to speak: She dropt her Lamp and dagger, and sank upon my bosom in silence. I raised her in my arms, and conveyed her to the Carriage. Theodore remained behind in order to release Dame Cunegonda. I also charged him with a letter to the Baroness explaining the whole affair, and entreating her good offices in reconciling Don Gaston to my union with his Daughter. I discovered to her my real name: I proved to her that my birth and expectations justified my pretending to her Niece, and assured her, though it was out of my power to return her love, that I would strive unceasingly to obtain her esteem and friendship.

I stepped into the Carriage, where Agnes was already seated. Theodore closed the door, and the Postillions drove away. At first I was delighted with the rapidity of our progress; But as soon as we were in no danger of pursuit, I called to the Drivers, and bad them moderate their pace. They strove in vain to obey me. The Horses refused to answer the rein, and continued to rush on with astonishing swiftness. The Postillions redoubled their efforts to stop them, but by kicking and plunging the Beasts soon released themselves from this restraint. Uttering a loud shriek, the Drivers were hurled upon the ground. Immediately thick clouds obscured the sky: The winds howled around us, the lightning flashed, and the Thunder roared tremendously. Never did I behold so frightful a Tempest! Terrified by the jar of contending elements, the Horses seemed every moment to increase their speed. Nothing could interrupt their career; They dragged the Carriage through Hedges and Ditches, dashed down the most dangerous precipices. and seemed to vye in swiftness with the rapidity of the winds.

All this while my Companion lay motionless in my arms. Truly alarmed by the magnitude of the danger, I was in vain attempting to recall her to her senses; when a loud crash announced, that a stop was put to our progress in the most disagreeable manner. The Carriage was shattered to pieces. In falling I struck my temple against a flint. The pain of the wound, the violence of the shock, and apprehension for the safety of Agnes combined to over-power me so compleatly, that my senses forsook me, and I lay without animation on the ground.

I probably remained for some time in this situation, since when I opened my eyes, it was broad day-light. Several Peasants were standing round me, and seemed disputing whether my recovery was possible. I spoke German tolerably well. As soon as I could utter an articulate sound, I enquired after Agnes. What was my surprise and distress, when assured by the Peasants, that nobody had been seen answering the description which I gave of her! They told me, that in going to their daily labour they had been alarmed by observing the fragments of my Carriage, and by hearing the groans of an Horse, the only one of the four which remained alive: The other Three lay dead by my side. Nobody was near me when they came up, and much time had been lost, before they succeeded in recovering me. Uneasy beyond expression respecting the fate of my Companion, I besought the Peasants to disperse themselves in search of her: I described her dress, and promised immense rewards to whoever brought me any intelligence. As for myself, it was impossible for me to join in the pursuit: I had broken two of my ribs in the fall: My arm being dislocated hung useless by my side; and my left leg was shattered so terribly, that I never expected to recover its use.

The Peasants complied with my request: All left me except Four, who made a litter of boughs, and prepared to convey me to the neighbouring Town. I enquired its name. It proved to be Ratisbon,* and I could scarcely persuade myself that I had travelled to such a distance in a single night. I told the Countrymen, that at one o'clock that morning I had past through the Village of Rosenwald.* They shook their heads wistfully, and made signs to each other, that I must certainly be delirious. I was conveyed to a decent Inn, and immediately put to bed. A Physician was sent for, who set my arm with success. He then examined my other hurts, and told me that I need be under no apprehension of the consequences of any of them; But ordered me to keep myself quiet, and be prepared for a tedious and painful cure. I answered him, that if He hoped to keep me quiet, He must first endeavour to procure me some news of a Lady, who had quitted Rosenwald in my company the night before, and had been with me at the moment when the Coach broke down. He smiled, and only replied by advising me to make myself easy, for that all proper care should be taken of me. As He quitted me, the Hostess met him at the door of the room.

'The Gentleman is not quite in his right senses;' I heard him say to her in a low voice; ' 'Tis the natural consequence of his fall, but that will soon be over.'

One after another the Peasants returned to the Inn, and informed me that no traces had been discovered of my unfortunate Mistress. Uneasiness now became despair. I entreated them to renew their search in the most urgent terms, doubling the promises which I had already made them. My wild and frantic manner confirmed the bye-standers in the idea of my being delirious. No signs of the Lady having appeared, they believed her to be a creature fabricated by my over-heated brain, and paid no attention to my entreaties. However, the Hostess assured me that a fresh enquiry should be made, but I found afterwards that her promise was only given to quiet me. No further steps were taken in the business.

Though my Baggage was left at Munich under the care of my French Servant, having prepared myself for a long journey, my purse was amply furnished: Besides my equipage proved me to be of distinction, and in consequence all possible attention was paid me at the Inn. The day passed away: Still no news arrived of Agnes. The anxiety of fear now gave place to despondency. I ceased to rave about her, and was plunged in the depth of melancholy reflections. Perceiving me to be silent and tranquil, my Attendants believed my delirium to have abated, and that my malady had taken a favourable turn. According to the Physician's order I swallowed a composing medicine; and as soon as the night shut in, my attendants withdrew, and left me to repose.

That repose I wooed in vain. The agitation of my bosom chased away sleep. Restless in my mind, in spite of the fatigue of my body I continued to toss about from side to side, till the Clock in a neighbouring Steeple struck 'One.' As I listened to the mournful hollow sound, and heard it die away in the wind, I felt a sudden chillness spread itself over my body. I shuddered without knowing wherefore; Cold dews poured down my forehead, and my hair stood bristling with alarm. Suddenly I heard slow and heavy steps ascending the stair-case. By an involuntary movement I started up in my bed, and drew back the curtain. A single rush-light, which glimmered upon the hearth shed a faint gleam through the apartment, which was hung with tapestry. The door was thrown open with violence. A figure entered, and drew near my Bed with solemn measured steps. With trembling apprehension I examined this midnight Visitor. God Almighty! It was the Bleeding Nun! It was my lost Companion! Her face was still veiled, but She no longer held her Lamp and dagger. She lifted up her veil slowly. What a sight presented itself to my startled eyes! I beheld before me an animated Corse. Her countenance was long and haggard; Her cheeks and lips were bloodless; The paleness of death was spread over her features, and her eye-balls fixed stedfastly upon me were lustreless and hollow.

I gazed upon the Spectre with horror too great to be described. My blood was frozen in my veins. I would have called for aid, but the sound expired, ere it could pass my lips. My nerves were bound up in impotence, and I remained in the same attitude inanimate as a Statue.

The visionary Nun looked upon me for some minutes in silence: There was something petrifying in her regard. At length in a low sepulchral voice She pronounced the following words.

> "Raymond! Raymond! Thou art mine!
> Raymond! Raymond! I am thine!
> In thy veins while blood shall roll,
> I am thine!
> Thou art mine!
> Mine thy body! Mine thy soul!——"

Breathless with fear, I listened while She repeated my own expressions. The Apparition seated herself opposite to me at the foot of the Bed, and was silent. Her eyes were fixed earnestly upon mine: They seemed endowed with the property of the Rattle-snake's,* for I strove in vain to look off her. My eyes were fascinated, and I had not the power of withdrawing them from the Spectre's.

In this attitude She remained for a whole long hour without speaking or moving; nor was I able to do either. At length the Clock struck two. The Apparition rose from her seat, and approached the side of the bed. She grasped with her icy fingers my hand which hung lifeless upon the Coverture, and pressing her cold lips to mine, again repeated,

"Raymond! Raymond! Thou art mine!
Raymond! Raymond! I am thine! &c.—"

She then dropped my hand, quitted the chamber with slow steps, and the Door closed after her. Till that moment the faculties of my body had been all suspended; Those of my mind had alone been waking. The charm now ceased to operate: The blood which had been frozen in my veins rushed back to my heart with violence: I uttered a deep groan, and sank lifeless upon my pillow.

The adjoining room was only separated from mine by a thin partition: It was occupied by the Host and his Wife: The Former was rouzed by my groan, and immediately hastened to my chamber: The Hostess soon followed him. With some difficulty they succeeded in restoring me to my senses, and immediately sent for the Physician, who arrived in all diligence. He declared my fever to be very much increased, and that if I continued to suffer such violent agitation, He would not take upon him to ensure my life. Some medicines which He gave me, in some degree tranquillized my spirits. I fell into a sort of slumber towards day-break; But fearful dreams prevented me from deriving any benefit from my repose. Agnes and the Bleeding Nun presented themselves by turns to my fancy, and combined to harass and torment me. I awoke fatigued and unrefreshed. My fever seemed rather augmented than diminished; The agitation of my mind impeded my fractured bones from knitting: I had frequent fainting fits, and during the whole day the Physician judged it expedient not to quit me for two hours together.

The singularity of my adventure made me determine to conceal it from every one, since I could not expect that a circumstance so strange should gain credit. I was very uneasy about Agnes. I knew not what She would think at not finding me at the rendez-vous, and dreaded her entertaining suspicions of my fidelity. However, I depended upon Theodore's discretion, and trusted, that my letter to the Baroness would convince her of the rectitude of my intentions. These considerations some-what lightened my inquietude upon her account: But the impression left upon my mind by my nocturnal Visitor, grew stronger with every succeeding moment. The night drew near; I dreaded its arrival. Yet I strove to persuade myself that the Ghost would appear no more, and at all events I desired, that a Servant might sit up in my chamber.

The fatigue of my body from not having slept on the former night co-operating with the strong opiates ad-ministered to me in profusion at length procured me that repose of which I was so much in need. I sank into a profound and tranquil slumber, and had already slept for some hours, when the neighbouring Clock rouzed me by striking 'One'. Its sound brought with it to my memory all the horrors of the night before. The same cold shivering seized me. I started up in my bed, and perceived the Servant fast asleep in an armed-Chair near me. I called him by his name: He made no answer. I shook him forcibly by the arm, and strove in vain to wake him. He was perfectly insensible to my efforts. I now heard the heavy steps ascending the stair-case; The Door was thrown open, and again the Bleeding Nun stood before me. Once more my limbs were chained in second infancy. Once more I heard those fatal words repeated,

"Raymond! Raymond! Thou art mine!
Raymond! Raymond! I am thine! &c.—"

The scene which had shocked me so sensibly on the former night, was again presented. The Spectre again pressed her lips to mine, again touched me with her rotting fingers, and as on her first appearance, quitted the chamber as soon as the Clock told 'Two.'

Even night was this repeated. Far from growing accustomed to the Ghost, every succeeding visit inspired me with greater horror. Her idea pursued me continually, and I became the prey of habitual melancholy. The constant agitation of my mind naturally retarded the re-establishment of my health. Several months elapsed before I was able to quit my bed; and when at length I was moved to a Sopha, I was so faint, spiritless, and emaciated, that I could not cross the room without assistance. The looks of my Attendants sufficiently denoted the little hope, which they entertained of my recovery. The profound sadness, which oppressed me without remission made the Physician consider me to be an Hypochondriac. The cause of my distress I carefully concealed in my own bosom, for I knew that no one could give me relief: The Ghost was not even visible to any eye but mine. I had frequently caused Attendants to sit up in my room: But the moment that the Clock struck 'One,' irresistible slumber seized them, nor left them till the departure of the Ghost.

You may be surprized, that during this time I made no enquiries after your Sister. Theodore, who with difficulty had discovered my abode, had quieted my apprehensions for her safety: At the same time He convinced me, that all attempts to release her from captivity must be fruitless, till I should be in a condition to return to Spain. The particulars of her adventure which I shall now relate to you, were partly communicated to me by Theodore, and partly by Agnes herself.

On the fatal night when her elopement was to have

taken place, accident had not permitted her to quit her chamber at the appointed time. At length She ventured into the haunted room, descended the stair-case leading into the Hall, found the Gates open as She expected, and left the Castle unobserved. What was her surprize at not finding me ready to receive her! She examined the Cavern, ranged through every Alley of the neighbouring wood, and passed two full hours in this fruitless enquiry. She could discover no traces either of me or of the Carriage. Alarmed and disappointed, her only resource was to return to the Castle before the Baroness missed her: But here She found herself in a fresh embarrassment. The Bell had already tolled 'Two:' The Ghostly hour was past, and the careful Porter had locked the folding gates. After much irresolution She ventured to knock softly. Luckily for her Conrad was still awake: He heard the noise, and rose, murmuring at being called up a second time. No sooner had He opened one of the Doors, and beheld the supposed Apparition waiting there for admittance, than He uttered a loud cry, and sank upon his knees. Agnes profited by his terror. She glided by him, flew to her own apartment, and having thrown off her Spectre's trappings, retired to bed endeavouring in vain to account for my disappearing.

In the mean while Theodore having seen my Carriage drive off with the false Agnes, returned joyfully to the Village. The next morning He released Cunegonda from her confinement, and accompanied her to the Castle. There He found the Baron, his Lady, and Don Gaston, disputing together upon the Porter's relation. All of them agreed in believing the existence of Spectres: But the Latter contended, that for a Ghost to knock for admittance was a proceeding till then unwitnessed, and totally incompatible with the immaterial nature of a Spirit. They were still discussing this subject, when the Page appeared with Cunegonda, and cleared up the mystery.

On hearing his deposition, it was agreed unanimously that the Agnes whom Theodore had seen step into my Carriage must have been the Bleeding Nun, and that the Ghost who had terrified Conrad was no other than Don Gaston's Daughter.

The first surprize which this discovery occasioned being over, the Baroness resolved to make it of use in persuading her Niece to take the veil. Fearing lest so advantageous an establishment for his Daughter should induce Don Gaston to renounce his resolution, She suppressed my letter, and continued to represent me as a needy unknown Adventurer. A childish vanity had led me to conceal my real name even from my Mistress; I wished to be loved for myself, not for being the Son and Heir of the Marquis de las Cisternas. The consequence was, that my rank was known to no one in the Castle except the Baroness, and She took good care to confine the knowledge to her own breast. Don Gaston having approved his Sister's design, Agnes was summoned to appear before them. She was taxed with having meditated an elopement, obliged to make a full confession, and was amazed at the gentleness with which it was received: But what was her affliction, when informed that the failure of her project must be attributed to me! Cunegonda, tutored by the Baroness, told her that when I released her, I had desired her to inform her Lady that our connexion was at an end, that the whole affair was occasioned by a false report, and that it by no means suited my circumstances to marry a Woman without fortune or expectations.

To this account my sudden disappearing gave but too great an air of probability. Theodore, who could have contradicted the story, by Donna Rodolpha's order was kept out of her sight: What proved a still greater confirmation of my being an Impostor, was the arrival of a letter from yourself declaring, that you had no sort of acquaintance with Alphonso d'Alvarada. These seeming proofs of my perfidy, aided by the artful insinuations of her Aunt, by Cunegonda's flattery, and her Father's threats and anger, entirely conquered your Sister's repugnance to a Convent. Incensed at my behaviour, and disgusted with the world in general, She consented to receive the veil. She past another Month at the Castle of Lindenberg, during which my non-appearance confirmed her in her resolution, and then accompanied Don Gaston into Spain. Theodore was now set at liberty. He hastened to Munich, where I had promised to let him hear from me; But finding from Lucas that I had never arrived there, He pursued his search with indefatigable perseverance, and at length succeeded in rejoining me at Ratisbon.

So much was I altered, that scarcely could He recollect my features: The distress visible upon his sufficiently testified how lively was the interest which He felt for me. The society of this amiable Boy, whom I had always considered rather as a Companion than a Servant, was now my only comfort. His conversation was gay yet sensible, and his observations shrewd and entertaining: He had picked up much more knowledge than is usual at his Age: But what rendered him most agreeable to me, was his having a delightful voice, and some skill in Music. He had also acquired some taste in poetry, and even ventured sometimes to write verses himself. He occasionally composed little Ballads in Spanish, his compositions were but indifferent, I must confess; yet they were pleasing to me from their novelty, and hearing him sing them to his guitar was the only amusement, which I was capable of receiving. Theodore perceived well enough that something preyed upon my mind; But as I concealed the cause of my grief even from him, Respect would not permit him to pry into my secrets.

One Evening I was lying upon my Sopha, plunged in

reflections very far from agreeable: Theodore amused himself by observing from the window a Battle between two Postillions, who were quarrelling in the Inn-yard.

'Ha! Ha!' cried He suddenly; 'Yonder is the Great Mogul.'*

'Who?' said I.

'Only a Man, who made me a strange speech at Munich.'

'What was the purport of it?'

'Now you put me in mind of it, Segnor, it was a kind of message to you; but truly it was not worth delivering. I believe the Fellow to be mad for my part. When I came to Munich in search of you, I found him living at 'The King of the Romans,' and the Host gave me an odd account of him. By his accent He is supposed to be a Foreigner, but of what Country nobody can tell. He seemed to have no acquaintance in the Town, spoke very seldom, and never was seen to smile. He had neither Servants or Baggage; But his Purse seemed well-furnished, and He did much good in the Town. Some supposed him to be an Arabian Astrologer, Others to be a Travelling Mountebank,* and many declared that He was Doctor Faustus,* whom the Devil had sent back to Germany. The Landlord, however told me, that He had the best reasons to believe him to be the Great Mogul incognito.'

'But the strange speech, Theodore.'

'True, I had almost forgotten the speech: Indeed for that matter, it would not have been a great loss, if I had forgotten it altogether. You are to know, Segnor, that while I was enquiring about you of the Landlord, this Stranger passed by. He stopped, and looked at me earnestly. 'Youth!' said He in a solemn voice, 'He whom you seek, has found that, which He would fain lose. My hand alone can dry up the blood: Bid your Master wish for me, when the Clock strikes, 'One.''

'How?' cried I, starting from my Sopha. [The words which Theodore had repeated, seemed to imply the Stranger's knowledge of my secret] 'Fly to him, my Boy! Entreat him to grant me one moment's conversation!'

Theodore was surprised at the vivacity of my manner: However, He asked no questions, but hastened to obey me. I waited his return impatiently. But a short space of time had elapsed when He again appeared, and ushered the expected Guest into my chamber. He was a Man of majestic presence. His countenance was strongly marked, and his eyes were large, black, and sparkling: Yet there was a something in his look, which the moment that I saw him, inspired me with a secret awe, not to say horror. He was drest plainly, his hair was unpowdered, and a band of black velvet which encircled his fore-head, spread over his features an additional gloom. His countenance wore the marks of profound melancholy; his step was slow, and his manner grave, stately, and solemn.

He saluted me with politeness; and having replied to the usual compliments of introduction, He motioned to Theodore to quit the chamber. The Page instantly with-drew.

'I know your business,' said He, without giving me time to speak. 'I have the power of releasing you from your nightly Visitor; But this cannot be done before Sunday. On the hour when the Sabbath Morning breaks, Spirits of darkness have least influence over Mortals. After Saturday the Nun shall visit you no more.'

'May I not enquire,' said I, 'by what means you are in possession of a secret, which I have carefully concealed from the knowledge of every one?'

'How can I be ignorant of your distress, when their cause at this moment stands beside you?'

I started. The Stranger continued.

'Though to you only visible for one hour in the twenty-four, neither day or night does She ever quit you; Nor will She ever quit you till you have granted her request.'

'And what is that request?'

'That She must herself explain: It lies not in my knowledge. Wait with patience for the night of Saturday: All shall be then cleared up.'

I dared not press him further. He soon after changed the conversation, and talked of various matters. He named People who had ceased to exist for many Centuries, and yet with whom He appeared to have been personally acquainted. I could not mention a Country however distant which He had not visited, nor could I sufficiently admire the extent, and variety of his information. I remarked to him that having travelled, seen, and known so much, must have given him infinite pleasure. He shook his head mournfully.

'No one,' He replied, 'is adequate to comprehending the misery of my lot! Fate obliges me to be constantly in movement:* I am not permitted to pass more than a fortnight in the same place. I have no Friend in the world, and from the restlessness of my destiny I never can acquire one. Fain would I lay down my miserable life, for I envy those who enjoy the quiet of the Grave: But Death eludes me, and flies from my embrace. In vain do I throw myself in the way of danger. I plunge into the Ocean; The Waves throw me back with abhorrence upon the shore: I rush into fire; The flames recoil at my approach: I oppose myself to the fury of Banditti; Their swords become blunted, and break against my breast: The hungry Tiger shudders at my approach, and the Alligator flies from a Monster more horrible than itself. God has set his seal upon me, and all his Creatures respect this fatal mark!'

He put his hand to the velvet, which was bound round

his fore-head. There was in his eyes an expression of fury, despair, and malevolence, that struck horror to my very soul. An involuntary convulsion made me shudder. The Stranger perceived it.

'Such is the curse imposed on me,' he continued: 'I am doomed to inspire all who look on me with terror and detestation. You already feel the influence of the charm, and with every succeeding moment will feel it more. I will not add to your sufferings by my presence. Farewell till Saturday. As soon as the Clock strikes twelve, expect me at your chamber-door.'

Having said this He departed, leaving me in astonishment at the mysterious turn of his manner and conversation.

His assurances that I should soon be relieved from the Apparition's visits, produced a good effect upon my constitution. Theodore, whom I rather treated as an adopted Child than a Domestic, was surprized at his return to observe the amendment in my looks. He congratulated me on this symptom of returning health, and declared himself delighted at my having received so much benefit from my conference with the Great Mogul. Upon enquiry I found that the Stranger had already past eight days in Ratisbon: According to his own account, therefore, He was only to remain there six days longer. Saturday was still at the distance of Three. Oh! with what impatience did I expect its arrival! In the interim, the Bleeding Nun continued her nocturnal visits; But hoping soon to be released from them altogether, the effects which they produced on me became less violent than before.

The wished-for night arrived. To avoid creating suspicion I retired to bed at my usual hour: But as soon as my Attendants had left me, I dressed myself again, and prepared for the Stranger's reception. He entered my room upon the turn of midnight. A small Chest was in his hand, which He placed near the Stove. He saluted me without speaking; I returned the compliment, observing an equal silence. He then opened his Chest. The first thing which He produced, was a small wooden Crucifix: He sank upon his knees, gazed upon it mournfully, and cast his eyes towards heaven. He seemed to be praying devoutly. At length He bowed his head respectfully, kissed the Crucifix thrice, and quitted his kneeling posture. He next drew from the Chest a covered Goblet: With the liquor which it contained, and which appeared to be blood, He sprinkled the floor, and then dipping in it one end of the Crucifix, He described a circle in the middle of the room. Round about this He placed various reliques, sculls, thigh-bones &c; I observed, that He disposed them all in the forms of Crosses. Lastly He took out a large Bible, and beckoned me to follow him into the Circle. I obeyed.

'Be cautious not to utter a syllable!' whispered the Stranger; 'Step not out of the circle, and as you love yourself, dare not to look upon my face!'

Holding the Crucifix in one hand, the Bible in the other, He seemed to read with profound attention. The Clock struck 'One'! As usual I heard the Spectre's steps upon the Stair-case: But I was not seized with the accustomed shivering. I waited her approach with confidence. She entered the room, drew near the Circle, and stopped. The Stranger muttered some words, to me unintelligible. Then raising his head from the Book, and extending the Crucifix towards the Ghost, He pronounced in a voice distinct and solemn,

'Beatrice! Beatrice! Beatrice!'

'What wouldst Thou?' replied the Apparition in a hollow faltering tone.

'What disturbs thy sleep? Why dost thou afflict and torture this Youth? How can rest be restored to thy unquiet Spirit?'

'I dare not tell!—I must not tell!—Fain would I repose in my Grave, but stern commands force me to prolong my punishment!'

'Knowest Thou this blood? Knowest Thou in whose veins it flowed? Beatrice! Beatrice! In his name I charge thee to answer me!'

'I dare not disobey my taskers.'

'Darest Thou disobey Me?'

He spoke in a commanding tone, and drew the sable band from his fore-head. In spite of his injunctions to the contrary, Curiosity would not suffer me to keep my eyes off his face. I raised them, and beheld a burning Cross impressed upon his brow. For the horror with which this object inspired me I cannot account, but I never felt its equal! My senses left me for some moments; A mysterious dread overcame my courage, and had not the Exorciser caught my hand, I should have fallen out of the Circle.

When I recovered myself, I perceived that the burning Cross had produced an effect no less violent upon the Spectre. Her countenance expressed reverence, and horror, and her visionary limbs were shaken by fear.

'Yes!' She said at length; 'I tremble at that mark!—I respect it!—I obey you! Know then, that my bones lie still unburied: They rot in the obscurity of Lindenberg Hole. None but this Youth has the right of consigning them to the Grave. His own lips have made over to me his body and his soul: Never will I give back his promise, never shall He know a night devoid of terror, unless He engages to collect my mouldering bones, and deposit them in the family vault of his Andalusian Castle. Then let thirty Masses be said for the repose of my Spirit, and I trouble this world no more. Now let me depart! Those flames are scorching!'

He let the hand drop slowly which held the Crucifix, and which till then He had pointed towards her. The apparition bowed her head, and her form melted into air. The Exorciser led me out of the Circle. He replaced the Bible &c. in the Chest, and then addressed himself to me, who stood near him speechless from astonishment.

'Don Raymond, you have heard the conditions on which repose is promised you. Be it your business to fulfil them to the letter. For me nothing more remains than to clear up the darkness still spread over the Spectre's History, and inform you that when living Beatrice bore the name of las Cisternas. She was the great Aunt of your Grand-father: In quality of your relation, her ashes demand respect from you, though the enormity of her crimes must excite your abhorrence. The nature of those crimes no one is more capable of explaining to you than myself: I was personally acquainted with the holy Man who proscribed her nocturnal riots in the Castle of Lindenberg, and I hold this narrative from his own lips.

'Beatrice de las Cisternas took the veil at an early age, not by her own choice, but at the express command of her Parents. She was then too young to regret the pleasures, of which her profession deprived her: But no sooner did her warm and voluptuous character begin to be developed, than She abandoned herself freely to the impulse of her passions, and seized the first opportunity to procure their gratification. This opportunity was at length presented, after many obstacles which only added new force to her desires. She contrived to elope from the Convent, and fled to Germany with the Baron Lindenberg. She lived at his Castle several months as his avowed Concubine: All Bavaria was scandalized by her impudent and abandoned conduct. Her feasts vied in luxury with Cleopatra's,* and Lindenberg became the Theatre of the most unbridled debauchery. Not satisfied with displaying the incontinence of a Prostitute, She professed herself an Atheist: She took every opportunity to scoff at her monastic vows, and loaded with ridicule the most sacred ceremonies of Religion.

'Possessed of a character so depraved, She did not long confine her affections to one object. Soon after her arrival at the Castle, the Baron's younger Brother attracted her notice by his strong-marked features, gigantic Stature, and Herculean limbs. She was not of an humour to keep her inclinations long unknown; But She found in Otto von Lindenberg her equal in depravity. He returned her passion just sufficiently to increase it; and when He had worked it up to the desired pitch, He fixed the price of his love at his Brother's murder. The Wretch consented to this horrible agreement. A night was pitched upon for perpetrating the deed. Otto, who resided on a small Estate a few miles distant from the Castle, promised that at One in the morning He would be waiting for her at Lindenberg Hole; that He would bring with him a party of chosen Friends, by whose aid He doubted not being able to make himself Master of the Castle; and that his next step should be the uniting her hand to his. It was this last promise, which over-ruled every scruple of Beatrice, since in spite of his affection for her, the Baron had declared positively, that He never would make her his Wife.

'The fatal night arrived. The Baron slept in the arms of his perfidious Mistress, when the Castle-Bell struck 'One.' Immediately Beatrice drew a dagger from underneath the pillow, and plunged it in her Paramour's heart. The Baron uttered a single dreadful groan, and expired. The Murderess quitted her bed hastily, took a Lamp in one hand, in the other the bloody dagger, and bent her course towards the cavern. The Porter dared not to refuse opening the Gates to one more dreaded in the Castle, than its Master. Beatrice reached Lindenberg Hole unopposed, where according to promise She found Otto waiting for her. He received, and listened to her narrative with transport: But ere She had time to ask why He came unaccompanied, He convinced her that He wished for no witnesses to their interview. Anxious to conceal his share in the murder, and to free himself from a Woman, whose violent and atrocious character made him tremble with reason for his own safety, He had resolved on the destruction of his wretched Agent. Rushing upon her suddenly, He wrested the dagger from her hand: He plunged it still reeking with his Brother's blood in her bosom, and put an end to her existence by repeated blows.

'Otto now succeeded to the Barony of Lindenberg. The murder was attributed solely to the fugitive Nun, and no one suspected him to have persuaded her to the action. But though his crime was unpunished by Man, God's justice permitted him not to enjoy in peace his blood-stained honours. Her bones lying still unburied in the Cave, the restless soul of Beatrice continued to inhabit the Castle. Drest in her religious habit in memory of her vows broken to heaven, furnished with the dagger which had drank the blood of her Paramour, and holding the Lamp which had guided her flying steps, every night did She stand before the Bed of Otto. The most dreadful confusion reigned through the Castle; The vaulted chambers resounded with shrieks and groans; And the Spectre, as She ranged along the antique Galleries, uttered an incoherent mixture of prayers and blasphemies. Otto was unable to withstand the shock, which He felt at this fearful Vision: Its horror increased with every succeeding appearance: His alarm at length became so insupportable, that his heart burst, and one morning He was found in his bed totally deprived of warmth and animation. His death did not put an end to the nocturnal riots. The bones of Beatrice continued to lie unburied, and her Ghost continued to haunt the Castle.

'The domains of Lindenberg now fell to a distant Relation. But terrified by the accounts given him of the Bleeding Nun [So was the Spectre called by the multitude,] the new Baron called to his assistance a celebrated Exorciser. This holy Man succeeded in obliging her to temporary repose; But though She discovered to him her history, He was not permitted to reveal it to others, or cause her skeleton to be removed to hallowed ground. That Office was reserved for you, and till your coming her Ghost was doomed to wander about the Castle, and lament the crime which She had there committed. However, the Exorciser obliged her to silence during his lifetime. So long as He existed, the haunted chamber was shut up, and the Spectre was invisible. At his death which happened in five years after, She again appeared, but only once on every fifth year, on the same day and at the same hour when She plunged her Knife in the heart of her sleeping Lover: She then visited the Cavern which held her mouldering skeleton, returned to the Castle as soon as the Clock struck 'Two,' and was seen no more till the next five years had elapsed.

'She was doomed to suffer during the space of a Century. That period is past. Nothing now remains but to consign to the Grave the ashes of Beatrice. I have been the means of releasing you from your visionary Tormentor; and amidst all the sorrows which oppress me, to think that I have been of use to you, is some consolation. Youth, farewell! May the Ghost of your Relation enjoy that rest in the Tomb, which the Almighty's vengeance has denied to me for ever!'

Here the Stranger prepared to quit the apartment.

'Stay yet one moment!' said I; 'You have satisfied my curiosity with regard to the Spectre, but you leave me in prey to yet greater respecting yourself. Deign to inform me, to whom I am under such real obligations. You mention circumstances long past, and persons long dead: You were personally acquainted with the Exorciser, who by your own account has been deceased near a Century. How am I to account for this? What means that burning Cross upon your fore-head, and why did the sight of it strike such horror to my soul?'

On these points He for some time refused to satisfy me. At length overcome by my entreaties, He consented to clear up the whole, on condition that I would defer his explanation till the next day. With this request I was obliged to comply, and He left me. In the Morning my first care was to enquire after the mysterious Stranger. Conceive my disappointment, when informed that He had already quitted Ratisbon. I dispatched messengers in pursuit of him but in vain. No traces of the Fugitive were discovered. Since that moment I never have heard any more of him, and 'tis most probable that I never shall.'

[Lorenzo here interrupted his Friend's narrative.

'How?' said He; 'You have never discovered who He was, or even formed a guess?'

'Pardon me,' replied the Marquis; 'When I related this adventure to my Uncle, the Cardinal-Duke, He told me that He had no doubt of this singular Man's being the celebrated Character known universally by the name of '*the wandering Jew*.'* His not being permitted to pass more than fourteen days on the same spot, the burning Cross impressed upon his fore-head, the effect which it produced upon the Beholders, and many other circumstances give this supposition the colour of truth. The Cardinal is fully persuaded of it; and for my own part I am inclined to adopt the only solution which offers itself to this riddle. I return to the narrative from which I have digressed.']

From this period I recovered my health so rapidly as to astonish my Physicians. The Bleeding Nun appeared no more, and I was soon able to set out for Lindenberg.

The Baron received me with open arms. I confided to him the sequel of my adventure; and He was not a little pleased to find, that his Mansion would be no longer troubled with the Phantom's quiennial visits. I was sorry to perceive, that absence had not weakened Donna Rodolpha's imprudent passion. In a private conversation, which I had with her during my short stay at the Castle, She renewed her attempts to persuade me to return her affection. Regarding her as the primary cause of all my sufferings, I entertained for her no other sentiment than disgust. The Skeleton of Beatrice was found in the place which She had mentioned. This being all that I sought at Lindenberg, I hastened to quit the Baron's domains, equally anxious to perform the obsequies of the murdered Nun, and escape the importunity of a Woman whom I detested. I departed, followed by Donna Rodolpha's menaces that my contempt should not be long unpunished.

I now bent my course towards Spain with all diligence. Lucas with my Baggage had joined me during my abode at Lindenberg. I arrived in my native Country without any accident, and immediately proceeded to my Father's Castle in Andalusia. The remains of Beatrice were deposited in the family vault, all due ceremonies performed, and the number of Masses said which She had required. Nothing now hindered me from employing all my endeavours to discover the retreat of Agnes. The Baroness had assured me, that her Niece had already taken the veil: This intelligence I suspected to have been forged by jealousy, and hoped to find my Mistress still at liberty to accept my hand. I enquired after her family; I found that before her Daughter could reach Madrid, Donna Inesilla was no more: You, my dear Lorenzo, were said to be abroad, but where I could not discover: Your Father was in a distant Province on a visit to the Duke de Medina, and as to Agnes no one could or would inform me what was become of her. Theodore according to promise had returned to Strasbourg, where He found his Grand-father dead, and Marguerite in possession of his fortune. All her persuations to remain with her were fruitless: He quitted her a second time, and followed me to Madrid. He exerted himself to the utmost in forwarding my search: But our united endeavours were unattended by success. The retreat, which concealed Agnes remained an impenetrable mystery, and I began to abandon all hopes of recovering her.

About eight months ago I was returning to my Hotel in a melancholy humour, having past the evening at the Play-House. The Night was dark, and I was unaccompanied. Plunged in reflections which were far from being agreeable, I perceived not that three Men had followed me from the Theatre; till, on turning into an unfrequented Street, they all attacked me at the same time with the utmost fury. I sprang back a few paces, drew my sword, and threw my cloak over my left arm. The obscurity of the night was in my favour. For the most part the blows of the Assassins, being aimed at random, failed to touch me. I at length was fortunate enough to lay one of my Adversaries at my feet; But before this I had already received so many wounds, and was so warmly pressed, that my destruction would have been inevitable, had not the clashing of swords called a Cavalier to my assistance. He ran towards me with his sword drawn: Several Domestics followed him with torches. His arrival made the combat equal: Yet would not the Bravoes abandon their design, till the Servants were on the point of joining us. They then fled away, and we lost them in the obscurity.

The Stranger now addressed himself to me with politeness, and enquired whether I was wounded. Faint with the loss of blood, I could scarcely thank him for his seasonable aid, and entreat him to let some of his Servants convey me to the Hotel de las Cisternas. I no sooner mentioned the name than He profest himself an acquaintance of my Father's, and declared that He would not permit my being transported to such a distance, before my wounds had been examined. He added, that his House was hard by, and begged me to accompany him thither. His manner was so earnest, that I could not reject his offer, and leaning upon his arm, a few minutes brought me to the Porch of a magnificent Hotel.

On entering the House, an old grey-headed Domestic came to welcome my Conductor: He enquired when the Duke, his Master, meant to quit the Country, and was answered that He would remain there yet some months. My Deliverer then desired the family-Surgeon to be summoned without delay. His orders were obeyed. I was seated upon a Sopha in a noble apartment; and my wounds being examined, they were declared to be very slight. The Surgeon, however, advised me not to expose myself to the night-air; and the Stranger pressed me so earnestly to take a bed in his House, that I consented to remain where I was for the present.

Being now left alone with my Deliverer, I took the opportunity of thanking him in more express terms, than I had done hitherto: But He begged me to be silent upon the subject.

'I esteem myself happy,' said He, 'in having had it in my power to render you this little service; and I shall think myself eternally obliged to my Daughter for detaining me so late at the Convent of St. Clare. The high esteem in which I have ever held the Marquis de las Cisternas, though accident has not permitted our being so intimate as I could wish, makes me rejoice in the opportunity of making his Son's acquaintance. I am certain that my Brother in whose House you now are, will lament his not being at Madrid to receive you himself: But in the Duke's absence I am Master of the family, and may assure you in his name, that every thing in the Hotel de Medina is perfectly at your disposal.'

Conceive my surprize, Lorenzo, at discovering in the person of my Preserver Don Gaston de Medina: It was only to be equalled by my secret satisfaction at the assurance, that Agnes inhabited the Convent of St. Clare. This latter sensation was not a little weakened, when in answer to my seemingly indifferent questions He told me, that his Daughter had really taken the veil. I suffered not my grief at this circumstance to take root in my mind: I flattered myself with the idea that my Uncle's credit at the Court of Rome would remove this obstacle, and that without difficulty I should obtain for my Mistress a dispensation from her vows.* Buoyed up with this hope I calmed the uneasiness of my bosom; and I redoubled my endeavours to appear grateful for the attention, and pleased with the society of Don Gaston.

A Domestic now entered the room, and informed me that the Bravo whom I had wounded, discovered some signs of life. I desired that He might be carried to my Father's Hotel, and that as soon as He recovered his voice, I would examine him respecting his reasons for attempting my life. I was answered, that He was already able to speak, though with difficulty: Don Gaston's curiosity made him press me to interrogate the Assassin in his presence, but this curiosity I was by no means inclined to gratify. One reason was, that doubting from whence the blow came, I was unwilling to place before Don Gaston's eyes the guilt of a Sister: Another was, that I feared to be recognized for Alphonso d'Alvarada, and precautions taken in consequence to keep me from the sight of Agnes. To avow my passion for his Daughter, and endeavour to make him enter into my schemes, what I knew of Don Gaston's character convinced me would be an imprudent step: and considering it to be essential that He should know me for no other than the Condé de las Cisternas, I was determined not to let him hear the Bravo's confession. I insinuated to him, that as I suspected a Lady to be concerned in the Business, whose name might accidentally escape from the Assassin, it was necessary for me to examine the Man in private. Don Gaston's delicacy would not permit his urging the point any longer, and in consequence the Bravo was conveyed to my Hotel.

The next Morning I took leave of my Host, who was to return to the Duke on the same day. My wounds had been so trifling, that except being obliged to wear my arm in a sling for a short time, I felt no inconvenience from the night's adventure. The Surgeon who examined the Bravo's wound declared it to be mortal: He had just time to confess, that He had been instigated to murder me by the revengeful Donna Rodolpha, and expired in a few minutes after.

All my thoughts were now bent upon getting to the speech of my lovely Nun. Theodore set himself to work, and for this time with better success. He attacked the Gardener of St. Clare so forcibly with bribes and promises, that the Old Man was entirely gained over to my interests; and it was settled, that I should be introduced into the Convent in the character of his Assistant. The plan was put into execution without delay. Disguised in a common habit, and a black patch covering one of my eyes, I was presented to the Lady Prioress, who condescended to approve of the Gardener's choice. I immediately entered upon my employment. Botany having been a favourite study with me, I was by no means at a loss in my new station. For some days I continued to work in the Convent-Garden without meeting the Object of my disguise: On the fourth Morning I was more successful. I heard the voice of Agnes, and was speeding towards the sound, when the sight of the Domina stopped me. I drew back with caution, and concealed myself behind a thick clump of Trees.

The Prioress advanced, and seated herself with Agnes on a Bench at no great distance. I heard her in an angry tone blame her Companion's continual melancholy: She told her that to weep the loss of any Lover in her situation was a crime; But that to weep the loss of a faithless one was folly and absurdity in the extreme. Agnes replied in so low a voice that I could not distinguish her words, but I perceived that She used terms of gentleness and submission. The conversation was interrupted by the arrival of a young Pensioner, who informed the Domina that She was waited for in the Parlour. The old Lady rose, kissed the cheek of Agnes, and retired. The new-comer remained. Agnes spoke much to her in praise of somebody whom I could not make out, but her Auditor seemed highly delighted, and interested by the conversation. The Nun showed her several letters; the Other perused them with evident pleasure, obtained permission to copy them, and withdrew for that purpose to my great satisfaction.

No sooner was She out of sight, than I quitted my concealment. Fearing to alarm my lovely Mistress, I drew near her gently, intending to discover myself by degrees. But who for a moment can deceive the eyes of love? She raised her head at my approach, and recognised me in spite of my disguise at a single glance. She rose hastily from her seat with an exclamation of surprize, and attempted to retire; But I followed her, detained her, and entreated to be heard. Persuaded of my falsehood She refused to listen to me, and ordered me positively to quit the Garden. It was now my turn to refuse. I protested, that however dangerous might be the consequences, I would not leave her till She had heard my justification. I assured her, that She had been deceived by the artifices of her Relations; that I could convince her beyond the power of doubt, that my passion had been pure and disinterested; and I asked her, what should induce me to seek her in the Convent, were I influenced by the selfish motives which my Enemies had ascribed to me.

My prayers, my arguments, and vows not to quit her, till She had promised to listen to me, united to her fears lest the Nuns should see me with her, to her natural curiosity, and to the effection which She still felt for me in spite of my supposed desertion, at length prevailed. She told me, that to grant my request at that moment was impossible; But She engaged to be in the same spot at eleven that night, and to converse with me for the last time. Having obtained this promise I released her hand, and She fled back with rapidity towards the Convent.

I communicated my success to my Ally, the old Gardener: He pointed out an hiding-place, where I might shelter myself till night without fear of a discovery. Thither I betook myself at the hour when I ought to have retired with my supposed Master, and waited impatiently for the appointed time. The chillness of the night was in my favour, since it kept the other Nuns confined to their Cells. Agnes alone was insensible of the inclemency of the Air, and before eleven joined me at the spot, which had witnessed our former interview. Secure from interruption I related to her the true cause of my disappearing on the fatal fifth of May. She was evidently much affected by my narrative: When it was concluded, She confessed the injustice of her suspicions, and blamed herself for having taken the veil through despair at my ingratitude.

'But now it is too late to repine!' She added; 'The die is thrown: I have pronounced my vows, and dedicated myself to the service of heaven. I am sensible, how ill I am calculated for a Convent. My disgust at a monastic life increases daily: Ennui and discontent are my constant Companions; and I will not conceal from you, that the passion which I formerly felt for one so near being my Husband is not yet extinguished in my bosom. But we must part! Insuperable Barriers divide us from each other, and on this side the Grave we must never meet again!'

I now exerted myself to prove, that our union was not so impossible as She seemed to think it. I vaunted to her the Cardinal-Duke of Lerma's influence* at the Court of Rome: I assured her, that I should easily obtain a dispensation from her vows; and I doubted not but Don Gaston would coincide with my views, when informed of my real name and long attachment. Agnes replied, that since I encouraged such an hope, I could know but little of her Father. Liberal and kind in every other respect, Superstition formed the only stain upon his character. Upon this head He was inflexible; He sacrificed his dearest interests to his scruples, and would consider it an insult to suppose him capable, of authorising his daughter to break her vows to heaven.

'But suppose,' said I interrupting her; 'Suppose, that He should disapprove of our union; Let him remain ignorant of my proceedings, till I have rescued you from the prison, in which you are now confined. Once my Wife, you are free from his authority: I need from him no pecuniary assistance; and when He sees his resentment to be unavailing, He will doubtless restore you to his favour. But let the worst happen; Should Don Gaston be irreconcileable, my Relations will vie with each other in making you forget his loss: and you will find in my Father a substitute for the Parent of whom I shall deprive you.'

'Don Raymond,' replied Agnes in a firm and resolute voice, 'I love my Father: He has treated me harshly in this one instance; but I have received from him in every other so many proofs of love, that his affection is become necessary to my existence. Were I to quit the Convent, He never would forgive me; nor can I think that on his death-bed He would leave me his curse, without shuddering at the very idea. Besides, I am conscious myself, that my vows are binding: Wilfully did I contract my engagement with heaven; I cannot break it without a crime. Then banish from your mind the idea of our being ever united. I am devoted to religion; and however I may grieve at our separation, I would oppose obstacles myself, to what I feel would render me guilty.'

I strove to over-rule these ill-grounded scruples: We were still disputing upon the subject, when the Convent-Bell summoned the Nuns to Matins. Agnes was obliged to attend them; But She left me not, till I had compelled her to promise, that on the following night She would be at the same place at the same hour. These meetings continued for several Weeks uninterrupted; and 'tis now, Lorenzo, that I must implore your indulgence. Reflect upon our situation, our youth, our long attachment: Weigh all the circumstances which attended our assignations, and you will confess the temptation to have been irresistible; you will even pardon me when I acknowledge, that in an unguarded moment the honour of Agnes was sacrificed to my passion.'

[Lorenzo's eyes sparkled with fury: A deep crimson spread itself over his face. He started from his seat, and attempted to draw his sword. The Marquis was aware of his movement, and caught his hand: He pressed it affectionately.

'My Friend! My Brother! Hear me to the conclusion! Till then restrain your passion, and be at least convinced, that if what I have related is criminal, the blame must fall upon me, and not upon your Sister.'

Lorenzo suffered himself to be prevailed upon by

Don Raymond's entreaties. He resumed his place, and listened to the rest of the narrative with a gloomy and impatient countenance. The Marquis thus continued.]

'Scarcely was the first burst of passion past, when Agnes recovering herself started from my arms with horror. She called me infamous Seducer, loaded me with the bitterest reproaches, and beat her bosom in all the wildness of delirium. Ashamed of my imprudence, I with difficulty found words to excuse myself. I endeavoured to console her; I threw myself at her feet, and entreated her forgiveness. She forced her hand from me, which I had taken, and would have prest to my lips.

'Touch me not!' She cried with a violence which terrified me; 'Monster of perfidy and ingratitude, how have I been deceived in you! I looked upon you as my Friend, my Protector: I trusted myself in your hands with confidence, and relying upon your honour thought that mine ran no risque. And 'tis by you, whom I adored, that I am covered with infamy! 'Tis by you that I have been seduced into breaking my vows to God, that I am reduced to a level with the basest of my sex! Shame upon you, Villain, you shall never see me more!'

She started from the Bank on which She was seated. I endeavoured to detain her; But She disengaged herself from me with violence, and took refuge in the Convent.

I retired, filled with confusion and inquietude. The next morning I failed not as usual to appear in the Garden; but Agnes was no where to be seen. At night I waited for her at the place where we generally met; I found no better success. Several days and nights passed away in the same manner. At length I saw my offended Mistress cross the walk, on whose borders I was working: She was accompanied by the same young Pensioner, on whose arm She seemed from weakness obliged to support herself. She looked upon me for a moment, but instantly turned her head away. I waited her return; But She passed on to the Convent without paying any attention to me, or the penitent looks with which I implored her forgiveness.

As soon as the Nuns were retired, the old Gardener joined me with a sorrowful air.

'Segnor,' said He, 'it grieves me to say, that I can be no longer of use to you. The Lady whom you used to meet, has just assured me, that if I admitted you again into the Garden, She would discover the whole business to the Lady Prioress. She bade me tell you also, that your presence was an insult, and that if you still possess the least respect for her, you will never attempt to see her more. Excuse me then for informing you, that I can favour your disguise no longer. Should the Prioress be acquainted with my conduct, She might not be contented with dismissing me her service: Out of revenge She might accuse me of having profaned the Convent, and cause me to be thrown into the Prisons of the Inquisition.'

Fruitless were my attempts to conquer his resolution. He denied me all future entrance into the Garden, and Agnes persevered in neither letting me see, or hear from her. In about a fortnight after a violent illness which had seized my Father, obliged me to set out for Andalusia. I hastened thither, and as I imagined, found the Marquis at the point of death. Though on its first appearance his complaint was declared mortal, He lingered out several Months; during which my attendance upon him during his malady, and the occupation of settling his affairs after his decease, permitted not my quitting Andalusia. Within these four days I returned to Madrid, and on arriving at my Hotel, I there found this letter waiting for me.

[Here the Marquis unlocked the drawer of a Cabinet: He took out a folded paper, which He presented to his Auditor. Lorenzo opened it, and recognised his Sister's hand. The Contents were as follows.

Into what an abyss of misery have you plunged me!
Raymond, you force me to become as criminal as
yourself. I had resolved never to see you more; if possible,
to forget you; If not, only to remember you with hate.
A Being for whom I already feel a Mother's tenderness,
solicits me to pardon my Seducer, and apply to his love
for the means of preservation. Raymond, your child lives
in my bosom. I tremble at the vengeance of the Prioress;
I tremble much for myself, yet more for the innocent
Creature whose existence depends upon mine. Both of
us are lost, should my situation be discovered. Advise
me then what steps to take, but seek not to see me. The
Gardener, who undertakes to deliver this, is dismissed,
and we have nothing to hope from that quarter: The
Man engaged in his place is of incorruptible fidelity.
The best means of conveying to me your answer, is by
concealing it under the great Statue of St. Francis,
which stands in the Capuchin-Cathedral. Thither I go
every Thursday to confession, and shall easily have an
opportunity of securing your letter. I hear, that you are
now absent from Madrid; Need I entreat you to write
the very moment of your return? I will not think it. Ah!
Raymond! Mine is a cruel situation! Deceived by my
nearest Relations, compelled to embrace a profession
the duties of which I am ill-calculated to perform,
conscious of the sanctity of those duties, and seduced into
violating them by One whom I least suspected of
perfidy, I am now obliged by circumstances to chuse
between death and perjury. Woman's timidity, and
maternal affection permit me not to balance in the
choice. I feel all the guilt into which I plunge myself,
when I yield to the plan which you before proposed to
me. My poor Father's death which has taken place since
we met, has removed one obstacle. He sleeps in his grave,
and I no longer dread his anger. But from the anger of
God, Oh! Raymond! who shall shield me? Who can

protect me against my conscience, against myself? I dare not dwell upon these thoughts; They will drive me mad. I have taken my resolution: Procure a dispensation from my vows; I am ready to fly with you. Write to me, my Husband! Tell me, that absence has not abated your love, tell me that you will rescue from death your unborn Child, and its unhappy Mother. I live in all the agonies of terror: Every eye which is fixed upon me, seems to read my secret and my shame. And you are the cause of those agonies! Oh! When my heart first loved you, how little did it suspect you of making it feel such pangs!

Agnes.

Having perused the letter, Lorenzo restored it in silence. The Marquis replaced it in the Cabinet, and then proceeded.]

'Excessive was my joy at reading this intelligence so earnestly-desired, so little expected. My plan was soon arranged. When Don Gaston discovered to me his Daughter's retreat, I entertained no doubt of her readiness to quit the Convent: I had, therefore, entrusted the Cardinal-Duke of Lerma with the whole affair, who immediately busied himself in obtaining the necessary Bull.* Fortunately I had afterwards neglected to stop his proceedings. Not long since I received a letter from him, stating that He expected daily to receive the order from the Court of Rome. Upon this I would willingly have relied: But the Cardinal wrote me word, that I must find some means of conveying Agnes out of the Convent, unknown to the Prioress. He doubted not but this Latter would be much incensed by losing a Person of such high rank from her society, and consider the renunciation of Agnes as an insult to her House. He represented her as a Woman of a violent and revengeful character, capable of proceeding to the greatest extremities.

It was therefore to be feared, lest by confining Agnes in the Convent She should frustrate my hopes, and render the Pope's mandate unavailing. Influenced by this consideration, I resolved to carry off my Mistress, and conceal her till the arrival of the expected Bull in the Cardinal-Duke's Estate. He approved of my design, and profest himself ready to give a shelter to the Fugitive. I next caused the new Gardener of St. Clare to be seized privately, and confined in my Hotel. By this means I became Master of the Key to the Garden-door, and I had now nothing more to do than prepare Agnes for the elopement. This was done by the letter, which you saw me deliver this Evening. I told her in it, that I should be ready to receive her at twelve tomorrow night, that I had secured the Key of the Garden, and that She might depend upon a speedy release.

You have now, Lorenzo, heard the whole of my long narrative. I have nothing to say in my excuse, save that my intentions towards your Sister have been ever the most honourable: That it has always been, and still is my design to make her my Wife: And that I trust, when you consider these circumstances, our youth, and our attachment, you will not only forgive our momentary lapse from virtue, but will aid me in repairing my faults to Agnes, and securing a lawful title to her person and her heart.

CHAPTER II

O You! whom Vanity's light bark conveys
On Fame's mad voyage by the wind of praise,
With what a shifting gale your course you ply,
For ever sunk too low, or borne too high!
Who pants for glory finds but short repose,
A breath revives him, and a breath o'er-throws.

Pope.*

HERE THE MARQUIS concluded his adventures. Lorenzo, before He could determine on his reply, past some moments in reflection. At length He broke silence.

'Raymond,' said He taking his hand, 'strict honour would oblige me to wash off in your blood the stain thrown upon my family; But the circumstances of your case forbid me to consider you as an Enemy. The temptation was too great to be resisted. 'Tis the superstition of my Relations which has occasioned these misfortunes, and they are more the Offenders than yourself and Agnes. What has past between you cannot be recalled, but may yet be repaired by uniting you to my Sister. You have ever been, you still continue to be, my dearest and indeed my only Friend. I feel for Agnes the truest affection, and there is no one on whom I would bestow her more willingly than on yourself. Pursue then your design. I will accompany you tomorrow night, and conduct her myself to the House of the Cardinal. My presence will be a sanction for her conduct, and prevent her incurring blame by her flight from the Convent.'

The Marquis thanked him in terms by no means deficient in gratitude. Lorenzo then informed him, that He had nothing more to apprehend from Donna Rodolpha's enmity. Five Months had already elapsed, since in an excess of passion She broke a blood-vessel, and expired in the course of a few hours. He then proceeded to mention the interests of Antonia. The Marquis was much surprized at hearing of this new Relation: His Father had carried his hatred of Elvira to the Grave, and had never given the least hint, that He knew what was become of his eldest Son's Widow. Don Raymond assured his Friend, that He was not mistaken in supposing him ready to acknowledge his Sister-in-law, and her amiable Daughter. The preparations for the elopement would not permit his visiting them the next day; But in the mean while He desired Lorenzo to assure them of his friendship, and to supply Elvira upon his account with any sums which She might want. This the Youth promised to do, as soon as her abode should be known to him: He then took leave of his future Brother, and returned to the Palace de Medina.

The day was already on the point of breaking, when the Marquis retired to his chamber. Conscious that his narrative would take up some hours, and wishing to secure himself from interruption, on returning to the Hotel He ordered his Attendants not to sit up for him. Consequently, He was somewhat surprised on entering his Anti-room, to find Theodore established there. The Page sat near a Table with a pen in his hand, and was so totally occupied by his employment, that He perceived not his Lord's approach. The Marquis stopped to observe him. Theodore wrote a few lines, then paused, and scratched out a part of the writing: Then wrote again, smiled, and seemed highly pleased with what He had been about. At last He threw down his pen, sprang from his chair, and clapped his hands together joyfully.

'There it is!' cried He aloud: 'Now they are charming!'

His transports were interrupted by a laugh from the Marquis, who suspected the nature of his employment.

'What is so charming, Theodore?'

The Youth started, and looked round. He blushed, ran to the Table, seized the paper on which He had been writing, and concealed it in confusion.

'Oh! my Lord, I knew not that you were so near me. Can I be of use to you? Lucas is already gone to bed.'

'I shall follow his example when I have given my opinion of your verses.'

'My verses, my Lord?'

'Nay, I am sure that you have been writing some, for nothing else could have kept you awake till this time of the morning. Where are they, Theodore? I shall like to see your composition.'

Theodore's cheeks glowed with still deeper crimson: He longed to show his poetry, but first chose to be pressed for it.

'Indeed, my Lord, they are not worthy your attention.'

'Not these verses, which you just now declared to be so charming? Come, come, let me see whether our opinions are the same. I promise, that you shall find in me an indulgent Critic.'

The Boy produced his paper with seeming reluctance; but the satisfaction which sparkled in his dark expressive eyes betrayed the vanity of his little bosom. The Marquis smiled while He observed the emotions of an heart, as yet but little skilled in veiling its sentiments. He seated himself upon a Sopha: Theodore, while Hope and fear contended on his anxious countenance, waited with inquietude for his Master's decision, while the Marquis read the following lines.

LOVE AND AGE

The night was dark; The wind blew cold;
Anacreon,* grown morose and old,
Sat by his fire, and fed the chearful flame:
Sudden the Cottage-door expands,

And lo! before him Cupid stands,
Casts round a friendly glance, and greets him by his name.

'What is it Thou?' the startled Sire
In sullen tone exclaimed, while ire
With crimson flushed his pale and wrinkled cheek:
'Wouldst Thou again with amorous rage
Inflame my bosom? Steeled by age,
Vain Boy, to pierce my breast thine arrows are too weak.

'What seek You in this desart drear?
No smiles or sports inhabit here;
Ne'er did these vallies witness dalliance sweet:
Eternal winter binds the plains;
Age in my house despotic reigns,
My Garden boasts no flower, my bosom boasts no heat.

'Begone, and seek the blooming bower,
Where some ripe Virgin courts thy power,
Or bid provoking dreams flit round her bed;
On Damon's amorous breast repose;
Wanton·on Chloe's lip of rose,
Or make her blushing cheek a pillow for thy head.

'Be such thy haunts; These regions cold
Avoid! Nor think grown wise and old
This hoary head again thy yoke shall bear:
Remembering that my fairest years
By Thee were marked with sighs and tears,
I think thy friendship false, and shun the guileful snare.

'I have not yet forgot the pains
I felt, while bound in Julia's chains;
The ardent flames with which my bosom burned;
The nights I passed deprived of rest;
The jealous pangs which racked my breast;
My disappointed hopes, and passion unreturned.

'Then fly, and curse mine eyes no more!
   Fly from my peaceful Cottage-door!
No day, no hour, no moment shalt Thou stay.
   I know thy falsehood, scorn thy arts,
   Distrust thy smiles, and fear thy darts;
Traitor, begone, and seek some other to betray!'

'Does Age, old Man, your wits confound?'
   Replied the offended God, and frowned;
[His frown was sweet as is the Virgin's smile!]
   'Do You to Me these words address?
   To Me, who do not love you less,
Though You my friendship scorn, and pleasures past revile!

'If one proud Fair you chanced to find,
   An hundred other Nymphs were kind,
Whose smiles might well for Julia's frowns atone:
   But such is Man! His partial hand
   Unnumbered favours writes on sand,
But stamps one little fault on solid lasting stone.

'Ingrate! Who led Thee to the wave,
   At noon where Lesbia loved to lave?
Who named the bower alone where Daphne lay?
   And who, when Cælia shrieked for aid,
   Bad you with kisses hush the Maid?
What other was't than Love, Oh! false Anacreon, say!

'Then You could call me—"Gentle Boy!
   "My only bliss! my source of joy!"—
Then You could prize me dearer than your soul!
   Could kiss, and dance me on your knees;
   And swear, not wine itself would please,
Had not the lip of Love first touched the flowing bowl!

'Must those sweet days return no more?
   Must I for aye your loss deplore,
Banished your heart, and from your favour driven?

Ah! no; My fears that smile denies;
  That heaving breast, those sparkling eyes
Declare me ever dear and all my faults forgiven.

  'Again beloved, esteemed, carest,
  Cupid shall in thine arms be prest,
Sport on thy knees, or on thy bosom sleep:
  My Torch thine age-struck heart shall warm;
  My Hand pale Winter's rage disarm,
And Youth and Spring shall here once more their revels
    keep.'—

  A feather now of golden hue
  He smiling from his pinion drew;
This to the Poet's hand the Boy commits;
  And straight before Anacreon's eyes
The fairest dreams of fancy rise,
  And round his favoured head wild inspiration flits.

  His bosom glows with amorous fire;
  Eager He grasps the magic lyre;
Swift o'er the tuneful chords his fingers move:
  The Feather plucked from Cupid's wing
  Sweeps the too-long-neglected string,
While soft Anacreon sings the power and praise of Love.

  Soon as that name was heard, the Woods
  Shook off their snows; The melting floods
Broke their cold chains, and Winter fled away.
  Once more the earth was deckt with flowers;
  Mild Zephyrs breathed through blooming bowers;
High towered the glorious Sun, and poured the blaze of day.

  Attracted by the harmonious sound,
  Sylvans and Fauns the Cot surround,
And curious crowd the Minstrel to behold:
  The Wood-nymphs haste the spell to prove;
  Eager They run; They list, they love,
And while They hear the strain, forget the Man is old.

Cupid, to nothing constant long,
  Perched on the Harp attends the song,
Or stifles with a kiss the dulcet notes:
  Now on the Poet's breast reposes,
  Now twines his hoary locks with roses,
Or borne on wings of gold in wanton circle floats.

  Then thus Anacreon—'I no more
  At other shrine my vows will pour,
Since Cupid deigns my numbers to inspire:
  From Phœbus or the blue-eyed Maid*
  Now shall my verse request no aid,
For Love alone shall be the Patron of my Lyre.

  'In lofty strain, of earlier days,
  I spread the King's or Hero's praise,
And struck the martial Chords with epic fire:
  But farewell, Hero! farewell, King!
  Your deeds my lips no more shall sing,
For Love alone shall be the subject of my Lyre.

The Marquis returned the paper with a smile of
encouragement.

'Your little poem pleases me much,' said He; 'However, you must not count my opinion for any-thing. I
am no judge of verses, and for my own part, never composed more than six lines in my life: Those six produced
so unlucky an effect, that I am fully resolved never to
compose another. But I wander from my subject. I was
going to say, that you cannot employ your time worse
than in making verses. An Author, whether good or bad,
or between both, is an Animal whom every body is
privileged to attack; For though All are not able to write
books, all conceive themselves able to judge them. A bad
composition carries with it its own punishment, contempt and ridicule. A good one excites envy, and entails
upon its Author a thousand mortifications. He finds

himself assailed by partial and ill-humoured Criticism:
One Man finds fault with the plan, Another with the
style, a Third with the precept, which it strives to in-
culcate; and they who cannot succeed in finding fault
with the Book, employ themselves in stigmatizing its
Author. They maliciously rake out from obscurity every
little circumstance, which may throw ridicule upon his
private character or conduct, and aim at wounding the
Man, since They cannot hurt the Writer. In short to
enter the lists of literature is wilfully to expose yourself
to the arrows of neglect, ridicule, envy, and disappointment. Whether you write well or ill, be assured that you
will not escape from blame; Indeed this circumstance
contains a young Author's chief consolation: He remembers that Lope de Vega and Calderona* had unjust
and envious Critics, and He modestly conceives himself
to be exactly in their predicament. But I am conscious,
that all these sage observations are thrown away upon
you. Authorship is a mania to conquer which no reasons
are sufficiently strong; and you might as easily persuade
me not to love, as I persuade you not to write. However,
if you cannot help being occasionally seized with a
poetical paroxysm, take at least the precaution of communicating your verses to none but those, whose
partiality for you secures their approbation.'

'Then, my Lord, you do not think these lines tolerable?' said Theodore with an humble and dejected air.

'You mistake my meaning. As I said before, they have
pleased me much; But my regard for you makes me
partial, and Others might judge them less favourably.
I must still remark, that even my prejudice in your
favour does not blind me so much, as to prevent my
observing several faults. For instance, you make a
terrible confusion of metaphors; You are too apt to make
the strength of your lines consist more in the words than
sense; Some of the verses only seem introduced in order to

rhyme with others; and most of the best ideas are borrowed from other Poets, though possibly you are unconscious of the theft yourself. These faults may occasionally be excused in a work of length; But a short Poem
must be correct and perfect.'

'All this is true, Segnor; But you should consider that
I only write for pleasure.'

'Your defects are the less excusable. Their incorrect-
ness may be forgiven, who work for money, who are
obliged to compleat a given task in a given time, and are
paid according to the bulk, not value of their productions.
But in those whom no necessity forces to turn Author,
who merely write for fame, and have full leisure to polish
their compositions, faults are impardonable, and merit
the sharpest arrows of criticism.'

The Marquis rose from the Sopha; the Page looked
discouraged and melancholy, and this did not escape his
Master's observation.

'However' added He smiling, 'I think that these lines
do you no discredit. Your versification is tolerably easy,
and your ear seems to be just. The perusal of your little
poem upon the whole gave me much pleasure; and if it
is not asking too great a favour, I shall be highly obliged
to you for a Copy.'

The Youth's countenance immediately cleared up. He
perceived not the smile, half approving, half ironical,
which accompanied the request, and He promised the
Copy with great readiness. The Marquis with-drew to
his chamber, much amused by the instantaneous effect
produced upon Theodore's vanity by the conclusion of
his Criticism. He threw himself upon his Couch; Sleep
soon stole over him, and his dreams presented him with
the most flattering pictures of happiness with Agnes.

On reaching the Hotel de Medina, Lorenzo's first care
was to enquire for Letters. He found several waiting for
him; but that which He sought, was not amongst them.

Leonella had found it impossible to write that evening. However, her impatience to secure Don Christoval's heart, on which She flattered herself with having made no slight impression, permitted her not to pass another day, without informing him where She was to be found. On her return from the Capuchin-Church, She had related to her Sister with exultation, how attentive an handsome Cavalier had been to her; as also how his Companion had undertaken to plead Antonia's cause with the Marquis de las Cisternas. Elvira received this intelligence with sensations very different from those with which it was communicated. She blamed her Sister's imprudence in confiding her history to an absolute Stranger, and expressed her fears, lest this inconsiderate step should prejudice the Marquis against her. The greatest of her apprehensions She concealed in her own breast. She had observed with inquietude, that at the mention of Lorenzo a deep blush spread itself over her Daughter's cheek. The timid Antonia dared not to pronounce his name: Without knowing wherefore, She felt embarrassed when He was made the subject of discourse, and endeavoured to change the conversation to Ambrosio. Elvira perceived the emotions of this young bosom: In consequence, She insisted upon Leonella's breaking her promise to the Cavaliers. A sigh, which on hearing this order escaped from Antonia, confirmed the wary Mother in her resolution.

Through this resolution Leonella was determined to break: She conceived it to be inspired by envy, and that her Sister dreaded her being elevated above her. Without imparting her design to any one, She took an opportunity of dispatching the following note to Lorenzo; It was delivered to him as soon as He woke.

'Doubtless, Segnor Don Lorenzo, you have frequently accused me of ingratitude and forgetfulness: But on the word of a Virgin, it was out of my power to perform my promise yesterday. I know not in what words to inform you, how strange a reception my Sister gave your kind wish to visit her. She is an odd Woman, with many good points about her; But her jealousy of me frequently makes her conceive notions quite unaccountable. On hearing that your Friend had paid some little attention to me, She immediately took the alarm: She blamed my conduct, and has absolutely forbidden me to let you know our abode. My strong sense of gratitude for your kind offers of service, and . . . Shall I confess it? my desire to behold once more the too amiable Don Christoval, will not permit my obeying her injunctions. I have therefore stolen a moment to inform you, that we lodge in the Strada di San Iago, four doors from the Palace d'Albornos, and nearly opposite to the Barber's Miguel Coello. Enquire for Donna Elvira Dalfa, since in compliance with her Father-in-law's order, my Sister continues to be called by her maiden name. At eight this evening you will be sure of finding us: But let not a word drop, which may raise a suspicion of my having written this letter. Should you see the Condé d'Ossorio, tell him . . . I blush while I declare it . . . Tell him that his presence will be but too acceptable to the sympathetic

Leonella.

The latter sentences were written in red ink, to express the blushes of her cheek, while She committed an outrage upon her virgin modesty.

Lorenzo had no sooner perused this note, than He set out in search of Don Christoval. Not being able to find him in the course of the day, He proceeded to Donna Elvira's alone to Leonella's infinite disappointment. The Domestic, by whom He sent up his name, having already declared his Lady to be at home, She had no excuse for refusing his visit: Yet She consented to receive it with much reluctance. That reluctance was increased by the changes which his approach produced in Antonia's countenance; nor was it by any means abated, when the Youth himself appeared. The symmetry of his person, animation of his features, and natural elegance of his manners and address, convinced Elvira that such a Guest must be dangerous for her Daughter. She resolved to treat him with distant politeness, to decline his services with gratitude for the tender of them, and to make him feel, without offence, that his future visits would be far from acceptable.

On his entrance He found Elvira who was indisposed, reclining upon a Sopha: Antonia sat by her embroidery frame, and Leonella, in a pastoral dress, held '*Montemayor's Diana*.'* In spite of her being the Mother of Antonia, Lorenzo could not help expecting to find in Elvira Leonella's true Sister, and the Daughter of 'as honest a pains-taking Shoe-maker, as any in Cordova.' A single glance was sufficient to undeceive him. He beheld a Woman whose features, though impaired by time and sorrow, still bore the marks of distinguished beauty: A serious dignity reigned upon her countenance, but was tempered by a grace and sweetness which rendered her truly enchanting. Lorenzo fancied that She must have resembled her Daughter in her youth, and readily excused the imprudence of the late Condé de las Cisternas. She desired him to be seated, and immediately resumed her place upon the Sopha.

Antonia received him with a simple reverence, and continued her work: Her cheeks were suffused with crimson, and She strove to conceal her emotion by leaning over her embroidery frame. Her Aunt also chose to play off her airs of modesty; She affected to blush and tremble, and waited with her eyes cast down to receive, as She expected, the compliments of Don Christoval. Finding after some time that no sign of his approach was given, She ventured to look round the room, and perceived with vexation that Medina was unaccompanied. Impatience would not permit her waiting for an explanation: Interrupting Lorenzo, who was delivering Raymond's message, She desired to know what was become of his Friend.

He, who thought it necessary to maintain himself in her good graces, strove to console her under her disappointment by committing a little violence upon truth.

'Ah! Segnora,' He replied in a melancholy voice 'How grieved will He be at losing this opportunity of paying you his respects! A Relation's illness has obliged him to quit Madrid in haste: But on his return, He will doubtless seize the first moment with transport to throw himself at your feet!'

As He said this, his eyes met those of Elvira: She punished his falsehood sufficiently by darting at him a look expressive of displeasure and reproach. Neither did the deceit answer his intention. Vexed and disappointed Leonella rose from her seat, and retired in dudgeon to her own apartment.

Lorenzo hastened to repair the fault, which had injured him in Elvira's opinion. He related his conversation with the Marquis respecting her: He assured her that Raymond was prepared to acknowledge her for his Brother's Widow; and that till it was in his power to pay his compliments to her in person, Lorenzo was commissioned to supply his place. This intelligence relieved Elvira from an heavy weight of uneasiness: She had now found a Protector for the fatherless Antonia, for whose future fortunes She had suffered the greatest apprehensions. She was not sparing of her thanks to him, who had interfered so generously in her behalf; But still She gave him no invitation to repeat his visit. However, when upon rising to depart He requested permission to enquire after her health occasionally, the polite earnestness of his manner, gratitude for his services, and respect for his Friend the Marquis, would not admit of a refusal. She consented reluctantly to receive him: He promised not to abuse her goodness, and quitted the House.

Antonia was now left alone with her Mother: A temporary silence ensued. Both wished to speak upon the same subject, but Neither knew how to introduce it. The one felt a bashfulness which sealed up her lips, and for which She could not account: The other feared to find her apprehensions true, or to inspire her Daughter with notions to which She might be still a Stranger. At length Elvira began the conversation.

'That is a charming young Man, Antonia; I am much pleased with him. Was He long near you yesterday in the Cathedral?'

'He quitted me not for a moment while I staid in the Church: He gave me his seat, and was very obliging and attentive.'

'Indeed? Why then have you never mentioned his name to me? Your Aunt lanched out in praise of his Friend, and you vaunted Ambrosio's eloquence: But Neither said a word of Don Lorenzo's person and accomplishments. Had not Leonella spoken of his readiness to undertake our cause, I should not have known him to be in existence.'

She paused. Antonia coloured, but was silent.

'Perhaps you judge him less favourably than I do. In my opinion his figure is pleasing, his conversation sensible, and manners engaging. Still He may have struck you differently: You may think him disagreeable, and . . .'.

'Disagreeable? Oh! dear Mother, how should I possibly think him so? I should be very ungrateful, were I not sensible of his kindness yesterday, and very blind if his merits had escaped me. His figure is so graceful, so noble! His manners so gentle, yet so manly! I never yet saw so many accomplishments united in one person, and I doubt whether Madrid can produce his equal.'

'Why then were you so silent in praise of this Phœnix of Madrid? Why was it concealed from me, that his society had afforded you pleasure?'

'In truth, I know not: You ask me a question, which I cannot resolve myself. I was on the point of mentioning him a thousand times: His name was constantly upon my lips, but when I would have pronounced it, I wanted courage to execute my design. However, if I did not speak of him, it was not that I thought of him the less.'

'That I believe; But shall I tell you why you wanted courage? It was because accustomed to confide to me your most secret thoughts, you knew not how to conceal, yet feared to acknowledge, that your heart nourished a sentiment, which you were conscious I should disapprove. Come hither to me, my Child.'

Antonia quitted her embroidery frame, threw herself upon her knees by the Sopha, and hid her face in her Mother's lap.

'Fear not, my sweet Girl! Consider me equally as your Friend and Parent, and apprehend no reproof from me. I have read the emotions of your bosom; you are yet ill skilled in concealing them, and they could not escape my attentive eye. This Lorenzo is dangerous to your repose; He has already made an impression upon your heart. 'Tis true, that I perceive easily that your affection is returned; But what can be the consequences of this attachment? You are poor and friendless, my Antonia; Lorenzo is the Heir of the Duke of Medina Celi. Even should Himself mean honourably, his Uncle never will consent to your union; Nor without that Uncle's consent, will I. By sad experience I know what sorrows She must endure, who marries into a family unwilling to receive her. Then struggle with your affection: Whatever pains it may cost you, strive to conquer it. Your heart is tender and susceptible: It has already received a strong impression; But when once convinced that you should not encourage such sentiments, I trust, that you have sufficient fortitude to drive them from your bosom.'

Antonia kissed her hand, and promised implicit obedience. Elvira then continued.

'To prevent your passion from growing stronger, it will be needful to prohibit Lorenzo's visits. The service which He has rendered me permits not my forbidding them positively; But unless I judge too favourably of his character, He will discontinue them without taking offence, if I confess to him my reasons, and throw myself entirely on his generosity. The next time that I see him, I will honestly avow to him the embarrassment which his presence occasions. How say you, my Child? Is not this measure necessary?'

Antonia subscribed to every thing without hesitation, though not without regret. Her Mother kissed her affectionately, and retired to bed. Antonia followed her example, and vowed so frequently never more to think of Lorenzo, that till Sleep closed her eyes She thought of nothing else.

While this was passing at Elvira's, Lorenzo hastened to rejoin the Marquis. Every thing was ready for the second elopement of Agnes; and at twelve the two Friends with a Coach and four were at the Garden-wall of the Convent. Don Raymond drew out his Key, and unlocked the door. They entered, and waited for some time in expectation of being joined by Agnes. At length the Marquis grew impatient: Beginning to fear that his second attempt would succeed no better than the first, He proposed to reconnoitre the Convent. The Friends advanced towards it. Every thing was still and dark. The Prioress was anxious to keep the story a secret, fearing lest the crime of one of its members should bring disgrace upon the whole community, or that the interposition of powerful Relations should deprive her vengeance of its intended victim. She took care therefore to give the Lover of Agnes no cause to suppose, that his design was discovered, and his Mistress on the point of suffering the punishment of her fault. The same reason made her reject the idea of arresting the unknown Seducer in the Garden; Such a proceeding would have created much disturbance, and the disgrace of her Convent would have been noised about Madrid. She contented herself with confining Agnes closely; As to the Lover She left him at liberty to pursue his designs. What She had expected was the result. The Marquis and Lorenzo waited in vain till the break of day: They then retired without noise, alarmed at the failure of their plan, and ignorant of the cause of its ill-success.

The next morning Lorenzo went to the Convent, and requested to see his Sister. The Prioress appeared at the Grate with a melancholy countenance: She informed him that for several days Agnes had appeared much agitated; That She had been prest by the Nuns in vain to reveal the cause, and apply to their tenderness for advice and consolation; That She had obstinately persisted in concealing the cause of her distress; But that on Thursday Evening it had produced so violent an effect upon her constitution, that She had fallen ill, and was actually confined to her bed. Lorenzo did not credit a syllable of this account: He insisted upon seeing his Sister; If She was unable to come to the Grate, He desired to be admitted to her Cell. The Prioress crossed herself! She was shocked at the very idea of a Man's profane eye pervading the interior of her holy Mansion, and professed herself astonished that Lorenzo could think of such a thing. She told him that his request could not be granted; But that if He returned the next day, She hoped that her beloved Daughter would then be sufficiently recovered to join him at the Parlour-grate.

With this answer Lorenzo was obliged to retire, unsatisfied and trembling for his Sister's safety.

He returned the next morning at an early hour. 'Agnes was worse; The Physician had pronounced her to be in imminent danger; She was ordered to remain quiet, and it was utterly impossible for her to receive her Brother's visit.' Lorenzo stormed at this answer, but there was no resource. He raved, He entreated, He threatened: No means were left untried to obtain a sight of Agnes. His endeavours were as fruitless as those of the day before, and He returned in despair to the Marquis. On his side, the Latter had spared no pains to discover what had occasioned his plot to fail: Don Christoval to whom the affair was now entrusted, endeavoured to worm out the secret from the Old Porteress of St. Clare, with whom He had formed an acquaintance; But She was too much upon her guard, and He gained from her no intelligence. The Marquis was almost distracted, and Lorenzo felt scarcely less inquietude. Both were convinced, that the purposed elopement must have been discovered: They doubted not but the malady of Agnes was a pretence, But they knew not by what means to rescue her from the hands of the Prioress.

Regularly every day did Lorenzo visit the Convent: As regularly was He informed that his Sister rather grew worse than better. Certain that her indisposition was feigned, these accounts did not alarm him: But his ignorance of her fate, and of the motives which induced the Prioress to keep her from him, excited the most serious uneasiness. He was still uncertain what steps He ought to take, when the Marquis received a letter from the Cardinal-Duke of Lerma. It inclosed the Pope's expected Bull, ordering that Agnes should be released from her vows, and restored to her Relations. This essential paper decided at once the proceedings of her Friends: They resolved that Lorenzo should carry it to the Domina without delay, and demand that his Sister should be instantly given up to him. Against this mandate illness could not be pleaded: It gave her Brother the power of removing her instantly to the Palace de Medina, and He determined to use that power on the following day.

His mind relieved from inquietude respecting his Sister, and his Spirits raised by the hope of soon restoring her to freedom, He now had time to give a few moments to love and to Antonia. At the same hour as on his former visit He repaired to Donna Elvira's: She had given orders for his admission. As soon as He was announced, her Daughter retired with Leonella, and when He entered the chamber, He found the Lady of the House alone. She received him with less distance than before, and desired him to place himself near her upon the Sopha. She then without losing time opened her business, as had been agreed between herself and Antonia.

'You must not think me ungrateful, Don Lorenzo, or forgetful how essential are the services, which you have rendered me with the Marquis. I feel the weight of my obligations; Nothing under the Sun should induce my taking the step to which I am now compelled, but the interest of my Child, of my beloved Antonia. My health is declining; God only knows, how soon I may be summoned before his Throne. My Daughter will be left without Parents, and should She lose the protection of the Cisternas family, without Friends. She is young and artless, uninstructed in the world's perfidy, and with charms sufficient to render her an object of seduction. Judge then, how I must tremble at the prospect before her! Judge, how anxious I must be to keep her from their society, who may excite the yet dormant passions of her bosom. You are amiable, Don Lorenzo: Antonia has a susceptible, a loving heart, and is grateful for the favours conferred upon us by your interference with the Marquis. Your presence makes me tremble: I fear, lest it should inspire her with sentiments which may embitter the remainder of her life, or encourage her to cherish hopes in her situation unjustifiable and futile. Pardon me, when I avow my terrors, and let my frankness plead in my excuse. I cannot forbid you my House, for gratitude restrains me; I can only throw myself upon your generosity, and entreat you to spare the feelings of an anxious, of a doting Mother. Believe me when I assure you, that I lament the necessity of rejecting your acquaintance; But there is no remedy, and Antonia's interest obliges me to beg you to forbear your visits. By complying with my request, you will increase the esteem which I already feel for you, and of which every thing convinces me, that you are truly deserving.'

'Your frankness charms me,' replied Lorenzo; 'You shall find, that in your favourable opinion of me you were not deceived. Yet I hope, that the reasons now in my power to allege, will persuade you to withdraw a request, which I cannot obey without infinite reluctance. I love your Daughter, love her most sincerely: I wish for no greater happiness than to inspire her with the same sentiments, and receive her hand at the Altar as her Husband. 'Tis true, I am not rich myself; My Father's death has left me but little in my own possession; But my expectations justify my pretending to the Condé de las Cisternas' Daughter.'

He was proceeding, but Elvira interrupted him.

'Ah! Don Lorenzo, you forget in that pompous title the meanness of my origin. You forget, that I have now past fourteen years in Spain, disavowed by my Husband's family, and existing upon a stipend barely sufficient for the support and education of my Daughter. Nay, I have even been neglected by most of my own Relations, who out of envy affect to doubt the reality of my marriage. My allowance being dis-continued at my Father-in-law's death, I was reduced to the very brink of want. In this situation I was found by my Sister, who amongst all her foibles possesses a warm, generous, and affectionate heart. She aided me with the little fortune which my Father left her, persuaded me to visit Madrid, and has supported my Child and myself since our quitting Murcia. Then consider not Antonia as descended from the Condé de la Cisternas: Consider her as a poor and unprotected Orphan, as the Grand-child of the Tradesman Torribio Dalfa, as the needy Pensioner of that Tradesman's Daughter. Reflect upon the difference between such a situation, and that of the Nephew and Heir of the potent Duke of Medina. I believe your intentions to be honourable; But as there are no hopes that your Uncle will approve of the union, I fore-see that the consequences of your attachment must be fatal to my Child's repose.'

'Pardon me, Segnora; You are mis-informed if you suppose the Duke of Medina to resemble the generality of Men. His sentiments are liberal and disinterested: He loves me well; and I have no reason to dread his forbidding the marriage, when He perceives that my happiness depends upon Antonia. But supposing him to refuse his sanction, what have I still to fear? My Parents are no more; My little fortune is in my own possession: It will be sufficient to support Antonia, and I shall exchange for her hand Medina's Dukedom without one sigh of regret.'

'You are young and eager; It is natural for you to entertain such ideas. But Experience has taught me to my cost, that curses accompany an unequal alliance. I married the Condé de las Cisternas in opposition to the will of his Relations; Many an heart-pang has punished me for the imprudent step. Where-ever we bent our course, a Father's execration pursued Gonzalvo. Poverty

over-took us, and no Friend was near to relieve our
wants. Still our mutual affection existed, but alas! not
without interruption. Accustomed to wealth and ease,
ill could my Husband support the transition to distress
and indigence. He looked back with repining to the
comforts which He once enjoyed. He regretted the
situation which for my sake He had quitted; and in
moments when Despair possessed his mind, has reproached me with having made him the Companion of
want and wretchedness! He has called me his bane! The
source of his sorrows, the cause of his destruction! Ah
God! He little knew, how much keener were my own
heart's reproaches! He was ignorant that I suffered
trebly, for myself, for my Children, and for him! 'Tis
true that his anger seldom lasted long: His sincere
affection for me soon revived in his heart; and then his
repentance for the tears which He had made me shed,
tortured me even more than his reproaches. He would
throw himself on the ground, implore my forgiveness in
the most frantic terms, and load himself with curses for
being the Murderer of my repose. Taught by experience
that an union contracted against the inclinations of
families on either side must be unfortunate, I will save
my Daughter from those miseries, which I have suffered.
Without your Uncle's consent, while I live, She never
shall be yours. Undoubtedly He will disapprove of the
union; His power is immense, and Antonia shall not be
exposed to his anger and persecution.'

'His persecution? How easily may that be avoided!
Let the worst happen, it is but quitting Spain. My
wealth may easily be realised; The Indian Islands will
offer us a secure retreat; I have an estate, though not of
value, in Hispaniola: Thither will we fly, and I shall
consider it to be my native Country, if it gives me
Antonia's undisturbed possession.'

'Ah! Youth, this is a fond romantic vision. Gonzalvo

thought the same. He fancied, that He could leave Spain without regret; But the moment of parting undeceived him. You know not yet what it is to quit your native land; to quit it, never to behold it more! You know not, what it is to exchange the scenes where you have passed your infancy, for unknown realms and barbarous climates! To be forgotten, utterly eternally forgotten by the Companions of your Youth! To see your dearest Friends, the fondest objects of your affection, perishing with diseases incidental to Indian atmospheres, and find yourself unable to procure for them necessary assistance! I have felt all this! My Husband and two sweet Babes found their Graves in Cuba: Nothing would have saved my young Antonia but my sudden return to Spain. Ah! Don Lorenzo, could you conceive what I suffered during my absence! Could you know, how sorely I regretted all that I left behind, and how dear to me was the very name of Spain! I envied the winds which blew towards it: And when the Spanish Sailor chaunted some well-known air as He past my window, tears filled my eyes, while I thought upon my native land. Gonzalvo too . . . My Husband . . .'.

Elvira paused. Her voice faltered, and She concealed her face with her hand-kerchief. After a short silence She rose from the Sopha, and proceeded.

'Excuse my quitting you for a few moments: The remembrance of what I have suffered has much agitated me, and I need to be alone. Till I return peruse these lines. After my Husband's death I found them among his papers; Had I known sooner that He entertained such sentiments, Grief would have killed me. He wrote these verses on his voyage to Cuba, when his mind was clouded by sorrow, and He forgot that He had a Wife and Children. What we are losing, ever seems to us the most precious: Gonzalvo was quitting Spain for ever, and therefore was Spain dearer to his eyes, than all else

which the World contained. Read them, Don Lorenzo;
They will give you some idea of the feelings of a banished
Man!'

Elvira put a paper into Lorenzo's hand, and retired
from the chamber. The Youth examined the contents,
and found them to be as follows.

THE EXILE

Farewell, Oh! native Spain! Farewell for ever!
   These banished eyes shall view thy coasts no more;
A mournful presage tells my heart, that never
   Gonzalvo's steps again shall press thy shore.

Hushed are the winds; While soft the Vessel sailing
   With gentle motion plows the unruffled Main,
I feel my bosom's boasted courage failing,
   And curse the waves which bear me far from Spain.

I see it yet! Beneath yon blue clear Heaven
   Still do the Spires, so well beloved, appear;
From yonder craggy point the gale of Even
   Still wafts my native accents to mine ear:

Propped on some moss-crowned Rock, and gaily singing,
   There in the Sun his nets the Fisher dries;
Oft have I heard the plaintive Ballad, bringing
   Scenes of past joys before my sorrowing eyes.

Ah! Happy Swain! He waits the accustomed hour,
   When twilight-gloom obscures the closing sky;
Then gladly seeks his loved paternal bower,
   And shares the feast his native fields supply:

Friendship and Love, his Cottage Guests, receive him
   With honest welcome and with smile sincere;
No threatening woes of present joys bereave him,
   No sigh his bosom owns, his cheek no tear.

Ah! Happy Swain! Such bliss to me denying,
    Fortune thy lot with envy bids me view;
Me, who from home and Spain an Exile flying,
    Bid all I value, all I love, adieu.

No more mine ear shall list the well-known ditty
    Sung by some Mountain-Girl, who tends her Goats,
Some Village-Swain imploring amorous pity,
    Or Shepherd chaunting wild his rustic notes:

No more my arms a Parent's fond embraces,
    No more my heart domestic calm, must know;
Far from these joys, with sighs which Memory traces,
    To sultry skies, and distant climes I go.

Where Indian Suns engender new diseases,
    Where snakes and tigers breed, I bend my way
To brave the feverish thirst no art appeases,
    The yellow plague, and madding blaze of day:

But not to feel slow pangs consume my liver,
    To die by piece-meal in the bloom of age,
My boiling blood drank by insatiate fever,
    And brain delirious with the day-star's rage,

Can make me know such grief, as thus to sever
    With many a bitter sigh, Dear Land, from Thee;
To feel this heart must doat on thee for ever,
    And feel, that all thy joys are torn from me!

Ah me! How oft will Fancy's spells in slumber
    Recall my native Country to my mind!
How oft regret will bid me sadly number
    Each lost delight and dear Friend left behind!

Wild Murcia's Vales, and loved romantic bowers,
    The River on whose banks a Child I played,
My Castle's antient Halls, its frowning Towers,
    Each much-regretted wood, and well-known Glade,

Dreams of the land where all my wishes centre,
  Thy scenes, which I am doomed no more to know,
Full oft shall Memory trace, my soul's Tormentor,
  And turn each pleasure past to present woe.

But Lo! The Sun beneath the waves retires;
  Night speeds apace her empire to restore:
Clouds from my sight obscure the village-spires,
  Now seen but faintly, and now seen no more.

Oh! breathe not, Winds! Still be the Water's motion!
  Sleep, sleep, my Bark, in silence on the Main!
So when to-morrow's light shall gild the Ocean,
  Once more mine eyes shall see the coast of Spain.

Vain is the wish! My last petition scorning,
  Fresh blows the Gale, and high the Billows swell:
Far shall we be before the break of Morning;
  Oh! then for ever, native Spain, farewell!

Lorenzo had scarcely time to read these lines, when Elvira returned to him: The giving a free course to her tears had relieved her, and her spirits had regained their usual composure.

'I have nothing more to say, my Lord,' said She; 'You have heard my apprehensions, and my reasons for begging you not to repeat your visits. I have thrown myself in full confidence upon your honour: I am certain, that you will not prove my opinion of you to have been too favourable.'

'But one question more, Segnora, and I leave you. Should the Duke of Medina approve my love, would my addresses be unacceptable to yourself and the fair Antonia?'

'I will be open with you, Don Lorenzo: There being little probability of such an union taking place, I fear that it is desired but too ardently by my Daughter. You have made an impression upon her young heart, which gives me the most serious alarm: To prevent that impression from growing stronger, I am obliged to decline your acquaintance. For me, you may be sure, that I should rejoice at establishing my Child so advantageously. Conscious that my constitution, impaired by grief and illness, forbids me to expect a long continuance in this world, I tremble at the thought of leaving her under the protection of a perfect Stranger. The Marquis de las Cisternas is totally unknown to me: He will marry; His Lady may look upon Antonia with an eye of displeasure, and deprive her of her only Friend. Should the Duke, your Uncle, give his consent, you need not doubt obtaining mine and my Daughter's: But without his, hope not for ours. At all events, what ever steps you may take, what ever may be the Duke's decision, till you know it let me beg your forbearing to strengthen by your presence Antonia's prepossession. If the sanction of your Relations authorises your addressing her as your Wife, my Doors fly open to you: If that sanction is refused, be satisfied to possess my esteem and gratitude, but remember, that we must meet no more.'

Lorenzo promised reluctantly to conform to this decree: But He added that He hoped soon to obtain that consent, which would give him a claim to the renewal of their acquaintance. He then explained to her why the Marquis had not called in person, and made no scruple of confiding to her his Sister's History. He concluded by saying, that He hoped to set Agnes at liberty the next day; and that as soon as Don Raymond's fears were quieted upon this subject, He would lose no time in assuring Donna Elvira of his friendship and protection.

The Lady shook her head.

'I tremble for your Sister,' said She; 'I have heard many traits of the Domina of St. Clare's character, from a Friend who was educated in the same Convent with

her. She reported her to be haughty, inflexible, superstitious, and revengeful. I have since heard, that She is
infatuated with the idea of rendering her Convent the
most regular in Madrid, and never forgave those whose
imprudence threw upon it the slightest stain. Though
naturally violent and severe, when her interests require
it, She well knows how to assume an appearance of
benignity. She leaves no means untried to persuade
young Women of rank to become Members of her
Community: She is implacable when once incensed, and
has too much intrepidity to shrink at taking the most
rigorous measures for punishing the Offender. Doubtless,
She will consider your Sister's quitting the Convent,
as a disgrace thrown upon it: She will use every artifice
to avoid obeying the mandate of his Holiness, and I
shudder to think, that Donna Agnes is in the hands of this
dangerous Woman.'

Lorenzo now rose to take leave. Elvira gave him her
hand at parting, which He kissed respectfully; and
telling her that He soon hoped for the permission to
salute that of Antonia, He returned to his Hotel. The
Lady was perfectly satisfied with the conversation, which
had past between them. She looked forward with satisfaction to the prospect of his becoming her Son-in-
law; But Prudence bad her conceal from her Daughter's
knowledge, the flattering hopes which Herself now ventured to entertain.

Scarcely was it day, and already Lorenzo was at the
Convent of St. Clare, furnished with the necessary
mandate. The Nuns were at Matins. He waited impatiently for the conclusion of the service, and at length
the Prioress appeared at the Parlour-Grate. Agnes was
demanded. The old Lady replied with a melancholy air,
that the dear Child's situation grew hourly more
dangerous; That the Physicians despaired of her life;
But that they had declared, the only chance for her

recovery to consist in keeping her quiet, and not to permit those to approach her whose presence was likely to agitate her. Not a word of all this was believed by Lorenzo, any more than He credited the expressions of grief and affection for Agnes, with which this account was interlarded. To end the business, He put the Pope's Bull into the hands of the Domina, and insisted, that ill or in health his Sister should be delivered to him without delay.

The Prioress received the paper with an air of humility: But no sooner had her eye glanced over the contents, than her resentment baffled all the efforts of Hypocrisy. A deep crimson spread itself over her face, and She darted upon Lorenzo looks of rage and menace.

'This order is positive,' said She in a voice of anger, which She in vain strove to disguise; 'Willingly would I obey it; But unfortunately it is out of my power.'

Lorenzo interrupted her by an exclamation of surprize.

'I repeat it, Segnor; to obey this order is totally out of my power. From tenderness to a Brother's feelings, I would have communicated the sad event to you by degrees, and have prepared you to hear it with fortitude. My measures are broken through: This order commands me to deliver up to you the Sister Agnes without delay; I am therefore obliged to inform you without circumlocution, that on Friday last She expired.'

Lorenzo started back with horror, and turned pale. A moment's recollection convinced him, that this assertion must be false, and it restored him to himself.

'You deceive me!' said He passionately; 'But five minutes past since you assured me, that though ill She was still alive. Produce her this instant! See her I must and will, and every attempt to keep her from me will be unavailing.'

'You forget yourself, Segnor; You owe respect to my

age as well as my profession. Your Sister is no more. If I at first concealed her death, it was from dreading, lest an event so unexpected should produce on you too violent an effect. In truth, I am but ill repaid for my attention. And what interest, I pray you, should I have in detaining her? To know her wish of quitting our society is a sufficient reason for me to wish her absence, and think her a disgrace to the Sister-hood of St. Clare: But She has forfeited my affection in a manner yet more culpable. Her crimes were great, and when you know the cause of her death, you will doubtless rejoice, Don Lorenzo, that such a Wretch is no longer in existence. She was taken ill on Thursday last on returning from confession in the Capuchin-Chapel. Her malady seemed attended with strange circumstances; But She persisted in concealing its cause: Thanks to the Virgin, we were too ignorant to suspect it! Judge then what must have been our consternation, our horror, when She was delivered the next day of a still-born Child, whom She immediately followed to the Grave. How, Segnor? Is it possible, that your countenance expresses no surprize, no indignation? Is it possible, that your Sister's infamy was known to you, and that still She possessed your affection? In that case, you have no need of my compassion. I can say nothing more, except repeat my inability of obeying the orders of his Holiness. Agnes is no more, and to convince you that what I say is true, I swear by our blessed Saviour, that three days have past since She was buried.'

Here She kissed a small crucifix, which hung at her girdle. She then rose from her chair, and quitted the Parlour. As She withdrew, She cast upon Lorenzo a scornful smile.

'Farewell, Segnor,' said She; 'I know no remedy for this accident: I fear that even a second Bull from the Pope will not procure your Sister's resurrection.'

Lorenzo also retired, penetrated with affliction: But Don Raymond's at the news of this event amounted to Madness. He would not be convinced that Agnes was really dead, and continued to insist, that the Walls of St. Clare still confined her. No arguments could make him abandon his hopes of regaining her: Every day some fresh scheme was invented for procuring intelligence of her, and all of them were attended with the same success.

On his part, Medina gave up the idea of ever seeing his Sister more: Yet He believed, that She had been taken off by unfair means. Under this persuasion, He encouraged Don Raymond's researches, determined, should He discover the least warrant for his suspicions, to take a severe vengeance upon the unfeeling Prioress. The loss of his Sister affected him sincerely; Nor was it the least cause of his distress, that propriety obliged him for some time to defer mentioning Antonia to the Duke. In the mean while his emissaries constantly surrounded Elvira's Door. He had intelligence of all the movements of his Mistress: As She never failed every Thursday to attend the Sermon in the Capuchin Cathedral, He was secure of seeing her once a week, though in compliance with his promise, He carefully shunned her observation. Thus two long Months passed away. Still no information was procured of Agnes: All but the Marquis credited her death; and now Lorenzo determined to disclose his sentiments to his Uncle. He had already dropt some hints of his intention to marry; They had been as favourably received as He could expect, and He harboured no doubt of the success of his application.

CHAPTER III

While in each other's arms entranced They lay,
They blessed the night, and curst the coming day.

Lee.*

THE BURST OF transport was past: Ambrosio's lust was satisfied; Pleasure fled, and Shame usurped her seat in his bosom. Confused and terrified at his weakness He drew himself from Matilda's arms. His perjury presented itself before him: He reflected on the scene which had just been acted, and trembled at the consequences of a discovery. He looked forward with horror; His heart was despondent, and became the abode of satiety and disgust. He avoided the eyes of his Partner in frailty; A melancholy silence prevailed, during which Both seemed busied with disagreable reflections.

Matilda was the first to break it. She took his hand gently, and pressed it to her burning lips.

'Ambrosio!' She murmured in a soft and trembling voice.

The Abbot started at the sound. He turned his eyes upon Matilda's: They were filled with tears; Her cheeks were covered with blushes, and her supplicating looks seemed to solicit his compassion.

'Dangerous Woman!' said He; 'Into what an abyss of misery have you plunged me! Should your sex be discovered, my honour, nay my life, must pay for the pleasure of a few moments. Fool that I was, to trust myself to your seductions! What can now be done? How can my offence be expiated? What atonement can purchase the pardon of my crime? Wretched Matilda, you have destroyed my quiet for ever!'

'To me these reproaches, Ambrosio? To me, who have sacrificed for you the world's pleasures, the luxury of wealth, the delicacy of sex, my Friends, my fortune, and my fame? What have you lost, which I preserved? Have *I* not shared in *your* guilt? Have *you* not shared in *my* pleasure? Guilt, did I say? In what consists ours, unless in the opinion of an ill-judging World? Let that World be ignorant of them, and our joys become divine and blameless! Unnatural were your vows of Celibacy; Man was not created for such a state; And were Love a crime, God never would have made it so sweet, so irresistible! Then banish those clouds from your brow, my Ambrosio! Indulge in those pleasures freely, without which life is a worthless gift: Cease to reproach me with having taught you, what is bliss, and feel equal transports with the Woman who adores you!'

As She spoke, her eyes were filled with a delicious languor. Her bosom panted: She twined her arms voluptuously round him, drew him towards her, and glewed her lips to his. Ambrosio again raged with desire: The die was thrown: His vows were already broken; He had already committed the crime, and why should He refrain from enjoying its reward? He clasped her to his breast with redoubled ardour. No longer repressed by the sense of shame, He gave a loose to his intemperate appetites: While the fair Wanton put every invention of lust in practice, every refinement in the art of pleasure, which might heighten the bliss of her possession, and render her Lover's transports still more exquisite. Ambrosio rioted in delights till then unknown to him: Swift fled the night, and the Morning blushed to behold him still clasped in the embraces of Matilda.

Intoxicated with pleasure, the Monk rose from the Syren's luxurious Couch.* He no longer reflected with shame upon his incontinence, or dreaded the vengeance of offended heaven. His only fear was, lest Death should rob him of enjoyments, for which his long Fast had only given a keener edge to his appetite. Matilda was still under the influence of poison, and the voluptuous Monk trembled less for his Preserver's life than his Concubine's. Deprived of her, He would not easily find another Mistress, with whom He could indulge his passions so fully, and so safely. He therefore pressed her with earnestness to use the means of preservation, which She had declared to be in her possession.

'Yes!' replied Matilda; 'Since you have made me feel that Life is valuable, I will rescue mine at any rate. No dangers shall appall me: I will look upon the consequences of my action boldly, nor shudder at the horrors which they present. I will think my sacrifice scarcely worthy to purchase your possession, and remember, that a moment past in your arms in *this* world, o'er-pays an age of punishment in the next. But before I take this step, Ambrosio, give me your solemn oath never to enquire, by what means I shall preserve myself.'

He did so in a manner the most binding.

'I thank you, my Beloved. This precaution is necessary, for though you know it not, you are under the command of vulgar prejudices: The Business on which I must be employed this night, might startle you from its singularity, and lower me in your opinion. Tell me; Are you possessed of the Key of the low door on the western side of the Garden?'

'The Door which opens into the burying-ground common to us and the Sister-hood of St. Clare?*I have not the Key, but can easily procure it.'

'You have only this to do. Admit me into the burying-ground at midnight; Watch while I descend into the vaults of St. Clare, lest some prying eye should observe my actions; Leave me there alone for an hour, and that life is safe, which I dedicate to your pleasures. To prevent creating suspicion do not visit me during the day.

Remember the Key, and that I expect you before twelve.
Hark! I hear steps approaching! Leave me; I will
pretend to sleep.'

The Friar obeyed, and left the Cell. As He opened the
door, Father Pablos made his appearance.

'I come,' said the Latter 'to enquire after the health of
my young Patient.'

'Hush!' replied Ambrosio, laying his finger upon his
lip; 'Speak softly; I am just come from him. He has
fallen into a profound slumber, which doubtless will be of
service to him. Do not disturb him at present, for He
wishes to repose.'

Father Pablos obeyed, and hearing the Bell ring,
accompanied the Abbot to Matins. Ambrosio felt
embarrassed, as He entered the Chapel. Guilt was new
to him, and He fancied that every eye could read the
transactions of the night upon his countenance. He
strove to pray; His bosom no longer glowed with devotion; His thoughts insensibly wandered to Matilda's
secret charms. But what He wanted in purity of heart,
He supplied by exterior sanctity. The better to cloak his
transgression, He redoubled his pretensions to the
semblance of virtue, and never appeared more devoted
to Heaven as since He had broken through his engagements. Thus did He unconsciously add Hypocrisy to
perjury and incontinence; He had fallen into the latter
errors from yielding to seduction almost irresistible; But
he was now guilty of a voluntary fault by endeavouring
to conceal those, into which Another had betrayed him.

The Matins concluded, Ambrosio retired to his Cell.
The pleasures which He had just tasted for the first time
were still impressed upon his mind. His brain was
bewildered, and presented a confused Chaos of remorse,
voluptuousness, inquietude, and fear. He looked back
with regret to that peace of soul, that security of virtue,
which till then had been his portion. He had indulged in

excesses whose very idea but four and twenty hours
before He had recoiled at with horror. He shuddered at
reflecting, that a trifling indiscretion on his part, or on
Matilda's, would overturn that fabric of reputation
which it had cost him thirty years to erect, and render
him the abhorrence of that People of whom He was then
the Idol. Conscience painted to him in glaring colours
his perjury and weakness; Apprehension magnified to
him the horrors of punishment, and He already fancied
himself in the prisons of the Inquisition. To these
tormenting ideas, succeeded Matilda's beauty, and those
delicious lessons, which once learnt can never be forgotten. A single glance thrown upon these reconciled
him with himself. He considered the pleasures of the
former night to have been purchased at an easy price by
the sacrifice of innocence and honour. Their very
remembrance filled his soul with ecstacy; He cursed his
foolish vanity, which had induced him to waste in
obscurity the bloom of life, ignorant of the blessings of
Love and Woman. He determined at all events to
continue his commerce with Matilda, and called every
argument to his aid, which might confirm his resolution.
He asked himself, provided his irregularity was unknown,
in what would his fault consist, and what consequences
He had to apprehend? By adhering strictly to every rule
of his order save Chastity, He doubted not to retain the
esteem of Men, and even the protection of heaven. He
trusted easily to be forgiven so slight and natural a
deviation from his vows: But He forgot that having
pronounced those vows, Incontinence, in Lay-men the
most venial of errors, became in his person the most
heinous of crimes.

Once decided upon his future conduct, his mind
became more easy. He threw himself upon his bed, and
strove by sleeping to recruit his strength exhausted by his
nocturnal excesses. He awoke refreshed, and eager for a

repetition of his pleasures. Obedient to Matilda's order, He visited not her Cell during the day. Father Pablos mentioned in the Refectory, that Rosario had at length been prevailed upon to follow his prescription; But that the medicine had not produced the slightest effect, and that He believed no mortal skill could rescue him from the Grave. With this opinion the Abbot agreed, and affected to lament the untimely fate of a Youth, whose talents had appeared so promising.

The night arrived. Ambrosio had taken care to procure from the Porter the Key of the low door opening into the Cemetery. Furnished with this, when all was silent in the Monastery, He quitted his Cell, and hastened to Matilda's. She had left her bed, and was drest before his arrival.

'I have been expecting you with impatience,' said She; 'My life depends upon these moments. Have you the Key?'

'I have.'

'Away then to the garden. We have no time to lose. Follow me!'

She took a small covered Basket from the Table. Bearing this in one hand, and the Lamp, which was flaming upon the Hearth, in the other, She hastened from the Cell. Ambrosio followed her. Both maintained a profound silence. She moved on with quick but cautious steps, passed through the Cloisters, and reached the Western side of the Garden. Her eyes flashed with a fire and wildness, which impressed the Monk at once with awe and horror. A determined desperate courage reigned upon her brow. She gave the Lamp to Ambrosio; Then taking from him the Key, She unlocked the low Door, and entered the Cemetery. It was a vast and spacious Square planted with yew-trees: Half of it belonged to the Abbey; The other half was the property of the Sister-hood of St. Clare, and was protected by a roof of Stone. The Division was marked by an iron railing, the wicket of which was generally left unlocked.

Thither Matilda bent her course. She opened the wicket, and sought for the door leading to the subterraneous Vaults, where reposed the mouldering Bodies of the Votaries of St. Clare. The night was perfectly dark; Neither Moon or Stars were visible. Luckily there was not a breath of Wind, and the Friar bore his Lamp in full security: By the assistance of its beams, the door of the Sepulchre was soon discovered. It was sunk within the hollow of a wall, and almost concealed by thick festoons of ivy hanging over it. Three steps of rough-hewn Stone conducted to it, and Matilda was on the point of descending them, when She suddenly started back.

'There are People in the Vaults!' She whispered to the Monk; 'Conceal yourself till they are past.

She took refuge behind a lofty and magnificent Tomb, erected in honour of the Convent's Foundress. Ambrosio followed her example, carefully hiding his Lamp, lest its beams should betray them. But a few moments had elapsed when the Door was pushed open leading to the subterraneous Caverns. Rays of light proceeded up the Stair-case: They enabled the concealed Spectators to observe two Females drest in religious habits, who seemed engaged in earnest conversation. The Abbot had no difficulty to recognize the Prioress of St. Clare in the first, and one of the elder Nuns in her Companion.

'Every thing is prepared,' said the Prioress; 'Her fate shall be decided to-morrow. All her tears and sighs will be unavailing. No! In five and twenty years that I have been Superior of this Convent, never did I witness a transaction more infamous!'

'You must expect much opposition to your will;' the Other replied in a milder voice; 'Agnes has many Friends in the Convent, and in particular the Mother

St. Ursula will espouse her cause most warmly. In truth, She merits to have Friends; and I wish, I could prevail upon you to consider her youth, and her peculiar situation. She seems sensible of her fault; The excess of her grief proves her penitence, and I am convinced that her tears flow more from contrition, than fear of punishment. Reverend Mother, would you be persuaded to mitigate the severity of your sentence, would you but deign to over-look this first transgression, I offer myself as the pledge of her future conduct.'

'Over-look it, say you? Mother Camilla, you amaze me! What? After disgracing me in the presence of Madrid's Idol, of the very Man on whom I most wished to impress an idea of the strictness of my discipline? How despicable must I have appeared to the reverend Abbot! No, Mother, No! I never can forgive the insult. I cannot better convince Ambrosio that I abhor such crimes, than by punishing that of Agnes with all the rigour of which our severe laws admit. Cease then your supplications; They will all be unavailing. My resolution is taken: To-morrow Agnes shall be made a terrible example of my justice and resentment.'

The Mother Camilla seemed not to give up the point, but by this time the Nuns were out of hearing. The Prioress unlocked the door which communicated with St. Clare's Chapel, and having entered with her Companion closed it again after them.

Matilda now asked, who was this Agnes with whom the Prioress was thus incensed, and what connexion She could have with Ambrosio. He related her adventure; and He added, that since that time his ideas having undergone a thorough revolution, He now felt much compassion for the unfortunate Nun.

'I design,' said He, 'to request an audience of the Domina to-morrow, and use every means of obtaining a mitigation of her sentence.'

'Beware of what you do!' interrupted Matilda; 'Your sudden change of sentiment may naturally create surprize, and may give birth to suspicions which it is most our interest to avoid. Rather redouble your outward austerity, and thunder out menaces against the errors of others, the better to conceal your own. Abandon the Nun to her fate. Your interfering might be dangerous, and her imprudence merits to be punished: She is unworthy to enjoy Love's pleasures, who has not wit enough to conceal them. But in discussing this trifling subject I waste moments which are precious. The night flies apace, and much must be done before morning. The Nuns are retired; All is safe. Give me the Lamp, Ambrosio. I must descend alone into these Caverns: Wait here, and if any one approaches, warn me by your voice; But as you value your existence, presume not to follow me. Your life would fall a victim to your imprudent curiosity.'

Thus saying She advanced towards the Sepulchre, still holding her Lamp in one hand, and her little Basket in the other. She touched the door: It turned slowly upon its grating hinges, and a narrow winding stair-case of black marble presented itself to her eyes. She descended it. Ambrosio remained above, watching the faint beams of the Lamp, as they still proceeded up the stairs. They disappeared, and He found himself in total darkness.

Left to himself He could not reflect without surprize on the sudden change in Matilda's character and sentiments. But a few days had past, since She appeared the mildest and softest of her sex, devoted to his will, and looking up to him as to a superior Being. Now She assumed a sort of courage and manliness in her manners and discourse but ill calculated to please him. She spoke no longer to insinuate, but command: He found himself unable to cope with her in argument, and was un-

willingly obliged to confess the superiority of her judgment. Every moment convinced him of the astonishing
powers of her mind: But what She gained in the opinion
of the Man, She lost with interest in the affection of the
Lover. He regretted Rosario, the fond, the gentle, and
submissive: He grieved, that Matilda preferred the
virtues of his sex to those of her own; and when He
thought of her expressions respecting the devoted Nun,
He could not help blaming them as cruel and unfeminine.
Pity is a sentiment so natural, so appropriate to the
female character, that it is scarcely a merit for a Woman
to possess it, but to be without it is a grievous crime.
Ambrosio could not easily forgive his Mistress for being
deficient in this amiable quality. However, though he
blamed her insensibility, He felt the truth of her observations; and though He pitied sincerely the unfortunate
Agnes, He resolved to drop the idea of interposing in her
behalf.

Near an hour had elapsed, since Matilda descended
into the Caverns; Still She returned not. Ambrosio's
curiosity was excited. He drew near the Stair-case. He
listened. All was silent, except that at intervals He caught
the sound of Matilda's voice, as it wound along the
subteraneous passages, and was re-echoed by the
Sepulchre's vaulted roofs. She was at too great a distance
for him to distinguish her words, and ere they reached
him they were deadened into a low murmur. He longed
to penetrate into this mystery. He resolved to disobey her
injunctions, and follow her into the Cavern. He advanced
to the Stair-case; He had already descended some steps,
when his courage failed him. He remembered Matilda's
menaces if He infringed her orders, and his bosom was
filled with a secret unaccountable awe. He returned up
the stairs, resumed his former station, and waited
impatiently for the conclusion of this adventure.

Suddenly He was sensible of a violent shock: An

earth-quake rocked the ground. The Columns, which supported the roof under which He stood, were so strongly shaken, that every moment menaced him with its fall, and at the same moment He heard a loud and tremendous burst of thunder. It ceased, and his eyes being fixed upon the Stair-case, He saw a bright column of light flash along the Caverns beneath. It was seen but for an instant. No sooner did it disappear, than all was once more quiet and obscure. Profound Darkness again surrounded him, and the silence of night was only broken by the whirring Bat, as She flitted slowly by him.

With every instant Ambrosio's amazement increased. Another hour elapsed, after which the same light again appeared and was lost again as suddenly. It was accompanied by a strain of sweet but solemn Music, which as it stole through the Vaults below, inspired the Monk with mingled delight and terror. It had not long been hushed, when He heard Matilda's steps upon the Stair-case. She ascended from the Cavern; The most lively joy animated her beautiful features.

'Did you see any thing?' She asked.

'Twice I saw a column of light flash up the Stair-case.'

'Nothing else?'

'Nothing.'

'The Morning is on the point of breaking. Let us retire to the Abbey, lest day-light should betray us.'

With a light step She hastened from the burying-ground. She regained her Cell, and the curious Abbot still accompanied her. She closed the door, and disembarrassed herself of her Lamp and Basket.

'I have succeeded!' She cried, throwing herself upon his bosom: 'Succeeded beyond my fondest hopes! I shall live, Ambrosio, shall live for you! The step, which I shuddered at taking, proves to me a source of joys inexpressible! Oh! that I dared communicate those joys to you! Oh! that I were permitted to share with you my power, and raise you as high above the level of your sex, as one bold deed has exalted me above mine!'

'And what prevents you, Matilda?' interrupted the Friar; 'Why is your business in the Cavern made a secret? Do you think me undeserving of your confidence? Matilda, I must doubt the truth of your affection, while you have joys in which I am forbidden to share.'

'You reproach me with injustice. I grieve sincerely, that I am obliged to conceal from you my happiness. But I am not to blame: The fault lies not in me, but in yourself, my Ambrosio! You are still too much the Monk. Your mind is enslaved by the prejudices of Education; And Superstition might make you shudder at the idea of that, which experience has taught me to prize and value. At present you are unfit to be trusted with a secret of such importance: But the strength of your judgment; and the curiosity which I rejoice to see sparkling in your eyes, makes me hope, that you will one day deserve my confidence. Till that period arrives, restrain your impatience. Remember that you have given me your solemn oath, never to enquire into this night's adventures. I insist upon your keeping this oath: For though' She added smiling, while She sealed his lips with a wanton kiss; 'Though I forgive your breaking your vows to heaven, I expect you to keep your vows to me.'

The Friar returned the embrace, which had set his blood on fire. The luxurious and unbounded excesses of the former night were renewed, and they separated not till the Bell rang for Matins.*

The same pleasures were frequently repeated. The Monks rejoiced in the feigned Rosario's unexpected recovery, and none of them suspected his real sex. The Abbot possessed his Mistress in tranquillity, and perceiving his frailty unsuspected, abandoned himself to his passions in full security. Shame and remorse no longer tormented him. Frequent repetitions made him familiar with sin, and his bosom became proof against the stings of Conscience. In these sentiments He was encouraged by Matilda; But She soon was aware that She had satiated her Lover by the unbounded freedom of her caresses. Her charms becoming accustomed to him, they ceased to excite the same desires, which at first they had inspired. The delirium of passion being past, He had leisure to observe every trifling defect: Where none were to be found, Satiety made him fancy them. The Monk was glutted with the fullness of pleasure: A Week had scarcely elapsed, before He was wearied of his Paramour: His warm constitution still made him seek in her arms the gratification of his lust: But when the moment of passion was over, He quitted her with disgust, and his humour, naturally inconstant, made him sigh impatiently for variety.

Possession, which cloys Man, only increases the affection of Woman. Matilda with every succeeding day grew more attached to the Friar. Since He had obtained her favours, He was become dearer to her than ever, and She felt grateful to him for the pleasures, in which they had equally been Sharers. Unfortunately as her passion grew ardent, Ambrosio's grew cold; The very marks of her fondness excited his disgust, and its excess served to extinguish the flame, which already burned but feebly in his bosom. Matilda could not but remark that her society seemed to him daily less agreeable: He was inattentive while She spoke: her musical talents, which She possessed in perfection, had lost the power of amusing him; Or if He deigned to praise them, his compliments were evidently forced and cold. He no longer gazed upon her with affection, or applauded her sentiments with a Lover's partiality. This Matilda well perceived, and redoubled her efforts to revive those sentiments, which He once had felt. She could not but fail, since He considered as importunities, the pains which She took to please him, and was disgusted by the very means which She used to recall the Wanderer. Still, however, their illicit Commerce continued: But it was clear, that He was led to her arms, not by love, but the cravings of brutal appetite. His constitution made a Woman necessary to him, and Matilda was the only one with whom He could indulge his passions safely: In spite of her beauty, He gazed upon every other Female with more desire; But fearing that his Hypocrisy should be made public, He confined his inclinations to his own breast.

It was by no means his nature to be timid: But his education had impressed his mind with fear so strongly, that apprehension was now become part of his character. Had his Youth been passed in the world, He would have shown himself possessed of many brilliant and manly qualities. He was naturally enterprizing, firm, and fearless: He had a Warrior's heart, and He might have shone with splendour at the head of an Army. There was no want of generosity in his nature: The Wretched never failed to find in him a compassionate Auditor: His abilities were quick and shining, and his judgment· vast, solid, and decisive. With such qualifications He would have been an ornament to his Country: That He possessed them, He had given proofs in his earliest infancy, and his Parents had beheld his dawning virtues with the fondest delight and admiration. Unfortunately, while yet a Child He was deprived of those Parents. He fell into the power of a Relation, whose only wish about him was never to hear of him more; For that purpose He gave him in charge to his Friend, the former Superior of the Capuchins. The Abbot, a very Monk, used all his endeavours to persuade the Boy, that happiness existed not without the walls of a Convent. He succeeded fully.

To deserve admittance into the order of St. Francis was Ambrosio's highest ambition. His Instructors carefully repressed those virtues, whose grandeur and disinterestedness were ill-suited to the Cloister. Instead of universal benevolence He adopted a selfish partiality for his own particular establishment: He was taught to consider compassion for the errors of Others as a crime of the blackest dye: The noble frankness of his temper was exchanged for servile humility; and in order to break his natural spirit, the Monks terrified his young mind, by placing before him all the horrors with which Superstition could furnish them: They painted to him the torments of the Damned in colours the most dark, terrible, and fantastic, and threatened him at the slightest fault with eternal perdition. No wonder, that his imagination constantly dwelling upon these fearful objects should have rendered his character timid and apprehensive. Add to this, that his long absence from the great world, and total unacquaintance with the common dangers of life made him form of them an idea far more dismal than the reality. While the Monks were busied in rooting out his virtues, and narrowing his sentiments, they allowed every vice which had fallen to his share, to arrive at full perfection. He was suffered to be proud, vain, ambitious, and disdainful: He was jealous of his Equals, and despised all merit but his own: He was implacable when offended, and cruel in his revenge. Still in spite of the pains taken to pervert them, his natural good qualities would occasionally break through the gloom cast over them so carefully: At such times the contest for superiority between his real and acquired character was striking and unaccountable to those unacquainted with his original disposition. He pronounced the most severe sentences upon Offenders, which the moment after Compassion induced him to mitigate: He undertook the most daring enterprizes, which the fear of their consequences soon obliged him to abandon: His in-born genius darted a brilliant light upon subjects the most obscure; and almost instantaneously his Superstition replunged them in darkness more profound than that from which they had just been rescued. His Brother Monks, regarding him as a Superior Being, remarked not this contradiction in their Idol's conduct. They were persuaded, that what He did must be right, and supposed him to have good reasons for changing his resolutions. The fact was, that the different sentiments, with which Education and Nature had inspired him, were combating in his bosom: It remained for his passions which as yet no opportunity had called into play, to decide the victory. Unfortunately his passions were the very worst Judges, to whom He could possibly have applied. His monastic seclusion had till now been in his favour, since it gave him no room for discovering his bad qualities. The superiority of his talents raised him too far above his Companions to permit his being jealous of them: His exemplary piety, persuasive eloquence, and pleasing manners had secured him universal Esteem, and consequently He had no injuries to revenge: His Ambition was justified by his acknowledged merit, and his pride considered as no more than proper confidence. He never saw, much less conversed with, the other sex: He was ignorant of the pleasures in Woman's power to bestow, and if He read in the course of his studies

'That Men were fond, He smiled, and wondered how!'*

For a time spare diet, frequent watching, and severe penance cooled and represt the natural warmth of his constitution: But no sooner did opportunity present itself, no sooner did He catch a glimpse of joys to which He was still a Stranger, than Religion's barriers were too feeble to resist the over-whelming torrent of his desires.

All impediments yielded before the force of his temperament, warm, sanguine, and voluptuous in the excess. As
yet his other passions lay dormant; But they only needed
to be once awakened, to display themselves with
violence as great and irresistible.

He continued to be the admiration of Madrid. The
Enthusiasm created by his eloquence seemed rather to
increase than diminish. Every Thursday, which was the
only day when He appeared in public, the Capuchin-
Cathedral was crowded with Auditors, and his discourse
was always received with the same approbation. He was
named Confessor to all the chief families in Madrid; and
no one was counted fashionable, who was injoined
penance by any other than Ambrosio. In his resolution
of never stirring out of his Convent He still persisted.
This circumstance created a still greater opinion of his
sanctity and self-denial. Above all the Women sang forth
his praises loudly, less influenced by devotion than by
his noble countenance, majestic air, and well-turned
graceful figure. The Abbey-door was thronged with
Carriages from morning to night; and the noblest and
fairest Dames of Madrid confessed to the Abbot their
secret peccadilloes. The eyes of the luxurious Friar
devoured their charms: Had his Penitents consulted
those Interpreters, He would have needed no other·
means of expressing his desires. For his misfortune, they
were so strongly persuaded of his continence, that the
possibility of his harbouring indecent thoughts never
once entered their imaginations. The climate's heat, 'tis
well known, operates with no small influence upon the
constitutions of the Spanish Ladies:* But the most
abandoned would have thought it an easier task to
inspire with passion the marble Statue of St. Francis, than
the cold and rigid heart of the immaculate Ambrosio.

On his part, the Friar was little acquainted with the
depravity of the world; He suspected not, that but few

of his Penitents would have rejected his addresses. Yet had He been better instructed on this head, the danger attending such an attempt would have sealed up his lips in silence. He knew that it would be difficult for a Woman to keep a secret so strange and so important as his frailty; and He even trembled, lest Matilda should betray him. Anxious to preserve a reputation which was infinitely dear to him, He saw all the risque of committing it to the power of some vain giddy Female; and as the Beauties of Madrid affected only his senses without touching his heart, He forgot them as soon as they were out of his sight. The danger of discovery, the fear of being repulsed, the loss of reputation, all these considerations counselled him to stifle his desires: And though He now felt for it the most perfect indifference, He was necessitated to confine himself to Matilda's person.

One morning, the confluence of Penitents was greater than usual. He was detained in the Confessional Chair till a late hour. At length the crowd was dispatched, and He prepared to quit the Chapel, when two Females entered, and drew near him with humility. They threw up their veils, and the youngest entreated him to listen to her for a few moments. The melody of her voice, of that voice to which no Man ever listened without interest, immediately caught Ambrosio's attention. He stopped. The Petitioner seemed bowed down with affliction: Her cheeks were pale, her eyes dimmed with tears, and her hair fell in disorder over her face and bosom. Still her countenance was so sweet, so innocent, so heavenly, as might have charmed an heart less susceptible, than that which panted in the Abbot's breast. With more than usual softness of manner He desired her to proceed, and heard her speak as follows with an emotion, which increased every moment.

'Reverend Father, you see an Unfortunate, threatened with the loss of her dearest, of almost her only Friend!

My Mother, my excellent Mother lies upon the bed of sickness. A sudden and dreadful malady seized her last night; and so rapid has been its progress, that the Physicians despair of her life. Human aid fails me; Nothing remains for me but to implore the mercy of Heaven. Father, all Madrid rings with the report of your piety and virtue. Deign to remember my Mother in your prayers: Perhaps they may prevail on the Almighty to spare her; and should that be the case, I engage myself every Thursday in the next three Months to illuminate the Shrine of St. Francis in his honour.'

'So!' thought the Monk; 'Here we have a second Vincentio della Ronda. Rosario's adventure began thus,' and He wished secretly, that this might have the same conclusion.

He acceded to the request. The Petitioner returned him thanks with every mark of gratitude, and then continued.

'I have yet another favour to ask. We are Strangers in Madrid; My Mother needs a Confessor, and knows not to whom She should apply. We understand that you never quit the Abbey, and Alas! my poor Mother is unable to come hither! If you would have the goodness, reverend Father, to name a proper person, whose wise and pious consolations may soften the agonies of my Parent's death-bed, you will confer an everlasting favour upon hearts not ungrateful.'

With this petition also the Monk complied. Indeed, what petition would He have refused, if urged in such enchanting accents? The suppliant was so interesting! Her voice was so sweet, so harmonious! Her very tears became her, and her affliction seemed to add new lustre to her charms. He promised to send to her a Confessor that same Evening, and begged her to leave her address. The Companion presented him with a Card on which it was written, and then with-drew with the fair Petitioner, who pronounced before her departure a thousand benedictions on the Abbot's goodness. His eyes followed her out of the Chapel. It was not till She was out of sight that He examined the Card, on which He read the following words.

'Donna Elvira Dalfa, Strada di San Iago, four doors from the Palace d'Albornos.'

The Suppliant was no other than Antonia, and Leonella was her Companion. The Latter had not consented without difficulty to accompany her Niece to the Abbey: Ambrosio had inspired her with such awe, that She trembled at the very sight of him. Her fears had conquered even her natural loquacity, and while in his presence She uttered not a single syllable.

The Monk retired to his Cell, whither He was pursued by Antonia's image. He felt a thousand new emotions springing in his bosom, and He trembled to examine into the cause which gave them birth. They were totally different from those inspired by Matilda, when She first declared her sex and her affection. He felt not the provocation of lust; No voluptuous desires rioted in his bosom; Nor did a burning imagination picture to him the charms, which Modesty had veiled from his eyes. On the contrary, what He now felt was a mingled sentiment of tenderness, admiration, and respect. A soft and delicious melancholy infused itself into his soul, and He would not have exchanged it for the most lively transports of joy. Society now disgusted him: He delighted in solitude, which permitted his indulging the visions of Fancy: His thoughts were all gentle, sad, and soothing, and the whole wide world presented him with no other object than Antonia.

'Happy Man!' He exclaimed in his romantic enthusiasm; 'Happy Man, who is destined to possess the heart of that lovely Girl! What delicacy in her features! What elegance in her form! How enchanting was the

timid innocence of her eyes, and how different from the
wanton expression, the wild luxurious fire, which sparkles
in Matilda's! Oh! sweeter must one kiss be snatched from
the rosy lips of the First, than all the full and lustful
favours bestowed so freely by the Second. Matilda gluts
me with enjoyment even to loathing, forces me to her
arms, apes the Harlot, and glories in her prostitution.
Disgusting! Did She know the inexpressible charm of
Modesty, how irresistibly it enthralls the heart of Man,
how firmly it chains him to the Throne of Beauty, She
never would have thrown it off. What would be too dear
a price for this lovely Girl's affections? What would I
refuse to sacrifice, could I be released from my vows, and
permitted to declare my love in the sight of earth and
heaven? While I strove to inspire her with tenderness,
with friendship and esteem, how tranquil and undisturbed would the hours roll away! Gracious God! To
see her blue down-cast eyes beam upon mine with timid
fondness! To sit for days, for years listening to that
gentle voice! To acquire the right of obliging her, and
hear the artless expressions of her gratitude! To watch
the emotions of her spotless heart! To encourage each
dawning virtue! To share in her joy when happy, to kiss
away her tears when distrest, and to see her fly to my
arms for comfort and support! Yes; If there is perfect
bliss on earth, 'tis his lot alone, who becomes that
Angel's Husband.'

While his fancy coined these ideas, He paced his Cell
with a disordered air. His eyes were fixed upon vacancy:
His head reclined upon his shoulder; A tear rolled down
his cheek, while He reflected that the vision of happiness
for him could never be realized.

'She is lost to me!' He continued; 'By marriage She
cannot be mine: And to seduce such innocence, to use
the confidence reposed in me to work her ruin. . . . Oh!
it would be a crime, blacker than yet the world ever

witnessed! Fear not, lovely Girl! Your virtue runs no
risque from me. Not for Indies would I make that gentle
bosom know the tortures of remorse.'

Again He paced his chamber hastily. Then stopping,
his eye fell upon the picture of his once-admired Madona.
He tore it with indignation from the wall: He threw it
on the ground, and spurned it from him with his foot.
'The Prostitute!'

Unfortunate Matilda! Her Paramour forgot, that for
his sake alone She had forfeited her claim to virtue; and
his only reason for despising her was, that She had loved
him much too well.

He threw himself into a Chair, which stood near the
Table. He saw the card with Elvira's address. He took it
up, and it brought to his recollection his promise respecting a Confessor. He passed a few minutes in doubt: But
Antonia's Empire over him was already too much
decided to permit his making a long resistance to the idea
which struck him. He resolved to be the Confessor himself. He could leave the Abbey unobserved without
difficulty: By wrapping up his head in his Cowl He hoped
to pass through the Streets without being recognised:
By taking these precautions, and by recommending
secrecy to Elvira's family, He doubted not to keep
Madrid in ignorance that He had broken his vow never
to see the outside of the Abbey-walls. Matilda was the
only person whose vigilance He dreaded: But by informing her at the Refectory, that during the whole of that
day Business would confine him to his Cell, He thought
himself secure from her wakeful jealousy. Accordingly
at the hours when the Spaniards are generally taking
their Siesta, He ventured to quit the Abbey by a private
door, the Key of which was in his possession. The Cowl
of his habit was thrown over his face: From the heat of
the weather the Streets were almost totally deserted:
The Monk met with few people, found the Strada di

San Iago, and arrived without accident at Donna
Elvira's door. He rang, was admitted, and immediately
ushered into an upper apartment.

It was here, that He ran the greatest risque of a
discovery. Had Leonella been at home, She would have
recognized him directly: Her communicative disposition
would never have permitted her to rest, till all Madrid
was informed that Ambrosio had ventured out of the
Abbey, and visited her Sister. Fortune here stood the
Monk's Friend. On Leonella's return home, She found
a letter instructing her, that a Cousin was just dead, who
had left what little He possessed between Herself and
Elvira. To secure this bequest She was obliged to set out
for Cordova without losing a moment. Amidst all her
foibles her heart was truly warm and affectionate, and
She was unwilling to quit her Sister in so dangerous a
state. But Elvira insisted upon her taking the journey,
conscious that in her Daughter's forlorn situation no
increase of fortune, however trifling, ought to be
neglected. Accordingly Leonella left Madrid, sincerely
grieved at her Sister's illness, and giving some few sighs
to the memory of the amiable but inconstant Don
Christoval. She was fully persuaded, that at first She had
made a terrible breach in his heart: But hearing nothing
more of him, She supposed that He had quitted the
pursuit, disgusted by the lowness of her origin, and
knowing upon other terms than marriage He had nothing to hope from such a Dragon of Virtue as She
professed herself; Or else, that being naturally capricious
and changeable, the remembrance of her charms had
been effaced from the Condé's heart by those of some
newer Beauty. Whatever was the cause of her losing him,
She lamented it sorely. She strove in vain, as She assured
every body who was kind enough to listen to her, to tear
his image from her too susceptible heart. She affected
the airs of a love-sick Virgin, and carried them all to the

most ridiculous excess. She heaved lamentable sighs, walked with her arms folded, uttered long soliloquies, and her discourse generally turned upon some forsaken Maid, who expired of a broken heart! Her fiery locks were always ornamented with a garland of willow; Every evening She was seen straying upon the Banks of a rivulet by Moon-light; and She declared herself a violent Admirer of murmuring Streams and Nightingales;

'Of lonely haunts, and twilight Groves,
'Places which pale Passion loves!'*

Such was the state of Leonella's mind, when obliged to quit Madrid. Elvira was out of patience at all these follies, and endeavoured at persuading her to act like a reasonable Woman. Her advice was thrown away: Leonella assured her at parting, that nothing could make her forget the perfidious Don Christoval. In this point She was fortunately mistaken. An honest Youth of Cordova, Journeyman to an Apothecary, found that her fortune would be sufficient to set him up in a genteel Shop of his own: In consequence of this reflection He avowed himself her Admirer. Leonella was not inflexible. The ardour of his sighs melted her heart, and She soon consented to make him the happiest of Mankind. She wrote to inform her Sister of her marriage; But, for reasons which will be explained here-after, Elvira never answered her letter.

Ambrosio was conducted into the Anti-chamber to that, where Elvira was reposing. The Female Domestic who had admitted him, left him alone, while She announced his arrival to her Mistress. Antonia who had been by her Mother's Bed-side, immediately came to him.

'Pardon me, Father,' said She advancing towards him; when recognizing his features She stopped suddenly, and uttered a cry of joy. 'Is it possible!' She continued;

'Do not my eyes deceive me? Has the worthy Ambrosio broken through his resolution, that He may soften the agonies of the best of Women? What pleasure will this visit give my Mother! Let me not delay for a moment the comfort, which your piety and wisdom will afford her.'

Thus saying, She opened the chamber-door, presented to her Mother her distinguished Visitor, and having placed an armed-chair by the side of the Bed, withdrew into another department.

Elvira was highly gratified by this visit: Her expectations had been raised high by general report, but She found them far exceeded. Ambrosio, endowed by nature with powers of pleasing, exerted them to the utmost while conversing with Antonia's Mother. With persuasive eloquence He calmed every fear, and dissipated every scruple: He bad her reflect on the infinite mercy of her Judge, despoiled Death of his darts and terrors, and taught her to view without shrinking the abyss of eternity, on whose brink She then stood. Elvira was absorbed in attention and delight: While She listened to his exhortations, confidence and comfort stole insensibly into her mind. She unbosomed to him without hesitation her cares and apprehensions. The latter respecting a future life He had already quieted: And He now removed the former, which She felt for the concerns of this. She trembled for Antonia. She had none to whose care She could recommend her, save to the Marquis de las Cisternas, and her Sister Leonella. The protection of the One was very uncertain; and as to the Other, though fond of her Niece Leonella was so thoughtless and vain, as to make her an improper person to have the sole direction of a Girl so young and ignorant of the World. The Friar no sooner learnt the cause of her alarms, than He begged her to make herself easy upon that head. He doubted not being able to secure for

Antonia a safe refuge in the House of one of his Penitents, the Marchioness of Villa-Franca: This was a Lady of acknowledged virtue, remarkable for strict principles and extensive charity. Should accident deprive her of this resource, He engaged to procure Antonia a reception in some respectable Convent: That is to say, in quality of boarder; for Elvira had declared herself no Friend to a monastic life, and the Monk was either candid or complaisant enough to allow, that her disapprobation was not unfounded.

These proofs of the interest which He felt for her, completely won Elvira's heart. In thanking him She exhausted every expression which Gratitude could furnish, and protested, that now She should resign herself with tranquillity to the Grave. Ambrosio rose to take leave: He promised to return the next day at the same hour, but requested that his visits might be kept secret.

'I am unwilling' said He, 'that my breaking through a rule imposed by necessity, should be generally known. Had I not resolved never to quit my Convent, except upon circumstances as urgent as that which has conducted me to your door, I should be frequently summoned upon insignificant occasions: That time would be engrossed by the Curious, the Unoccupied, and the fanciful, which I now pass at the Bed-side of the Sick, in comforting the expiring Penitent, and clearing the passage to Eternity from Thorns.'

Elvira commended equally his prudence and compassion, promising to conceal carefully the honour of his visits. The Monk then gave her his benediction, and retired from the chamber.

In the Anti-room He found Antonia: He could not refuse himself the pleasure of passing a few moments in her society. He bad her take comfort, for that her Mother seemed composed and tranquil, and He hoped that She might yet do well. He enquired who attended her, and engaged to send the Physician of his Convent to see her, one of the most skilful in Madrid. He then launched out in Elvira's commendation, praised her purity and fortitude of mind, and declared, that She had inspired him with the highest esteem and reverence. Antonia's innocent heart swelled with gratitude: Joy danced in her eyes, where a tear still sparkled. The hopes which He gave her of her Mother's recovery, the lively interest which He seemed to feel for her, and the flattering way in which She was mentioned by him, added to the report of his judgment and virtue, and to the impression made upon her by his eloquence, confirmed the favourable opinion with which his first. appearance had inspired Antonia. She replied with diffidence, but without restraint: She feared·not to relate to him all her little sorrows, all her little fears and anxieties; and She thanked him for his goodness with all the genuine warmth, which favours kindle in a young and innocent heart. Such alone know how to estimate benefits at their full value. They who are conscious of Mankind's perfidy and selfishness, ever receive an obligation with apprehension and distrust: They suspect, that some secret motive must lurk behind it: They express their thanks with restraint and caution, and fear to praise a kind action to its full extent, aware that some future day a return may be required. Not so Antonia; She thought, the world was composed only of those who resembled her, and that vice existed was to her still a secret. The Monk had been of service to her; He said, that He wished her well; She was grateful for his kindness, and thought that no terms were strong enough to be the vehicle of her thanks. With what delight did Ambrosio listen to the declaration of her artless gratitude! The natural grace of her manners, the unequalled sweetness of her voice, her modest vivacity, her unstudied elegance, her expressive countenance, and intelligent eyes united to inspire him with pleasure and admiration: While the solidity and correctness of her remarks received additional beauty from the unaffected simplicity of the language, in which they were conveyed.

Ambrosio was at length obliged to tear himself from this conversation, which possessed for him but too many charms. He repeated to Antonia his wishes, that his visits should not be made known, which desire She promised to observe. He then quitted the House, while his Enchantress hastened to her Mother, ignorant of the mischief which her Beauty had caused. She was eager to know Elvira's opinion of the Man whom She had praised in such enthusiastic terms, and was delighted to find it equally favourable, if not even more so, than her own.

'Even before He spoke,' said Elvira, 'I was prejudiced in his favour: The fervour of his exhortations, dignity of his manner, and closeness of his reasoning, were very far from inducing me to alter my opinion. His fine and full-toned voice struck me particularly; But surely, Antonia, I have heard it before. It seemed perfectly familiar to my ear. Either I must have known the Abbot in former times, or his voice bears a wonderful resemblance to that of some other, to whom I have often listened. There were certain tones which touched my very heart, and made me feel sensations so singular, that I strive in vain to account for them.'

'My dearest Mother, it produced the same effect upon me: Yet certainly neither of us ever heard his voice till we came to Madrid. I suspect, that what we attribute to his voice, really proceeds from his pleasant manners, which forbid our considering him as a Stranger. I know not why, but I feel more at my ease while conversing with him, than I usually do with people who are unknown to me. I feared not to repeat to him all my childish thoughts; and some-how I felt confident that He would hear my folly with indulgence. Oh! I was not deceived in him! He listened to me with such an air of kindness and attention! He answered me with such gentleness, such condescension! He did not call me an Infant, and treat me with contempt, as our cross old Confessor at the Castle used to do. I verily believe, that if I had lived in Murcia a thousand years, I never should have liked that fat old Father Dominic!'

'I confess, that Father Dominic had not the most pleasing manners in the world; But He was honest, friendly, and well-meaning.'

'Ah! my dear Mother, those qualities are so common!'

'God grant, my Child, that Experience may not teach you to think them rare and precious: I have found them but too much so! But tell me, Antonia; Why is it impossible for me to have seen the Abbot before?'

'Because since the moment when He entered the Abbey, He has never been on the outside of its walls. He told me just now, that from his ignorance of the Streets, He had some difficulty to find the Strada di San Iago, though so near the Abbey.'

'All this is possible, and still I may have seen him *before* He entered the Abbey: In order to come out, it was rather necessary that He should first go in.'

'Holy Virgin! As you say, that is very true.—Oh! But might He not have been born in the Abbey?'

Elvira smiled.

'Why not very easily.'

'Stay, Stay! Now I recollect how it was. He was put into the Abbey quite a Child; The common People say, that He fell from heaven, and was sent as a present to the Capuchins by the Virgin.'

'That was very kind of her. And so He fell from heaven, Antonia? He must have had a terrible tumble.'

'Many do not credit this, and I fancy, my dear Mother, that I must number you among the Unbelievers. Indeed, as our Land-lady told my Aunt, the general idea is, that his Parents, being poor and unable to maintain him, left him just born at the Abbey-door. The late Superior from pure charity had him educated in the Convent, and He proved to be a model of virtue, and piety, and learning, and I know not what else besides: In consequence, He was first received as a Brother of the order, and not long ago was chosen Abbot. However, whether this account or the other is the true one, at least all agree that when the Monks took him under their care, He could not speak: Therefore, you could not have heard his voice before He entered the Monastery, because at that time He had no voice at all.'

'Upon my word, Antonia, you argue very closely! Your conclusions are infallible! I did not suspect you of being so able a Logician.'

'Ah! You are mocking me! But so much the better. It delights me to see you in spirits: Besides you seem tranquil and easy, and I hope, that you will have no more convulsions. Oh! I was sure the Abbot's visit would do you good!'

'It has indeed done me good, my Child. He has quieted my mind upon some points which agitated me, and I already feel the effects of his attention. My eyes grow heavy, and I think I can sleep a little. Draw the curtains, my Antonia: But if I should not wake before midnight, do not sit up with me, I charge you.'

Antonia promised to obey her, and having received her blessing drew the curtains of the Bed. She then seated herself in silence at her embroidery frame, and beguiled the hours with building Castles in the air. Her spirits were enlivened by the evident change for the better in Elvira, and her fancy presented her with visions bright and pleasing. In these dreams Ambrosio made no despicable figure. She thought of him with joy and gratitude; But for every idea which fell to the Friar's share, at least two were unconsciously bestowed upon

Lorenzo. Thus passed the time, till the Bell in the neighbouring Steeple of the Capuchin-Cathedral announced the hour of midnight: Antonia remembered her Mother's injunctions, and obeyed them, though with reluctance. She undrew the curtains with caution. Elvira was enjoying a profound and quiet slumber; Her cheek glowed with health's returning colours: A smile declared, that her dreams were pleasant, and as Antonia bent over her, She fancied that She heard her name pronounced. She kissed her Mother's fore-head softly, and retired to her chamber. There She knelt before a Statue of St. Rosolia,* her Patroness; She recommended herself to the protection of heaven, and as had been her custom from infancy, concluded her devotions by chaunting the following Stanzas.

MIDNIGHT HYMN

Now all is hushed; The solemn chime
No longer swells the nightly gale:
Thy awful presence, Hour sublime,
With spotless heart once more I hail.

'Tis now the moment still and dread,
When Sorcerers use their baleful power;
When Graves give up their buried dead
To profit by the sanctioned hour:

From guilt and guilty thoughts secure,
To duty and devotion true,
With bosom light and conscience pure,
Repose, thy gentle aid I woo.

Good Angels, take my thanks, that still
The snares of vice I view with scorn;
Thanks, that to-night as free from ill
I sleep, as when I woke at morn.

Yet may not my unconscious breast
Harbour some guilt to me unknown?
Some wish impure, which unreprest
You blush to see, and I to own?

If such there be, in gentle dream
Instruct my feet to shun the snare;
Bid truth upon my errors beam,
And deign to make me still your care.

Chase from my peaceful bed away
The witching Spell, a foe to rest,
The nightly Goblin, wanton Fay,
The Ghost in pain, and Fiend unblest:

Let not the Tempter in mine ear
Pour lessons of unhallowed joy;
Let not the Night-mare, wandering near
My Couch, the calm of sleep destroy;

Let not some horrid dream affright
With strange fantastic forms mine eyes;
But rather bid some vision bright
Display the bliss of yonder skies.

Show me the crystal Domes of Heaven,
The worlds of light where Angels lie;
Shew me the lot to Mortals given,
Who guiltless live, who guiltless die.

Then show me how a seat to gain
Amidst those blissful realms of Air;
Teach me to shun each guilty stain,
And guide me to the good and fair.

So every morn and night, my Voice
To heaven the grateful strain shall raise;
In You as Guardian Powers rejoice,
Good Angels, and exalt your praise:

So will I strive with zealous fire
Each vice to shun, each fault correct;
Will love the lessons you inspire,
And Prize the virtues you protect.

Then when at length by high command
My body seeks the Grave's repose,
When Death draws nigh with friendly hand
My failing Pilgrim eyes to close;

Pleased that my soul has 'scaped the wreck,
Sighless will I my life resign,
And yield to God my Spirit back,
As pure as when it first was mine.

Having finished her usual devotions, Antonia retired
to bed. Sleep soon stole over her senses; and for several
hours She enjoyed that calm repose which innocence
alone can know, and for which many a Monarch with
pleasure would exchange his Crown.

CHAPTER IV

―――Ah! how dark
These long-extended realms and rueful wastes;
Where nought but silence reigns, and night, dark night,
Dark as was Chaos ere the Infant Sun
Was rolled together, or had tried its beams
Athwart the gloom profound! The sickly Taper
By glimmering through thy low-browed misty vaults,
Furred round with mouldy damps, and ropy slime,
Lets fall a supernumerary horror,
And only serves to make Thy night more irksome!

                                        Blair.*

RETURNED UNDISCOVERED TO the Abbey, Ambrosio's mind was filled with the most pleasing images. He was wilfully blind to the danger of exposing himself to Antonia's charms: He only remembered the pleasure which her society had afforded him, and rejoiced in the prospect of that pleasure being repeated. He failed not to profit by Elvira's indisposition to obtain a sight of her Daughter every day. At first He bounded his wishes to inspire Antonia with friendship: But no sooner was He convinced that She felt that sentiment in its fullest extent, than his aim became more decided, and his attentions assumed a warmer colour. The innocent familiarity with which She treated him, encouraged his desires: Grown used to her modesty, it no longer commanded the same respect and awe: He still admired it, but it only made him more anxious to deprive her of that quality, which formed her principal charm. Warmth of passion, and natural penetration, of which latter unfortunately both for himself and Antonia He possessed an ample share, supplied a knowledge of the arts of seduction. He easily distinguished the emotions which were favourable to his designs, and seized every means with avidity of infusing corruption into Antonia's bosom. This He found no easy matter. Extreme simplicity prevented her from perceiving the aim to which the Monk's insinuations tended; But the excellent morals which She owed to Elvira's care, the solidity and correctness of her understanding, and a strong sense of what was right implanted in her heart by Nature, made her feel that his precepts must be faulty. By a few simple words She frequently overthrew the whole bulk of his sophistical arguments, and made him conscious how weak they were when opposed to Virtue and Truth. On such occasion He took refuge in his eloquence; He over-powered her with a torrent of Philosophical paradoxes, to which, not understanding them, it was impossible for her to reply; And thus though He did not convince her that his reasoning was just, He at least prevented her from discovering it to be false. He perceived that her respect for his judgment augmented daily, and doubted not with time to bring her to the point desired.

He was not unconscious, that his attempts were highly criminal: He saw clearly the baseness of seducing the innocent Girl: But his passion was too violent to permit his abandoning his design. He resolved to pursue it, let the consequences be what they might. He depended upon finding Antonia in some unguarded moment; And seeing no other Man admitted into her society, nor hearing any mentioned either by her or by Elvira, He imagined that her young heart was still unoccupied. While He waited for the opportunity of satisfying his unwarrantable lust, every day increased his coldness for Matilda. Not a little was this occasioned by the consciousness of his faults to her. To hide them from her He was not sufficiently master of himself: Yet He dreaded, lest in a transport of jealous rage She should betray the secret, on which his character and even his life depended.

Matilda could not but remark his indifference: He was conscious that She remarked it, and fearing her reproaches shunned her studiously. Yet when He could not avoid her, her mildness might have convinced him that He had nothing to dread from her resentment. She had resumed the character of the gentle interesting Rosario: She taxed him not with ingratitude; But her eyes filled with involuntary tears, and the soft melancholy of her countenance and voice uttered complaints far more touching than words could have conveyed. Ambrosio was not unmoved by her sorrow; But unable to remove its cause, He forbore to show that it affected him. As her conduct convinced him that He needed not fear her vengeance, He continued to neglect her, and avoided her company with care. Matilda saw, that She in vain attempted to regain his affections: Yet She stifled the impulse of resentment, and continued to treat her inconstant Lover with her former fondness and attention.

By degrees Elvira's constitution recovered itself. She was no longer troubled with convulsions, and Antonia ceased to tremble for her Mother. Ambrosio beheld this re-establishment with displeasure. He saw, that Elvira's knowledge of the world would not be the Dupe of his sanctified demeanour, and that She would easily perceive his views upon her Daughter. He resolved therefore, before She quitted her chamber, to try the extent of his influence over the innocent Antonia.

One evening, when He had found Elvira almost perfectly restored to health, He quitted her earlier than was his usual custom. Not finding Antonia in the Anti-Chamber, He ventured to follow her to her own. It was only separated from her Mother's by a Closet, in which Flora, the Waiting-Woman, generally slept. Antonia sat upon a Sopha with her back towards the door, and read attentively. She heard not his approach, till He had seated himself by her. She started, and welcomed him with a look of pleasure: Then rising, She would have conducted him to the sitting-room; But Ambrosio taking her hand, obliged her by gentle violence to resume her place. She complied without difficulty: She knew not, that there was more impropriety in conversing with him in one room than another. She thought herself equally secure of his principles and her own, and having replaced herself upon the Sopha, She began to prattle to him with her usual ease and vivacity.

He examined the Book which She had been reading, and had now placed upon the Table. It was the Bible.

'How!' said the Friar to himself; 'Antonia reads the Bible, and is still so ignorant?'

But, upon a further inspection, He found that Elvira had made exactly the same remark. That prudent Mother, while She admired the beauties of the sacred writings, was convinced, that unrestricted no reading more improper could be permitted a young Woman. Many of the narratives can only tend to excite ideas the worst calculated for a female breast: Every thing is called plainly and roundly by its name; and the annals of a Brothel would scarcely furnish a greater choice of indecent expressions. Yet this is the Book, which young Women are recommended to study; which is put into the hands of Children, able to comprehend little more than those passages of which they had better remain ignorant; and which but too frequently inculcates the first rudiments of vice, and gives the first alarm to the still sleeping passions. Of this was Elvira so fully convinced, that She would have preferred putting into her Daughter's hands 'Amadis de Gaul,' or 'The Valiant Champion, Tirante the White;' and would sooner have authorised her studying the lewd exploits of 'Don Galaor,' or the lascivious jokes of the 'Damsel Plazer di mi vida.' She had in consequence made two resolutions respecting the Bible. The first was, that Antonia should not read it, till

She was of an age to feel its beauties, and profit by its morality: The second, that it should be copied out with her own hand, and all improper passages either altered or omitted. She had adhered to this determination, and such was the Bible which Antonia was reading: It had been lately delivered to her, and She perused it with an avidity, with a delight that was inexpressible. Ambrosio perceived his mistake, and replaced the Book upon the Table.

Antonia spoke of her Mother's health with all the enthusiastic joy of a youthful heart.

'I admire your filial affection,' said the Abbot; 'It proves the excellence and sensibility of your character; It promises a treasure to him, whom Heaven has destined to possess your affections. The Breast, so capable of fondness for a Parent, what will it feel for a Lover? Nay, perhaps, what feels it for one even now? Tell me, my lovely Daughter; Have you known, what it is to love? Answer me with sincerity: Forget my habit, and consider me only as a Friend.'

'What it is to love?' said She, repeating his question; 'Oh! yes, undoubtedly; I have loved many, many People.'

'That is not what I mean. The love of which I speak, can be felt only for one. Have you never seen the Man, whom you wished to be your Husband?'

'Oh! No, indeed!'

This was an untruth, but She was unconscious of its falsehood: She knew not the nature of her sentiments for Lorenzo; and never having seen him since his first visit to Elvira, with every day his Image grew less feebly impressed upon her bosom. Besides, She thought of an Husband with all a Virgin's terror, and negatived the Friar's demand without a moment's hesitation.

'And do you not long to see that Man, Antonia? Do you feel no void in your heart, which you fain would have filled up? Do you heave no sighs for the absence of some one dear to you, but who that some one is, you know not? Perceive you not that what formerly could please, has charms for you no longer? That a thousand new wishes, new ideas, new sensations, have sprang in your Bosom, only to be felt, never to be described? Or while you fill every other heart with passion, is it possible that your own remains insensible and cold? It cannot be! That melting eye, that blushing cheek, that enchanting voluptuous melancholy which at times over-spreads your features, all these marks belye your words. You love, Antonia, and in vain would hide it from me.'

'Father, you amaze me! What is this love of which you speak? I neither know its nature, nor if I felt it, why I should conceal the sentiment.'

'Have you seen no Man, Antonia, whom though never seen before, you seemed long to have sought? Whose form, though a Stranger's, was familiar to your eyes? The sound of whose voice soothed you, pleased you, penetrated to your very soul? In whose presence you rejoiced, for whose absence you lamented? With whom your heart seemed to expand, and in whose bosom with confidence unbounded you reposed the cares of your own? Have you not felt all this, Antonia?'

'Certainly I have: The first time that I saw you, I felt it.'

Ambrosio started. Scarcely dared He credit his hearing.

'Me, Antonia?' He cried, his eyes sparkling with delight and impatience, while He seized her hand, and pressed it rapturously to his lips. 'Me, Antonia? You felt these sentiments for me?'

'Even with more strength than you have described. The very moment that I beheld you, I felt so pleased, so interested! I waited so eagerly to catch the sound of your voice, and when I heard it, it seemed so sweet! It spoke to me a language till then so unknown! Methought, it told me a thousand things which I wished to hear! It seemed as if I had long known you; as if I had a right to your friendship, your advice, and your protection. I wept when you departed, and longed for the time which should restore you to my sight.'

'Antonia! my charming Antonia!' exclaimed the Monk, and caught her to his bosom; 'Can I believe my senses? Repeat it to me, my sweet Girl! Tell me again that you love me, that you love me truly and tenderly!'

'Indeed, I do: Let my Mother be excepted, and the world holds no one more dear to me!'

At this frank avowal Ambrosio no longer possessed himself; Wild with desire, He clasped the blushing Trembler in his arms. He fastened his lips greedily upon hers, sucked in her pure delicious breath, violated with his bold hand the treasures of her bosom, and wound around him her soft and yielding limbs. Startled, alarmed, and confused at his action, surprize at first deprived her of the power of resistance. At length recovering herself, She strove to escape from his embrace.

'Father! .... Ambrosio!' She cried; 'Release me, for God's sake!'

But the licentious Monk heeded not her prayers: He persisted in his design, and proceeded to take still greater liberties. Antonia prayed, wept, and struggled: Terrified to the extreme, though at what She knew not, She exerted all her strength to repulse the Friar, and was on the point of shrieking for assistance, when the chamber-door was suddenly thrown open. Ambrosio had just sufficient presence of mind to be sensible of his danger. Reluctantly He quitted his prey, and started hastily from the Couch. Antonia uttered an exclamation of joy, flew towards the door, and found herself clasped in the arms of her Mother.

Alarmed at some of the Abbot's speeches, which Antonia had innocently repeated, Elvira resolved to ascertain the truth of her suspicions. She had known enough of Mankind, not to be imposed upon by the Monk's reputed virtue. She reflected on several circumstances, which though trifling, on being put together seemed to authorize her fears. His frequent visits, which as far as She could see, were confined to her family; His evident emotion, whenever She spoke of Antonia; His being in the full prime and heat of Manhood; and above all, his pernicious philosophy communicated to her by Antonia, and which accorded but ill with his conversation in her presence, all these circumstances inspired her with doubts respecting the purity of Ambrosio's friendship. In consequence, She resolved, when He should next be alone with Antonia, to endeavour at surprizing him. Her plan had succeeded. 'Tis true, that when She entered the room, He had already abandoned his prey; But the disorder of her Daughter's dress, and the shame and confusion stamped upon the Friar's countenance sufficed to prove, that her suspicions were but too well-founded. However, She was too prudent to make those suspicions known. She judged, that to unmask the Imposter would be no easy matter, the public being so much prejudiced in his favour: and having but few Friends, She thought it dangerous to make herself so powerful an Enemy. She affected therefore not to remark his agitation, seated herself tranquilly upon the Sopha, assigned some trifling reason for having quitted her room unexpectedly, and conversed on various subjects with seeming confidence and ease.

Re-assured by her behaviour, the Monk began to recover himself. He strove to answer Elvira without appearing embarrassed: But He was still too great a novice in dissimulation, and He felt, that He must look confused and awkward. He soon broke off the conversation, and rose to depart. What was his vexation, when on taking leave, Elvira told him in polite terms, that being now perfectly re-established, She thought it an injustice to deprive Others of his company, who might be more in need of it! She assured him of her eternal gratitude, for the benefit which during her illness She had derived from his society and exhortations: And She lamented that her domestic affairs, as well as the multitude of business which his situation must of necessity impose upon him, would in future deprive her of the pleasure of his visits. Though delivered in the mildest language this hint was too plain to be mistaken. Still He was preparing to put in a remonstrance, when an expressive look from Elvira stopped him short. He dared not press her to receive him, for her manner convinced him that He was discovered: He submitted without reply, took an hasty leave, and retired to the Abbey, his heart filled with rage and shame, with bitterness and disappointment.

Antonia's mind felt relieved by his departure; Yet She could not help lamenting, that She was never to see him more. Elvira also felt a secret sorrow; She had received too much pleasure from thinking him her Friend, not to regret the necessity of changing her opinion: But her mind was too much accustomed to the fallacy of worldly friendships to permit her present disappointment to weigh upon it long. She now endeavoured to make her Daughter aware of the risque, which She had ran: But She was obliged to treat the subject with caution, lest in removing the bandage of ignorance, the veil of innocence should be rent away. She therefore contented herself with warning Antonia to be upon her guard, and ordering her, should the Abbot persist in his visits, never to receive them but in company. With this injunction Antonia promised to comply.

Ambrosio hastened to his Cell. He closed the door after him, and threw himself upon the bed in despair. The impulse of desire, the stings of disappointment, the shame of detection, and the fear of being publicly unmasked, rendered his bosom a scene of the most horrible confusion. He knew not what course to pursue. Debarred the presence of Antonia, He had no hopes of satisfying that passion, which was now become a part of his existence. He reflected, that his secret was in a Woman's power: He trembled with apprehension when He beheld the precipice before him, and with rage, when He thought that had it not been for Elvira, He should now have possessed the object of his desires. With the direct imprecations He vowed vengeance against her; He swore, that cost what it would, He still would possess Antonia. Starting from the Bed He paced the chamber with disordered steps, howled with impotent fury, dashed himself violently against the walls, and indulged all the transports of rage and madness.

He was still under the influence of this storm of passions, when He heard a gentle knock at the door of his Cell. Conscious that his voice must have been heard, He dared not refuse admittance to the Importuner: He strove to compose himself, and to hide his agitation. Having in some degree succeeded, He drew back the bolt: The door opened, and Matilda appeared.

At this precise moment there was no one with whose presence He could better have dispensed. He had not sufficient command over himself to conceal his vexation. He started back, and frowned.

'I am busy,' said He in a stern and hasty tone; 'Leave me!'

Matilda heeded him not: She again fastened the door, and then advanced towards him with an air gentle and supplicating.

'Forgive me, Ambrosio,' said She; 'For your own sake I must not obey you. Fear no complaints from me; I come not to reproach you with your ingratitude. I pardon you from my heart, and since your love can no longer be mine, I request the next best gift, your confidence and friendship. We cannot force our inclinations; The little beauty which you once saw in me, has perished with its novelty, and if it can no longer excite desire, mine is the fault, not yours. But why persist in shunning me? Why such anxiety to fly my presence? You have sorrows, but will not permit me to share them; You have disappointments, but will not accept my comfort; You have wishes, but forbid my aiding your pursuits. 'Tis of this which I complain, not of your indifference to my person. I have given up the claims of the Mistress, but nothing shall prevail on me to give up those of the Friend.'

Her mildness had an instantaneous effect upon Ambrosio's feelings.

'Generous Matilda!' He replied, taking her hand, 'How far do you rise superior to the foibles of your sex! Yes, I accept your offer. I have need of an adviser, and a Confident: In you I find every needful quality united. But to aid my pursuits . . . . Ah! Matilda, it lies not in your power!'

'It lies in no one's power but mine. Ambrosio, your secret is none to me; Your every step, your every action has been observed by my attentive eye. You love.'

'Matilda!'

'Why conceal it from me? Fear not the little jealousy, which taints the generality of Women: My soul disdains so despicable a passion. You love, Ambrosio; Antonia Dalfa is the object of your flame. I know every circumstance respecting your passion: Every conversation has been repeated to me. I have been informed of your attempt to enjoy Antonia's person, your disappointment, and dismission from Elvira's House. You now despair of possessing your Mistress; But I come to revive your hopes, and point out the road to success.'

'To success? Oh! impossible!'

'To them who dare nothing is impossible. Rely upon me, and you may yet be happy. The time is come,

Ambrosio, when regard for your comfort and tranquillity compels me to reveal a part of my History, with which you are still unacquainted. Listen, and do not interrupt me: Should my confession disgust you, remember that in making it my sole aim is to satisfy your wishes, and restore that peace to your heart, which at present has abandoned it. I formerly mentioned, that my Guardian was a Man of uncommon knowledge: He took pains to instil that knowledge into my infant mind. Among the various sciences which curiosity had induced him to explore, He neglected not that, which by most is esteemed impious, and by many chimerical. I speak of those arts, which relate to the world of Spirits. His deep researches into causes and effects, his unwearied application to the study of natural philosophy,* his profound and unlimited knowledge of the properties and virtues of every gem which enriches the deep, of every herb which the earth produces, at length procured him the distinction, which He had sought so long, so earnestly. His curiosity was fully slaked, his ambition amply gratified. He gave laws to the elements; He could reverse the order of nature; His eye read the mandates of futurity, and the infernal Spirits were submissive to his commands. Why shrink you from me? I understand that enquiring look. Your suspicions are right, though your terrors are unfounded. My Guardian concealed not from me his most precious acquisition. Yet had I never seen *you*, I should never have exerted my power. Like you I shuddered at the thoughts of Magic: Like you I had formed a terrible idea of the consequences of raising a dæmon. To preserve that life which your love had taught me to prize, I had recourse to means which I trembled at employing. You remember that night, which I past in St. Clare's Sepulchre? Then was it, that surrounded by mouldering bodies, I dared to perform those mystic rites, which summoned to my aid a fallen Angel. Judge what must have been my joy at discovering, that my terrors were imaginary: I saw the Dæmon obedient to my orders; I saw him trembling at my frown, and found, that instead of selling my soul to a Master, my courage had purchased for myself a Slave.'

'Rash Matilda! What have you done? You have doomed yourself to endless perdition; You have bartered for momentary power eternal happiness! If on witchcraft depends the fruition of my desires, I renounce your aid most absolutely. The consequences are too horrible: I doat upon Antonia, but am not so blinded by lust, as to sacrifice for her enjoyment my existence both in this world and the next.'

'Ridiculous prejudices! Oh! blush, Ambrosio, blush at being subjected to their dominion. Where is the risque of accepting my offers? What should induce my persuading you to this step, except the wish of restoring you to happiness and quiet. If there is danger, it must fall upon me: It is I, who invoke the ministry of the Spirits; Mine therefore will be the crime, and yours the profit. But danger there is none: The Enemy of Mankind is my Slave, not my Sovereign. Is there no difference between giving and receiving laws, between serving and commanding? Awake from your idle dreams, Ambrosio! Throw from you these terrors so ill-suited to a soul like yours; Leave them for common Men, and dare to be happy! Accompany me this night to St. Clare's Sepulchre, witness my incantations, and Antonia is your own.'

'To obtain her by such means I neither can, or will. Cease then to persuade me, for I dare not employ Hell's agency.'

'You *dare* not? How have you deceived me! That mind which I esteemed so great and valiant, proves to be feeble, puerile, and grovelling, a slave to vulgar errors, and weaker than a Woman's.'

'What? Though conscious of the danger, wilfully shall

I expose myself to the Seducer's arts? Shall I renounce for ever my title to salvation? Shall my eyes seek a sight, which I know will blast them? No, no, Matilda; I will not ally myself with God's Enemy.'

'Are you then God's Friend at present? Have you not broken your engagements with him, renounced his service, and abandoned yourself to the impulse of your passions? Are you not planning the destruction of innocence, the ruin of a Creature, whom He formed in the mould of Angels? If not of Dæmons, whose aid would you invoke to forward this laudable design? Will the Seraphims protect it, conduct Antonia to your arms, and sanction with their ministry your illicit pleasures? Absurd! But I am not deceived, Ambrosio! It is not virtue, which makes you reject my offer: You *would* accept it, but you *dare* not. 'Tis not the crime which holds your hand, but the punishment; 'Tis not respect for God which restrains you, but the terror of his vengeance! Fain would you offend him in secret, but you tremble to profess yourself his Foe. Now shame on the coward soul, which wants the courage either to be a firm Friend, or open Enemy!'

'To look upon guilt with horror, Matilda, is in itself a merit: In this respect I glory to confess myself a Coward. Though my passions have made me deviate from her laws, I still feel in my heart an innate love of virtue. But it ill becomes you to tax me with my perjury: You, who first seduced me to violate my vows; You, who first rouzed my sleeping vices, made me feel the weight of Religion's chains, and bad me be convinced that guilt had pleasures. Yet though my principles have yielded to the force of temperament, I still have sufficient grace to shudder at Sorcery, and avoid a crime so monstrous, so unpardonable!'

'Unpardonable, say you? Where then is your constant boast of the Almighty's infinite mercy? Has He of late set bounds to it? Receives He no longer a Sinner with joy? You injure him, Ambrosio; You will always have time to repent, and He have goodness to forgive. Afford him a glorious opportunity to exert that goodness: The greater your crime, the greater his merit in pardoning. Away then with these childish scruples: Be persuaded to your good, and follow me to the Sepulchre.'

'Oh! cease, Matilda! That scoffing tone, that bold and impious language is horrible in every mouth, but most so in a Woman's. Let us drop a conversation, which excites no other sentiments than horror and disgust. I will not follow you to the Sepulchre, or accept the services of your infernal Agents. Antonia shall be mine, but mine by human means.'

'Then yours She will never be! You are banished her presence; Her Mother has opened her eyes to your designs, and She is now upon her guard against them. Nay more, She loves another. A Youth of distinguished merit, possesses her heart, and unless you interfere, a few days will make her his Bride. This intelligence was brought me by my invisible Servants, to whom I had recourse on first perceiving your indifference. They watched your every action, related to me all that past at Elvira's, and inspired me with the idea of favouring your designs. Their reports have been my only comfort. Though you shunned my presence, all your proceedings were known to me: Nay, I was constantly with you in some degree, thanks to this precious gift!'

With these words She drew from beneath her habit a mirror of polished steel, the borders of which were marked with various strange and unknown characters.

'Amidst all my sorrows, amidst all my regrets for your coldness, I was sustained from despair by the virtues of this Talisman. On pronouncing certain words the Person appears in it, on whom the Observer's thoughts are bent: thus though *I* was exiled from *your* sight, you, Ambrosio, were ever present to mine.'

The Friar's curiosity was excited strongly.

'What you relate is incredible! Matilda, are you not amusing yourself with my credulity?'

'Be your own eyes the Judge.'

She put the Mirror into his hand. Curiosity induced him to take it, and Love, to wish that Antonia might appear. Matilda pronounced the magic words. Immediately, a thick smoke rose from the characters traced upon the borders, and spread itself over the surface. It dispersed again gradually; A confused mixture of colours and images presented themselves to the Friar's eyes, which at length arranging themselves in their proper places, He beheld in miniature Antonia's lovely form.

The scene was a small closet belonging to her apartment. She was undressing to bathe herself. The long tresses of her hair were already bound up. The amorous Monk had full opportunity to observe the voluptuous contours and admirable symmetry of her person. She threw off her last garment, and advancing to the Bath prepared for her, She put her foot into the water. It struck cold, and She drew it back again. Though unconscious of being observed, an in-bred sense of modesty induced her to veil her charms; and She stood hesitating upon the brink, in the attitude of the Venus de Medicis. At this moment a tame Linnet flew towards her, nestled its head between her breasts, and nibbled them in wanton play. The smiling Antonia strove in vain to shake off the Bird, and at length raised her hands to drive it from its delightful harbour. Ambrosio could bear no more: His desires were worked up to phrenzy.

'I yield!' He cried, dashing the mirror upon the ground: 'Matilda, I follow you! Do with me what you will!'

She waited not to hear his consent repeated. It was already midnight. She flew to her Cell, and soon returned with her little basket and the Key of the Cemetery, which had remained in her possession since her first visit to the Vaults. She gave the Monk no time for reflection.

'Come!' She said, and took his hand; 'Follow me, and witness the effects of your resolve!'

This said, She drew him hastily along. They passed into the Burying-ground unobserved, opened the door of the Sepulchre, and found themselves at the head of the subterraneous Stair-case. As yet the beams of the full Moon had guided their steps, but that resource now failed them. Matilda had neglected to provide herself with a Lamp. Still holding Ambrosio's hand She descended the marble steps; But the profound obscurity with which they were over-spread, obliged them to walk slow and cautiously.

'You tremble!' said Matilda to her Companion; 'Fear not; The destined spot is near.'

They reached the foot of the Stair-case, and continued to proceed, feeling their way along the Walls. On turning a corner suddenly, they descried faint gleams of light, which seemed burning at a distance. Thither they bent their steps: The rays proceeded from a small sepulchral Lamp, which flamed unceasingly before the Statue of St. Clare. It tinged with dim and cheerless beams the massy Columns which supported the Roof, but was too feeble to dissipate the thick gloom, in which the Vaults above were buried.

Matilda took the Lamp.

'Wait for me!' said She to the Friar; 'In a few moments I am here again.'

With these words She hastened into one of the passages which branched in various directions from this spot, and formed a sort of Labyrinth. Ambrosio was now left alone: Darkness the most profound surrounded him, and encouraged the doubts, which began to revive in his bosom. He had been hurried away by the delirium of the moment: The shame of betraying his terrors, while in Matilda's presence, had induced him to repress them; But now that he was abandoned to himself, they resumed their former ascendancy. He trembled at the scene, which He was soon to witness. He knew not how far the delusions of Magic might operate upon his mind, and possibly might force him to some deed, whose commission would make the breach between himself and Heaven irreparable. In this fearful dilemma, He would have implored God's assistance, but was conscious that He had forfeited all claim to such protection. Gladly would He have returned to the Abbey; But as He had past through innumerable Caverns and winding passages, the attempt of regaining the Stairs was hopeless. His fate was determined: No possibility of escape presented itself: He therefore combated his apprehensions, and called every argument to his succour, which might enable him to support the trying scene with fortitude. He reflected, that Antonia would be the reward of his daring: He inflamed his imagination by enumerating her charms. He persuaded himself, that, [as Matilda had observed,] He always should have time sufficient for repentance, and that as He employed *her* assistance, not that of the Dæmons, the crime of Sorcery could not be laid to his charge. He had read much respecting witchcraft: He understood that unless a formal Act was signed renouncing his claim to salvation, Satan would have no power over him. He was fully determined not to execute any such act, whatever threats might be used, or advantages held out to him.

Such were his meditations, while waiting for Matilda. They were interrupted by a low murmur, which seemed at no great distance from him. He was startled. He listened. Some minutes past in silence, after which the murmur was repeated. It appeared to be the groaning of one in pain. In any other situation, this circumstance would only have excited his attention and curiosity: In the present, his predominant sensation was that of terror. His imagination totally engrossed by the ideas of sorcery and Spirits, He fancied that some unquiet Ghost was wandering near him; or else, that Matilda had fallen a Victim to her presumption, and was perishing under the cruel fangs of the Dæmons. The noise seemed not to approach, but continued to be heard at intervals. Sometimes it became more audible, doubtless, as the sufferings of the person who uttered the groans became more acute and insupportable. Ambrosio now and then thought, that He could distinguish accents; and once in particular He was almost convinced, that He heard a faint voice exclaim,

'God! Oh! God! No hope! No succour!'

Yet deeper groans followed these words. They died away gradually, and universal silence again prevailed.

'What can this mean?' thought the bewildered Monk.

At that moment an idea which flashed into his mind, almost petrified him with horror. He started, and shuddered at himself.

'Should it be possible!' He groaned involuntarily; 'Should it but be possible, Oh! what a Monster am I!'

He wished to resolve his doubts, and to repair his fault, if it were not too late already: But these generous and compassionate sentiments were soon put to flight by the return of Matilda. He forgot the groaning Sufferer, and remembered nothing but the danger and embarrassment of his own situation. The light of the returning Lamp gilded the walls, and in a few moments after Matilda stood beside him. She had quitted her religious habit: She was now cloathed in a long sable Robe, on which was traced in gold embroidery a variety of unknown characters: It was fastened by a girdle of precious stones, in which was fixed a poignard. Her neck and arms were uncovered. In her hand She bore a golden wand. Her hair was loose and flowed wildly upon her shoulders; Her eyes sparkled with terrific expression; and her whole Demeanour was calculated to inspire the beholder with awe and admiration.

'Follow me!' She said to the Monk in a low and solemn voice; 'All is ready!'

His limbs trembled, while He obeyed her. She led him through various narrow-passages; and on every side as they past along, the beams of the Lamp displayed none but the most revolting objects; Skulls, Bones, Graves, and Images whose eyes seemed to glare on them with horror and surprize. At length they reached a spacious Cavern, whose lofty roof the eye sought in vain to discover. A profound obscurity hovered through the void. Damp vapours struck cold to the Friar's heart; and He listened sadly to the blast, while it howled along the lonely Vaults. Here Matilda stopped. She turned to Ambrosio. His cheeks and lips were pale with apprehension. By a glance of mingled scorn and anger She reproved his pusillanimity, but She spoke not. She placed the Lamp upon the ground, near the Basket. She motioned that Ambrosio should be silent, and began the mysterious rites. She drew a circle round him, another round herself, and then taking a small Phial from the Basket, poured a few drops upon the ground before her. She bent over the place, muttered some indistinct sentences, and immediately a pale sulphurous flame arose from the ground. It increased by degrees, and at length spread its waves over the whole surface, the circles alone excepted in which stood Matilda and the Monk. It then ascended the huge Columns of unhewn stone, glided along the roof, and formed the Cavern into an immense chamber totally covered with blue trembling fire. It emitted no heat: On the contrary, the extreme chillness of the place seemed to augment with every moment. Matilda continued her incantations: At intervals She took various articles from the Basket, the nature and name of most of which were unknown to the Friar: But among the few which He distinguished, He particularly observed three human fingers, and an Agnus Dei*which She broke in pieces. She threw them all into the flames which burned before her, and they were instantly consumed.

The Monk beheld her with anxious curiosity. Suddenly She uttered a loud and piercing shriek. She appeared to be seized with an access of delirium; She tore her hair, beat her bosom, used the most frantic gestures, and drawing the poignard from her girdle plunged it into her left arm. The blood gushed out plentifully, and as She stood on the brink of the circle, She took care that it should fall on the outside. The flames retired from the spot on which the blood was pouring. A volume of dark clouds rose slowly from the ensanguined earth, and ascended gradually, till it reached the vault of the Cavern. At the same time a clap of thunder was heard: The echo pealed fearfully along the subterraneous passages, and the ground shook beneath the feet of the Enchantress.

It was now that Ambrosio repented of his rashness. The solemn singularity of the charm had prepared him for something strange and horrible. He waited with fear for the Spirit's appearance, whose coming was announced by thunder and earthquakes. He looked wildly round him, expecting that some dreadful Apparition would meet his eyes, the sight of which would drive him mad. A cold shivering seized his body, and He sank upon one knee, unable to support himself.

'He comes!' exclaimed Matilda in a joyful accent.

Ambrosio started, and expected the Dæmon with terror. What was his surprize, when the Thunder ceasing to roll, a full strain of melodious Music sounded in the air. At the same time the cloud dispersed, and He beheld a Figure more beautiful, than Fancy's pencil ever drew. It was a Youth seemingly scarce eighteen, the perfection of whose form and face was unrivalled. He was perfectly naked: A bright Star sparkled upon his fore-head; Two crimson wings extended themselves from his shoulders; and his silken locks were confined by a band of many-coloured fires, which played round his head, formed themselves into a variety of figures, and shone with a brilliance far surpassing that of precious Stones. Circlets of Diamonds were fastened round his arms and ankles, and in his right hand He bore a silver branch, imitating Myrtle.* His form shone with dazzling glory: He was surrounded by clouds of rose-coloured light, and at the moment that He appeared, a refreshing air breathed perfumes through the Cavern. Enchanted at a vision so contrary to his expectations, Ambrosio gazed upon the Spirit with delight and wonder: Yet however beautiful the Figure, He could not but remark a wildness in the Dæmon's eyes, and a mysterious melancholy impressed upon his features, betraying the Fallen Angel, and inspiring the Spectators with secret awe.

The Music ceased. Matilda addressed herself to the Spirit: She spoke in a language unintelligible to the Monk, and was answered in the same. She seemed to insist upon something, which the Dæmon was unwilling to grant. He frequently darted upon Ambrosio angry glances, and at such times the Friar's heart sank within him. Matilda appeared to grow incensed. She spoke in a loud and commanding tone, and her gestures declared, that She was threatening him with her vengeance. Her menaces had the desired effect: The Spirit sank upon his knee, and with a submissive air presented to her the branch of Myrtle. No sooner had She received it, than the Music was again heard; A thick cloud spread itself over the Apparition; The blue flames disappeared, and total obscurity reigned through the Cave. The Abbot moved not from his place: His faculties were all bound up in pleasure, anxiety, and surprize. At length the darkness dispersing, He perceived Matilda standing near him in her religious habit, with the Myrtle in her hand. No traces of the incantation, and the Vaults were only illuminated by the faint rays of the sepulchral Lamp.

'I have succeeded,' said Matilda, 'though with more difficulty than I expected. Lucifer, whom I summoned to my assistance, was at first unwilling to obey my commands: To enforce his compliance I was constrained to have recourse to my strongest charms. They have produced the desired effect, but I have engaged never more to invoke his agency in your favour. Beware then, how you employ an opportunity which never will return. My magic arts will now be of no use to you: In future you can only hope for supernatural aid, by invoking the Dæmons yourself, and accepting the conditions of their service. This you will never do: You want strength of mind to force them to obedience, and unless you pay their established price, they will not be your voluntary Servants. In this one instance they consent to obey you: I offer you the means of enjoying your Mistress, and be careful not to lose the opportunity. Receive this constellated Myrtle: While you bear this in your hand, every door will fly open to you. It will procure you access to-morrow night to Antonia's chamber: Then breathe upon it thrice, pronounce her name, and place it upon her pillow. A death-like slumber will immediately seize upon her, and deprive her of the power of resisting your attempts. Sleep will hold her till break of Morning. In this state you may satisfy your desires without danger of being discovered; since when day-light shall dispel the effects of the enchantment, Antonia will perceive her dishonour, but be ignorant of the Ravisher. Be happy then, my Ambrosio, and let this service convince you, that my friendship is disinterested and pure. The night must be near expiring: Let us return to the Abbey, lest our absence should create surprize.'

The Abbot received the talisman with silent gratitude. His ideas were too much bewildered by the adventures of the night, to permit his expressing his thanks audibly, or indeed as yet to feel the whole value of her present. Matilda took up her Lamp and Basket, and guided her Companion from the mysterious Cavern. She restored the Lamp to its former place, and continued her route in darkness, till She reached the foot of the Stair-case. The first beams of the rising Sun darting down it facilitated the ascent. Matilda and the Abbot hastened out of the Sepulchre, closed the door after them, and soon regained the Abbey's western Cloister. No one met them, and they retired unobserved to their respective Cells.

The confusion of Ambrosio's mind now began to appease. He rejoiced in the fortunate issue of his adventure, and reflecting upon the virtues of the Myrtle, looked upon Antonia as already in his power. Imagination retraced to him those secret charms, betrayed to him by the Enchanted Mirror, and He waited with impatience for the approach of midnight.

END OF THE SECOND VOLUME

VOLUME III

CHAPTER I

The crickets sing, and Man's o'er-laboured sense
Repairs itself by rest: Our Tarquin thus
Did softly press the rushes, ere He wakened
The chastity He wounded—Cytherea,
How bravely thou becom'st thy bed! Fresh Lily!
And whiter than the sheets!

Cymbeline.*

ALL THE RESEARCHES of the Marquis de las Cisternas proved vain: Agnes was lost to him for ever. Despair produced so violent an effect upon his constitution, that the consequence was a long and severe illness. This prevented him from visiting Elvira, as He had intended; and She being ignorant of the cause of his neglect, it gave her no trifling uneasiness. His Sister's death had prevented Lorenzo from communicating to his Uncle his designs respecting Antonia: The injunctions of her Mother forbad his presenting himself to her without the Duke's consent; and as She heard no more of him or his proposals, Elvira conjectured that He had either met with a better match, or had been commanded to give up all thoughts of her Daughter. Every day made her more uneasy respecting Antonia's fate: While She retained the Abbot's protection, She bore with fortitude the disappointment of her hopes with regard to Lorenzo and the Marquis. That resource now failed her. She was convinced that Ambrosio had meditated her Daughter's ruin: And when She reflected that her death would leave Antonia friendless, and unprotected in a world so base, so perfidious and depraved, her heart swelled with the

bitterness of apprehension. At such times She would sit
for hours gazing upon the lovely Girl; and seeming to
listen to her innocent prattle, while in reality her thoughts
dwelt upon the sorrows, into which a moment would
suffice to plunge her. Then She would clasp her in her
arms suddenly, lean her head upon her Daughter's
bosom, and bedew it with her tears.

An event was in preparation, which had She known it,
would have relieved her from her inquietude. Lorenzo
now waited only for a favourable opportunity to inform
the Duke of his intended marriage: However, a circumstance which occurred at this period, obliged him to
delay his explanation for a few days longer.

Don Raymond's malady seemed to gain ground.
Lorenzo was constantly at his bed-side, and treated him
with a tenderness truly fraternal. Both the cause and
effects of the disorder were highly afflicting to the Brother
of Agnes: yet Theodore's grief was scarcely less sincere.
That amiable Boy quitted not his Master for a moment,
and put every means in practice to console and alleviate
his sufferings. The Marquis had conceived so rooted an
affection for his deceased Mistress, that it was evident to
all that He never could survive her loss: Nothing could
have prevented him from sinking under his grief, but
the persuasion of her being still alive, and in need of his
assistance. Though convinced of its falsehood, his Attendants encouraged him in a belief, which formed his only
comfort. He was assured daily, that fresh perquisitions
were making respecting the fate of Agnes: Stories were
invented recounting the various attempts made to get
admittance into the Convent; and circumstances were
related, which though they did not promise her absolute recovery, at least were sufficient to keep his
hopes alive. The Marquis constantly fell into the most
terrible access of passion, when informed of the failure of
these supposed attempts. Still He would not credit that

the succeeding ones would have the same fate, but flattered himself that the next would prove more fortunate.

Theodore was the only one, who exerted himself to realize his Master's Chimœras.* He was eternally busied in planning schemes for entering the Convent, or at least of obtaining from the Nuns some intelligence of Agnes. To execute these schemes was the only inducement, which could prevail on him to quit Don Raymond. He became a very Proteus,* changing his shape every day; but all his metamorphoses were to very little purpose: He regularly returned to the Palace de las Cisternas without any intelligence to confirm his Master's hopes. One day He took it into his head to disguise himself as a Beggar. He put a patch over his left eye, took his Guitar in hand, and posted himself at the Gate of the Convent.

'If Agnes is really confined in the Convent,' thought He, 'and hears my voice, She will recollect it, and possibly may find means to let me know, that She is here.'

With this idea He mingled with a crowd of Beggars, who assembled daily at the Gate of St. Clare to receive Soup, which the Nuns were accustomed to distribute at twelve o'clock. All were provided with jugs or bowls to carry it away; But as Theodore had no utensil of this kind, He begged leave to eat his portion at the Convent-door. This was granted without difficulty: His sweet voice, and in spite of his patched eye his engaging countenance, won the heart of the good old Porteress, who aided by a Lay-Sister was busied in serving to each his Mess. Theodore was bad to stay till the Others should depart, and promised that his request should then be granted. The Youth desired no better, since it was not to eat Soup that He presented himself at the Convent. He thanked the Porteress for her permission, retired from the Door, and seating himself upon a large stone, amused himself in tuning his Guitar while the Beggars were served.

As soon as the Crowd was gone, Theodore was beckoned to the Gate, and desired to come in. He obeyed with infinite readiness, but affected great respect at passing the hallowed Threshold, and to be much daunted by the presence of the Reverend Ladies. His feigned timidity flattered the vanity of the Nuns, who endeavoured to re-assure him. The Porteress took him into her own little Parlour: In the mean while, the Lay-Sister went to the Kitchen, and soon returned with a double portion of Soup, of better quality than what was given to the Beggars. His Hostess added some fruits and confections from her own private store, and Both encouraged the Youth to dine heartily. To all these attentions He replied with much seeming gratitude, and abundance of blessings upon his benefactresses. While He ate, the Nuns admired the delicacy of his features, the beauty of his hair, and the sweetness and grace which accompanied all his actions. They lamented to each other in whispers, that so charming a Youth should be exposed to the seductions of the World, and agreed, that He would be a worthy Pillar of the Catholic Church. They concluded their conference by resolving, that Heaven would be rendered a real service, if they entreated the Prioress to intercede with Ambrosio for the Beggar's admission into the order of Capuchins.

This being determined, the Porteress who was a person of great influence in the Convent, posted away in all haste to the Domina's Cell. Here She made so flaming a narrative of Theodore's merits, that the old Lady grew curious to see him. Accordingly the Porteress was commissioned to convey him to the Parlour-grate. In the interim, the supposed Beggar was sifting the Lay-Sister with respect to the fate of Agnes: Her evidence only corroborated the Domina's assertions. She said, that Agnes had been taken ill on returning from confession, had never quitted her bed from that moment, and that

She had herself been present at the Funeral. She even attested having seen her dead body, and assisted with her own hands in adjusting it upon the Bier. This account discouraged Theodore: Yet as He had pushed the adventure so far, He resolved to witness its conclusion.

The Porteress now returned, and ordered him to follow her. He obeyed, and was conducted into the Parlour, where the Lady Prioress was already posted at the Grate. The Nuns surrounded her, who all flocked with eagerness to a scene which promised some diversion. Theodore saluted them with profound respect, and his presence had the power to smooth for a moment even the stern brow of the Superior. She asked several questions respecting his Parents, his religion, and what had reduced him to a state of Beggary. To these demands his answers were perfectly satisfactory and perfectly false. He was then asked his opinion of a monastic life: He replied in terms of high estimation and respect for it. Upon this, the Prioress told him, that his obtaining an entrance into a religious order was not impossible; that her recommendation would not permit his poverty to be an obstacle, and that if She found him deserving it, He might depend in future upon her protection. Theodore assured her that to merit her favour would be his highest ambition; and having ordered him to return next day, when She would talk with him further, the Domina quitted the Parlour.

The Nuns, whom respect for the Superior had till then kept silent, now crowded all together to the Grate, and assailed the Youth with a multitude of questions. He had already examined each with attention: Alas! Agnes was not amongst them. The Nuns heaped question upon question so thickly, that it was scarcely possible for him to reply. One asked where He was born, since his accent declared him to be a Foreigner: Another wanted to know, why He wore a patch upon his left eye: Sister Helena en-

quired whether He had not a Sister like him, because
She should like such a Companion; and Sister Rachael
was fully persuaded, that the Brother would be the
pleasanter Companion of the Two. Theodore amused
himself with retailing to the credulous Nuns for truths
all the strange stories which his imagination could invent.
He related to them his supposed adventures, and penetrated every Auditor with astonishment, while He talked
of Giants, Savages, Ship-wrecks, and Islands inhabited

'By Anthropophagi, and Men whose heads
Do grow beneath their shoulders,'*

With many other circumstances to the full as remarkable.
He said, that He was born in Terra Incognita, was
educated at an Hottentot University, and had past two
years among the Americans of Silesia.*

'For what regards the loss of my eye' said He, 'it was a
just punishment upon me for disrespect to the Virgin,
when I made my second pilgrimage to Loretto.* I stood
near the Altar in the miraculous Chapel: The Monks
were proceeding to array the Statue in her best apparel.
The Pilgrims were ordered to close their eyes during this
ceremony: But though by nature extremely religious,
curiosity was too powerful. At the moment . . . . . I shall
penetrate you with horror, reverend Ladies, when I
reveal my crime! . . . . At the moment that the Monks
were changing her shift, I ventured to open my left eye,
and gave a little peep towards the Statue. That look was
my last! The Glory which surrounded the Virgin was too
great to be supported. I hastily shut my sacrilegious eye,
and never have been able to unclose it since!'

At the relation of this miracle the Nuns all crossed
themselves, and promised to intercede with the blessed
Virgin for the recovery of his sight. They expressed their
wonder at the extent of his travels, and at the strange

adventures which He had met with at so early an age.
They now remarked his Guitar, and enquired whether he
was an adept in Music. He replied with modesty that it
was not for him to decide upon his talents, but requested
permission to appeal to them as Judges. This was granted
without difficulty.

'But at least,' said the old Porteress, 'take care not to
sing any thing profane.'

'You may depend upon my discretion,' replied Theodore: 'You shall hear, how dangerous it is for young
Women to abandon themselves to their passions, illus-
trated by the adventure of a Damsel, who fell suddenly in
love with an unknown Knight.'

'But is the adventure true?' enquired the Porteress.

'Every word of it. It happened in Denmark, and the
Heroine was thought so beautiful, that She was known by
no other name but that of "the lovely Maid".'

'In Denmark, say you?' mumbled an old Nun; 'Are
not the People all Blacks in Denmark?'

'By no means, reverend Lady; They are of a delicate
pea-green with flame-coloured hair and whiskers.'

'Mother of God! Pea-green?' exclaimed Sister Helena;
'Oh! 'tis impossible!'

'Impossible?' said the Porteress with a look of contempt and exultation: 'Not at all: When I was a young
Woman, I remember seeing several of them myself.'

Theodore now put his instrument in proper order. He
had read the story of a King of England, whose prison
was discovered by a Minstrel; and He hoped that the
same scheme would enable him to discover Agnes,
should She be in the Convent. He chose a Ballad, which
She had taught him herself in the Castle of Lindenberg:
She might possibly catch the sound, and He hoped to
hear her replying to some of the Stanzas. His Guitar was
now in tune, and He prepared to strike it.

'But before I begin,' said He 'it is necessary to inform

you, Ladies, that this same Denmark is terribly infested
by Sorcerers, Witches, and Evil Spirits. Every element
possesses its appropriate Dæmons. The Woods are
haunted by a malignant power, called "the Erl- or
Oak-King:" He it is who blights the Trees, spoils the
Harvest, and commands the Imps and Goblins: He
appears in the form of an old Man of majestic figure,
with a golden Crown and long white beard: His principal amusement is to entice young Children from their
Parents, and as soon as He gets them into his Cave, He
tears them into a thousand pieces—The Rivers are governed by another Fiend, called "the Water-King:" His
province is to agitate the deep, occasion ship-wrecks,
and drag the drowning Sailors beneath the waves: He
wears the appearance of a Warrior, and employs himself
in luring young Virgins into his snare: What He does
with them, when He catches them in the water, Reverend
Ladies, I leave for you to imagine—"The Fire-King"
seems to be a Man all formed of flames: He raises the
Meteors and wandering lights, which beguile Travellers
into ponds and marshes, and He directs the lightning
where it may do most mischief—The last of these ele-
mentary Dæmons is called "the Cloud-King;" His
figure is that of a beautiful Youth, and He is distinguished by two large sable Wings: Though his outside is
so enchanting, He is not a bit better disposed than the
Others: He is continually employed in raising Storms,
tearing up Forests by the roots, and blowing Castles and
Convents about the ears of their Inhabitants—The First
has a Daughter, who is Queen of the Elves and Fairies;
The Second has a Mother, who is a powerful Enchantress: Neither of these Ladies are worth more than the
Gentlemen: I do not remember to have heard any family
assigned to the two other Dæmons, but at present I have
no business with any of them, except the Fiend of the
Waters. He is the Hero of my Ballad; but I thought it

necessary before I began, to give you some account of his proceedings—'

Theodore then played a short symphony; After which, stretching his voice to its utmost extent to facilitate its reaching the ear of Agnes, He sang the following Stanzas.

THE WATER-KING*
A DANISH BALLAD

With gentle murmur flowed the Tide,
While by the fragrant flowery side
The lovely Maid with carols gay
To Mary's Church pursued her way.

The Water-Fiend's malignant eye
Along the Banks beheld her hie;
Straight to his Mother-witch He sped,
And thus in suppliant accents said.

'Oh! Mother! Mother! now advise,
How I may yonder Maid surprize:
Oh! Mother! Mother! Now explain,
How I may yonder Maid obtain.'

The Witch She gave him armour white;
She formed him like a gallant Knight;
Of water clear next made her hand
A Steed, whose housings were of sand.

The Water-King then swift He went;
To Mary's Church his steps He bent:
He bound his Courser to the Door,
And paced the Church-yard three times four.

His Courser to the door bound He,
And paced the Church-yard four time three:
Then hastened up the Aisle, where all
The People flocked, both great and small.

The Priest said, as the Knight drew near,
'And wherefore comes the white Chief here?'
The lovely Maid She smiled aside;
'Oh! would I were the white Chief's Bride!'

He stept o'er Benches one and two;
'Oh! lovely Maid, I die for You!'
He stept o'er Benches two and three;
'Oh! lovely Maiden, go with me!'

Then sweet She smiled, the lovely Maid,
And while She gave her hand, She said,
'Betide me joy, betide me woe,
O'er Hill, o'er dale, with thee I go.'

The Priest their hands together joins:
They dance, while clear the moon-beam shines;
And little thinks the Maiden bright,
Her Partner is the Water-spright.

Oh! had some spirit deigned to sing,
'Your Partner is the Water-King!'
The Maid had fear and hate confest,
And cursed the hand which then She prest.

But nothing giving cause to think,
How near She strayed to danger's brink,
Still on She went, and hand in hand
The Lovers reached the yellow sand.

'Ascend this Steed with me, my Dear;
We needs must cross the streamlet here;
Ride boldly in; It is not deep;
The winds are hushed, the billows sleep.'

Thus spoke the Water-King. The Maid
Her Traitor-Bride-groom's wish obeyed:
And soon She saw the Courser lave
Delighted in his parent wave.

'Stop! Stop! my Love! The waters blue
E'en now my shrinking foot bedew!'
'Oh! lay aside your fears, sweet Heart!
We now have reached the deepest part.'

'Stop! Stop! my Love! For now I see
The waters rise above my knee.'
'Oh! lay aside your fears, sweet Heart!
We now have reached the deepest part.'

'Stop! Stop! for God's sake, stop! For Oh!
The waters o'er my bosom flow!'—
Scarce was the word pronounced, when Knight
And Courser vanished from her sight.

She shrieks, but shrieks in vain; for high
The wild winds rising dull the cry;
The Fiend exults; The Billows dash,
And o'er their hapless Victim wash.

Three times while struggling with the stream,
The lovely Maid was heard to scream;
But when the Tempest's rage was o'er,
The lovely Maid was seen no more.

Warned by this Tale, ye Damsels fair,
To whom you give your love beware!
Believe not every handsome Knight,
And dance not with the Water-Spright!

The Youth ceased to sing. The Nuns were delighted
with the sweetness of his voice, and masterly manner of
touching the Instrument: But however acceptable this
applause would have been at any other time, at present
it was insipid to Theodore. His artifice had not succeeded.
He paused in vain between the Stanzas: No voice replied
to his, and He abandoned the hope of equalling Blondel.
The Convent-Bell now warned the Nuns, that it was

time to assemble in the Refectory. They were obliged to
quit the Grate; They thanked the Youth for the entertainment which his Music had afforded them, and
charged him to return the next day. This He promised:
The Nuns, to give him the greater inclination to keep his
word, told him that He might always depend upon the
Convent for his meals, and each of them made him some
little present. One gave him a box of sweetmeats;
Another, an Agnus Dei; Some brought reliques of
Saints, waxen Images, and consecrated Crosses; and
Others presented him with pieces of those works in which
the Religious excel, such as embroidery, artificial flowers,
lace, and needle-work. All these He was advised to sell,
in order to put himself into better case; and He was
assured that it would be easy to dispose of them, since the
Spaniards hold the performances of the Nuns in high
estimation. Having received these gifts with seeming
respect and gratitude, He remarked, that having no
Basket, He knew not how to convey them away. Several
of the Nuns were hastening in search of one, when they were
stopped by the return of an elderly Woman, whom
Theodore had not till then observed: Her mild countenance, and respectable air prejudiced him immediately
in her favour.

'Hah!' said the Porteress; 'Here comes the Mother
St. Ursula with a Basket.'

The Nun approached the Grate, and presented the
Basket to Theodore: It was of willow, lined with blue
satin, and upon the four sides were painted scenes from
the legend of St. Genevieve.

'Here is my gift,' said She, as She gave it into his hand;
'Good Youth, despise it not; Though its value seems
insignificant, it has many hidden virtues.'

She accompanied these words with an expressive look.
It was not lost upon Theodore; In receiving the present,
He drew as near the Grate as possible.

'Agnes!' She whispered in a voice scarcely intelligible.

Theodore, however, caught the sound: He concluded that some mystery was concealed in the Basket, and his heart beat with impatience and joy. At this moment the Domina returned. Her air was gloomy and frowning, and She looked if possible more stern than ever.

'Mother St. Ursula, I would speak with you in private.'

The Nun changed colour, and was evidently disconcerted.

'With me?' She replied in a faltering voice.

The Domina motioned that She must follow her, and retired. The Mother St. Ursula obeyed her; Soon after the Refectory Bell ringing a second time, the Nuns quitted the Grate, and Theodore was left at liberty to carry off his prize. Delighted that at length He had obtained some intelligence for the Marquis, He flew rather than ran, till He reached the Hotel de las Cisternas. In a few minutes He stood by his Master's Bed with the Basket in his hand. Lorenzo was in the chamber, endeavouring to reconcile his Friend to a misfortune, which He felt himself but too severely. Theodore related his adventure, and the hopes which had been created by the Mother St. Ursula's gift. The Marquis started from his pillow: That fire which since the death of Agnes had been extinguished, now revived in his bosom, and his eyes sparkled with the eagerness of expectation. The emotions which Lorenzo's countenance betrayed, were scarcely weaker, and He waited with inexpressible impatience for the solution of this mystery. Raymond caught the basket from the hands of his Page: He emptied the contents upon the bed, and examined them with minute attention. He hoped that a letter would be found at the bottom; Nothing of the kind appeared. The search was resumed, and still with no better success. At length Don Raymond observed, that one corner of the blue satin lining was unripped; He tore it open hastily, and drew forth a small scrap of

paper neither folded or sealed. It was addressed to the
Marquis de las Cisternas, and the contents were as
follows.

Having recognised your Page, I venture to send these
few lines. Procure an order from the Cardinal-Duke for
seizing my Person, and that of the Domina; But let it
not be executed till Friday at midnight. It is the Festival
of St. Clare: There will be a procession of Nuns by
torch-light, and I shall be among them. Beware not to
let your intention be known: Should a syllable be
dropt to excite the Domina's suspicions, you will never
hear of me more. Be cautious, if you prize the memory of
Agnes, and wish to punish her Assassins. I have that to
tell, will freeze your blood with horror.   St. Ursula.

No sooner had the Marquis read the note, than He fell
back upon his pillow deprived of sense or motion. The
hope failed him which till now had supported his existence; and these lines convinced him but too positively
that Agnes was indeed no more. Lorenzo felt this circumstance less forcibly, since it had always been his idea that
his Sister had perished by unfair means. When He found
by the Mother St. Ursula's letter how true were his suspicions, the confirmation excited no other sentiment in
his bosom, than a wish to punish the Murderers as they
deserved. It was no easy task to recall the Marquis to
himself. As soon as He recovered his speech, He broke
out into execrations against the Assassins of his Beloved,
and vowed to take upon them a signal vengeance. He
continued to rave and torment himself with impotent
passion, till his constitution enfeebled by grief and illness
could support itself no longer, and He relapsed into
insensibility. His melancholy situation sincerely affected
Lorenzo, who would willingly have remained in the
apartment of his Friend; But other cares now demanded

his presence. It was necessary to procure the order for seizing the Prioress of St. Clare. For this purpose, having committed Raymond to the care of the best Physicians in Madrid, He quitted the Hotel de las Cisternas, and bent his course towards the Palace of the Cardinal-Duke.

His disappointment was excessive, when He found that affairs of State had obliged the Cardinal to set out for a distant Province. It wanted but five to Friday: Yet by travelling day and night, He hoped to return in time for the Pilgrimage of St. Clare. In this He succeeded. He found the Cardinal-Duke; and represented to him the supposed culpability of the Prioress, as also the violent effects which it had produced upon Don Raymond. He could have used no argument so forcible as this last. Of all his Nephews, the Marquis was the only one to whom the Cardinal-Duke was sincerely attached: He perfectly doated upon him, and the Prioress could have committed no greater crime in his eyes, than to have endangered the life of the Marquis. Consequently, He granted the order of arrest without difficulty: He also gave Lorenzo a letter to a principal Officer of the Inquisition,* desiring him to see his mandate executed. Furnished with these papers, Medina hastened back to Madrid, which He reached on the Friday a few hours before dark. He found the Marquis somewhat easier, but so weak and exhausted, that without great exertion He could neither speak or more. Having past an hour by his Bed-side, Lorenzo left him to communicate his design to his Uncle, as also to give Don Ramirez de Mello the Cardinal's letter. The First was petrified with horror, when He learnt the fate of his unhappy Niece: He encouraged Lorenzo to punish her Assassins, and engaged to accompany him at night to St. Clare's Convent. Don Ramirez promised his firmest support, and selected a band of trusty Archers to prevent opposition on the part of the Populace.

But while Lorenzo was anxious to unmask one reli-

gious Hypocrite, He was unconscious of the sorrows
prepared for him by Another. Aided by Matilda's
infernal Agents, Ambrosio had resolved upon the innocent Antonia's ruin. The moment destined to be so fatal
to her arrived. She had taken leave of her Mother for the
night. As She kissed her, She felt an unusual despondency
infuse itself into her bosom. She left her, and returned to
her instantly, threw herself into her maternal arms, and
bathed her cheek with tears: She felt uneasy at quitting
her, and a secret presentiment assured her that never
must they meet again. Elvira observed, and tried to
laugh her out of this childish prejudice: She chid her
mildly for encouraging such ungrounded sadness, and
warned her how dangerous it was to encourage such
ideas.

To all her remonstrances She received no other answer,
than,

'Mother! Dear Mother! Oh! would to God, it were
Morning!'

Elvira, whose inquietude respecting her Daughter,
was a great obstacle to her perfect re-establishment, was
still labouring under the effects of her late severe illness.
She was this Evening more than usually indisposed, and
retired to bed before her accustomed hour. Antonia
withdrew from her Mother's chamber with regret, and
till the Door closed, kept her eyes fixed upon her with
melancholy expression. She retired to her own apartment; Her heart was filled with bitterness: It seemed to
her that all her prospects were blasted, and the world
contained nothing for which it was worth existing. She
sank into a Chair, reclined her head upon her arm, and
gazed upon the floor with a vacant stare, while the most
gloomy images floated before her fancy. She was still
in this state of insensibility, when She was disturbed by
hearing a strain of soft Music breathed beneath her
window. She rose, drew near the Casement, and opened

it to hear it more distinctly. Having thrown her veil over her face, She ventured to look out. By the light of the Moon She perceived several Men below with Guitars and Lutes in their hands; and at a little distance from them stood Another wrapped in his cloak, whose stature and appearance bore a strong resemblance to Lorenzo's. She was not deceived in this conjecture. It was indeed Lorenzo himself, who bound by his word not to present himself to Antonia without his Uncle's consent, endeavoured by occasional Serenades, to convince his Mistress that his attachment still existed. His stratagem had not the desired effect. Antonia was far from supposing, that this nightly music was intended as a compliment to her: She was too modest to think herself worthy such attentions; and concluding them to be addressed to some neighbouring Lady, She grieved to find that they were offered by Lorenzo.

The air which was played, was plaintive and melodious. It accorded with the state of Antonia's mind, and She listened with pleasure. After a symphony of some length, it was succeeded by the sound of voices, and Antonia distinguished the following words.

SERENADE

Chorus

Oh! Breathe in gentle strain, my Lyre!
'Tis here that Beauty loves to rest:
Describe the pangs of fond desire,
Which rend a faithful Lover's breast.

Song

In every heart to find a Slave,
In every Soul to fix his reign,
In bonds to lead the wise and brave,
And make the Captives kiss his chain,
Such is the power of Love, and Oh!
I grieve so well Love's power to know.

In sighs to pass the live-long day,
To taste a short and broken sleep,
For one dear Object far away,
All others scorned, to watch and weep,
Such are the pains of Love, and Oh!
I grieve so well Love's pains to know!

To read consent in virgin eyes,
To press the lip ne'er prest till then,
To hear the sigh of transport rise,
And kiss, and kiss, and kiss again,
Such are thy pleasures, Love; But Oh!
When shall my heart thy pleasures know?

Chorus

Now hush, my Lyre! My voice be still!
Sleep, gentle Maid! May fond desire
With amorous thoughts thy visions fill,
Though still my voice, and hushed my Lyre.

The Music ceased: The Performers dispersed, and
silence prevailed through the Street. Antonia quitted the
window with regret: She as usual recommended herself
to the protection of St. Rosolia, said her accustomed
prayers, and retired to bed. Sleep was not long absent,
and his presence relieved her from her terrors and inquietude.

It was almost two o'clock, before the lustful Monk
ventured to bend his steps towards Antonia's dwelling.
It has been already mentioned, that the Abbey was at no
great distance from the Strada di San Iago. He reached
the House unobserved. Here He stopped, and hesitated
for a moment. He reflected on the enormity of the crime,
the consequences of a discovery, and the probability,
after what had passed, of Elvira's suspecting him to be
her Daughter's Ravisher: On the other hand it was sug-

gested, that She could do no more than suspect; that no
proofs of his guilt could be produced; that it would seem
impossible for the rape to have been committed without
Antonia's knowing when, where, or by whom; and
finally, He believed that his fame was too firmly established to be shaken by the unsupported accusations of
two unknown Women. This latter argument was perfectly false: He knew not how uncertain is the air of
popular applause, and that a moment suffices to make
him to-day the detestation of the world, who yesterday
was its Idol. The result of the Monk's deliberations was,
that He should proceed in his enterprize. He ascended
the steps leading to the House. No sooner did He touch
the door with the silver Myrtle, than it flew open, and
presented him with a free passage. He entered, and the
door closed after him of its own accord.

Guided by the moon-beams, He proceeded up the
Stair-case with slow and cautious steps. He looked round
him every moment with apprehension and anxiety. He
saw a Spy in every shadow, and heard a voice in every
murmur of the night-breeze. Consciousness of the guilty
business on which He was employed appalled his heart,
and rendered it more timid than a Woman's. Yet still He
proceeded. He reached the door of Antonia's chamber.
He stopped, and listened. All was hushed within. The
total silence persuaded him that his intended Victim was
retired to rest, and He ventured to lift up the Latch. The
door was fastened, and resisted his efforts: But no sooner
was it touched by the Talisman, than the Bolt flew back.
The Ravisher stept on, and found himself in the chamber,
where slept the innocent Girl, unconscious how dangerous
a Visitor was drawing near her Couch. The door closed
after him, and the Bolt shot again into its fastening.

Ambrosio advanced with precaution. He took care
that not a board should creak under his foot, and held in
his breath as He approached the Bed. His first attention

was to perform the magic ceremony, as Matilda had charged him: He breathed thrice upon the silver Myrtle, pronounced over it Antonia's name, and laid it upon her pillow. The effects which it had already produced, permitted not his doubting its success in prolonging the slumbers of his devoted Mistress. No sooner was the enchantment performed, than He considered her to be absolutely in his power, and his eyes flamed with lust and impatience. He now ventured to cast a glance upon the sleeping Beauty. A single Lamp, burning before the Statue of St. Rosolia, shed a faint light through the room, and permitted him to examine all the charms of the lovely Object before him. The heat of the weather had obliged her to throw off part of the Bed-cloathes: Those which still covered her, Ambrosio's insolent hand hastened to remove. She lay with her cheek reclining upon one ivory arm; The Other rested on the side of the Bed with graceful indolence. A few tresses of her hair had escaped from beneath the Muslin which confined the rest, and fell carelessly over her bosom, as it heaved with slow and regular suspiration. The warm air had spread her cheek with higher colour than usual. A smile inexpressibly sweet played round her ripe and coral lips, from which every now and then escaped a gentle sigh or an half-pronounced sentence. An air of enchanting innocence and candour pervaded her whole form; and there was a sort of modesty in her very nakedness, which added fresh stings to the desires of the lustful Monk.

He remained for some moments devouring those charms with his eyes, which soon were to be subjected to his ill-regulated passions. Her mouth half-opened seemed to solicit a kiss: He bent over her; he joined his lips to hers, and drew in the fragrance of her breath with rapture. This momentary pleasure increased his longing for still greater. His desires were raised to that frantic

height, by which Brutes are agitated. He resolved not to
delay for one instant longer the accomplishment of his
wishes, and hastily proceeded to tear off those garments,
which impeded the gratification of his lust.

'Gracious God!' exclaimed a voice behind him; 'Am
I not deceived? Is not this an illusion?'

Terror, confusion, and disappointment accompanied
these words, as they struck Ambrosio's hearing. He
started, and turned towards it. Elvira stood at the door
of the chamber, and regarded the Monk with looks of
surprize and detestation.

A frightful dream had represented to her Antonia on
the verge of a precipice. She saw her trembling on the
brink: Every moment seemed to threaten her fall, and
She heard her exclaim with shrieks, 'Save me, Mother!
Save me!—Yet a moment, and it will be too late!'
Elvira woke in terror. The vision had made too strong an
impression upon her mind, to permit her resting till
assured of her Daughter's safety. She hastily started from
her Bed, threw on a loose night-gown, and passing
through the Closet in which slept the Waiting-woman,
She reached Antonia's chamber just in time to rescue
her from the grasp of the Ravisher.

His shame and her amazement seemed to have petrified into Statues both Elvira and the Monk: They remained gazing upon each other in silence. The Lady was
the first to recover herself.

'It is no dream!' She cried; 'It is really Ambrosio, who
stands before me! It is the Man whom Madrid esteems a
Saint, that I find at this late hour near the Couch of my
unhappy Child! Monster of Hypocrisy! I already suspected your designs, but forbore your accusation in pity to
human frailty. Silence would now be criminal: The
whole City shall be informed of your incontinence. I will
unmask you, Villain, and convince the Church what a
Viper She cherishes in her bosom.'

Pale and confused the baffled Culprit stood trembling before her. He would fain have extenuated his offence, but could find no apology for his conduct: He could produce nothing but broken sentences, and excuses which contradicted each other. Elvira was too justly incensed to grant the pardon which He requested. She protested that She would raise the neighbourhood, and make him an example to all future Hypocrites. Then hastening to the Bed, She called to Antonia to wake; and finding that her voice had no effect, She took her arm, and raised her forcibly from the pillow. The charm operated too powerfully. Antonia remained insensible, and on being released by her Mother, sank back upon the pillow.

'This slumber cannot be natural!' cried the amazed Elvira, whose indignation increased with every moment. 'Some mystery is concealed in it; But tremble, Hypocrite; all your villainy shall soon be unravelled! Help! Help!' She exclaimed aloud; 'Within there! Flora! Flora!'

'Hear me for one moment, Lady!' cried the Monk, restored to himself by the urgency of the danger; 'By all that is sacred and holy, I swear that your Daughter's honour is still unviolated. Forgive my transgression! Spare me the shame of a discovery, and permit me to regain the Abbey undisturbed. Grant me this request in mercy! I promise not only that Antonia shall be secure from me in future, but that the rest of my life shall prove . . . . . .'

Elvira interrupted him abruptly.

'Antonia secure from you? *I* will secure her! You shall betray no longer the confidence of Parents! Your iniquity shall be unveiled to the public eye: All Madrid shall shudder at your perfidy, your hypocrisy and incontinence. What Ho! there! Flora! Flora, I say!'

While She spoke thus, the remembrance of Agnes

struck upon his mind. Thus had She sued to him for
mercy, and thus had He refused her prayer! It was now
his turn to suffer, and He could not but acknowledge
that his punishment was just. In the mean while Elvira
continued to call Flora to her assistance; but her voice
was so choaked with passion, that the Servant who was
buried in profound slumber, was insensible to all her
cries: Elvira dared not go towards the Closet in which
Flora slept, lest the Monk should take that opportunity to
escape. Such indeed was his intention: He trusted, that
could He reach the Abbey unobserved by any other than
Elvira, her single testimony would not suffice to ruin a
reputation, so well established as his was in Madrid.
With this idea He gathered up such garments as He had
already thrown off, and hastened towards the Door.
Elvira was aware of his design; She followed him, and
ere He could draw back the bolt, seized him by the arm,
and detained him.

'Attempt not to fly!' said She; 'You quit not this room
without Witnesses of your guilt.'

Ambrosio struggled in vain to disengage himself.
Elvira quitted not her hold, but redoubled her cries for
succour. The Friar's danger grew more urgent. He expected every moment to hear people assembling at her
voice; And worked up to madness by the approach of
ruin, He adopted a resolution equally desperate and
savage. Turning round suddenly, with one hand He
grasped Elvira's throat so as to prevent her continuing
her clamour, and with the other, dashing her violently
upon the ground, He dragged her towards the Bed.
Confused by this unexpected attack, She scarcely had
power to strive at forcing herself from his grasp: While
the Monk, snatching the pillow from beneath her
Daughter's head, covering with it Elvira's face, and
pressing his knee upon her stomach with all his strength,
endeavoured to put an end to her existence. He succeeded

but too well. Her natural strength increased by the excess of anguish, long did the Sufferer struggle to disengage herself, but in vain. The Monk continued to kneel upon her breast, witnessed without mercy the convulsive trembling of her limbs beneath him, and sustained with inhuman firmness the spectacle of her agonies, when soul and body were on the point of separating. Those agonies at length were over. She ceased to struggle for life. The Monk took off the pillow, and gazed upon her. Her face was covered with a frightful blackness: Her limbs moved no more; The blood was chilled in her veins; Her heart had forgotten to beat, and her hands were stiff and frozen. Ambrosio beheld before him that once noble and majestic form, now become a Corse, cold, senseless and disgusting.

This horrible act was no sooner perpetrated, than the Friar beheld the enormity of his crime. A cold dew flowed over his limbs; his eyes closed; He staggered to a chair, and sank into it almost as lifeless, as the Unfortunate who lay extended at his feet. From this state He was rouzed by the necessity of flight, and the danger of being found in Antonia's apartment. He had no desire to profit by the execution of his crime. Antonia now appeared to him an object of disgust. A deadly cold had usurped the place of that warmth, which glowed in his bosom: No ideas offered themselves to his mind but those of death and guilt, of present shame and future punishment. Agitated by remorse and fear He prepared for flight: Yet his terrors did not so compleatly master his recollection, as to prevent his taking the precautions necessary for his safety. He replaced the pillow upon the bed, gathered up his garments, and with the fatal Talisman in his hand, bent his unsteady steps towards the door. Bewildered by fear, He fancied that his flight was opposed by Legions of Phantoms; Where-ever He turned, the disfigured Corse seemed to lie in his passage, and it was long before He succeeded in reaching the door. The enchanted Myrtle produced its former effect. The door opened, and He hastened down the stair-case. He entered the Abbey unobserved, and having shut himself into his Cell, He abandoned his soul to the tortures of unavailing remorse, and terrors of impending detection.

CHAPTER II

> Tell us, ye Dead, will none of you in pity
> To those you left behind disclose the secret?
> O! That some courteous Ghost would blab it out,
> What 'tis you are, and we must shortly be.
> I've heard, that Souls departed have sometimes
> Fore-warned Men of their deaths: 'Twas kindly done
> To knock, and give the alarum.
>
> Blair.*

AMBROSIO SHUDDERED AT himself, when He reflected on his rapid advances in iniquity. The enormous crime which He had just committed, filled him with real horror. The murdered Elvira was continually before his eyes, and his guilt was already punished by the agonies of his conscience. Time, however, considerably weakened these impressions: One day passed away, another followed it, and still not the least suspicion was thrown upon him. Impunity reconciled him to his guilt: He began to resume his spirits; and as his fears of detection died away, He paid less attention to the reproaches of remorse. Matilda exerted herself to quiet his alarms. At the first intelligence of Elvira's death, She seemed greatly affected, and joined the Monk in deploring the unhappy

catastrophe of his adventure: But when She found his
agitation to be somewhat calmed, and himself better disposed to listen to her arguments, She proceeded to mention his offence in milder terms, and convince him that
He was not so highly culpable as He appeared to consider himself. She represented, that He had only availed
himself of the rights which Nature allows to every one,
those of self-preservation: That either Elvira or himself
must have perished, and that her inflexibility and resolution to ruin him had deservedly marked her out for
the Victim. She next stated, that as He had before
rendered himself suspected to Elvira, it was a fortunate
event for him that her lips were closed by death; since
without this last adventure, her suspicions if made public
might have produced very disagreeable consequences.
He had therefore freed himself from an Enemy, to whom
the errors of his conduct were sufficiently known to make
her dangerous, and who was the greatest obstacle to his
designs upon Antonia. Those designs She encouraged
him not to abandon. She assured him, that no longer
protected by her Mother's watchful eye, the Daughter
would fall an easy conquest; and by praising and enumerating Antonia's charms, She strove to rekindle the
desires of the Monk. In this endeavour She succeeded
but too well.

As if the crimes into which his passion had seduced
him, had only increased its violence, He longed more
eagerly than ever to enjoy Antonia. The same success in
concealing his present guilt, He trusted, would attend his
future. He was deaf to the murmurs of conscience, and
resolved to satisfy his desires at any price. He waited only
for an opportunity of repeating his former enterprize;
But to procure that opportunity by the same means was
now impracticable. In the first transports of despair
He had dashed the enchanted Myrtle into a thousand
pieces: Matilda told him plainly, that He must expect no

further assistance from the infernal Powers, unless He was willing to subscribe to their established conditions. This Ambrosio was determined not to do: He persuaded himself that, however great might be his iniquity, so long as he preserved his claim to salvation, He need not despair of pardon. He therefore resolutely refused to enter into any bond or compact with the Fiends; and Matilda finding him obstinate upon this point, forbore to press him further. She exerted her invention to discover some means of putting Antonia into the Abbot's power: Nor was it long before that means presented itself.

While her ruin was thus meditating, the unhappy Girl herself suffered severely from the loss of her Mother. Every morning on waking, it was her first care to hasten to Elvira's chamber. On that which followed Ambrosio's fatal visit, She woke later than was her usual custom: Of this She was convinced by the Abbey-Chimes. She started from her bed, threw on a few loose garments hastily, and was speeding to enquire how her Mother had passed the night, when her foot struck against something which lay in her passage. She looked down. What was her horror at recognizing Elvira's livid Corse! She uttered a loud shriek, and threw herself upon the floor. She clasped the inanimate form to her bosom, felt that it was dead-cold, and with a movement of disgust, of which She was not the Mistress, let it fall again from her arms. The cry had alarmed Flora, who hastened to her assistance. The sight which She beheld penetrated her with horror; but her alarm was more audible than Antonia's. She made the House ring with her lamentations, while her Mistress almost suffocated with grief could only mark her distress by sobs and groans. Flora's shrieks soon reached the ears of the Hostess, whose terror and surprize were excessive on learning the cause of this disturbance. A Physician was immediately sent for: But on the first moment of beholding the Corse, He declared that Elvira's recovery was beyond the power of art. He proceeded therefore to give his assistance to Antonia, who by this time was truly in need of it. She was conveyed to bed, while the Landlady busied herself in giving orders for Elvira's Burial. Dame Jacintha was a plain good kind of Woman, charitable, generous, and devout: But her intellects were weak, and She was a Miserable Slave to fear and superstition. She shuddered at the idea of passing the night in the same House with a dead Body: She was persuaded that Elvira's Ghost would appear to her, and no less certain, that such a visit would kill her with fright. From this persuasion, She resolved to pass the night at a Neighbour's, and insisted that the Funeral should take place the next day. St. Clare's Cemetery being the nearest, it was determined that Elvira should be buried there. Dame Jacintha engaged to defray every expence attending the burial. She knew not in what circumstances Antonia was left, but from the sparing manner in which the Family had lived, She concluded them to be indifferent. Consequently, She entertained very little hope of ever being recompensed; But this consideration prevented her not from taking care that the Interment was performed with decency, and from showing the unfortunate Antonia all possible respect.

Nobody dies of mere grief; Of this Antonia was an instance. Aided by her youth and healthy constitution, She shook off the malady, which her Mother's death had occasioned; But it was not so easy to remove the disease of her mind. Her eyes were constantly filled with tears: Every trifle affected her, and She evidently nourished in her bosom a profound and rooted melancholy. The slightest mention of Elvira, the most trivial circumstance recalling that beloved Parent to her memory, was sufficient to throw her into serious agitation. How much would her grief have been increased, had She known the agonies which terminated her Mother's existence! But of this no one entertained the least suspicion. Elvira was subject to strong convulsions: It was supposed, that aware of their approach, She had dragged herself to her Daughter's chamber in hopes of assistance; that a sudden access of her fits had seized her, too violent to be resisted by her already enfeebled state of health; and that She had expired, ere She had time to reach the medicine which generally relieved her, and which stood upon a shelf in Antonia's room. This idea was firmly credited by the few people, who interested themselves about Elvira: Her Death was esteemed a natural event, and soon forgotten by all save by her, who had but too much reason to deplore her loss.

In truth Antonia's situation was sufficiently embarrassing and unpleasant. She was alone in the midst of a dissipated and expensive City; She was ill provided with money, and worse with Friends. Her aunt Leonella was still at Cordova, and She knew not her direction. Of the Marquis de las Cisternas She heard no news: As to Lorenzo, She had long given up the idea of possessing any interest in his bosom. She knew not to whom She could address herself in her present dilemma. She wished to consult Ambrosio; But She remembered her Mother's injunctions to shun him as much as possible, and the last conversation which Elvira had held with her upon the subject, had given her sufficient lights respecting his designs, to put her upon her guard against him in future. Still all her Mother's warnings could not make her change her good opinion of the Friar. She continued to feel, that his friendship and society were requisite to her happiness: She looked upon his failings with a partial eye, and could not persuade herself, that He really had intended her ruin. However, Elvira had positively commanded her to drop his acquaintance, and She had too much respect for her orders to disobey them.

At length She resolved to address herself for advice

and protection to the Marquis de las Cisternas, as being her nearest Relation. She wrote to him, briefly stating her desolate situation; She besought him to compassionate his Brother's Child, to continue to her Elvira's pension, and to authorise her retiring to his old Castle in Murcia, which till now had been her retreat. Having sealed her letter, She gave it to the trusty Flora, who immediately set out to execute her commission. But Antonia was born under an unlucky Star. Had She made her application to the Marquis but one day sooner, received as his Niece and placed at the head of his Family, She would have escaped all the misfortunes, with which She was now threatened. Raymond had always intended to execute this plan: But first, his hopes of making the proposal to Elvira through the lips of Agnes, and afterwards, his disappointment at losing his intended Bride, as well as the severe illness which for some time had confined him to his Bed, made him defer from day to day the giving an Asylum in his House to his Brother's Widow. He had commissioned Lorenzo to supply her liberally with money: But Elvira, unwilling to receive obligations from that Nobleman, had assured him that She needed no immediate pecuniary assistance. Consequently, the Marquis did not imagine, that a trifling delay on his part could create any embarrassment; and the distress and agitation of his mind might well excuse his negligence.

Had He been informed that Elvira's death had left her Daughter Friendless and unprotected, He would doubtless have taken such measures, as would have ensured her from every danger: But Antonia was not destined to be so fortunate. The day on which She sent her letter to the Palace de las Cisternas, was that following Lorenzo's departure from Madrid. The Marquis was in the first paroxysms of despair at the conviction, that Agnes was indeed no more: He was delirious, and his life being in danger, no one was suffered to approach him. Flora was informed, that He was incapable of attending to Letters, and that probably a few hours would decide his fate. With this unsatisfactory answer She was obliged to return to her Mistress, who now found herself plunged into greater difficulties than ever.

Flora and Dame Jacintha exerted themselves to console her. The Latter begged her to make herself easy, for that as long as She chose to stay with her, She would treat her like her own Child. Antonia, finding that the good Woman had taken a real affection for her, was somewhat comforted by thinking, that She had at least one Friend in the World. A Letter was now brought to her, directed to Elvira. She recognized Leonella's writing, and opening it with joy, found a detailed account of her Aunt's adventures at Cordova. She informed her Sister that She had recovered her Legacy, had lost her heart, and had received in exchange that of the most amiable of Apothecaries, past, present, and to come. She added, that She should be at Madrid on the Tuesday night, and meant to have the pleasure of presenting her Caro Sposo* in form. Though her nuptials were far from pleasing Antonia, Leonella's speedy return gave her Niece much delight. She rejoiced in thinking, that She should once more be under a Relation's care. She could not but judge it to be highly improper, for a young Woman to be living among absolute Strangers, with no one to regulate her conduct, or protect her from the insults to which in her defenceless situation She was exposed. She therefore looked forward with impatience to the Tuesday night.

It arrived. Antonia listened anxiously to the Carriages, as they rolled along the Street. None of them stopped, and it grew late without Leonella's appearing. Still Antonia resolved to sit up till her Aunt's arrival, and in spite of all her remonstrances Dame Jacintha and

Flora insisted upon doing the same. The hours passed on slow and tediously. Lorenzo's departure from Madrid had put a stop to the nightly Serenades: She hoped in vain to hear the usual sound of Guitars beneath her window. She took up her own, and struck a few chords: But Music that evening had lost its charms for her, and She soon replaced the Instrument in its case. She seated herself at her embroidery frame, but nothing went right: The silks were missing, the thread snapped every moment, and the needles were so expert at falling, that they seemed to be animated. At length a flake of wax fell from the Taper which stood near her upon a favourite wreath of Violets: This compleatly discomposed her; She threw down her needle, and quitted the frame. It was decreed, that for that night nothing should have the power of amusing her. She was the prey of Ennui, and employed herself in making fruitless wishes for the arrival of her Aunt.

As She walked with a listless air up and down the chamber, the Door caught her eye conducting to that which had been her Mother's. She remembered that Elvira's little Library was arranged there, and thought that She might possibly find in it, some Book to amuse her till Leonella should arrive. Accordingly She took her Taper from the table, passed through the little Closet, and entered the adjoining apartment. As She looked around her, the sight of this room brought to her recollection a thousand painful ideas. It was the first time of her entering it since her Mother's death. The total silence prevailing through the chamber, the Bed despoiled of its furniture, the cheerless hearth where stood an extinguished Lamp, and a few dying Plants in the window, which since Elvira's loss had been neglected, inspired Antonia with a melancholy awe. The gloom of night gave strength to this sensation. She placed her light upon the Table, and sank into a large chair, in which She had seen her Mother seated a thousand and a thousand times. She was never to see her seated there again! Tears unbidden streamed down her cheek, and She abandoned herself to the sadness, which grew deeper with every moment.

Ashamed of her weakness, She at length rose from her seat: She proceeded to seek for what had brought her to this melancholy scene. The small collection of Books was arranged upon several shelves in order. Antonia examined them without finding any thing likely to interest her, till She put her hand upon a volume of old Spanish Ballads. She read a few Stanzas of one of them: They excited her curiosity. She took down the Book, and seated herself to peruse it with more ease. She trimmed the Taper, which now drew towards its end, and then read the following Ballad.

ALONZO THE BRAVE, AND FAIR IMOGINE*

A Warrior so bold, and a Virgin so bright
   Conversed, as They sat on the green:
They gazed on each other with tender delight;
Alonzo the Brave was the name of the Knight,
   The Maid's was the Fair Imogine.

'And Oh!' said the Youth, 'since to-morrow I go
   To fight in a far distant land,
Your tears for my absence soon leaving to flow,
Some Other will court you, and you will bestow
   On a wealthier Suitor your hand.'

'Oh! hush these suspicions,' Fair Imogine said,
   'Offensive to Love and to me!
For if ye be living, or if ye be dead,
I swear by the Virgin, that none in your stead
   Shall Husband of Imogine be

'If e'er I by lust or by wealth led aside
  Forget my Alonzo the Brave,
God grant, that to punish my falsehood and pride
Your Ghost at the Marriage may sit by my side,
May tax me with perjury, claim me as Bride,
  And bear me away to the Grave!'

To Palestine hastened the Hero so bold;
  His Love, She lamented him sore:
But scarce had a twelve-month elapsed, when behold,
A Baron all covered with jewels and gold
  Arrived at Fair Imogine's door.

His treasure, his presents, his spacious domain
  Soon made her untrue to her vows:
He dazzled her eyes; He bewildered her brain;
He caught her affections so light and so vain,
  And carried her home as his Spouse.

And now had the Marriage been blest by the Priest;
  The revelry now was begun:
The Tables, they groaned with the weight of the Feast;
Nor yet had the laughter and merriment ceased,
  When the Bell of the Castle told,—'One!'

Then first with amazement Fair Imogine found
  That a Stranger was placed by her side:
His air was terrific; He uttered no sound;
He spoke not, He moved not, He looked not around,
  But earnestly gazed on the Bride.

His vizor was closed, and gigantic his height;
  His armour was sable to view:
All pleasure and laughter were hushed at his sight;
The Dogs as They eyed him drew back in affright;
  The Lights in the chamber burned blue!

His presence all bosoms appeared to dismay;
  The Guests sat in silence and fear.

At length spoke the Bride, while She trembled; 'I pray,
Sir Knight, that your Helmet aside you would lay,
  And deign to partake of our chear.'

The Lady is silent: The Stranger complies.
  His vizor He slowly unclosed:
Oh! God! what a sight met Fair Imogine's eyes!
What words can express her dismay and surprize,
  When a Skeleton's head was exposed.

All present then uttered a terrified shout;
  All turned with disgust from the scene.
The worms, They crept in, and the worms, They crept out,
And sported his eyes and his temples about,
  While the Spectre addressed Imogine.

'Behold me, Thou false one! Behold me!' He cried;
  'Remember Alonzo the Brave!
God grants, that to punish thy falsehood and pride
My Ghost at thy marriage should sit by thy side,
Should tax thee with perjury, claim thee as Bride
  And bear thee away to the Grave!'

Thus saying, his arms round the Lady He wound,
  While loudly She shrieked in dismay;
Then sank with his prey through the wide-yawning ground:
Nor ever again was Fair Imogine found,
  Or the Spectre who bore her away.

Not long lived the Baron; and none since that time
  To inhabit the Castle presume:
For Chronicles tell, that by order sublime
There Imogine suffers the pain of her crime,
  And mourns her deplorable doom.

At midnight four times in each year does her Spright
  When Mortals in slumber are bound,
Arrayed in her bridal apparel of white,
Appear in the Hall with the Skeleton-Knight,
  And shriek, as He whirls her around

While They drink out of skulls newly torn from the grave,
  Dancing round them the Spectres are seen:
Their liquor is blood, and this horrible Stave
They howl.—'To the health of Alonzo the Brave,
  And his Consort, the False Imogine!'*

The perusal of this story was ill calculated to dispel
Antonia's melancholy. She had naturally a strong
inclination to the marvellous; and her Nurse who believed firmly in Apparitions, had related to her when
an Infant so many horrible adventures of this kind, that
all Elvira's attempts had failed to eradicate their impressions from her Daughter's mind. Antonia still nourished
a superstitious prejudice in her bosom: She was often
susceptible of terrors, which when She discovered their
natural and insignificant cause made her blush at her
own weakness. With such a turn of mind, the adventure
which She had just been reading, sufficed to give her
apprehensions the alarm. The hour and the scene
combined to authorize them. It was the dead of night:
She was alone, and in the chamber once occupied by
her deceased Mother. The weather was comfortless and
stormy: The wind howled around the House, the doors
rattled in their frames, and the heavy rain pattered
against the windows. No other sound was heard. The
Taper, now burnt down to the socket, sometimes flaring
upwards shot a gleam of light through the room, then
sinking again seemed upon the point of expiring. Antonia's
heart throbbed with agitation: Her eyes wandered
fearfully over the objects around her, as the trembling
flame illuminated them at intervals. She attempted to
rise from her seat; But her limbs trembled so violently,
that She was unable to proceed. She then called Flora,
who was in a room at no great distance: But agitation
choked her voice, and her cries died away in hollow
murmurs.

She passed some minutes in this situation, after which her terrors began to diminish. She strove to recover herself, and acquire strength enough to quit the room: Suddenly She fancied, that She heard a low sigh drawn near her. This idea brought back her former weakness. She had already raised herself from her seat, and was on the point of taking the Lamp from the Table. The imaginary noise stopped her: She drew back her hand, and supported herself upon the back of a Chair. She listened anxiously, but nothing more was heard.

'Gracious God!' She said to herself; 'What could be that sound? Was I deceived, or did I really hear it?'

Her reflections were interrupted by a noise at the door scarcely audible: It seemed as if somebody was whispering. Antonia's alarm increased: Yet the Bolt She knew to be fastened, and this idea in some degree re-assured her. Presently the Latch was lifted up softly, and the Door moved with caution backwards and forwards. Excess of terror now supplied Antonia with that strength, of which She had till then been deprived. She started from her place, and made towards the Closet door, whence She might soon have reached the chamber where She expected to find Flora and Dame Jacintha. Scarcely had She reached the middle of the room, when the Latch was lifted up a second time. An involuntary movement obliged her to turn her head. Slowly and gradually the Door turned upon its hinges, and standing upon the Threshold She beheld a tall thin Figure, wrapped in a white shroud which covered it from head to foot.

This vision arrested her feet: She remained as if petrified in the middle of the apartment. The Stranger with measured and solemn steps drew near the Table. The dying Taper darted a blue and melancholy flame as the Figure advanced towards it. Over the Table was fixed a small Clock; The hand of it was upon the stroke of three. The Figure stopped opposite to the Clock: It raised its right arm, and pointed to the hour, at the same time looking earnestly upon Antonia, who waited for the conclusion of this scene, motionless and silent.

The figure remained in this posture for some moments. The clock struck. When the sound had ceased, the Stranger advanced yet a few steps nearer Antonia.

'Yet three days,' said a voice faint, hollow, and sepulchral; 'Yet three days, and we meet again!'

Antonia shuddered at the words.

'We meet again?' She pronounced at length with difficulty: 'Where shall we meet? Whom shall I meet?'

The figure pointed to the ground with one hand, and with the other raised the Linen which covered its face.

'Almighty God! My Mother!'

Antonia shrieked, and fell lifeless upon the floor.

Dame Jacintha who was at work in a neighbouring chamber, was alarmed by the cry: Flora was just gone down stairs to fetch fresh oil for the Lamp, by which they had been sitting. Jacintha therefore hastened alone to Antonia's assistance, and great was her amazement to find her extended upon the floor. She raised her in her arms, conveyed her to her apartment, and placed her upon the Bed still senseless. She then proceeded to bathe her temples, chafe her hands, and use all possible means of bringing her to herself. With some difficulty She succeeded. Antonia opened her eyes, and looked round her wildly.

'Where is She?' She cried in a trembling voice; 'Is She gone? Am I safe? Speak to me! Comfort me! Oh! speak to me for God's sake!'

'Safe from whom, my Child?' replied the astonished Jacintha; 'What alarms you? Of whom are you afraid?'

'In three days! She told me that we should meet in three days! I heard her say it! I saw her, Jacintha, I saw her but this moment!'

She threw herself upon Jacintha's bosom.

'You saw her? Saw whom?'

'My Mother's Ghost!'

'Christ Jesus!' cried Jacintha, and starting from the Bed, let fall Antonia upon the pillow, and fled in consternation out of the room.

As She hastened down stairs, She met Flora ascending them.

'Go to your Mistress, Flora,' said She; 'Here are rare doings! Oh! I am the most unfortunate Woman alive! My House is filled with Ghosts and dead Bodies, and the Lord knows what besides; Yet I am sure, nobody likes such company, less than I do. But go your way to Donna Antonia, Flora, and let me go mine.'

Thus saying, She continued her course to the Streetdoor, which She opened, and without allowing herself time to throw on her veil, She made the best of her way to the Capuchin-Abbey. In the mean while, Flora hastened to her Lady's chamber, equally surprized and alarmed at Jacintha's consternation. She found Antonia lying upon the bed insensible. She used the same means for her recovery that Jacintha had already employed; But finding that her Mistress only recovered from one fit to fall into another, She sent in all haste for a Physician. While expecting his arrival, She undrest Antonia, and conveyed her to Bed.

Heedless of the storm, terrified almost out of her senses, Jacintha ran through the Streets, and stopped not till She reached the Gate of the Abbey. She rang loudly at the bell, and as soon as the Porter appeared, She desired permission to speak to the Superior. Ambrosio was then conferring with Matilda upon the means of procuring access to Antonia. The cause of Elvira's death remaining unknown, He was convinced that crimes were not so swiftly followed by punishment, as his Instructors the Monks had taught him, and as till then He had himself believed. This persuasion made him resolve upon Antonia's ruin, for the enjoyment of whose person dangers and difficulties only seemed to have increased his passion. The Monk had already made one attempt to gain admission to her presence; But Flora had refused him in such a manner as to convince him, that all future endeavours must be vain. Elvira had confided her suspicions to that trusty Servant: She had desired her never to leave Ambrosio alone with her Daughter, and if possible to prevent their meeting altogether. Flora promised to obey her, and had executed her orders to the very letter. Ambrosio's visit had been rejected that morning, though Antonia was ignorant of it. He saw that to obtain a sight of his Mistress by open means was out of the question; and both Himself and Matilda had consumed the night, in endeavouring to invent some plan, whose event might be more successful. Such was their employment, when a Lay-Brother entered the Abbot's Cell, and informed him, that a Woman calling herself Jacintha Zuniga requested audience for a few minutes.

Ambrosio was by no means disposed to grant the petition of his Visitor. He refused it positively, and bad the Lay-Brother tell the Stranger to return the next day. Matilda interrupted him.

'See this Woman,' said She in a low voice; 'I have my reasons.'

The Abbot obeyed her, and signified that He would go to the Parlour immediately. With this answer the Lay-Brother with-drew. As soon as they were alone Ambrosio enquired, why Matilda wished him to see this Jacintha.

'She is Antonia's Hostess,' replied Matilda; 'She may possibly be of use to you: but let us examine her, and learn what brings her hither.'

They proceeded together to the Parlour, where Jacintha was already waiting for the Abbot. She had conceived a great opinion of his piety and virtue; and supposing him to have much influence over the Devil, thought that it must be an easy matter for him to lay Elvira's Ghost in the Red Sea. Filled with this persuasion She had hastened to the Abbey. As soon as She saw the Monk enter the Parlour, She dropped upon her knees, and began her story as follows.

'Oh! Reverend Father! Such an accident! Such an adventure! I know not what course to take, and unless you can help me, I shall certainly go distracted. Well, to be sure, never was Woman so unfortunate, as myself! All in my power to keep clear of such abomination have I done, and yet that all is too little. What signifies my telling my beads four times a day, and observing every fast prescribed by the Calendar? What signifies my having made three Pilgrimages to St. James of Compostella,* and purchased as many pardons from the Pope, as would buy off Cain's punishment?*Nothing prospers with me! All goes wrong, and God only knows, whether any thing will ever go right again! Why now, be your Holiness the Judge. My Lodger dies in convulsions; Out of pure kindness I bury her at my own expence; [Not that She is any Relation of mine, or that I shall be benefited a single pistole by her death: I got nothing by it, and therefore you know, reverend Father, that her living or dying was just the same to me. But that is nothing to the purpose; To return to what I was saying,] I took care of her funeral, had every thing performed decently and properly, and put myself to expence enough, God knows! And how do you think the Lady repays me for my kindness? Why truly by refusing to sleep quietly in her comfortable deal Coffin, as a peaceable well-disposed Spirit ought to do, and coming to plague me, who never wish to set eyes on her again. Forsooth, it well becomes her to go racketing about my House at midnight, popping into her Daughter's room through the Key-hole, and frightening the poor Child out of her wits! Though She be a Ghost, She might be more civil than to bolt into a Person's House, who likes her company so little. But as for me, reverend Father, the plain state of the case is this: If She walks into my House, I must walk out of it, for I cannot abide such Visitors, not I! Thus you see, your Sanctity, that without your assistance I am ruined and undone for ever. I shall be obliged to quit my House; Nobody will take it, when 'tis known that She haunts it, and then I shall find myself in a fine situation! Miserable Woman that I am! What shall I do! What will become of me!'

Here She wept bitterly, wrung her hands, and begged to know the Abbot's opinion of her case.

'In truth, good Woman,' replied He, 'It will be difficult for me to relieve you, without knowing what is the matter with you. You have forgotten to tell me what has happened, and what it is you want.'

'Let me die' cried Jacintha, 'but your Sanctity is in the right! This then is the fact stated briefly. A lodger of mine is lately dead, a very good sort of Woman that I must needs say for her as far as my knowledge of her went, though that was not a great way: She kept me too much at a distance; for indeed She was given to be upon the high ropes, and whenever I ventured to speak to her, She had a look with her, which always made me feel a little queerish, God forgive me for saying so. However, though She was more stately than needful, and affected to look down upon me [Though if I am well informed, I come of as good Parents as She could do for her ears, for her Father was a Shoe-maker at Cordova, and Mine was an Hatter at Madrid, aye, and a very creditable Hatter too, let me tell you,] Yet for all her pride, She was a quiet well-behaved Body, and I never wish to have a better Lodger. This makes me wonder the more at her not sleeping quietly in her Grave: But there is no trusting to people in this world! For my part, I never saw her do amiss, except on the Friday before her death. To be sure,

I was then much scandalized by seeing her eat the wing of a Chicken! "How, Madona Flora!" quoth I; [Flora, may it please your Reverence, is the name of the waiting Maid]—"How, Madona Flora!" quoth I; "Does your Mistress eat flesh upon Fridays? Well! Well! See the event, and then remember, that Dame Jacintha warned you of it!" These were my very words, but Alas! I might as well have held my tongue! Nobody minded me; and Flora, who is somewhat pert and snappish, [More is the pity, say I] told me, that there was no more harm in eating a Chicken, than the egg from which it came. Nay She even declared, that if her Lady added a slice of bacon, She would not be an inch nearer Damnation, God protect us! A poor ignorant sinful soul! I protest to your Holiness, I trembled to hear her utter such blasphemies, and expected every moment to see the ground open and swallow her up, Chicken and all! For you must know, worshipful Father, that while She talked thus, She held the plate in her hand, on which lay the identical roast Fowl. And a fine Bird it was, that I must say for it! Done to a turn, for I super-intended the cooking of it myself: It was a little Gallician* of my own raising, may it please your Holiness, and the flesh was as white as an egg-shell, as indeed Donna Elvira told me herself. "Dame Jacintha," said She, very good-humouredly, though to say the truth, She was always very polite to me . . . . .'

Here Ambrosio's patience failed him. Eager to know Jacintha's business in which Antonia seemed to be concerned, He was almost distracted while listening to the rambling of this prosing old Woman. He interrupted her, and protested that if She did not immediately tell her story and have done with it, He should quit the Parlour, and leave her to get out of her difficulties by herself. This threat had the desired effect. Jacintha related her business in as few words as She could manage; But her account was still so prolix that Ambrosio had need of his patience to bear him to the conclusion.

'And so, your Reverence,' said She, after relating Elvira's death and burial, with all their circumstances; 'And so, your Reverence, upon hearing the shriek, I put away my work, and away posted I to Donna Antonia's chamber. Finding nobody there, I past on to the next; But I must own, I was a little timorous at going in, for this was the very room, where Donna Elvira used to sleep. However, in I went, and sure enough there lay the young Lady at full length upon the floor, as cold as a stone, and as white as a sheet. I was surprized at this, as your Holiness may well suppose; But Oh me! how I shook, when I saw a great tall figure at my elbow whose head touched the ceiling! The face was Donna Elvira's, I must confess; But out of its mouth came clouds of fire, its arms were loaded with heavy chains which it rattled piteously, and every hair on its head was a Serpent as big as my arm! At this I was frightened enough, and began to say my Ave-Maria: But the Ghost interrupting me uttered three loud groans, and roared out in a terrible voice, "Oh! That Chicken's wing! My poor soul suffers for it!" As soon as She had said this, the Ground opened, the Spectre sank down, I heard a clap of thunder, and the room was filled with a smell of brimstone. When I recovered from my fright, and had brought Donna Antonia to herself, who told me that She had cried out upon seeing her Mother's Ghost, [And well might She cry, poor Soul! Had I been in her place, I should have cried ten times louder] it directly came into my head, that if any one had power to quiet this Spectre, it must be your Reverence. So hither I came in all diligence, to beg that you will sprinkle my House with holy water, and lay the Apparition in the Red Sea.'

Ambrosio stared at this strange story, which He could not credit.

'Did Donna Antonia also see the Ghost?' said He.

'As plain as I see you, Reverend Father!'

Ambrosio paused for a moment. Here was an opportunity offered him of gaining access to Antonia, but He hesitated to employ it. The reputation which He enjoyed in Madrid was still dear to him; and since He had lost the reality of virtue, it appeared as if its semblance was become more valuable. He was conscious, that publicly to break through the rule never to quit the Abbey-precincts, would derogate much from his supposed austerity. In visiting Elvira, He had always taken care to keep his features concealed from the Domestics. Except by the Lady, her Daughter, and the faithful Flora, He was known in the Family by no other name than that of Father Jerome. Should He comply with Jacintha's request, and accompany her to her House, He knew that the violation of his rule could not be kept a secret. However, his eagerness to see Antonia obtained the victory: He even hoped, that the singularity of this adventure would justify him in the eyes of Madrid: But whatever might be the consequences, He resolved to profit by the opportunity which chance had presented to him. An expressive look from Matilda confirmed him in this resolution.

'Good Woman,' said He to Jacintha, 'what you tell me is so extraordinary that I can scarcely credit your assertions. However, I will comply with your request. Tomorrow after Matins you may expect me at your House: I will then examine into what I can do for you, and if it is in my power, will free you from this unwelcome Visitor. Now then go home, and peace be with you!'

'Home?' exclaimed Jacintha; 'I go home? Not I by my troth! except under your protection, I set no foot of mine within the threshold. God help me, the Ghost may meet me upon the Stairs, and whisk me away with her to

the devil! Oh! That I had accepted young Melchior
Basco's offer! Then I should have had somebody to
protect me; But now I am a lone Woman, and meet with
nothing but crosses and misfortunes! Thank Heaven, it is
not yet too late to repent! There is Simon Gonzalez will
have me any day of the week, and if I live till day-break,
I will marry him out of hand: An Husband I will have,
that is determined, for now this Ghost is once in my
House, I shall be frightened out of my wits to sleep alone.
But for God's sake, reverend Father, come with me now.
I shall have no rest till the House is purified, or the poor
young Lady either. The dear Girl! She is in a piteous
taking: I left her in strong convulsions, and I doubt, She
will not easily recover her fright.'

The Friar started, and interrupted her hastily.

'In convulsions, say you? Antonia in convulsions?
Lead on, good Woman! I follow you this moment!'

Jacintha insisted upon his stopping to furnish himself
with the vessel of holy water: With this request He complied. Thinking herself safe under his protection should a
Legion of Ghosts attack her, the old Woman returned
the Monk a profusion of thanks, and they departed
together for the Strada di San Iago.

So strong an impression had the Spectre made upon
Antonia, that for the first two or three hours the Physician
declared her life to be in danger. The fits at length
becoming less frequent induced him to alter his opinion.
He said, that to keep her quiet was all that was necessary;
and He ordered a medicine to be prepared which would
tranquillize her nerves, and procure her that repose,
which at present She much wanted. The sight of Ambrosio, who now appeared with Jacintha at her Bed-side,
contributed essentially to compose her ruffled spirits.
Elvira had not sufficiently explained herself upon the
nature of his designs, to make a Girl so ignorant of the
world as her Daughter, aware how dangerous was his

acquaintance. At this moment, when penetrated with horror at the scene which had just past, and dreading to contemplate the Ghost's prediction, her mind had need of all the succours of friendship and religion, Antonia regarded the Abbot with an eye doubly partial. That strong prepossession in his favour still existed, which She had felt for him at first sight: She fancied, yet knew not wherefore, that his presence was a safe-guard to her from every danger, insult, or misfortune. She thanked him gratefully for his visit, and related to him the adventure, which had alarmed her so seriously.

The Abbot strove to re-assure her, and convince her that the whole had been a deception of her over-heated fancy. The solitude in which She had passed the Evening, the gloom of night, the Book which She had been reading, and the Room in which She sat, were all calculated to place before her such a vision. He treated the idea of Ghosts with ridicule, and produced strong arguments to prove the fallacy of such a system. His conversation tranquillized and comforted her, but did not convince her. She could not believe, that the Spectre had been a mere creature of her imagination; Every circumstance was impressed upon her mind too forcibly, to permit her flattering herself with such an idea. She persisted in asserting, that She had really seen her Mother's Ghost, had heard the period of her dissolution announced and declared, that She never should quit her bed alive. Ambrosio advised her against encouraging these sentiments, and then quitted her chamber, having promised to repeat his visit on the morrow. Antonia received this assurance with every mark of joy: But the Monk easily perceived, that He was not equally acceptable to her Attendant. Flora obeyed Elvira's injunctions with the most scrupulous observance. She examined every circumstance with an anxious eye likely in the least to prejudice her young Mistress, to whom She had been attached for

many years. She was a Native of Cuba, had followed
Elvira to Spain, and loved the young Antonia with a
Mother's affection. Flora quitted not the room for a
moment, while the Abbot remained there: She watched
his every word, his every look, his every action. He saw
that her suspicious eye was always fixed upon him, and
conscious that his designs would not bear inspection so
minute, He felt frequently confused and disconcerted.
He was aware, that She doubted the purity of his intentions; that She would never leave him alone with Antonia, and his Mistress defended by the presence of this
vigilant Observer, He despaired of finding the means to
gratify his passion.

As He quitted the House, Jacintha met him, and
begged, that some Masses might be sung for the repose
of Elvira's soul, which She doubted not was suffering in
Purgatory. He promised not to forget her request; But
He perfectly gained the old Woman's heart, by engaging
to watch during the whole of the approaching night in
the haunted chamber. Jacintha could find no terms
sufficiently strong to express her gratitude, and the
Monk departed loaded with her benedictions.

It was broad day, when He returned to the Abbey.
His first care was to communicate what had past to his
Confident. He felt too sincere a passion for Antonia to
have heard unmoved the prediction of her speedy death,
and He shuddered at the idea of losing an object so
dear to him. Upon this head Matilda re-assured him.
She confirmed the arguments, which Himself had already
used: She declared Antonia to have been deceived by
the wandering of her brain, by the Spleen which opprest her at the moment, and by the natural turn of
her mind to superstition, and the marvellous. As to
Jacintha's account, the absurdity refuted itself; The
Abbot hesitated not to believe, that She had fabricated
the whole story, either confused by terror, or hoping to

make him comply more readily with her request. Having
over-ruled the Monk's apprehensions, Matilda continued thus.

'The prediction and the Ghost are equally false; But
it must be your care, Ambrosio, to verify the first.
Antonia within three days must indeed be dead to the
world; But She must live for you. Her present illness,
and this fancy which She has taken into her head, will
colour a plan, which I have long meditated, but which
was impracticable without your procuring access to
Antonia. She shall be yours, not for a single night, but
for ever. All the vigilance of her Duenna shall not avail
her: You shall riot unrestrained in the charms of your
Mistress. This very day must the scheme be put in execution, for you have no time to lose. The Nephew of the
Duke of Medina Celi prepares to demand Antonia for his
Bride: In a few days She will be removed to the Palace of.
her Relation, the Marquis de las Cisternas, and there
She will be secure from your attempts. Thus during your
absence have I been informed by my Spies, who are ever
employed in bringing me intelligence for your service.
Now then listen to me. There is a juice extracted from
certain herbs known but to few, which brings on the
Person who drinks it the exact image of Death. Let this
be administered to Antonia: You may easily find means
to pour a few drops into her medicine. The effect will be
throwing her into strong convulsions for an hour: After
which her blood will gradually cease to flow, and heart to
beat; A mortal paleness will spread itself over her features, and She will appear a Corse to every eye. She has
no Friends about her: You may charge yourself unsuspected with the superintendence of her funeral, and cause
her to be buried in the Vaults of St. Clare. Their solitude
and easy access render these Caverns favourable to your
designs. Give Antonia the soporific draught this Evening:
Eight and forty hours after She has drank it, Life will

revive to her bosom. She will then be absolutely in your power: She will find all resistance unavailing, and necessity will compel her to receive you in her arms.'

'Antonia will be in my power!' exclaimed the Monk; 'Matilda, you transport me! At length then happiness will be mine, and that happiness will be Matilda's gift, will be the gift of friendship! I shall clasp Antonia in my arms, far from every prying eye, from every tormenting Intruder! I shall sigh out my soul upon her bosom; Shall teach her young heart the first rudiments of pleasure, and revel uncontrouled in the endless variety of her charms! And shall this delight indeed by mine? Shall I give the reins to my desires, and gratify every wild tumultuous wish? Oh! Matilda, how can I express to you my gratitude?'

'By profiting by my counsels. Ambrosio, I live but to serve you: Your interest and happiness are equally mine. Be your person Antonia's, but to your friendship and your heart I still assert my claim. Contributing to yours forms now my only pleasure. Should my exertions procure the gratification of your wishes, I shall consider my trouble to be amply repaid. But let us lose no time. The liquor of which I spoke, is only to be found in St. Clare's Laboratory. Hasten then to the Prioress; Request of her admission to the Laboratory, and it will not be denied. There is a Closet at the lower end of the great Room, filled with liquids of different colours and qualities. The Bottle in question stands by itself upon the third shelf on the left. It contains a greenish liquor: Fill a small phial with it when you are unobserved, and Antonia is your own.'

The Monk hesitated not to adopt this infamous plan. His desires, but too violent before, had acquired fresh vigour from the sight of Antonia. As He sat by her bedside, accident had discovered to him some of those charms, which till then had been concealed from him:

He found them even more perfect, than his ardent imagination had pictured them. Sometimes her white and polished arm was displayed in arranging the pillow: Sometimes a sudden movement discovered part of her swelling bosom: But where-ever the new-found charm presented itself, there rested the Friar's gloting eyes. Scarcely could He master himself sufficiently to conceal his desires from Antonia and her vigilant Duenna. Inflamed by the remembrance of these beauties, He entered into Matilda's scheme without hesitation.

No sooner were Matins over, than He bent his course towards the Convent of St. Clare: His arrival threw the whole Sisterhood into the utmost amazement. The Prioress was sensible of the honour done her Convent by his paying it his first visit, and strove to express her gratitude by every possible attention. He was paraded through the Garden, shown all the reliques of Saints and Martyrs, and treated with as much respect and distinction as had He been the Pope himself. On his part, Ambrosio received the Domina's civilities very graciously, and strove to remove her surprize at his having broken through his resolution. He stated, that among his penitents, illness prevented many from quitting their Houses. These were exactly the People, who most needed his advice and the comforts of Religion: Many representations had been made to him upon this account, and though highly repugnant to his own wishes, He had found it absolutely necessary for the service of heaven to change his determination, and quit his beloved retirement. The Prioress applauded his zeal in his profession and his charity towards Mankind: She declared, that Madrid was happy in possessing a Man so perfect and irreproachable. In such discourse, the Friar at length reached the Laboratory. He found the Closet: The Bottle stood in the place which Matilda had described, and the Monk seized an opportunity to fill his

phial unobserved with the soporific liquor. Then having
partaken of a Collation in the Refectory, He retired from
the Convent pleased with the success of his visit, and
leaving the Nuns delighted by the honour conferred upon
them.

He waited till Evening, before He took the road to
Antonia's dwelling. Jacintha welcomed him with transport, and besought him not to forget his promise to pass
the night in the haunted Chamber: That promise He
now repeated. He found Antonia tolerably well, but still
harping upon the Ghost's prediction. Flora moved not
from her Lady's Bed, and by symptoms yet stronger than
on the former night testified her dislike to the Abbot's
presence. Still Ambrosio affected not to observe them.
The Physician arrived, while He was conversing with
Antonia. It was dark already; Lights were called for,
and Flora was compelled to descend for them herself.
However, as She left a third Person in the room, and
expected to be absent but a few minutes, She believed
that She risqued nothing in quitting her post. No sooner
had She left the room, than Ambrosio moved towards the
Table, on which stood Antonia's medicine: It was placed
in a recess of the window. The Physician seated in an
armed-chair, and employed in questioning his Patient,
paid no attention to the proceedings of the Monk.
Ambrosio seized the opportunity: He drew out the fatal
Phial, and let a few drops fall into the medicine. He then
hastily left the Table, and returned to the seat which He
had quitted. When Flora made her appearance with
lights, every thing seemed to be exactly as She had left it.

The Physician declared, that Antonia might quit her
chamber the next day with perfect safety. He recommended her following the same prescription, which on
the night before had procured her a refreshing sleep:
Flora replied, that the draught stood ready upon the
Table: He advised the Patient to take it without delay,

and then retired. Flora poured the medicine into a Cup, and presented it to her Mistress. At that moment Ambrosio's courage failed him. Might not Matilda have deceived him? Might not Jealousy have persuaded her to destroy her Rival, and substitute poison in the room of an opiate? This idea appeared so reasonable, that He was on the point of preventing her from swallowing the medicine. His resolution was adopted too late: The Cup was already emptied, and Antonia restored it into Flora's hands. No remedy was now to be found: Ambrosio could only expect the moment impatiently, destined to decide upon Antonia's life or death, upon his own happiness or despair.

Dreading to create suspicion by his stay, or betray himself by his mind's agitation, He took leave of his Victim, and withdrew from the room. Antonia parted from him with less cordiality than on the former night. Flora had represented to her Mistress, that to admit his visits was to disobey her Mother's orders: She described to her his emotion on entering the room, and the fire which sparkled in his eyes, while He gazed upon her. This had escaped Antonia's observation, but not her Attendant's; Who explaining the Monk's designs and their probable consequences in terms much clearer than Elvira's, though not quite so delicate, had succeeded in alarming her young Lady, and persuading her to treat him more distantly than She had done hitherto. The idea of obeying her Mother's will at once determined Antonia. Though She grieved at losing his society, She conquered herself sufficiently to receive the Monk with some degree of reserve and coldness. She thanked him with respect and gratitude for his former visits, but did not invite his repeating them in future. It now was not the Friar's interest to solicit admission to her presence, and He took leave of her, as if not designing to return. Fully persuaded that the acquaintance which She dreaded was now at an end, Flora was so much worked upon by his easy compliance, that She began to doubt the justice of her suspicions. As She lighted him down Stairs, She thanked him for having endeavoured to root out from Antonia's mind her superstitious terrors of the Spectre's prediction: She added, that as He seemed interested in Donna Antonia's welfare, should any change take place in her situation, She would be careful to let him know it. The Monk in replying took pains to raise his voice, hoping that Jacintha would hear it. In this He succeeded; As He reached the foot of the Stairs with his Conductress, the Landlady failed not to make her appearance.

'Why surely you are not going away, reverend Father?' cried She; 'Did you not promise to pass the night in the haunted Chamber? Christ Jesus! I shall be left alone with the Ghost, and a fine pickle I shall be in by morning! Do all I could, say all I could, that obstinate old Brute, Simon Gonzalez, refused to marry me to-day; And before to-morrow comes, I suppose, I shall be torn to pieces, by the Ghosts, and Goblins, and Devils, and what not! For God's sake, your Holiness, do not leave me in such a woeful condition! On my bended knees I beseech you to keep your promise: Watch this night in the haunted chamber; Lay the Apparition in the Red Sea, and Jacintha remembers you in her prayers to the last day of her existence!'

This request Ambrosio expected and desired; Yet He affected to raise objections, and to seem unwilling to keep his word. He told Jacintha that the Ghost existed no where but in her own brain, and that her insisting upon his staying all night in the House was ridiculous and useless. Jacintha was obstinate: She was not to be convinced, and pressed him so urgently not to leave her a prey to the Devil, that at length He granted her request. All this show of resistance imposed not upon Flora, who was naturally of a suspicious temper. She suspected the Monk to be acting a part very contrary to his own inclinations, and that He wished for no better than to remain where He was. She even went so far as to believe, that Jacintha was in his interest; and the poor old Woman was immediately set down, as no better than a Procuress. While She applauded herself for having penetrated into this plot against her Lady's honour, She resolved in secret to render it fruitless.

'So then,' said She to the Abbot with a look half-satirical and half indignant; 'So then you mean to stay here to-night? Do so, in God's name! Nobody will prevent you. Sit up to watch for the Ghost's arrival: I shall sit up too, and the Lord grant, that I may see nothing worse than a Ghost! I quit not Donna Antonia's Bed-side during this blessed night: Let me see any one dare to enter the room, and be He mortal or immortal, be He Ghost, Devil, or Man, I warrant his repenting that ever He crossed the threshold!'

This hint was sufficiently strong, and Ambrosio understood its meaning. But instead of showing that He perceived her suspicions; He replied mildly that He approved the Duenna's precautions, and advised her to persevere in her intention. This, She assured him faithfully, that He might depend upon her doing. Jacintha then conducted him into the chamber where the Ghost had appeared, and Flora returned to her Lady's.

Jacintha opened the door of the haunted room with a trembling hand: She ventured to peep in; But the wealth of India would not have tempted her to cross the threshold. She gave the Taper to the Monk, wished him well through the adventure, and hastened to be gone. Ambrosio entered. He bolted the door, placed the light upon the Table, and seated himself in the Chair which on the former night had sustained Antonia. In spite of Matilda's assurances that the Spectre was a mere crea-

tion of fancy, his mind was impressed with a certain
mysterious horror. He in vain endeavoured to shake it
off. The silence of the night, the story of the Apparition,
the chamber wainscotted with dark oak pannells, the
recollection which it brought with it of the murdered
Elvira, and his incertitude respecting the nature of the
drops given by him to Antonia, made him feel uneasy at
his present situation. But He thought much less of the
Spectre, than of the poison. Should He have destroyed
the only object, which rendered life dear to him; Should
the Ghost's prediction prove true; Should Antonia in
three days be no more, and He the wretched cause of her
death . . . . . . The supposition was too horrible to dwell
upon. He drove away these dreadful images, and as often
they presented themselves again before him. Matilda
had assured him, that the effects of the Opiate would be
speedy. He listened with fear, yet with eagerness, expecting to hear some disturbance in the adjoining chamber.
All was still silent. He concluded, that the drops had not
begun to operate. Great was the stake, for which He now
played: A moment would suffice to decide upon his
misery or happiness. Matilda had taught him the means
of ascertaining, that life was not extinct for ever: Upon
this assay depended all his hopes. With every instant his
impatience redoubled; His terrors grew more lively, his
anxiety more awake. Unable to bear this state of inserti-
tude, He endeavoured to divert it by substituting the
thoughts of Others to his own. The Books, as was before
mentioned, were ranged upon shelves near the Table:
This stood exactly opposite to the Bed, which was
placed in an Alcove near the Closet-door. Ambrosio took
down a Volume, and seated himself by the Table: But
his attention wandered from the Pages before him.
Antonia's image and that of the murdered Elvira persisted to force themselves before his imagination. Still He
continued to read, though his eyes ran over the charac-

ters, without his mind being conscious of their import.

Such was his occupation, when He fancied that He heard a foot-step. He turned his head, but nobody was to be seen. He resumed his Book; But in a few minutes after the same sound was repeated, and followed by a rustling noise close behind him. He now started from his seat, and looking round him, perceived the Closet-door standing half-unclosed. On his first entering the room He had tried to open it, but found it bolted on the inside.

'How is this?' said He to himself; 'How comes this door unfastened?'

He advanced towards it: He pushed it open, and looked into the closet: No one was there. While He stood irresolute, He thought, that He distinguished a groaning in the adjacent chamber: It was Antonia's, and He supposed, that the drops began to take effect: But upon listening more attentively, He found the noise to be caused by Jacintha, who had fallen asleep by the Lady's Bed-side, and was snoring most lustily. Ambrosio drew back, and returned to the other room, musing upon the sudden opening of the Closet-door, for which He strove in vain to account.

He paced the chamber up and down in silence. At length He stopped, and the Bed attracted his attention. The curtain of the Recess was but half-drawn. He sighed involuntarily.

'That Bed,' said He in a low voice, 'That Bed was Elvira's! There has She past many a quiet night, for She was good and innocent. How sound must have been her sleep! And yet now She sleeps sounder! Does She indeed sleep? Oh! God grant, that She may! What if She rose from her Grave at this sad and silent hour? What if She broke the bonds of the Tomb, and glided angrily before my blasted eyes? Oh! I never could support the sight! Again to see her form distorted by dying agonies, her blood-swollen veins, her livid countenance, her eyes bursting from their sockets with pain! To hear her speak of future punishment, menace me with Heaven's vengeance, tax me with the crimes I have committed, with those I am going to commit . . . . . Great God! What is that?'

As He uttered these words, his eyes which were fixed upon the Bed, saw the curtain shaken gently backwards and forwards. The Apparition was recalled to his mind, and He almost fancied that He beheld Elvira's visionary form reclining upon the Bed. A few moments consideration sufficed to re-assure him.

'It was only the wind,' said He, recovering himself.

Again He paced the chamber; But an involuntary movement of awe and inquietude constantly led his eye towards the Alcove. He drew near it with irresolution. He paused before He ascended the few steps which led to it. He put out his hand thrice to remove the curtain, and as often drew it back.

'Absurd terrors!' He cried at length, ashamed of his own weakness——

Hastily he mounted the steps; When a Figure drest in white started from the Alcove, and gliding by him, made with precipitation towards the Closet. Madness and despair now supplied the Monk with that courage, of which He had till then been destitute. He flew down the steps, pursued the Apparition, and attempted to grasp it.

'Ghost, or Devil, I hold you!' He exclaimed, and seized the Spectre by the arm.

'Oh! Christ Jesus!' cried a shrill voice; 'Holy Father, how you gripe me! I protest, that I meant no harm!'

This address, as well as the arm which He held, convinced the Abbot that the supposed Ghost was substantial flesh and blood. He drew the Intruder towards the Table, and holding up the light, discovered the features of . . . . . . Madona Flora!

Incensed at having been betrayed by this trifling

cause into fears so ridiculous, He asked her sternly, what business had brought her to that chamber. Flora, ashamed at being found out, and terrified at the severity of Ambrosio's looks, fell upon her knees, and promised to make a full confession.

'I protest, reverend Father,' said She, 'that I am quite grieved at having disturbed you: Nothing was further from my intention. I meant to get out of the room as quietly as I got in; and had you been ignorant that I watched you, you know, it would have been the same thing, as if I had not watched you at all. To be sure, I did very wrong in being a Spy upon you, that I cannot deny; But Lord! your Reverence, how can a poor weak Woman resist curiosity? Mine was so strong to know what you were doing, that I could not but try to get a little peep, without any body knowing any thing about it. So with that I left old Dame Jacintha sitting by my Lady's Bed, and I ventured to steal into the Closet. Being unwilling to interrupt you, I contented myself at first with putting my eye to the Key-hole; But as I could see nothing by this means, I undrew the bolt, and while your back was turned to the Alcove, I whipt me in softly and silently. Here I lay snug behind the curtain, till your Reverence found me out, and seized me ere I had time to regain the Closet-door. This is the whole truth, I assure you, Holy Father, and I beg your pardon a thousand times for my impertinence.'

During this speech the Abbot had time to recollect himself: He was satisfied with reading the penitent Spy a lecture upon the dangers of curiosity, and the meanness of the action in which She had been just discovered. Flora declared herself fully persuaded, that She had done wrong; She promised never to be guilty of the same fault again, and was retiring very humble and contrite to Antonia's chamber, when the Closet-door was suddenly thrown open, and in rushed Jacintha pale and out of breath.

'Oh! Father! Father!' She cried in a voice almost choked with terror; 'What shall I do! What shall I do! Here is a fine piece of work! Nothing but misfortunes! Nothing but dead people, and dying people! Oh! I shall go distracted! I shall go distracted!'

'Speak! Speak!' cried Flora and the Monk at the same time; 'What has happened? What is the matter?'

'Oh! I shall have another Corse in my House! Some Witch has certainly cast a spell upon it, upon me, and upon all about me! Poor Donna Antonia! There She lies in just such convulsions, as killed her Mother! The Ghost told her true! I am sure, the Ghost has told her true!'

Flora ran, or rather flew to her Lady's chamber: Ambrosio followed her, his bosom trembling with hope and apprehension. They found Antonia as Jacintha had described, torn by racking convulsions from which they in vain endeavoured to relieve her. The Monk dispatched Jacintha to the Abbey in all haste, and commissioned her to bring Father Pablos back with her, without losing a moment.

'I will go for him,' replied Jacintha, 'and tell him to come hither; But as to bringing him myself, I shall do no such thing. I am sure that the House is bewitched, and burn me if ever I set foot in it again.'

With this resolution She set out for the Monastery, and delivered to Father Pablos the Abbot's orders. She then betook herself to the House of old Simon Gonzalez, whom She resolved never to quit, till She had made him her Husband, and his dwelling her own.

Father Pablos had no sooner beheld Antonia, than He pronounced her incurable. The convulsions continued for an hour: During that time her agonies were much milder than those, which her groans created in the Abbot's heart. Her every pang seemed a dagger in his bosom, and He cursed himself a thousand times for having adopted so barbarous a project. The hour being expired, by degrees the Fits became less frequent, and Antonia less agitated. She felt that her dissolution was approaching, and that nothing could save her.

'Worthy Ambrosio,' She said in a feeble voice, while She pressed his hand to her lips; 'I am now at liberty to express, how grateful is my heart for your attention and kindness. I am upon the bed of death; Yet an hour, and I shall be no more. I may therefore acknowledge without restraint, that to relinquish your society was very painful to me: But such was the will of a Parent, and I dared not disobey. I die without repugnance: There are few, who will lament my leaving them; There are few, whom I lament to leave. Among those few, I lament for none more than for yourself; But we shall meet again, Ambrosio! We shall one day meet in heaven: There shall our friendship be renewed, and my Mother shall view it with pleasure!'

She paused. The Abbot shuddered when She mentioned Elvira: Antonia imputed his emotion to pity and concern for her.

'You are grieved for me, Father,' She continued; 'Ah! sigh not for my loss. I have no crimes to repent, at least none of which I am conscious, and I restore my soul without fear to him from whom I received it. I have but few requests to make: Yet let me hope that what few I have shall be granted. Let a solemn Mass be said for my soul's repose, and another for that of my beloved Mother. Not, that I doubt her resting in her Grave: I am now convinced that my reason wandered, and the falsehood of the Ghost's prediction is sufficient to prove my error. But every one has some failing: My Mother may have had hers, though I knew them not: I therefore wish a Mass to be celebrated for her repose, and the expence may be defrayed by the little wealth of which I am possessed. Whatever may then remain, I bequeath to my

Aunt Leonella. When I am dead, let the Marquis de las Cisternas know, that his Brother's unhappy family can no longer importune him. But disappointment makes me unjust: They tell me, that He is ill, and perhaps had it been in his power, He wished to have protected me. Tell him then, Father, only that I am dead, and that if He had any faults to me, I forgave him from my heart. This done, I have nothing more to ask for, than your prayers: Promise to remember my requests, and I shall resign my life without a pang or sorrow.'

Ambrosio engaged to comply with her desires, and proceeded to give her absolution. Every moment announced the approach of Antonia's fate: Her sight failed; Her heart beat sluggishly; Her fingers stiffened, and grew cold, and at two in the morning She expired without a groan. As soon as the breath had forsaken her body, Father Pablos retired, sincerely affected at the melancholy scene. On her part, Flora gave way to the most unbridled sorrow. Far different concerns employed Ambrosio: He sought for the pulse whose throbbing, so Matilda had assured him, would prove Antonia's death but temporal. He found it; He pressed it; It palpitated beneath his hand, and his heart was filled with ecstacy. However, He carefully concealed his satisfaction at the success of his plan. He assumed a melancholy air, and addressing himself to Flora, warned her against abandoning herself to fruitless sorrow. Her tears were too sincere to permit her listening to his counsels, and She continued to weep unceasingly. The Friar withdrew, first promising to give orders himself about the Funeral, which, out of consideration for Jacintha as He pretended, should take place with all expedition. Plunged in grief for the loss of her beloved Mistress, Flora scarcely attended to what He said. Ambrosio hastened to command the Burial. He obtained permission from the Prioress, that the Corse should be deposited in St. Clare's Sepulchre: and on the

Friday Morning, every proper and needful ceremony being performed, Antonia's body was committed to the Tomb.

On the same day Leonella arrived at Madrid, intending to present her young Husband to Elvira. Various circumstances had obliged her to defer her journey from Tuesday to Friday, and She had no opportunity of making this alteration in her plans known to her Sister. As her heart was truly affectionate, and as She had ever entertained a sincere regard for Elvira and her Daughter, her surprize at hearing of their sudden and melancholy fate was fully equalled by her sorrow and disappointment. Ambrosio sent to inform her of Antonia's bequest: At her solication, He promised, as soon as Elvira's trifling debts were discharged, to transmit to her the remainder. This being settled, no other business detained Leonella in Madrid, and She returned to Cordova with all diligence.

CHAPTER III

> Oh! could I worship aught beneath the skies,
> That earth hath seen or fancy could devise,
> Thine altar, sacred Liberty, should stand,
> Built by no mercenary vulgar hand,
> With fragrant turf, and flowers as wild and fair,
> As ever dressed a bank, or scented summer air.
>
> Cowper.*

HIS WHOLE ATTENTION bent upon bringing to justice the Assassins of his Sister, Lorenzo little thought, how severely his interest was suffering in another quarter. As was before mentioned, He returned not to Madrid till the evening of that day, on which Antonia was buried. Signifying to the Grand Inquisitor the order of the Cardinal-Duke [a ceremony not to be neglected, when a Member of the Church was to be arrested publicly] communicating his design to his Uncle and Don Ramirez, and assembling a troop of Attendants sufficiently to prevent opposition, furnished him with full occupation during the few hours preceding midnight. Consequently, He had no opportunity to enquire about his Mistress, and was perfectly ignorant both of her death and her Mother's.

The Marquis was by no means out of danger: His delirium was gone, but had left him so much exhausted, that the Physicians declined pronouncing upon the consequences likely to ensue. As for Raymond himself, He wished for nothing more earnestly than to join Agnes in the grave. Existence was hateful to him : He saw nothing in the world deserving his attention; and He hoped to hear that Agnes was revenged, and himself given over in the same moment.

Followed by Raymond's ardent prayers for success, Lorenzo was at the Gates of St. Clare a full hour before the time appointed by the Mother St. Ursula. He was accompanied by his Uncle, by Don Ramirez de Mello, and a party of chosen Archers. Though in considerable numbers their appearance created no surprize: A great Crowd was already assembled before the Convent-doors, in order to witness the Procession. It was naturally supposed, that Lorenzo and his Attendants were conducted thither by the same design. The Duke of Medina being recognised, the People drew back, and made way for his party to advance. Lorenzo placed himself opposite to the great Gate, through which the Pilgrims were to pass. Convinced that the Prioress could not escape him, He waited patiently for her appearance, which She was expected to make exactly at Midnight.

The Nuns were employed in religious duties established in honour of St. Clare, and to which no Prophane was ever admitted. The Chapel-windows were illuminated. As they stood on the outside, the Auditors heard the full swell of the organ, accompanied by a chorus of female voices, rise upon the stillness of the night. This died away, and was succeeded by a single strain of harmony: It was the voice of her who was destined to sustain in the procession the character of St. Clare. For this office the most beautiful Virgin of Madrid was always selected, and She upon whom the choice fell, esteemed it as the highest of honours. While listening to the Music, whose melody distance only seemed to render sweeter, the Audience was wrapped up in profound attention. Universal silence prevailed through the Crowd, and every heart was filled with reverence for religion. Every heart but Lorenzo's. Conscious that among those who chaunted the praises of their God so sweetly, there were some who cloaked with devotion the foulest sins, their hymns inspired him with detestation at their Hypocrisy. He had long observed with disapprobation and contempt the superstition, which governed Madrid's Inhabitants. His good sense had pointed out to him the artifices of the Monks, and the gross absurdity of their miracles, wonders, and supposititious reliques. He blushed to see his Countrymen the Dupes of deceptions so ridiculous, and only wished for an opportunity to free them from their monkish fetters. That opportunity, so long desired in vain, was at length presented to him. He resolved not to let it slip, but to set before the People in glaring colours, how enormous were the abuses but too frequently practised in Monasteries, and how unjustly public esteem was bestowed indiscriminately upon all who wore a religious habit. He longed for the moment destined to unmask the

Hypocrites, and convince his Countrymen, that a sanctified exterior does not always hide a virtuous heart.

The service lasted, till Midnight was announced by
the Convent-Bell. That sound being heard, the Music
ceased: The voices died away softly, and soon after the
lights disappeared from the Chapel-windows. Lorenzo's
heart beat high, when He found the execution of his plan
to be at hand. From the natural superstition of the People
He had prepared himself for some resistance. But He
trusted that the Mother St. Ursula would bring good
reasons to justify his proceeding. He had force with him
to repel the first impulse of the Populace, till his arguments should be heard: His only fear was, lest the
Domina, suspecting his design, should have spirited away
the Nun, on whose deposition every thing depended.
Unless the Mother St. Ursula should be present, He could
only accuse the Prioress upon suspicion; and this reflection
gave him some little apprehension for the success of his
enterprize. The tranquillity which seemed to reign through
the Convent, in some degree re-assured him: Still He
expected the moment eagerly, when the presence of his
Ally should deprive him of the power of doubting.

The Abbey of Capuchins was only separated from
the Convent by the Garden and Cemetery. The Monks
had been invited to assist at the Pilgrimage. They now
arrived, marching two by two with lighted Torches in
their hands, and chaunting Hymns in honour of St.
Clare. Father Pablos was at their head, the Abbot having
excused himself from attending. The people made way
for the holy Train, and the Friars placed themselves in
ranks on either side of the great Gates. A few minutes
sufficed to arrange the order of the Procession. This being
settled, the Convent-doors were thrown open, and again
the female Chorus sounded in full melody. First appeared a Band of Choristers: As soon as they had passed,
the Monks fell in two by two, and followed with steps

slow and measured. Next came the Novices; They bore
no Tapers, as did the Professed, but moved on with
eyes bent downwards, and seemed to be occupied by
telling their Beads. To them succeeded a young and
lovely Girl, who represented St. Lucia:*She held a golden
bason in which were two eyes: Her own were covered by
a velvet bandage, and She was conducted by another
Nun habited as an Angel. She was followed by St.
Catherine,* a palm-branch in one hand, a flaming Sword
in the other: She was robed in white, and her brow was
ornamented with a sparkling Diadem. After her appeared St. Genevieve, surrounded by a number of Imps,
who putting themselves into grotesque attitudes, drawing
her by the robe, and sporting round her with antic
gestures, endeavoured to distract her attention from the
Book, on which her eyes were constantly fixed. These
merry Devils greatly entertained the Spectators, who
testified their pleasure by repeated bursts of Laughter.
The Prioress had been careful to select a Nun whose
disposition was naturally solemn and saturnine. She had
every reason to be satisfied with her choice: The drolle-
ries of the Imps were entirely thrown away, and St.
Genevieve moved on without discomposing a muscle.

Each of these Saints was separated from the Other by
a band of Choristers, exalting her praise in their Hymns,
but declaring her to be very much inferior to St. Clare,
the Convent's avowed Patroness. These having passed,
a long train of Nuns appeared, bearing like the Choristers each a burning Taper. Next came the reliques of
St. Clare, inclosed in vases equally precious for their
materials and workmanship: But they attracted not
Lorenzo's attention. The Nun who bore the heart,
occupied him entirely. According to Theodore's description, He doubted not her being the Mother St. Ursula.
She seemed to look round with anxiety. As He stood
foremost in the rank by which the procession past, her

eye caught Lorenzo's. A flush of joy overspread her till then pallid cheek. She turned to her Companion eagerly.

'We are safe!' He heard her whisper; ''tis her Brother!'

His heart being now at ease, Lorenzo gazed with tranquillity upon the remainder of the show. Now appeared its most brilliant ornament. It was a Machine fashioned like a throne, rich with jewels, and dazzling with light. It rolled onwards upon concealed wheels, and was guided by several lovely Children, dressed as Seraphs. The summit was covered with silver clouds, upon which reclined the most beautiful form that eyes ever witnessed. It was a Damsel representing St. Clare: Her dress was of inestimable price, and round her head a wreath of Diamonds formed an artificial glory: But all these ornaments yielded to the lustre of her charms. As She advanced, a murmur of delight ran through the Crowd. Even Lorenzo confessed secretly, that He never beheld more perfect beauty, and had not his heart been Antonia's, it must have fallen a sacrifice to this enchanting Girl. As it was, He considered her only as a fine Statue: She obtained from him no tribute save cold admiration, and when She had passed him, He thought of her no more.

'Who is She?' asked a By-stander in Lorenzo's hearing.

'One, whose beauty you must often have heard celebrated. Her name is Virginia de Villa-Franca: She is a Pensioner of St. Clare's Convent, a Relation of the Prioress, and has been selected-with justice as the ornament of the Procession.'

The Throne moved onwards. It was followed by the Prioress herself: She marched at the head of the remaining Nuns with a devout and sanctified air, and closed the procession. She moved on slowly: Her eyes were raised to heaven: Her countenance calm and tranquil seemed abstracted from all sublunary things, and no feature betrayed her secret pride at displaying the pomp and opulence of her Convent. She passed along, accompanied by the prayers and benedictions of the Populace: But how great was the general confusion and surprize, when Don Ramirez starting forward, challenged her as his Prisoner.

For a moment amazement held the Domina silent and immoveable: But no sooner did She recover herself, than She exclaimed against sacrilege and impiety, and called the People to rescue a Daughter of the Church. They were eagerly preparing to obey her; when Don Ramirez, protected by the Archers from their rage, commanded them to forbear, and threatened them with the severest vengeance of the Inquisition. At that dreaded word every arm fell, every sword shrunk back into its scabbard. The Prioress herself turned pale, and trembled. The general silence convinced her that She had nothing to hope but from innocence, and She besought Don Ramirez in a faultering voice, to inform her of what crime She was accused.

'That you shall know in time,' replied He; 'But first I must secure the Mother St. Ursula.'

'The Mother St. Ursula?' repeated the Domina faintly.

At this moment casting her eyes round, She saw near her Lorenzo and the Duke, who had followed Don Ramirez.

'Ah! great God!' She cried, clasping her hands together with a frantic air; 'I am betrayed!'

'Betrayed?' replied St. Ursula, who now arrived conducted by some of the Archers, and followed by the Nun her Companion in the procession: 'Not betrayed, but discovered. In me recognise your Accuser: You know not, how well I am instructed in your guilt!—Segnor!' She continued, turning to Don Ramirez; 'I commit myself to your custody. I charge the Prioress of St. Clare with murder, and stake my life for the justice of my accusation.'

A general cry of surprize was uttered by the whole Audience, and an explanation was demanded loudly. The trembling Nuns, terrified at the noise and universal confusion, had dispersed, and fled different ways. Some regained the Convent; Others sought refuge in the dwellings of their Relations; and Many, only sensible of their present danger, and anxious to escape from the tumult, ran through the Streets, and wandered, they knew not whither. The lovely Virginia was one of the first to fly: And in order that She might be better seen and heard, the People desired that St. Ursula should harangue them from the vacant Throne. The Nun complied; She ascended the glittering Machine, and then addressed the surrounding multitude as follows.

'However strange and unseemly may appear my conduct, when considered to be adopted by a Female and a Nun, necessity will justify it most fully. A secret, an horrible secret weighs heavy upon my soul: No rest can be mine till I have revealed it to the world, and satisfied that innocent blood which calls from the Grave for vengeance. Much have I dared to gain this opportunity of lightening my conscience. Had I failed in my attempt to reveal the crime, had the Domina but suspected that the mystery was none to me, my ruin was inevitable. Angels who watch unceasingly over those who deserve their favour, have enabled me to escape detection: I am now at liberty to relate a Tale, whose circumstances will freeze every honest soul with horror. Mine is the task to rend the veil from Hypocrisy, and show misguided Parents to what dangers the Woman is exposed, who falls under the sway of a monastic Tyrant.

'Among the Votaries of St. Clare, none was more lovely, none more gentle, than Agnes de Medina. I knew her well; She entrusted to me every secret of her heart; I was her Friend and Confident, and I loved her with sincere affection. Nor was I singular in my attachment.

Her piety unfeigned, her willingness to oblige, and her angelic disposition, rendered her the Darling of all that was estimable in the Convent. The Prioress herself, proud, scrupulous and forbidding, could not refuse Agnes that tribute of approbation, which She bestowed upon no one else. Every one has some fault: Alas! Agnes had her weakness! She violated the laws of our order, and incurred the inveterate hate of the unforgiving Domina. St. Clare's rules are severe: But grown antiquated and neglected, many of late years have either been forgotten, or changed by universal consent into milder punishments. The penance, adjudged to the crime of Agnes, was most cruel, most inhuman! The law had been long exploded: Alas! It still existed, and the revengeful Prioress now determined to revive it. This law decreed, that the Offender should be plunged into a private dungeon, expressly constituted to hide from the world for ever the Victim of Cruelty and tyrannic superstition. In this dreadful abode She was to lead a perpetual solitude, deprived of all society, and believed to be dead by those, whom affection might have prompted to attempt her rescue. Thus was She to languish out the remainder of her days, with no other food than bread and water, and no other comfort than the free indulgence of her tears.'

The indignation created by this account was so violent, as for some moments to interrupt St. Ursula's narrative. When the disturbance ceased, and silence again prevailed through the Assembly, She continued her discourse, while at every word the Domina's countenance betrayed her increasing terrors.

'A Council of the twelve elder Nuns was called: I was of the number. The Prioress in exaggerated colours described the offence of Agnes, and scrupled not to propose the revival of this almost forgotten law. To the shame of our sex be it spoken, that either so absolute was the Domina's will in the Convent, or so much had disappointment, solitude, and self-denial hardened their hearts and sowered their tempers, that this barbarous proposal was assented to by nine voices out of the twelve. I was not one of the nine. Frequent opportunities had convinced me of the virtues of Agnes, and I loved and pitied her most sincerely. The Mothers Bertha and Cornelia joined my party: We made the strongest opposition possible, and the Superior found herself compelled to change her intention. In spite of the majority in her favour, She feared to break with us openly. She knew, that supported by the Medina family, our forces would be too strong for her to cope with: And She also knew, that after being once imprisoned and supposed dead, should Agnes be discovered, her ruin would be inevitable. She therefore gave up her design, though which much reluctance. She demanded some days to reflect upon a mode of punishment, which might be agreeable to the whole Community; and She promised, that as soon as her resolution was fixed, the same Council should be again summoned. Two days passed away: On the Evening of the Third it was announced, that on the next day Agnes should be examined; and that according to her behaviour on that occasion, her punishment should be either strengthened or mitigated.

'On the night preceding this examination, I stole to the Cell of Agnes at an hour, when I supposed the other Nuns to be buried in sleep. I comforted her to the best of my power: I bad her take courage, told her to rely upon the support of her friends, and taught her certain signs, by which I might instruct her to answer the Domina's questions by an assent or negative. Conscious, that her Enemy would strive to confuse, embarrass, and daunt her, I feared her being ensnared into some confession prejudicial to her interests. Being anxious to keep my visit secret, I stayed with Agnes but a short time. I bad her not let her spirits be cast down; I mingled my tears

with those, which streamed down her cheek, embraced
her fondly, and was on the point of retiring, when I heard
the sound of steps approaching the Cell. I started back. A
Curtain which veiled a large Crucifix offered me a
retreat, and I hastened to place myself behind it. The
door opened. The Prioress entered, followed by four
other Nuns. They advanced towards the bed of Agnes.
The Superior reproached her with her errors in the
bitterest terms: She told her, that She was a disgrace to
the Convent, that She was resolved to deliver the world
and herself from such a Monster, and commanded her to
drink the contents of a Goblet now presented to her by
one of the Nuns. Aware of the fatal properties of the
liquor, and trembling to find herself upon the brink of
Eternity, the unhappy Girl strove to excite the Domina's
pity by the most affecting prayers. She sued for life in
terms which might have melted the heart of a Fiend: She
promised to submit patiently to any punishment, to
shame, imprisonment, and torture, might She but be
permitted to live! Oh! might She but live another month,
or week, or day! Her merciless Enemy listened to her
complaints unmoved: She told her, that at first She
meant to have spared her life, and that if She had altered
her, intention, She had to thank the opposition of her
Friends. She continued to insist upon her swallowing the
poison: She bad her recommend herself to the Almighty's
mercy, not to hers, and assured her that in an hour She
would be numbered with the Dead. Perceiving that it was
vain to implore this unfeeling Woman, She attempted to
spring from her bed, and call for assistance: She hoped,
if She could not escape the fate announced to her, at least
to have witnesses of the violence committed. The Prioress
guessed her design. She seized her forcibly by the arm,
and pushed her back upon her pillow. At the same time
drawing a dagger, and placing it at the breast of the
unfortunate Agnes, She protested that if She uttered a

single cry, or hesitated a single moment to drink the
poison, She would pierce her heart that instant. Already
half-dead with fear, She could make no further resistance. The Nun approached with the fatal Goblet. The
Domina obliged her to take it, and swallow the contents.
She drank, and the horrid deed was accomplished. The
Nuns then seated themselves round the Bed. They
answered her groans with reproaches; They interrupted
with sarcasms the prayers in which She recommended
her parting soul to mercy: They threatened her with
heaven's vengeance and eternal perdition: They bad her
despair of pardon, and strowed with yet sharper thorns
Death's painful pillow. Such were the sufferings of this
young Unfortunate, till released by fate from the malice
of her Tormentors. She expired in horror of the past, in
fears for the future; and her agonies were such as must
have amply gratified the hate and vengeance of her
Enemies. As soon as her Victim ceased to breathe, the
Domina retired, and was followed by her Accomplices.

'It was now that I ventured from my concealment. I
dared not to assist my unhappy Friend, aware, that without preserving her, I should only have brought on myself
the same destruction. Shocked and terrified beyond
expression at this horrid scene, scarcely had I sufficient
strength to regain my Cell. As I reached the door of that
of Agnes, I ventured to look towards the bed, on which
lay her lifeless body, once so lovely and so sweet! I
breathed a prayer for her departed Spirit, and vowed to
revenge her death by the shame and punishment of her
Assassins. With danger and difficulty have I kept my
oath. I unwarily dropped some words at the funeral of
Agnes, while thrown off my guard by excessive grief,
which alarmed the guilty conscience of the Prioress. My
every action was observed; My every step was traced. I
was constantly surrounded by the Superior's spies. It
was long before I could find the means of conveying to

the unhappy Girl's Relations an intimation of my secret. It was given out, that Agnes had expired suddenly: This account was credited not only by her Friends in Madrid, but even by those within the Convent. The poison had left no marks upon her body: No one suspected the true cause of her death, and it remained unknown to all, save the Assassins and Myself.

'I have no more to say: For what I have already said, I will answer with my life. I repeat, that the Prioress is a Murderess; That She has driven from the world, perhaps from heaven, an Unfortunate whose offence was light and venial; that She has abused the power intrusted to her hands, and has been a Tyrant, a Barbarian, and an Hypocrite. I also accuse the four Nuns, Violante, Camilla, Alix, and Mariana, as being her Accomplices, and equally criminal.'

Here St. Ursula ended her narrative. It created horror and surprize throughout: But when She related the inhuman murder of Agnes, the indignation of the Mob was so audibly testified, that it was scarcely possible to hear the conclusion. This confusion increased with every moment: At length a multitude of voices exclaimed, that the Prioress should be given up to their fury. To this Don Ramirez refused to consent positively. Even Lorenzo bad the People remember, that She had undergone no trial, and advised them to leave her punishment to the Inquisition. All representations were fruitless: The disturbance grew still more violent, and the Populace more exasperated. In vain did Ramirez attempt to convey his Prisoner out of the Throng. Wherever He turned, a band of Rioters barred his passage, and demanded her being delivered over to them more loudly than before. Ramirez ordered his Attendants to cut their way through the multitude: Oppressed by numbers, it was impossible for them to draw their swords. He threatened the Mob with the vengeance of the Inquisition: But in this moment of popular phrenzy even this dreadful name had lost its effect. Though regret for his Sister made him look upon the Prioress with abhorrence, Lorenzo could not help pitying a Woman in a situation so terrible: But in spite of all his exertions, and those of the Duke, of Don Ramirez, and the Archers, the People continued to press onwards. They forced a passage through the Guards who protected their destined Victim, dragged her from her shelter, and proceeded to take upon her a most summary and cruel vengeance. Wild with terror, and scarcely knowing what She said, the wretched Woman shrieked for a moment's mercy: She protested that She was innocent of the death of Agnes, and could clear herself from the suspicion beyond the power of doubt. The Rioters heeded nothing but the gratification of their barbarous vengeance. They refused to listen to her: They showed her every sort of insult, loaded her with mud and filth, and called her by the most opprobrious appellations. They tore her one from another, and each new Tormentor was more savage than the former. They stifled with howls and execrations her shrill cries for mercy; and dragged her through the Streets, spurning her, trampling her, and treating her with every species of cruelty which hate or vindictive fury could invent. At length a Flint, aimed by some well-directing hand, struck her full upon the temple. She sank upon the ground bathed in blood, and in a few minutes terminated her miserable existence. Yet though She no longer felt their insults, the Rioters still exercised their impotent rage upon her lifeless body. They beat it, trod upon it, and ill-used it, till it became no more than a mass of flesh, unsightly, shapeless, and disgusting.

Unable to prevent this shocking event, Lorenzo and his Friends had beheld it with the utmost horror: But they were rouzed from their compelled inactivity, on hearing that the Mob was attacking the Convent of St. Clare. The incensed Populace, confounding the innocent with the guilty, had resolved to sacrifice all the Nuns of that order to their rage, and not to leave one stone of the building upon another. Alarmed at this intelligence, they hastened to the Convent, resolved to defend it if possible, or at least to rescue the Inhabitants from the fury of the Rioters. Most of the Nuns had fled, but a few still remained in their habitation. Their situation was truly dangerous. However, as they had taken the precaution of fastening the inner Gates, with this assistance Lorenzo hoped to repel the Mob, till Don Ramirez should return to him with a more sufficient force.

Having been conducted by the former disturbance to the distance of some Streets from the Convent, He did not immediately reach it: When He arrived, the throng surrounding it was so excessive, as to prevent his approaching the Gates. In the interim, the Populace besieged the Building with persevering rage: They battered the walls, threw lighted torches in at the windows, and swore that by break of day not a Nun of St. Clare's order should be left alive. Lorenzo had just succeeded in piercing his way through the Crowd, when one of the Gates was forced open. The Rioters poured into the interior part of the Building, where they exercised their vengeance upon every thing which found itself in their passage. They broke the furniture into pieces, tore down the pictures, destroyed the reliques, and in their hatred of her Servant forgot all respect to the Saint. Some employed themselves in searching out the Nuns, Others in pulling down parts of the Convent, and Others again in setting fire to the pictures and valuable furniture, which it contained. These Latter produced the most decisive desolation: Indeed the consequences of their action were more sudden, than themselves had expected or wished. The Flames rising from the burning piles caught part of the Building, which being old and dry, the conflagration spread with rapidity from room to room.

The Walls were soon shaken by the devouring element:
The Columns gave way: The Roofs came tumbling down
upon the Rioters, and crushed many of them beneath
their weight. Nothing was to be heard but shrieks and
groans; The Convent was wrapped in flames, and the
whole presented a scene of devastation and horror.

Lorenzo was shocked at having been the cause, however innocent, of this frightful disturbance: He endeavoured to repair his fault by protecting the helpless
Inhabitants of the Convent. He entered it with the
Mob, and exerted himself to repress the prevailing Fury,
till the sudden and alarming progress of the flames compelled him to provide for his own safety. The People now
hurried out, as eagerly as they had before thronged in;
But their numbers clogging up the door-way, and the
fire gaining upon them rapidly, many of them perished
ere they had time to effect their escape. Lorenzo's good
fortune directed him to a small door in a farther Aisle of
the Chapel. The bolt was already undrawn: He opened
the door, and found himself at the foot of St. Clare's
Sepulchre.

Here He stopped to breathe. The Duke and some of
his Attendants had followed him, and thus were in
security for the present. They now consulted, what steps
they should take to escape from this scene of disturbance: But their deliberations were considerably interrupted by the sight of volumes of fire rising from amidst
the Convent's massy walls, by the noise of some heavy
Arch tumbling down in ruins, or by the mingled shrieks
of the Nuns and Rioters, either suffocating in the press,
perishing in the flames, or crushed beneath the weight of
the falling Mansion.

Lorenzo enquired, whither the Wicket led? He was
answered, to the Garden of the Capuchins, and it was
resolved to explore an out-let upon that side. Accordingly the Duke raised the Latch, and passed into the

adjoining Cemetery. The Attendants followed without ceremony. Lorenzo, being the last, was also on the point of quitting the Colonnade, when He saw the door of the Sepulchre opened softly. Some-one looked out, but on perceiving Strangers uttered a loud shriek, started back again, and flew down the marble Stairs.

'What can this mean?' cried Lorenzo; 'Here is some mystery concealed. Follow me without delay!'

Thus saying, He hastened into the Sepulchre, and pursued the person who continued to fly before him. The Duke knew not the cause of his exclamation, but supposing that He had good reasons for it, he followed him without hesitation. The Others did the same, and the whole Party soon arrived at the foot of the Stairs. The upper door having been left open, the neighbouring flames darted from above a sufficient light to enable Lorenzo's catching a glance of the Fugitive running through the long passages and distant Vaults: But when a sudden turn deprived him of this assistance, total darkness succeeded, and He could only trace the object of his enquiry by the faint echo of retiring feet. The Pursuers were now compelled to proceed with caution: As well as they could judge, the Fugitive also seemed to slacken pace, for they heard the steps follow each other at longer intervals. They at length were bewildered by the Labyrinth of passages, and dispersed in various directions. Carried away by his eagerness to clear up this mystery, and to penetrate into which He was impelled by a movement secret and unaccountable, Lorenzo heeded not this circumstance till He found himself in total solitude. The noise of foot-steps had ceased. All was silent around, and no clue offered itself to guide him to the flying Person. He stopped to reflect on the means most likely to aid his pursuit. He was persuaded, that no common cause would have induced the Fugitive to seek that dreary place at an hour so unusual: The cry which

He had heard, seemed uttered in a voice of terror, and He was convinced that some mystery was attached to this event. After some minutes past in hesitation He continued to proceed, feeling his way along the walls of the passage. He had already past some time in this slow progress, when He descried a spark of light glimmering at a distance. Guided by this observation, and having drawn his sword, He bent his steps towards the place, whence the beam seemed to be emitted.

It proceeded from the Lamp, which flamed before St. Clare's Statue. Before it stood several Females, their white Garments streaming in the blast, as it howled along the vaulted dungeons. Curious to know what had brought them together in this melancholy spot, Lorenzo drew near with precaution. The Strangers seemed earnestly engaged in conversation. They heard not Lorenzo's steps, and He approached unobserved, till He could hear their voices distinctly.

'I protest,' continued She who was speaking when He arrived, and to whom the rest were listening with great attention; 'I protest, that I saw them with my own eyes. I flew down the steps; They pursued me, and I escaped falling into their hands with difficulty. Had it not been for the Lamp, I should never have found you.'

'And what could bring them hither?' said another in a trembling voice; 'Do you think, that they were looking for us?'

'God grant, that my fears may be false,' rejoined the First; 'But I doubt they are Murderers! If they discover us, we are lost! As for me, my fate is certain: My affinity to the Prioress will be a sufficient crime to condemn me; and though till now these Vaults have afforded me a retreat. . . . .'

Here looking up, her eye fell upon Lorenzo, who had continued to approach softly.

'The Murderers!' She cried—

She started away from the Statue's Pedestal on which
She had been seated, and attempted to escape by
flight. Her Companions at the same moment uttered a
terrified scream, while Lorenzo arrested the Fugitive
by the arm. Frightened and desperate She sank upon her
knees before him.

'Spare me!' She exclaimed; 'For Christ's sake, spare
me! I am innocent, indeed, I am!'

While She spoke, her voice was almost choaked with
fear. The beams of the Lamp darting full upon her face
which was unveiled, Lorenzo recognized the beautiful
Virginia de Villa-Franca. He hastened to raise her from
the ground, and besought her to take courage. He promised to protect her from the Rioters, assured her that
her retreat was still a secret, and that She might depend
upon his readiness to defend her to the last drop of his
blood. During this conversation, the Nuns had thrown
themselves into various attitudes: One knelt, and addressed herself to heaven; Another hid her face in the
lap of her Neighbour; Some listened motionless with fear
to the discourse of the supposed Assassin; while Others
embraced the Statue of St. Clare, and implored her protection with frantic cries. On perceiving their mistake,
they crowded round Lorenzo, and heaped benedictions
on him by dozens. He found, that on hearing the threats
of the Mob, and terrified by the cruelties, which from the
Convent Towers they had seen inflicted on the Superior,
many of the Pensioners and Nuns had taken refuge in the
Sepulchre. Among the former was to be reckoned the
lovely Virginia. Nearly related to the Prioress, She had
more reason than the rest to dread the Rioters, and now
besought Lorenzo earnestly not to abandon her to their
rage. Her Companions, most of whom were Women of
noble family, made the same request, which He readily
granted. He promised not to quit them, till He had seen
each of them safe in the arms of her Relations: But He

advised their deferring to quit the Sepulchre for some time longer, when the popular fury should be somewhat calmed, and the arrival of military force have dispersed the multitude.

'Would to God!' cried Virginia, 'That I were already safe in my Mother's embraces! How say you, Segnor; Will it be long, ere we may leave this place? Every moment that I pass here, I pass in torture!'

'I hope, not long,' said He; 'But till you can can proceed with security, this Sepulchre will prove an impenetrable asylum. Here you run no risque of a discovery, and I would advise your remaining quiet for the next two or three hours.'

'Two or three hours?' exclaimed Sister Helena; 'If I stay another hour in these vaults, I shall expire with fear! Not the wealth of worlds should bribe me to undergo again, what I have suffered since my coming hither. Blessed Virgin! To be in this melancholy place in the middle of night, surrounded by the mouldering bodies of my deceased Companions, and expecting every moment to be torn in pieces by their Ghosts who wander about me, and complain, and groan, and wail in accents that make my blood run cold, ... Christ Jesus! It is enough to drive me to madness!'

'Excuse me,' replied Lorenzo, 'if I am surprised, that while menaced by real woes you are capable of yielding to imaginary dangers. These terrors are puerile and groundless: Combat them, holy Sister; I have promised to guard you from the Rioters, but against the attacks of superstition you must depend for protection upon yourself. The idea of Ghosts is ridiculous in the extreme; And if you continue to be swayed by ideal terrors . . . . . .'

'Ideal?' exclaimed the Nuns with one voice; 'Why we heard it ourselves, Segnor! Every one of us heard it! It was frequently repeated, and it sounded every time more melancholy and deep. You will never persuade me, that we could all have been deceived. Not we, indeed; No, no; Had the noise been merely created by fancy . . . .'

'Hark! Hark!' interrupted Virginia in a voice of terror; 'God preserve us! There it is again!'

The Nuns clasped their hands together, and sank upon their knees. Lorenzo looked round him eagerly, and was on the point of yielding to the fears, which already had possessed the Women. Universal silence prevailed. He examined the Vault, but nothing was to be seen. He now prepared to address the Nuns, and ridicule their childish apprehensions, when his attention was arrested by a deep and long-drawn groan.

'What was that?' He cried, and started.

'There, Segnor!' said Helena; 'Now you must be convinced! You have heard the noise yourself! Now judge, whether our terrors are imaginary. Since we have been here, that groaning has been repeated almost every five minutes. Doubtless, it proceeds from some Soul in pain, who wishes to be prayed out of purgatory: But none of us here dares ask it the question. As for me, were I to see an Apparition, the fright, I am very certain, would kill me out of hand.'

As She said this, a second groan was heard yet more distinctly. The Nuns crossed themselves, and hastened to repeat their prayers against evil Spirits. Lorenzo listened attentively. He even thought, that He could distinguish sounds, as of one speaking in complaint; But distance rendered them inarticulate. The noise seemed to come from the midst of the small Vault in which He and the Nuns then were, and which a multitude of passages branching out in various directions, formed into a sort of Star. Lorenzo's curiosity which was ever awake, made him anxious to solve this mystery. He desired that silence might be kept. The Nuns obeyed him. All was hushed, till the general stillness was again disturbed by the groaning, which was repeated several times successively. He perceived it to be most audible, when upon following the sound He was conducted close to the shrine of St. Clare.

'The noise comes from hence,' said He; 'Whose is this Statue?'

Helena, to whom He addressed the question, paused for a moment. Suddenly She clapped her hands together.

'Aye!' cried She, 'it must be so. I have discovered the meaning of these groans.'

The Nuns crowded round her, and besought her eagerly to explain herself. She gravely replied, that for time immemorial the Statue had been famous for performing miracles: From this She inferred, that the Saint was concerned at the conflagration of a Convent which She protected, and expressed her grief by audible lamentations. Not having equal faith in the miraculous Saint, Lorenzo did not think this solution of the mystery quite so satisfactory, as the Nuns, who subscribed to it without hesitation. In one point, 'tis true, that He agreed with Helena. He suspected that the groans proceeded from the Statue: The more He listened, the more was He confirmed in this idea. He drew nearer to the Image, designing to inspect it more closely: But perceiving his intention, the Nuns besought him for God's sake to desist, since if He touched the Statue, his death was inevitable.

'And in what consists the danger?' said He.

'Mother of God! In what?' replied Helena, ever eager to relate a miraculous adventure; 'If you had only heard the hundredth part of those marvellous Stories about this Statue, which the Domina used to recount! She assured us often and often, that if we only dared to lay a finger upon it, we might expect the most fatal consequences. Among other things She told us, that a Robber having entered these Vaults by night, He observed yonder Ruby, whose value is inestimable. Do you see it, Segnor? It sparkles upon the third finger of the hand, in which She holds a crown of Thorns. This Jewel naturally excited the Villain's cupidity. He resolved to make himself Master of it. For this purpose He ascended the Pedestal: He supported himself by grasping the Saint's right arm, and extended his own towards the Ring. What was his surprize, when He saw the Statue's hand raised in a posture of menace, and heard her lips pronounce his eternal perdition! Penetrated with awe and consternation, He desisted from his attempt, and prepared to quit the Sepulchre. In this He also failed. Flight was denied him. He found it impossible to disengage the hand, which rested upon the right arm of the Statue. In vain did He struggle: He remained fixed to the Image, till the insupportable and fiery anguish which darted itself through his veins, compelled his shrieking for assistance. The Sepulchre was now filled with Spectators. The Villain confessed his sacrilege, and was only released by the separation of his hand from his body. It has remained ever since fastened to the Image. The Robber turned Hermit, and led ever after an exemplary life: But yet the Saint's decree was performed, and Tradition says, that He continues to haunt this Sepulchre, and implore St. Clare's pardon with groans and lamentations. Now I think of it, those which we have just heard, may very possibly have been uttered by the Ghost of this Sinner: But of this I will not be positive. All that I can say is, that since that time no one has ever dared to touch the Statue: Then do not be fool-hardy, good Segnor! For the love of heaven, give up your design, nor expose yourself unnecessarily to certain destruction.'

Not being convinced that his destruction would be so certain, as Helena seemed to think it, Lorenzo persisted in his resolution. The Nuns besought him to desist in piteous terms, and even pointed out the Robber's hand, which in effect was still visible upon the arm of the Statue. This proof, as they imagined, must convince him.

It was very far from doing so; and they were greatly
scandalized when he declared his suspicion, that the
dried and shrivelled fingers had been placed there by
order of the Prioress. In spite of their prayers and threats
He approached the Statue. He sprang over the iron Rails
which defended it, and the Saint under-went a thorough
examination. The Image at first appeared to be of Stone,
but proved on further inspection to be formed of no more
solid materials than coloured Wood. He shook it, and
attempted to move it; But it appeared to be of a piece
with the Base which it stood upon. He examined it over
and over: Still no clue guided him to the solution of this
mystery, for which the Nuns were become equally
solicitous, when they saw that He touched the Statue with
impunity. He paused, and listened: The groans were
repeated at intervals, and He was convinced of being in
the spot nearest to them. He mused upon this singular
event, and ran over the Statue with enquiring eyes.
Suddenly they rested upon the shrivelled hand. It struck
him, that so particular an injunction was not given
without cause, not to touch the arm of the Image. He
again ascended the Pedestal; He examined the object of
his attention, and discovered a small knob of iron concealed between the Saint's shoulder, and what was
supposed to have been the hand of the Robber. This
observation delighted him. He applied his fingers to the
knob, and pressed it down forcibly. Immediately a
rumbling noise was heard within the Statue, as if a chain
tightly stretched was flying back. Startled at the sound
the timid Nuns started away, prepared to hasten from
the Vault at the first appearance of danger. All remaining
quiet and still, they again gathered round Lorenzo, and
beheld his proceedings with anxious curiosity.

Finding that nothing followed this discovery, He
descended. As He took his hand from the Saint, She
trembled beneath his touch. This created new terrors in

the Spectators, who believed the Statue to be animated. Lorenzo's ideas upon the subject were widely different. He easily comprehended, that the noise which He had heard, was occasioned by his having loosened a chain, which attached the Image to its Pedestal. He once more attempted to move it, and succeeded without much exertion. He placed it upon the ground, and then perceived the Pedestal to be hollow, and covered at the opening with an heavy iron grate.

This excited such general curiosity, that the Sisters forgot both their real and imaginary dangers. Lorenzo proceeded to raise the Grate, in which the Nuns assisted him to the utmost of their strength. The attempt was accomplished, with little difficulty. A deep abyss now presented itself before them, whose thick obscurity the eye strove in vain to pierce. The rays of the Lamp were too feeble to be of much assistance. Nothing was discernible, save a flight of rough unshapen steps, which sank into the yawning Gulph, and were soon lost in darkness. The groans were heard no more; But All believed them to have ascended from this Cavern. As He bent over it, Lorenzo fancied, that He distinguished something bright twinkling through the gloom. He gazed attentively upon the spot where it showed itself, and was convinced, that He saw a small spark of light, now visible, now disappearing. He communicated this circumstance to the Nuns: They also perceived the spark; But when He declared his intention to descend into the Cave, they united to oppose his resolution. All their remonstrances could not prevail on him to alter it. None of them had courage enough to accompany him; neither could He think of depriving them of the Lamp. Alone therefore, and in darkness, He prepared to pursue his design, while the Nuns were contented to offer up prayers for his success and safety.

The steps were so narrow and uneven, that to descend

them was like walking down the side of a precipice. The obscurity by which He was surrounded, rendered his footing insecure. He was obliged to proceed with great caution, lest He should miss the steps, and fall into the Gulph below him. This He was several times on the point of doing. However, He arrived sooner upon solid ground than He had expected: He now found, that the thick darkness and impenetrable mists which reigned through the Cavern, had deceived him into the belief of its being much more profound, than it proved upon inspection. He reached the foot of the Stairs unhurt: He now stopped, and looked round for the spark, which had before caught his attention. He sought it in vain: All was dark and gloomy. He listened for the groans; But his ear caught no sound, except the distant murmur of the Nuns above, as in low voices they repeated their Ave-Marias. He stood irresolute to which side He should address his steps. At all events He determined to proceed: He did so, but slowly, fearing lest instead of approaching, He should be retiring from the object of his search. The groans seemed to announce one in pain, or at least in sorrow, and He hoped to have the power of relieving the Mourner's calamities. A plaintive tone, sounding at no great distance, at length reached his hearing; He bent his course joyfully towards it. It became more audible as He advanced; and He soon beheld again the spark of light, which a low projecting Wall had hitherto concealed from him.

It proceeded from a small Lamp which was placed upon an heap of stones, and whose faint and melancholy rays served rather to point out, than dispell the horrors of a narrow gloomy dungeon formed in one side of the Cavern; It also showed several other recesses of similar construction, but whose depth was buried in obscurity. Coldly played the light upon the damp walls, whose dew-stained surface gave back a feeble reflection. A thick and

pestilential fog clouded the height of the vaulted dungeon. As Lorenzo advanced, He felt a piercing chillness
spread itself through his veins. The frequent groans still
engaged him to move forwards. He turned towards them,
and by the Lamp's glimmering beams beheld in a corner
of this loathsome abode, a Creature stretched upon a
bed of straw, so wretched, so emaciated, so pale, that He
doubted to think her Woman. She was half-naked: Her
long dishevelled hair fell in disorder over her face, and
almost entirely concealed it. One wasted Arm hung
listlessly upon a tattered rug, which covered her convul-
sed and shivering limbs: The Other was wrapped round
a small bundle, and held it closely to her bosom. A large
Rosary lay near her: Opposite to her was a Crucifix, on
which She bent her sunk eyes fixedly, and by her side
stood a Basket and a small Earthen Pitcher.

Lorenzo stopped: He was petrified with horror. He
gazed upon the miserable Object with disgust and pity.
He trembled at the spectacle; He grew sick at heart:
His strength failed him, and his limbs were unable to
support his weight. He was obliged to lean against the
low Wall which was near him, unable to go forward,
or to address the Sufferer. She cast her eyes towards the
Stair-case: The Wall concealed Lorenzo, and She observed him not.

'No one comes!' She at length murmured.

As She spoke, her voice was hollow, and rattled in her
throat: She signed bitterly.

'No one comes!' She repeated; 'No! They have forgotten me! They will come no more!'

She paused for a moment: Then continued mournfully.

'Two days! Two long, long days, and yet no food! And
yet no hope, no comfort! Foolish Woman! How can I
wish to lengthen a life so wretched! Yet such a death! O!
God! To perish by such a death! To linger out such ages

in torture! Till now, I knew not what it was to hunger!
Hark! No. No one comes! They will come no more!'

She was silent. She shivered, and drew the rug over her
naked shoulders.

'I am very cold! I am still unused to the damps of this
dungeon! 'Tis strange: But no matter. Colder shall I
soon be, and yet not feel it—I shall be cold, cold as Thou
art!'

She looked at the bundle, which lay upon her breast.
She bent over it, and kissed it: Then drew back hastily,
and shuddered with disgust.

'It was once so sweet! It would have been so lovely, so
like him! I have lost it for ever! How a few days have
changed it! I should not know it again myself! Yet it is
dear to me! God! how dear! I will forget what it is:
I will only remember what it was, and love it as well, as
when it was so sweet! so lovely! so like him! I thought,
that I had wept away all my tears, but here is one still
lingering.'

She wiped her eyes with a tress of her hair. She put out
her hand for the Pitcher, and reached it with difficulty.
She cast into it a look of hopeless enquiry. She sighed,
and replaced it upon the ground.

'Quite a void! Not a drop! Not one drop left to cool
my scorched-up burning palate! Now would I give treasures for a draught of water! And they are God's Servants, who make me suffer thus! They think themselves
holy, while they torture me like Fiends! They are cruel
and unfeeling; And 'tis they who bid me repent; And 'tis
they, who threaten me with eternal perdition! Saviour,
Saviour! You think not so!'

She again fixed her eyes upon the Crucifix, took her
Rosary, and while She told her beads, the quick motion
of her lips declared her to be praying with fervency.

While He listened to her melancholy accents, Lorenzo's
sensibility became yet more violently affected. The first

sight of such misery had given a sensible shock to his feelings: But that being past, He now advanced towards the Captive. She heard his steps, and uttering a cry of joy, dropped the Rosary.

'Hark! Hark! Hark!' She cried: 'Some one comes!'

She strove to raise herself, but her strength was unequal to the attempt: She fell back, and as She sank again upon the bed of straw, Lorenzo heard the rattling of heavy chains. He still approached, while the Prisoner thus continued.

'Is it you, Camilla? You are come then at last? Oh! it was time! I thought that you had forsaken me; that I was doomed to perish of hunger. Give me to drink, Camilla, for pity's sake! I am faint with long fasting, and grown so weak that I cannot raise myself from the ground. Good Camilla, give me to drink, lest I expire before you!'

Fearing that surprize in her enfeebled state might be fatal, Lorenzo was at a loss how to address her.

'It is not Camilla,' said He at length, speaking in a slow and gentle voice.

'Who is it then?' replied the Sufferer: 'Alix, perhaps, or Violante. My eyes are grown so dim and feeble, that I cannot distinguish your features. But which-ever it is, if your breast is sensible of the least compassion, if you are not more cruel than Wolves and Tigers, take pity on my sufferings. You know, that I am dying for want of sustenance. This is the third day, since these lips have received nourishment. Do you bring me food? Or come you only to announce my death, and learn how long I have yet to exist in agony?'

'You mistake my business,' replied Lorenzo; 'I am no Emissary of the cruel Prioress. I pity your sorrows, and come hither to relieve them.'

'To relieve them?' repeated the Captive; 'Said you, to relieve them?'

At the same time starting from the ground, and supporting herself upon her hands, She gazed upon the Stranger earnestly.

'Great God! It is no illusion! A Man! Speak! Who are you? What brings you hither? Come you to save me, to restore me to liberty, to life and light? Oh! speak, speak quickly, lest I encourage an hope whose disappointment will destroy me.'

'Be calm!' replied Lorenzo in a voice soothing and compassionate; 'The Domina of whose cruelty you complain, has already paid the forfeit of her offences: You have nothing more to fear from her. A few minutes will restore you to liberty, and the embraces of your Friends from whom you have been secluded. You may rely upon my protection. Give me your hand, and be not fearful. Let me conduct you where you may receive those attentions which your feeble state requires.'

'Oh! Yes! Yes! Yes!' cried the Prisoner with an exulting shriek; 'There is a God then, and a just one! Joy! Joy! I shall once more breath the fresh air, and view the light of the glorious sun-beams! I will go with you! Stranger, I will go with you! Oh! Heaven will bless you for pitying an Unfortunate! But this too must go with me,' She added pointing to the small bundle, which She still clasped to her bosom; 'I cannot part with this. I will bear it away: It shall convince the world, how dreadful are the abodes so falsely termed religious. Good Stranger, lend me your hand to rise: I am faint with want, and sorrow, and sickness, and my forces have quite forsaken me! So, that is well!'

As Lorenzo stooped to raise her, the beams of the Lamp struck full upon his face.

'Almighty God!' She exclaimed; 'Is it possible! That look! Those features! Oh! Yes, it is, it is . . . . .'

She extended her arms to throw them round him; But her enfeebled frame was unable to sustain the emotions, which agitated her bosom. She fainted, and again sank upon the bed of straw.

Lorenzo was surprised at her last exclamation. He thought that He had before heard such accents as her hollow voice had just formed, but where He could not remember. He saw, that in her dangerous situation immediate physical aid was absolutely necessary, and He hastened to convey her from the dungeon. He was at first prevented from doing so by a strong chain fastened round the prisoner's body, and fixing her to the neighbouring Wall. However, his natural strength being aided by anxiety to relieve the Unfortunate, He soon forced out the Staple, to which one end of the Chain was attached. Then taking the Captive in his arms, He bent his course towards the Stair-case. The rays of the Lamp above, as well as the murmur of female voices, guided his steps. He gained the Stairs, and in a few minutes after arrived at the iron-grate.

The Nuns during his absence had been terribly tormented by curiosity and apprehension: They were equally surprised and delighted on seeing him suddenly emerge from the Cave. Every heart was filled with compassion for the miserable Creature, whom He bore in his arms. While the Nuns, and Virginia in particular employed themselves in striving to re-call her to her senses, Lorenzo related in few words the manner of his finding her. He then observed to them that by this time the tumult must have been quelled, and that He could now conduct them to their Friends without danger. All were eager to quit the Sepulchre: Still to prevent all possibility of ill-usage, they besought Lorenzo to venture out first alone, and examine, whether the Coast was clear. With this request He complied. Helena offered to conduct him to the Stair-case, and they were on the point of departing, when a strong light flashed from several passages upon the adjacent walls. At the same time Steps were heard of people approaching hastily, and whose number seemed to be considerable. The Nuns were greatly alarmed at this circumstance: They supposed their retreat to be discovered, and the Rioters to be advancing in pursuit of them. Hastily quitting the Prisoner who remained insensible, they crowded round Lorenzo, and claimed his promise to protect them. Virginia alone forgot her own danger by striving to relieve the sorrows of Another. She supported the Sufferer's head upon her knees, bathing her temples with rose-water, chafing her cold hands, and sprinkling her face with tears which were drawn from her by compassion. The Strangers approaching nearer, Lorenzo was enabled to dispel the fears of the Suppliants. His name, pronounced by a number of voices among which He distinguished the Duke's, pealed along the Vaults, and convinced him that He was the object of their search. He communicated this intelligence to the Nuns, who received it with rapture. A few moments after confirmed his idea. Don Ramirez, as well as the Duke, appeared, followed by Attendants with Torches. They had been seeking him through the Vaults, in order to let him know that the Mob was dispersed, and the riot entirely over. Lorenzo recounted briefly his adventure in the Cavern, and explained, how much the Unknown was in want of medical assistance. He besought the Duke to take charge of her, as well as of the Nuns and Pensioners.

'As for me,' said He, 'Other cares demand my attention. While you with one half of the Archers convey these Ladies to their respective homes, I wish the other half to be left with me. I will examine the Cavern below, and pervade the most secret recesses of the Sepulchre. I cannot rest till convinced, that yonder wretched Victim was the only one confined by Superstition in these vaults.'

The Duke applauded his intention. Don Ramirez offered to assist him in his enquiry, and his proposal was accepted with gratitude. The Nuns having made their acknowledgments to Lorenzo, committed themselves to the care of his Uncle, and 'were conducted from the Sepulchre. Virginia requested that the Unknown might be given to her in charge, and promised to let Lorenzo know, whenever She was sufficiently recovered to accept his visits. In truth, She made this promise more from consideration for herself, than for either Lorenzo or the Captive. She had witnessed his politeness, gentleness, and intrepidity with sensible emotion. She wished earnestly to preserve his acquaintance; and in addition to the sentiments of pity which the Prisoner excited, She hoped that her attention to this Unfortunate would raise her a degree in the esteem of Lorenzo. She had no occasion to trouble herself upon this head. The kindness already displayed by her, and the tender concern which She had shown for the Sufferer had gained her an exalted place in his good graces. While occupied in alleviating the Captive's sorrows, the nature of her employment adorned her with new charms, and rendered her beauty a thousand times more interesting. Lorenzo viewed her with admiration and delight: He considered her as a ministering Angel descended to the aid of afflicted innocence; nor could his heart have resisted her attractions, had it not been steeled by the remembrance of Antonia.

The Duke now conveyed the Nuns in safety to the Dwellings of their respective Friends. The rescued Prisoner was still insensible, and gave no signs of life, except by occasional groans. She was borne upon a sort of litter; Virginia who was constantly by the side of it, was apprehensive that exhausted by long abstinence, and shaken by the sudden change from bonds and darkness to liberty and light, her frame would never get the better of the shock. Lorenzo and Don Ramirez still remained in the Sepulchre. After deliberating upon their proceedings, it was resolved that to prevent losing time, the Archers should be divided into two Bodies: That with one Don Ramirez should examine the cavern, while Lorenzo with the other might penetrate into the further Vaults. This being arranged, and his Followers being provided with Torches, Don Ramirez advanced to the Cavern. He had already descended some steps, when He heard People approaching hastily from the interior part of the Sepulchre. This surprized him, and He quitted the Cave precipitately.

'Do you hear foot-steps?' said Lorenzo; 'Let us bend our course towards them. 'Tis from this side, that they seem to proceed.'

At that moment a loud and piercing shriek induced him to quicken his steps.

'Help! Help, for God's sake! cried a voice, whose melodious tone penetrated Lorenzo's heart with terror.

He flew towards the cry with the rapidity of lightning, and was followed by Don Ramirez with equal swiftness.

CHAPTER IV

Great Heaven! How frail thy creature Man is made!
How by himself insensibly betrayed!
In our own strength unhappily secure,
Too little cautious of the adverse power,
On pleasure's flowery brink we idly stray,
Masters as yet of our returning way:
Till the strong gusts of raging passion rise,
Till the dire Tempest mingles earth and skies,
And swift into the boundless Ocean borne,
Our foolish confidence too late we mourn:
Round our devoted heads the billows beat,
And from our troubled view the lessening lands retreat.

Prior.*

ALL THIS WHILE, Ambrosio was unconscious of the dreadful scenes which were passing so near. The execution of his designs upon Antonia employed his every thought. Hitherto, He was satisfied with the success of his plans. Antonia had drank the opiate, was buried in the vaults of St. Clare, and absolutely in his disposal. Matilda, who was well acquainted with the nature and effects of the soporific medicine, had computed that it would not cease to operate till one in the Morning. For that hour He waited with impatience. The Festival of St. Clare presented him with a favourable opportunity of consummating his crime. He was certain that the Friars and Nuns would be engaged in the Procession, and that He had no cause to dread an interruption: From appearing himself at the head of his Monks, He had desired to be excused. He doubted not, that being beyond the reach of help, cut off from all the world, and totally in his power, Antonia would comply with his desires. The affection which She had ever exprest for him, warranted this persuasion: But He resolved that should She prove obstinate, no consideration whatever should prevent him from enjoying her. Secure from a discovery, He shuddered not at the idea of employing force: Of if He felt any repugnance, it arose not from a principle of shame or compassion, but from his feeling for Antonia the most sincere and ardent affection, and wishing to owe her favours to no one but herself.

The Monks quitted the Abbey at midnight. Matilda was among the Choristers, and led the chaunt. Ambrosio was left by himself, and at liberty to pursue his own inclinations. Convinced that no one remained behind to watch his motions, or disturb his pleasures, He now hastened to the Western Aisles. His heart beating with hope not unmingled with anxiety, He crossed the Garden, unlocked the door which admitted him into the Cemetery, and in a few minutes He stood before the Vaults. Here He paused. He looked round him with suspicion, conscious that his business was unfit for any other eye. As He stood in hesitation, He heard the melancholy shriek of the screech-Owl: The wind rattled loudly against the windows of the adjacent Convent, and as the current swept by him, bore with it the faint notes of the chaunt of Choristers. He opened the door cautiously, as if fearing to be over-heard: He entered; and closed it again after him. Guided by his Lamp, He threaded the long passages, in whose windings Matilda had instructed him, and reached the private Vault which contained his sleeping Mistress.

Its entrance was by no means easy to discover: But this was no obstacle to Ambrosio, who at the time of Antonia's Funeral had observed it too carefully to be deceived. He found the door, which was unfastened, pushed it open, and descended into the dungeon. He approached the humble Tomb, in which Antonia reposed. He had provided himself with an iron crow and a pick-axe; But this precaution was unnecessary. The Grate was slightly fastened on the outside: He raised it, and placing the Lamp upon its ridge, bent silently over the Tomb. By the side of three putrid half-corrupted Bodies lay the sleeping Beauty.* A lively red, the fore-runner of returning animation, had already spread itself over her cheek; and as wrapped in her shroud She reclined upon her funeral Bier, She seemed to smile at the Images of Death around her. While He gazed upon their rotting bones and disgusting figures, who perhaps were once as sweet and lovely, Ambrosio thought upon Elvira, by him reduced to the same state. As the memory of that horrid act glanced upon his mind, it was clouded with a gloomy horror. Yet it served but to strengthen his resolution to destroy Antonia's honour.

'For your sake, Fatal Beauty!' murmured the Monk, while gazing on his devoted prey; 'For your sake, have I committed this murder, and sold myself to eternal tortures. Now you are in my power: The produce of my guilt will at least be mine. Hope not that your prayers breathed in tones of unequalled melody, your bright eyes filled with tears, and your hands lifted in supplication, as when seeking in penitence the Virgin's pardon; Hope not, that your moving innocence, your beauteous grief, or all your suppliant arts shall ransom you from my embraces. Before the break of day, mine you must, and mine you shall be!'

He lifted her still motionless from the Tomb: He seated himself upon a bank of Stone, and supporting her in his arms, watched impatiently for the symptoms of returning animation. Scarcely could He command his passions sufficiently, to restrain himself from enjoying her while yet insensible. His natural lust was increased in ardour by the difficulties, which had opposed his satisfying it: As also by his long abstinence from Woman, since from the moment of resigning her claim to his love, Matilda had exiled him from her arms for ever.

'I am no Prostitute, Ambrosio;' Had She told him, when in the fullness of his lust He demanded her favours with more than usual earnestness; 'I am now no more than your Friend, and will not be your Mistress. Cease then to solicit my complying with desires, which insult me. While your heart was mine, I gloried in your embraces: Those happy times are past: My person is become indifferent to you, and 'tis necessity, not love, which makes you seek my enjoyment. I cannot yield to a request, so humiliating to my pride.'

Suddenly deprived of pleasures, the use of which had made them an absolute want, the Monk felt this restraint severely. Naturally addicted to the gratification of the senses, in the full vigour of manhood, and heat of blood, He had suffered his temperament to acquire such ascendency, that his lust was become madness. Of his fondness for Antonia, none but the grosser particles remained: He longed for the possession of her person; and even the gloom of the vault, the surrounding silence, and the resistance which He expected from her, seemed to give a fresh edge to his fierce and unbridled desires.

Gradually He felt the bosom which rested against his, glow with returning warmth. Her heart throbbed again; Her blood flowed swifter, and her lips moved. At length She opened her eyes, but still opprest and bewildered by the effects of the strong opiate, She closed them again immediately. Ambrosio watched her narrowly, nor permitted a movement to escape him. Perceiving that She was fully restored to existence, He caught her in rapture to his bosom, and closely pressed his lips to hers. The suddenness of his action sufficed to dissipate the fumes, which obscured Antonia's reason. She hastily raised herself, and cast a wild look round her. The strange Images which presented themselves on every side contributed to confuse her. She put her hand to her head, as if to settle her disordered imagination. At length She took it away, and threw her eyes through the dungeon a second time. They fixed upon the Abbot's face.

'Where am I?' She said abruptly. 'How came I here? Where is my Mother? Methought, I saw her! Oh! a dream, a dreadful dreadful dream told me ...... But where am I? Let me go! I cannot stay here!'

She attempted to rise, but the Monk prevented her.

'Be calm, lovely Antonia!' He replied; 'No danger is near you: Confide in my protection. Why do you gaze on me so earnestly? Do you not know me? Not know your Friend? Ambrosio?'

'Ambrosio? My Friend? Oh! yes, yes; I remember ...... But why am I here? Who has brought me? Why are you with me? Oh! Flora bad me beware ...... ! Here are nothing but Graves, and Tombs, and Skeletons! This place frightens me! Good Ambrosio take me away from it, for it recalls my fearful dream! Methought I was dead, and laid in my grave! Good Ambrosio, take me from hence. Will you not? Oh! will you not? Do not look on me thus! Your flaming eyes terrify me! Spare me, Father! Oh! spare me for God's sake!'

'Why these terrors, Antonia?' rejoined the Abbot, folding her in his arms, and covering her bosom with kisses which She in vain struggled to avoid: 'What fear you from me, from one who adores you? What matters it where you are? This Sepulchre seems to me Love's bower; This gloom is the friendly night of mystery, which He spreads over our delights! Such do I think it, and such must my Antonia. Yes, my sweet Girl! Yes! Your veins shall glow with fire, which circles in mine, and my transports shall be doubled by your sharing them!'

While He spoke thus, He repeated his embraces, and permitted himself the most indecent liberties. Even Antonia's ignorance was not proof against the freedom of his behaviour. She was sensible of her danger, forced herself from his arms, and her shroud being her only garment, She wrapped it closely round her.

'Unhand me, Father!' She cried, her honest indignation tempered by alarm at her unprotected position; 'Why have you brought me to this place? Its appearance freezes me with horror! Convey me from hence, if you have the least sense of pity and humanity! Let me return to the House, which I have quitted I know not how; But stay here one moment longer, I neither will, or ought.'

Though the Monk was somewhat startled by the resolute tone in which this speech was delivered, it produced upon him no other effect than surprize. He caught her hand, forced her upon his knee, and gazing upon her with gloting eyes, He thus replied to her.

'Compose yourself, Antonia. Resistance is unavailing, and I need disavow my passion for you no longer. You are imagined dead: Society is for ever lost to you. I possess you here alone; You are absolutely in my power, and I burn with desires, which I must either gratify, or die: But I would owe my happiness to yourself. My lovely Girl! My adorable Antonia! Let me instruct you in joys to which you are still a Stranger, and teach you to feel those pleasures in my arms, which I must soon enjoy in yours. Nay, this struggling is childish,' He continued, seeing her repell his caresses, and endeavour to escape from his grasp; 'No aid is near: Neither heaven or earth shall save you from my embraces. Yet why reject pleasures so sweet, so rapturous? No one observes us: Our loves will be a secret to all the world: Love and opportunity invite your giving loose to your passions. Yield to them, my Antonia! Yield to them, my lovely Girl! Throw your arms thus fondly round me; Join your lips thus closely to mine! Amidst all her gifts, has Nature denied her most precious, the sensibility of Pleasure? Oh! impossible! Every feature, look, and motion declares you formed to bless, and to be blessed yourself! Turn not on me those supplicating eyes: Consult your own charms; They will tell you, that I am proof against entreaty. Can I relinquish these limbs so white, so soft, so delicate; These swelling breasts, round, full, and elastic! These lips fraught with such inexhaustible sweetness? Can I relinquish these treasures, and leave them to another's enjoyment? No, Antonia; never, never! I swear it by this kiss, and this! and this!'

With every moment the Friar's passion became more ardent, and Antonia's terror more intense. She struggled to disengage herself from his arms: Her exertions were unsuccessful; and finding that Ambrosio's conduct became still freer, She shrieked for assistance with all her strength. The aspect of the Vault, the pale glimmering of the Lamp, the surrounding obscurity, the sight of the Tomb, and the objects of mortality which met her eyes on either side, were ill-calculated to inspire her with those emotions, by which the Friar was agitated. Even his caresses terrified her from their fury, and created no other sentiment than fear. On the contrary, her alarm, her evident disgust, and incessant opposition, seemed only to inflame the Monk's desires, and supply his brutality with additional strength. Antonia's shrieks were unheard: Yet She continued them, nor abandoned her endeavours to escape, till exhausted and out of breath She sank from his arms upon her knees, and once more had recourse to prayers and supplications. This attempt had no better success than the former. On the contrary, taking advantage of her situation, the Ravisher threw himself by her side: He clasped her to his bosom almost lifeless with terror, and faint with struggling. He stifled her cries with kisses, treated her with the rudeness of an unprincipled Barbarian, proceeded from freedom to freedom, and in the violence of his lustful delirium, wounded and bruised her tender limbs. Heedless of her tears, cries and entreaties, He gradually made himself

Master of her person, and desisted not from his prey, till He had accomplished his crime and the dishonour of Antonia.

Scarcely had He succeeded in his design, than He shuddered at himself and the means by which it was effected. The very excess of his former eagerness to possess Antonia now contributed to inspire him with disgust; and a secret impulse made him feel, how base and unmanly was the crime, which He had just committed. He started hastily from her arms. She, who so lately had been the object of his adoration, now raised no other sentiment in his heart than aversion and rage. He turned away from her; or if his eyes rested upon her figure involuntarily, it was only to dart upon her looks of hate. The Unfortunate had fainted ere the completion of her disgrace: She only recovered life to be sensible of her misfortune. She remained stretched upon the earth in silent despair: The tears chased each other slowly down her cheeks, and her bosom heaved with frequent sobs. Oppressed with grief, She continued for some time in this state of torpidity. At length She rose with difficulty, and dragging her feeble steps towards the door, prepared to quit the dungeon.

The sound of her foot-steps rouzed the Monk from his sullen apathy. Starting from the Tomb against which He reclined, while his eyes wandered over the images of corruption contained in it, He pursued the Victim of his brutality, and soon over-took her. He seized her by the arm, and violently forced her back into the dungeon.

'Whither go you?' He cried in a stern voice; 'Return this instant!'

Antonia trembled at the fury of his countenance.

'What would you more?' She said with timidity: 'Is not my ruin compleated? Am I not undone, undone for ever? Is not your cruelty contented, or have I yet more to suffer? Let me depart. Let me return to my home, and weep unrestrained my shame and my affliction!'

'Return to your home?' repeated the Monk, with bitter and contemptuous mockery; Then suddenly his eyes flaming with passion, 'What? That you may denounce me to the world? That you may proclaim me an Hypocrite, a Ravisher, a Betrayer, a Monster of cruelty, lust, and ingratitude? No, no, no! I know well the whole weight of my offences; Well, that your complaints would be too just, and my crimes too notorious! You shall not from hence to tell Madrid that I am a Villain; that my conscience is loaded with sins, which make me despair of Heaven's pardon. Wretched Girl, you must stay here with me! Here amidst these lonely Tombs, these images of Death, these rotting loathsome corrupted bodies! Here shall you stay, and witness my sufferings; witness, what it is to die in the horrors of despondency, and breathe the last groan in blasphemy and curses! And who·am I to thank for this? What seduced me into crimes, whose bare remembrance makes me shudder? Fatal Witch! was it not thy beauty? Have you not plunged my soul into infamy? Have you not made me a perjured Hypocrite, a Ravisher, an Assassin! Nay, at this moment, does not that angel look bid me despair of God's forgiveness? Oh! when I stand before his judgment-throne, that look will suffice to damn me! You will tell my Judge, that you were happy, till *I* saw you; that you were innocent, till *I* polluted you! You will come with those tearful eyes, those cheeks pale and ghastly, those hands lifted in supplication, as when you sought from me that mercy which I gave not! Then will my perdition be certain! Then will come your Mother's Ghost, and hurl me down into the dwellings of Fiends, and flames, and Furies, and everlasting torments! And 'tis you, who will accuse me! 'Tis you, who will cause my eternal anguish! You, wretched Girl! You! You!'

As He thundered out these words, He violently grasped

Antonia's arm, and spurned the earth with delirious fury.

Supposing his brain to be turned, Antonia sank in terror upon her knees: She lifted up her hands, and her voice almost died away, ere She could give it utterance.

'Spare me! Spare me!' She murmured with difficulty.

'Silence!' cried the Friar madly, and dashed her upon the ground——

He quitted her, and paced the dungeon with a wild and disordered air. His eyes rolled fearfully: Antonia trembled, whenever She met their gaze. He seemed to meditate on something horrible, and She gave up all hopes of escaping from the Sepulchre with life. Yet in harbouring this idea, She did him injustice. Amidst the horror and disgust to which his soul was a prey, pity for his Victim still held a place in it. The storm of passion once over, He would have given worlds had He possest them, to have restored to her that innocence, of which his unbridled lust had deprived her. Of the desires which had urged him to the crime, no trace was left in his bosom: The wealth of India would not have tempted him to a second enjoyment of her person. His nature seemed to revolt at the very idea, and fain would He have wiped from his memory the scene which had just past. As his gloomy rage abated, in proportion did his compassion augment for Antonia. He stopped, and would have spoken to her words of comfort; But He knew not from whence to draw them, and remained gazing upon her with mournful wildness. Her situation seemed so hopeless, so woe-begone, as to baffle mortal power to relieve her. What could He do for her? Her peace of mind was lost, her honour irreparably ruined. She was cut off for ever from society, nor dared He give her back to it. He was conscious, that were She to appear in the world again, his guilt would be revealed, and his punishment inevitable. To one so laden with crimes, Death came

armed with double terrors. Yet should He restore
Antonia to light, and stand the chance of her betraying
him, how miserable a prospect would present itself
before her. She could never hope to be creditably established; She would be marked with infamy, and condemned to sorrow and solitude for the remainder of her
existence. What was the alternative? A resolution far
more terrible for Antonia, but which at least would in-
sure the Abbot's safety. He determined to leave the
world persuaded of her death, and to retain her a captive
in this gloomy prison: There He proposed to visit her
every night, to bring her food, to profess his penitence,
and mingle his tears with hers. The Monk felt that this
resolution was unjust and cruel; but it was his only means
to prevent Antonia, from publishing his guilt and her own
infamy. Should He release her, He could not depend
upon her silence: His offence was too flagrant to permit
his hoping for her forgiveness. Besides, her re-appearing
would excite universal curiosity, and the violence of her
affliction would prevent her from concealing its cause.
He determined therefore, that Antonia should remain a
Prisoner in the dungeon.

He approached her with confusion painted on his
countenance. He raised her from the ground. Her hand
trembled, as He took it, and He dropped it again as if
He had touched a Serpent. Nature seemed to recoil at
the touch. He felt himself at once repulsed from and
attracted towards her, yet could account for neither
sentiment. There was something in her look which
penetrated him with horror; and though his understanding was still ignorant of it, Conscience pointed out
to him the whole extent of his crime. In hurried accents
yet the gentlest He could find, while his eye was averted,
and his voice scarcely audible, He strove to console her
under a misfortune which now could not be avoided. He
declared himself sincerely penitent, and that He would

gladly shed a drop of his blood, for every tear which his barbarity had forced from her. Wretched and hopeless, Antonia listened to him in silent grief: But when He announced her confinement in the Sepulchre, that dreadful doom to which even death seemed preferable, roused her from her insensibility at once. To linger out a life of misery in a narrow loathsome Cell, known to exist by no human Being save her Ravisher, surrounded by mouldering Corses, breathing the pestilential air of corruption, never more to behold the light, or drink the pure gale of heaven, the idea was more terrible than She could support. It conquered even her abhorrence of the Friar. Again She sank upon her knees: She besought his compassion in terms the most pathetic and urgent. She promised, would He but restore her to liberty, to conceal her injuries from the world; to assign any reason for her re-appearance, which He might judge proper; and in order to prevent the least suspicion from falling upon him, She offered to quit Madrid immediately. Her entreaties were so urgent, as to make a considerable impression upon the Monk. He reflected, that as her person no longer excited his desires, He had no interest in keeping her concealed as He had at first intended; that He was adding a fresh injury, to those which She had already suffered; and that if She adhered to her promises, whether She was confined or at liberty, his life and reputation were equally secure. On the other hand, He trembled lest in her affliction Antonia should unintentionally break her engagement; or that her excessive simplicity and ignorance of deceit should permit some one more artful to surprize her secret. However well-founded were these apprehensions, compassion, and a sincere wish to repair his fault as much as possible solicited his complying with the prayers of his Suppliant. The difficulty of colouring Antonia's unexpected return to life, after her supposed death and public interment, was the only point which kept him irresolute. He was still pondering on the means of removing this obstacle, when He heard the sound of feet approaching with precipitation. The door of the Vault was thrown open, and Matilda rushed in, evidently much confused and terrified.

On seeing a Stranger enter, Antonia uttered a cry of joy: But her hopes of receiving succour from him were soon dissipated. The supposed Novice, without expressing the least surprize at finding a Woman alone with the Monk, in so strange a place, and at so late an hour, addressed him thus without losing a moment.

'What is to be done, Ambrosio? We are lost, unless some speedy means is found of dispelling the Rioters. Ambrosio, the Convent of St. Clare is on fire; The Prioress has fallen a victim to the fury of the Mob. Already is the Abbey menaced with a similar fate. Alarmed at the threats of the People, the Monks seek for you everywhere. They imagine, that your authority alone will suffice to calm this disturbance. No one knows, what is become of you, and your absence creates universal astonishment and despair. I profited by the confusion, and fled hither to warn you of the danger.'

'This will soon be remedied,' answered the Abbot; 'I will hasten back to my Cell: a trivial reason will account for my having been missed.'

'Impossible!' rejoined Matilda: 'The Sepulchre is filled with Archers. Lorenzo de Medina, with several Officers of the Inquisition, searches through the Vaults, and pervades every passage. You will be intercepted in your flight; Your reasons for being at this late hour in the Sepulchre will be examined; Antonia will be found, and then you are undone for ever!'

'Lorenzo de Medina? Officers of the Inquisition? What brings them here? Seek they for me? Am I then suspected? Oh! speak, Matilda! Answer me, in pity!'

'As yet they do not think of you, but I fear, that they will ere long. Your only chance of escaping their notice rests upon the difficulty of exploring this Vault. The door is artfully hidden: Haply it may not be observed, and we may remain concealed till the search is over.'

'But Antonia . . . . . Should the Inquisitors draw near, and her cries be heard . . . .'

'Thus I remove that danger!' interrupted Matilda.

At the same time drawing a poignard, She rushed upon her devoted prey.

'Hold! Hold!' cried Ambrosio, seizing her hand, and wresting from it the already lifted weapon. 'What would you do, cruel Woman? The Unfortunate has already suffered but too much, thanks to your pernicious consels! Would to God, that I had never followed them! Would to God, that I had never seen your face!'

Matilda darted upon him a look of scorn.

'Absurd!' She exclaimed with an air of passion and majesty, which impressed the Monk with awe. 'After robbing her of all that made it dear, can you fear to deprive her of a life so miserable? But 'tis well! Let her live to convince you of your folly. I abandon you to your evil destiny! I disclaim your alliance! Who trembles to commit so insignificant a crime, deserves not my protection. Hark! Hark! Ambrosio; Hear you not the Archers? They come, and your destruction is inevitable!'

At this moment the Abbot heard the sound of distant voices. He flew to close the door on whose concealment his safety depended, and which Matilda had neglected to fasten. Ere He could reach it, He saw Antonia glide suddenly by him, rush through the door, and fly towards the noise with the swiftness of an arrow. She had listened attentively to Matilda: She heard Lorenzo's name mentioned, and resolved to risque every thing to throw herself under his protection. The door was open. The sounds convinced her, that the Archers could be at no great distance. She mustered up her little remaining strength, rushed by the Monk ere He perceived her design, and bent her course rapidly towards the voices. As soon as He recovered from his first surprize, the Abbot failed not to pursue her. In vain did Antonia redouble her speed, and stretch every nerve to the utmost. Her Enemy gained upon her every moment: She heard his steps close after her, and felt the heat of his breath glow upon her neck. He over-took her; He twisted his hand in the ringlets of her streaming hair, and attempted to drag her back with him to the dungeon. Antonia resisted with all her strength: She folded her arms round a Pillar which supported the roof, and shrieked loudly for assistance. In vain did the Monk strive to threaten her to silence.

'Help!' She continued to exclaim; 'Help! Help! for God's sake!'

Quickened by her cries, the sound of foot-steps was heard approaching. The Abbot expected every moment to see the Inquisitors arrive. Antonia still resisted, and He now enforced her silence by means the most horrible and inhuman. He still grasped Matilda's dagger: Without allowing himself a moment's reflection, He raised it, and plunged it twice in the bosom of Antonia! She shrieked, and sank upon the ground. The Monk endeavoured to bear her away with him, but She still embraced the Pillar firmly. At that instant the light of approaching Torches flashed upon the Walls. Dreading a discovery, Ambrosio was compelled to abandon his Victim, and hastily fled back to the Vault, where He had left Matilda.

He fled not unobserved. Don Ramirez happening to arrive the first, perceived a Female bleeding upon the ground, and a Man flying from the spot, whose confusion betrayed him for the Murderer. He instantly pursued the Fugitive with some part of the Archers, while the Others remained with Lorenzo to protect the wounded Stranger.

They raised her, and supported her in their arms. She had fainted from excess of pain, but soon gave signs of returning life. She opened her eyes, and on lifting up her head, the quantity of fair hair fell back which till then had obscured her features.

'God Almighty! It is Antonia!'

Such was Lorenzo's exclamation, while He snatched her from the Attendant's arms, and clasped her in his own.

Though aimed by an uncertain hand, the poignard had answered but too well the purpose of its Employer. The wounds were mortal, and Antonia was conscious, that She never could recover. Yet the few moments which remained for her, were moments of happiness. The concern exprest upon Lorenzo's countenance, the frantic fondness of his complaints, and his earnest enquiries respecting her wounds, convinced her beyond a doubt that his affections were her own. She would not be removed from the Vaults, fearing lest motion should only hasten her death; and She was unwilling to lose those moments, which She past in receiving proofs of Lorenzo's love, and assuring him of her own. She told him, that had She still been undefiled She might have lamented the loss of life; But that deprived of honour and branded with shame, Death was to her a blessing: She could not have been his Wife, and that hope being denied her, She resigned herself to the Grave without one sigh of regret. She bad him take courage, conjured him not to abandon himself to fruitless sorrow, and declared that She mourned to leave nothing in the whole world, but him. While every sweet accent increased rather than lightened Lorenzo's grief, She continued to converse with him till the moment of dissolution. Her voice grew faint and scarcely audible; A thick cloud spread itself over her eyes; Her heart beat slow and irregular, and every instant seemed to announce that her fate was near at hand.

She lay, her head reclining upon Lorenzo's bosom, and her lips still murmuring to him words of comfort. She was interrupted by the Convent-Bell, as tolling at a distance, it struck the hour. Suddenly Antonia's eyes sparkled with celestial brightness: Her frame seemed to have received new strength and animation. She started from her Lover's arms.

'Three o'clock!' She cried; 'Mother, I come!'

She clasped her hands, and sank lifeless upon the ground. Lorenzo in agony threw himself beside her: He tore his hair, beat his breast, and refused to be separated from the Corse. At length his force being exhausted, He suffered himself to be led from the Vault, and was conveyed to the Palace de Medina scarcely more alive than the unfortunate Antonia.

In the mean while, though closely pursued, Ambrosio succeeded in regaining the Vault. The Door was already fastened when Don Ramirez arrived, and much time elapsed, ere the Fugitive's retreat was discovered. But nothing can resist perseverance. Though so artfully concealed, the Door could not escape the vigilance of the Archers. They forced it open, and entered the Vault to the infinite dismay of Ambrosio and his Companion. The Monk's confusion, his attempt to hide himself, his rapid flight, and the blood sprinkled upon his cloaths, left no room to doubt his being Antonia's Murderer. But when He was recognized for the immaculate Ambrosio, 'The Man of Holiness,' the Idol of Madrid, the faculties of the Spectators were chained up in surprize, and scarcely could they persuade themselves that what they saw was no vision. The Abbot strove not to vindicate himself, but preserved a sullen silence. He was secured and bound. The same precaution was taken with Matilda: Her Cowl being removed, the delicacy of her features and profusion of her golden hair betrayed her sex, and this incident created fresh amazement. The dagger was also found in the Tomb, where the Monk had thrown it; and the dungeon having undergone a thorough search, the two Culprits were conveyed to the prisons of the Inquisition.

Don Ramirez took care, that the populace should remain ignorant both of the crimes and profession of the Captives. He feared a repetition of the riots, which had followed the apprehending the Prioress of St. Clare. He contented himself with stating to the Capuchins, the guilt of their Superior. To avoid the shame of a public accusation, and dreading the popular fury from which they had already saved their Abbey with much difficulty, the Monks readily permitted the Inquisitors to search their Mansion without noise. No fresh discoveries were made. The effects found in the Abbot's and Matilda's Cells were seized, and carried to the Inquisition to be produced in evidence. Every thing else remained in its former position, and order and tranquillity once more prevailed through Madrid.

St. Clare's Convent was completely ruined by the united ravages of the Mob and conflagration. Nothing remained of it but the principal Walls, whose thickness and solidity had preserved them from the flames. The Nuns who had belonged to it, were obliged in consequence to disperse themselves into other Societies: But the prejudice against them ran high, and the Superiors were very unwilling to admit them. However, most of them being related to Families the most distinguished for their riches birth and power, the several Convents were compelled to receive them, though they did it with a very ill grace. This prejudice was extremely false and unjustifiable: After a close investigation, it was proved that All in the Convent were persuaded of the death of Agnes, except the four Nuns whom St. Ursula had pointed out. These had fallen Victims to the popular fury; as had also several who were perfectly innocent and unconscious of the whole affair. Blinded by resentment, the

Mob had sacrificed every Nun who fell into their hands:
They who escaped were entirely indebted to the Duke de
Medina's prudence and moderation. Of this they were
conscious, and felt for that Nobleman a proper sense of
gratitude.

Virginia was not the most sparing of her thanks: She
wished equally to make a proper return for his attentions, and to obtain the good graces of Lorenzo's Uncle.
In this She easily succeeded. The Duke beheld her
beauty with wonder and admiration; and while his eyes
were enchanted with her Form, the sweetness of her
manners and her tender concern for the suffering Nun
prepossessed his heart in her favour. This Virginia had
discernment enough to perceive, and She redoubled her
attention to the Invalid. When He parted from her at the
door of her Father's Palace, the Duke entreated permission to enquire occasionally after her health. His request was readily granted: Virginia assured him, that the
Marquis de Villa-Franca would be proud of an opportunity to thank him in person for the protection afforded
to her. They now separated, He enchanted with her
beauty and gentleness, and She much pleased with him
and more with his Nephew.

On entering the Palace, Virginia's first care was to
summon the family Physician, and take care of her unknown charge. Her Mother hastened to share with her
the charitable office. Alarmed by the riots, and trembling
for his Daughter's safety, who was his only child, the
Marquis had flown to St. Clare's Convent, and was still
employed in seeking her. Messengers were now dispatched on all sides to inform him, that He would find
her safe at his Hotel, and desire him to hasten thither
immediately. His absence gave Virginia liberty to bestow
her whole attention upon her Patient; and though much
disordered herself by the adventures of the night, no
persuasion could induce her to quit the bed-side of the

Sufferer. Her constitution being much enfeebled by want and sorrow, it was some time before the Stranger was restored to her senses. She found great difficulty in swallowing the medicines prescribed to her: But this obstacle being removed, She easily conquered her disease which proceeded from nothing but weakness. The attention which was paid her, the wholesome food to which She had been long a Stranger, and her joy at being restored to liberty, to society, and, as She dared to hope, to Love, all this combined to her speedy re-establishment. From the first moment of knowing her, her melancholy situation, her sufferings almost unparalleled had engaged the affections of her amiable Hostess: Virginia felt for her the most lively interest; But how was She delighted, when her Guest being sufficiently recovered to relate her History, She recognized in the captive Nun the Sister of Lorenzo!

This victim of monastic cruelty was indeed no other than the unfortunate Agnes. During her abode in the Convent, She had been well known to Virginia: But her emaciated form, her features altered by affliction, her death universally credited, and her over-grown and matted hair which hung over her face and bosom in disorder, at first had prevented her being recollected. The Prioress had put every artifice in practice to induce Virginia to take the veil; for the Heiress of Villa-Franca would have been no despicable acquisition. Her seeming kindness and unremitted attention so far succeeded, that her young Relation began to think seriously upon compliance. Better instructed in the disgust and ennui of a monastic life, Agnes had penetrated the designs of the Domina: She trembled for the innocent Girl, and endeavoured to make her sensible of her error. She painted in their true colours the numerous inconveniencies attached to a Convent, the continued restraint, the low jealousies, the petty intrigues, the servile court and gross flattery expected by the Superior. She then bad Virginia reflect on the brilliant prospect which presented itself before hèr: The Idol of her Parents, the admiration of Madrid, endowed by nature and education with every perfection of person and mind, She might look forward to an establishment the most fortunate. Her riches furnished her with the means of exercising in their fullest extent, charity and benevolence, those virtues so dear to her; and her stay in the world, would enable her discovering Objects worthy her protection, which could not be done in the seclusion of a Convent.

Her persuasions induced Virginia to lay aside all thoughts of the Veil: But another argument, not used by Agnes, had more weight with her than all the others put together. She had seen Lorenzo, when He visited his Sister at the Grate. His Person pleased her, and her conversations with Agnes generally used to terminate in some question about her Brother. She, who doted upon Lorenzo, wished for no better than an opportunity to trumpet out his praise. She spoke of him in terms of rapture; and to convince her Auditor, how just were his sentiments, how cultivated his mind, and elegant his expressions, She showed her at different times the letters, which She received from him. She soon perceived that from these communications the heart of her young Friend had imbibed impressions, which She was far from intending to give, but was truly happy to discover. She could not have wished her Brother a more desirable union: Heiress of Villa-Franca, virtuous, affectionate, beautiful, and accomplished, Virginia seemed calculated to make him happy. She sounded her Brother upon the subject, though without mentioning names or circumstances. He assured her in his answers that his heart and hand were totally disengaged, and She thought, that upon these grounds She might proceed without danger. She in consequence endeavoured to strengthen the dawning passion of her Friend. Lorenzo was made the constant topic of her discourse; and the avidity with which her Auditor listened, the sighs which frequently escaped from her bosom, and the eagerness with which upon any digression She brought back the conversation to the subject whence it had wandered, sufficed to convince Agnes, that her Brother's addresses would be far from disagreeable. She at length ventured to mention her wishes to the Duke: Though a Stranger to the Lady herself, He knew enough of her situation to think her worthy his Nephew's hand. It was agreed between him and his Niece, that She should insinuate the idea to Lorenzo, and She only waited his return to Madrid to propose her Friend to him as his Bride. The unfortunate events which took place in the interim, prevented her from executing her design. Virginia wept her loss sincerely, both as a Companion, and as the only Person to whom She could speak of Lorenzo. Her passion continued to prey upon her heart in secret, and She had almost determined to confess her sentiments to her Mother, when accident once more threw their object in her way. The sight of him so near her, his politeness, his compassion, his intrepidity, had combined to give new ardour to her affection. When She now found her Friend and Advocate restored to her, She looked upon her as a Gift from Heaven; She ventured to cherish the hope of being united to Lorenzo, and resolved to use with him his Sister's influence.

Supposing that before her death Agnes might possibly have made the proposal, the Duke had placed all his Nephew's hints of marriage to Virginia's account: Consequently, He gave them the most favourable reception. On returning to his Hotel, the relation given him of Antonia's death, and Lorenzo's behaviour on the occasion, made evident his mistake. He lamented the circumstances; But the unhappy Girl being effectually out of the way, He trusted that his designs would yet be executed. 'Tis true, that Lorenzo's situation just then ill-suited him for a Bridegroom. His hopes disappointed at the moment when He expected to realize them, and the dreadful and sudden death of his Mistress had affected him very severely. The Duke found him upon the Bed of sickness. His Attendants expressed serious apprehensions for his life; But the Uncle entertained not the same fears. He was of opinion, and not unwisely, that 'Men have died, and worms have eat them; but not for Love!'* He therefore flattered himself, that however deep might be the impression made upon his Nephew's heart, Time and Virginia would be able to efface it. He now hastened to the afflicted Youth, and endeavoured to console him: He sympathised in his distress, but encouraged him to resist the encroachments of despair. He allowed that He could not but feel shocked at an event so terrible, nor could He blame his sensibility; But He besought him not to torment himself with vain regrets, and rather to struggle with affliction, and preserve his life, if not for his own sake, at least for the sake of those who were fondly attached to him. While He laboured thus to make Lorenzo forget Antonia's loss, the Duke paid his court assiduously to Virginia, and seized every opportunity to advance his Nephew's interest in her heart.

It may easily be expected, that Agnes was not long without enquiring after Don Raymond. She was shocked to hear the wretched situation to which grief had reduced him; Yet She could not help exulting secretly, when She reflected, that his illness proved the sincerity of his love. The Duke undertook the office himself, of announcing to the Invalid the happiness which awaited him. Though He omitted no precaution to prepare him for such an event, at this sudden change from despair to happiness Raymond's transports were so violent, as nearly to have proved fatal to him. These once passed, the tranquillity of his mind, the assurance of felicity, and above all the presence of Agnes, [Who was no sooner re-established by the care of Virginia and the Marchioness, than She hastened to attend her Lover] soon enabled him to overcome the effects of his late dreadful malady. The calm of his soul communicated itself to his body, and He recovered with such rapidity as to create universal surprize.

No so Lorenzo. Antonia's death accompanied with such terrible circumstances weighed upon his mind heavily. He was worn down to a shadow. Nothing could give him pleasure. He was persuaded with difficulty to swallow nourishment sufficient for the support of life, and a consumption was apprehended. The society of Agnes formed his only comfort. Though accident had never permitted their being much together, He entertained for her a sincere friendship and attachment. Perceiving how necessary She was to him, She seldom quitted his chamber. She listened to his complaints with unwearied attention, and soothed him by the gentleness of her manners, and by sympathising with his distress. She still inhabited the Palace de Villa-Franca, the Possessors of which treated her with marked affection. The Duke had intimated to the Marquis his wishes respecting Virginia. The match was unexceptionable: Lorenzo was Heir to his Uncle's immense property, and was distinguished in Madrid for his agreeable person, extensive knowledge, and propriety of conduct: Add to this, that the Marchioness had discovered, how strong was her Daughter's prepossession in his favour.

In consequence the Duke's proposal was accepted without hesitation: Every precaution was taken, to induce Lorenzo's seeing the Lady with those sentiments, which She so well merited to excite. In her visits to her Brother Agnes was frequently accompanied by the Marchioness; and as soon as He was able to move into his Anti-chamber, Virginia under her mother's protection was sometimes permitted to express her wishes for his recovery. This She did with such delicacy, the manner in which She mentioned Antonia was so tender and soothing, and when She lamented her Rival's melancholy fate, her bright eyes shone so beautiful through her tears, that Lorenzo could not behold, or listen to her without emotion. His Relations, as well as the Lady, perceived that with every day her society seemed to give him fresh pleasure, and that He spoke of her in terms of stronger admiration. However, they prudently kept their observations to themselves. No word was dropped, which might lead him to suspect their designs. They continued their former conduct and attention, and left Time to ripen into a warmer sentiment, the friendship which He already felt for Virginia.

In the mean while, her visits became more frequent; and latterly there was scarce a day, of which She did not pass some part by the side of Lorenzo's Couch. He gradually regained his strength, but the progress of his recovery was slow and doubtful. One evening He seemed to be in better spirits than usual: Agnes and her Lover, the Duke, Virginia, and her Parents were sitting round him. He now for the first time entreated his Sister to inform him, how She had escaped the effects of the poison, which St. Ursula had seen her swallow. Fearful of recalling those scenes to his mind in which Antonia had perished, She had hitherto concealed from him the history of her sufferings. As He now started the subject himself, and thinking that perhaps the narrative of her sorrows might draw him from the contemplation of those on which He dwelt too constantly, She immediately complied with his request. The rest of the company had already heard her story; But the interest which all present felt for its Heroine made them anxious to hear it repeated. The whole society seconding Lorenzo's en-

treaties, Agnes obeyed. She first recounted the discovery
which had taken place in the Abbey-Chapel, the
Domina's resentment, and the mid-night scene of which
St. Ursula had been a concealed witness. Though the
Nun had already described this latter event, Agnes now
related it more circumstantially and at large: After
which She proceeded in her narrative as follows.

Conclusion of the History of Agnes de Medina

My supposed death was attended with the greatest
agonies. Those moments which I believed my last, were
embittered by the Domina's assurances, that I could not
e cape perdition; and as my eyes closed, I heard her rage
exhale itself in curses, on my offence. The horror of this
situation, of a death-bed from which hope was banished,
of a sleep from which I was only to wake to find myself
the prey of flames and Furies, was more dreadful than I
can describe. When animation revived in me, my soul
was still impressed with these terrible ideas: I looked
round with fear, expecting to behold the Ministers of
divine vengeance. For the first hour, my senses were so
bewildered, and my brain so dizzy, that I strove in vain
to arrange the strange images which floated in wild
confusion before me. If I endeavoured to raise myself
from the ground, the wandering of my head deceived me.
Every thing around me seemed to rock, and I sank once
more upon the earth. My weak and dazzled eyes were
unable to bear a nearer approach to a gleam of light,
which I saw trembling above me. I was compelled to
close them again, and remain motionless in the same
posture.

A full hour elapsed, before I was sufficiently myself to
examine the surrounding Objects. When I did examine
them, what terror filled my bosom I found myself extended upon a sort of wicker Couch: It had six handles to

it, which doubtless had served the Nuns to convey me to
my grave. I was covered with a linen cloth: Several faded
flowers were strown over me: On one side lay a small
wooden Crucifix; On the other, a Rosary of large Beads.
Four low narrow walls confined me. The top was also
covered, and in it was practised a small grated Door:
Through this was admitted the little air, which circulated in this miserable place. A faint glimmering of
light which streamed through the Bars, permitted me to
distinguish the surrounding horrors. I was opprest by a
noisome suffocating smell; and perceiving that the grated
door was unfastened, I thought that I might possibly
effect my escape. As I raised myself with this design, my
hand rested upon something soft: I grasped it, and advanced it towards the light. Almighty God! What was
my disgust, my consternation! In spite of its putridity,
and the worms which preyed upon it, I perceived a corrupted human head, and recognised the features of a
Nun who had died some months before! I threw it
from me, and sank almost lifeless upon my Bier.

When my strength returned, this circumstance, and
the consciousness of being surrounded by the loathsome
and mouldering Bodies of my Companions, increased my
desire to escape from my fearful prison. I again moved
towards the light. The grated door was within my reach:
I lifted it without difficulty; Probably it had been left
unclosed to facilitate my quitting the dungeon. Aiding
myself by the irregularity of the Walls some of whose
stones projected beyond the rest, I contrived to ascend
them, and drag myself out of my prison. I now found
Myself in a Vault tolerably spacious. Several Tombs,
similar in appearance to that whence I had just escaped,
were ranged along the sides in order, and seemed to be
considerably sunk within the earth. A sepulchral Lamp
was suspended from the roof by an iron chain, and shed a
gloomy light through the dungeon. Emblems of Death

were seen on every side: Skulls, shoulder-blades, thigh-bones, and other leavings of Mortality were scattered upon the dewy ground. Each Tomb was ornamented with a large Crucifix, and in one corner stood a wooden Statue of St. Clare. To these objects I at first paid no attention: A Door, the only outlet from the Vault, had attracted my eyes. I hastened towards it, having wrapped my winding-sheet closely round me. I pushed against the door, and to my inexpressible terror found that it was fastened on the outside.

I guessed immediately, that the Prioress mistaking the nature of the liquor which She had compelled me to drink, instead of poison had administered a strong Opiate. From this I concluded, that being to all appearance dead I had received the rites of burial; and that deprived of the power of making my existence known, it would be my fate to expire of hunger. This idea penetrated me with horror, not merely for my own sake, but that of the innocent Creature, who still lived within my bosom. I again endeavoured to open the door, but it resisted all my efforts. I stretched my voice to the extent of its compass, and shrieked for aid: I was remote from the hearing of every one: No friendly voice replied to mine. A profound and melancholy silence prevailed through the Vault, and I despaired of liberty. My long abstinence from food now began to torment me. The tortures which hunger inflicted on me, were the most painful and insupportable: Yet they seemed to increase with every hour which past over my head. Sometimes I threw myself upon the ground, and rolled upon it wild and desperate: Sometimes starting up, I returned to the door, again strove to force it open, and repeated my fruitless cries for succour. Often was I on the point of striking my temple against the sharp corner of some Monument, dashing out my brains, and thus terminating my woes at once; But still the remembrance of my Baby vanquished my resolution:

I trembled at a deed, which equally endangered my
Child's existence and my own. Then would I vent my
anguish in loud exclamations and passionate complaints; and then again my strength failing me, silent
and hopeless I would sit me down upon the base of St.
Clare's Statue, fold my arms, and abandon myself to
sullen despair. Thus passed several wretched hours.
Death advanced towards me with rapid strides, and I
expected that every succeeding moment would be that of
my dissolution. Suddenly a neighbouring Tomb caught
my eye: A Basket stood upon it, which till then I had not
observed. I started from my seat: I made towards it as
swiftly as my exhausted frame would permit. How
eagerly did I seize the Basket, on finding it to contain a
loaf of coarse bread and a small bottle of water.

I threw myself with avidity upon these humble aliments. They had to all appearance been placed in the
Vault for several days; The bread was hard, and the
water tainted; Yet never did I taste food to me so delicious. When the cravings of appetite were satisfied, I
busied myself with conjectures upon this new circumstance: I debated whether the Basket had been placed
there with a view to my necessity. Hope answered my
doubts in the affirmative. Yet who could guess me to be
in need of such assistance? If my existence was known,
why was I detained in this gloomy Vault? If I was kept a
Prisoner, what meant the ceremony of committing me
to the Tomb? Or if I was doomed to perish with hunger,
to whose pity was I indebted for provisions placed within
my reach? A Friend would not have kept my dreadful
punishment a secret; Neither did it seem probable, that
an Enemy would have taken pains to supply me with the
means of existence. Upon the whole I was inclined to
think, that the Domina's designs upon my life had been
discovered by some one of my Partizans in the Convent,
who had found means to substitute an opiate for poison:

That She had furnished me with food to support me, till She could effect my delivery: And that She was then employed in giving intelligence to my Relations of my danger, and pointing out a way to release me from captivity. Yet why then was the quality of my provisions so coarse? How could my Friend have entered the Vault without the Domina's knowledge? And if She had entered, why was the Door fastened so carefully? These reflections staggered me: Yet still this idea was the most favourable to my hopes, and I dwelt upon it in preference.

My meditations were interrupted by the sound of distant foot-steps. They approached, but slowly. Rays of light now darted through the crevices of the Door. Uncertain whether the Persons who advanced, came to relieve me, or were conducted by some other motive to the Vault, I failed not to attract their notice by loud cries for help. Still the sounds drew near: The light grew stronger: At length with inexpressible pleasure I heard the Key turning in the Lock. Persuaded that my deliverance was at hand, I flew towards the Door with a shriek of joy. It opened: But all my hopes of escape died away, when the Prioress appeared followed by the same four Nuns, who had been witnesses of my supposed death. They bore torches in their hands, and gazed upon me in fearful silence.

I started back in terror. The Domina descended into the Vault, as did also her Companions. She bent upon me a stern resentful eye, but expressed no surprize at finding me still living. She took the seat which I had just quitted: The door was again closed, and the Nuns ranged themselves behind their Superior, while the glare of their torches, dimmed by the vapours and dampness of the Vault, gilded with cold beams the surrounding Monuments. For some moments all preserved a dead and solemn silence. I stood at some distance from the

Prioress. At length She beckoned me to advance. Trembling at the severity of her aspect my strength scarce sufficed me to obey her. I drew near, but my limbs were unable to support their burthen. I sank upon my knees; I clasped my hands, and lifted them up to her for mercy, but had no power to articulate a syllable.

She gazed upon me with angry eyes.

'Do I see a Penitent, or a Criminal?' She said at length; 'Are those hands raised in contrition for your crimes, or in fear of meeting their punishment? Do those tears acknowledge the justice of your doom, or only solicit mitigation of your sufferings? I fear me, 'tis the latter!'

She paused, but kept her eye still fixt upon mine.

'Take courage;' She continued: 'I wish not for your death, but your repentance. The draught which I administered, was no poison, but an opiate. My intention in deceiving you, was to make you feel the agonies of a guilty conscience, had Death overtaken you suddenly, while your crimes were still unrepented. You have suffered those agonies: I have brought you to be familiar with the sharpness of death, and I trust, that your momentary anguish will prove to you an eternal benefit. It is not my design to destroy your immortal soul; or bid you seek the grave, burthened with the weight of sins unexpiated. No, Daughter, far from it: I will purify you with wholesome chastisement, and furnish you with full leisure for contrition and remorse. Hear then my sentence; The ill-judged zeal of your Friends delayed its execution, but cannot now prevent it. All Madrid believes you to be no more; Your Relations are thoroughly persuaded of your death, and the Nuns your Partizans have assisted at your funeral. Your existence can never be suspected: I have taken such precautions, as must render it an impenetrable mystery. Then abandon all thoughts of a World from which you are eternally separated, and em-

ploy the few hours which are allowed you, in preparing
for the next.'

This exordium led me to expect something terrible. I
trembled, and would have spoken to deprecate her
wrath: but a motion of the Domina commanded me to
be silent. She proceeded.

'Though of late years unjustly neglected, and now
opposed by many of our mis-guided Sisters, [whom Heaven convert!] it is my intention to revive the laws of our
order in their full force. That against incontinence is
severe, but no more than so monstrous an offence demands: Submit to it, Daughter, without resistance; You
will find the benefit of patience and resignation in a
better life than this. Listen then to the sentence of St.
Clare. Beneath these Vaults there exist Prisons, intended
to receive such criminals as yourself: Artfully is their
entrance concealed, and She who enters them, must
resign all hopes of liberty. Thither must you now be
conveyed. Food shall be supplied you, but not sufficient
for the indulgence of appetite: You shall have just enough
to keep together body and soul, and its quality shall be
the simplest and coarsest. Weep, Daughter, weep, and
moisten your bread with your tears: God knows, that
you have ample cause for sorrow! Chained down in one
of these secret dungeons, shut out from the world and
light for ever, with no comfort but religion, no society
but repentance, thus must you groan away the remainder
of your days. Such are St. Clare's orders; Submit to them
without repining. Follow me!'

Thunder-struck at this barbarous decree, my little
remaining strength abandoned me. I answered only by
falling at her feet, and bathing them with tears. The
Domina, unmoved by my affliction, rose from her seat
with a stately air. She repeated her commands in an
absolute tone: But my excessive faintness made me
unable to obey her. Mariana and Alix raised me from

the ground, and carried me forwards in their arms. The Prioress moved on, leaning upon Violante, and Camilla preceded her with a Torch. Thus passed our sad procession along the passages, in silence only broken by my sighs and groans. We stopped before the principal shrine of St. Clare. The Statue was removed from its Pedestal, though how I knew not. The Nuns afterwards raised an iron grate till then concealed by the Image, and let it fall on the other side with a loud crash. The awful sound, repeated by the vaults above, and Caverns below me, rouzed me from the despondent apathy in which I had been plunged. I looked before me: An abyss presented itself to my affrighted eyes, and a steep and narrow Staircase, whither my Conductors were leading me. I shrieked, and started back. I implored compassion, rent the air with my cries, and summoned both heaven and earth to my assistance. In vain! I was hurried down the Staircase, and forced into one of the Cells which lined the Cavern's sides.

My blood ran cold, as I gazed upon this melancholy abode. The cold vapours hovering in the air, the walls green with damp, the bed of Straw so forlorn and comfortless, the Chain destined to bind me for ever to my prison, and the Reptiles of every description which as the torches advanced towards them, I descried hurrying to their retreats, struck my heart with terrors almost too exquisite for nature to bear. Driven by despair to madness, I burst suddenly from the Nuns who held me: I threw myself upon my knees before the Prioress, and besought her mercy in the most passionate and frantic terms.

'If not on me,' said I, 'look at least with pity on that innocent Being, whose life is attached to mine! Great is my crime, but let not my Child suffer for it! My Baby has committed no fault: Oh! spare me for the sake of my unborn Offspring, whom ere it tastes life your severity dooms to destruction!'

The Prioress drew back haughtily: She forced her habit from my grasp, as if my touch had been contagious.

'What?' She exclaimed with an exasperated air; 'What? Dare you plead for the produce of your shame? Shall a Creature be permitted to live, conceived in guilt so monstrous? Abandoned Woman, speak for him no more! Better that the Wretch should perish than live: Begotten in perjury, incontinence, and pollution, It cannot fail to prove a Prodigy of vice. Hear me, thou Guilty! Expect no mercy from me either for yourself, or Brat. Rather pray, that Death may seize you before you produce it; Or if it must see the light, that its eyes may immediately be closed again for ever! No aid shall be given you in your labour; Bring your Offspring into the world yourself, Feed it yourself, Nurse it yourself, Bury it yourself: God grant that the latter may happen soon, lest you receive comfort from the fruit of your iniquity!'

This inhuman speech, the threats which it contained, the dreadful sufferings foretold to me by the Domina, and her prayers for my Infant's death, on whom though unborn I already doated, were more than my exhausted frame could support. Uttering a deep groan, I fell senseless at the feet of my unrelenting Enemy. I know not how long I remained in this situation; But I imagine, that some time must have elapsed before my recovery, since it sufficed the Prioress and her Nuns to quit the Cavern. When my senses returned, I found myself in silence and solitude. I heard not even the retiring foot-steps of my Persecutors. All was hushed, and all was dreadful! I had been thrown upon the bed of Straw: The heavy Chain which I had already eyed with terror, was wound around my waist, and fastened me to the Wall. A Lamp glimmering with dull, melancholy rays through my dungeon, permitted my distinguishing all its horrors: It was separated from the Cavern by a low and irregular Wall of Stone: A large Chasm was left open in it which formed the entrance, for door there was none. A leaden Crucifix was in front of my straw Couch. A tattered rug lay near me, as did also a Chaplet of Beads; and not far from me stood a pitcher of water, and a wicker-Basket containing a small loaf, and a bottle of oil to supply my Lamp.

With a despondent eye did I examine this scene of suffering: When I reflected, that I was doomed to pass in it the remainder of my days, my heart was rent with bitter anguish. I had once been taught to look forward to a lot so different! At one time my prospects had appeared so bright, so flattering! Now all was lost to me. Friends, comfort, society, happiness, in one moment I was deprived of all! Dead to the world, Dead to pleasure, I lived to nothing but the sense of misery. How fair did that world seem to me, from which I was for ever excluded! How many loved objects did it contain, whom I never should behold again! As I threw a look of terror round my prison, as I shrunk from the cutting wind, which howled through my subterraneous dwelling, the change seemed so striking, so abrupt, that I doubted its reality. That the Duke de Medina's Niece, that the destined Bride of the Marquis de las Cisternas, One bred up in affluence, related to the noblest families in Spain, and rich in a multitude of affectionate Friends, that She should in one moment become a Captive, separated from the world for ever, weighed down with chains, and reduced to support life with the coarsest aliments, appeared a change so sudden and incredible, that I believed myself the sport of some frightful vision. Its continuance convinced me of my mistake with but too much certainty. Every morning my hopes were disappointed. At length I abandoned all idea of escaping: I resigned myself to my fate, and only expected Liberty when She came the Companion of Death.

My mental anguish, and the dreadful scenes in which I had been an Actress, advanced the period of my labour.

In solitude and misery, abandoned by all, unassisted by Art, uncomforted by Friendship, with pangs which if witnessed would have touched the hardest heart, was I delivered of my wretched burthen. It came alive into the world; But I knew not how to treat it, or by what means to preserve its existence. I could only bathe it with tears, warm it in my bosom, and offer up prayers for its safety. I was soon deprived of this mournful employment: The want of proper attendance, my ignorance how to nurse it, the bitter cold of the dungeon, and the unwholesome air which inflated its lungs, terminated my sweet Babe's short and painful existence. It expired in a few hours after its birth, and I witnessed its death with agonies which beggar all description.

But my grief was unavailing. My Infant was no more; nor could all my sighs impart to its little tender frame the breath of a moment. I rent my winding-sheet, and wrapped in it my lovely Child. I placed it on my bosom, its soft arm folded round my neck, and its pale cold cheek resting upon mine. Thus did its lifeless limbs repose, while I covered it with kisses, talked to it, wept, and moaned over it without remission, day or night. Camilla entered my prison regularly once every twenty-four hours, to bring me food. In spite of her flinty nature, She could not behold this spectacle unmoved. She feared, that grief so excessive would at length turn my brain, and in truth I was not always in my proper senses. From a principle of compassion She urged me to permit the Corse to be buried: But to this I never would consent. I vowed not to part with it while I had life: Its presence was my only comfort, and no persuasion could induce me to give it up. It soon became a mass of putridity, and to every eye was a loathsome and disgusting Object; To every eye, but a Mother's. In vain did human feelings bid me recoil from this emblem of mortality with repugnance: I with-stood, and vanquished that repugnance. I persisted in holding

my Infant to my bosom, in lamenting it, loving it,
adoring it! Hour after hour have I passed upon my sorry
Couch, contemplating what had once been my Child: I
endeavoured to retrace its features through the livid corruption, with which they were over-spread: During my
confinement this sad occupation was my only delight;
and at that time Worlds should not have bribed me to
give it up. Even when released from my prison, I brought
away my Child in my arms. The representations of my
two kind Friends,"—[Here She took the hands of the
Marchioness and Virginia, and pressed them alternately
to her lips]—"at length persuaded me to resign my unhappy Infant to the Grave. Yet I parted from it with
reluctance: However, reason at length prevailed; I
suffered it to be taken from me, and it now reposes in
consecrated ground.*

I before mentioned, that regularly once a day Camilla
brought me food. She sought not to embitter my sorrows
with reproach: She bad me, 'tis true, resign all hopes of
liberty and worldly happiness; But She encouraged me
to bear with patience my temporary distress, and advised
me to draw comfort from religion. My situation evidently
affected her more, than She ventured to express: But She
believed, that to extenuate my fault would make me less
anxious to repent it. Often while her lips painted the
enormity of my guilt in glaring colours, her eyes betrayed,
how sensible She was to my sufferings. In fact I am certain that none of my Tormentors, [for the three other
Nuns entered my prison occasionally] were so much
actuated by the spirit of oppressive cruelty, as by the idea
that to afflict my body was the only way to preserve my
soul. Nay, even this persuasion might not have had such
weight with them, and they might have thought my
punishment too severe, had not their good dispositions
been represt by blind obedience to their Superior. Her
resentment existed in full force. My project of elopement

having been discovered by the Abbot of the Capuchins, She supposed herself lowered in his opinion by my disgrace, and in consequence her hate was inveterate. She told the Nuns to whose custody I was committed, that my fault was of the most heinous nature, that no sufferings could equal the offence, and that nothing could save me from eternal perdition, but punishing my guilt with the utmost severity. The Superior's word is an oracle to but too many of a Convent's Inhabitants. The Nuns believed whatever the Prioress chose to assert: Though contradicted by reason and charity, they hesitated not to admit the truth of her arguments. They followed her injunctions to the very letter, and were fully persuaded, that to treat me with lenity, or to show the least pity for my woes, would be a direct means to destroy my chance for salvation.

Camilla being most employed about me, was particularly charged by the Prioress to treat me with harshness. In compliance with these orders, She frequently strove to convince me, how just was my punishment, and how enormous was my crime: She bad me think myself too happy in saving my soul by mortifying my body, and even threatened me sometimes with eternal perdition. Yet as I before observed, She always concluded by words of encouragement and comfort; and though uttered by Camilla's lips, I easily recognised the Domina's expressions. Once, and once only, the Prioress visited me in my dungeon. She then treated me with the most unrelenting cruelty: She loaded me with reproaches, taunted me with my frailty, and when I implored her mercy, told me to ask it of heaven, since I deserved none on earth. She even gazed upon my lifeless Infant without emotion; and when She left me, I heard her charge Camilla to increase the hardships of my Captivity. Unfeeling Woman! But let me check my resentment: She has expiated her errors by her sad and unexpected death. Peace be with her; and may her crimes be forgiven in heaven, as I forgive her my sufferings on earth!

Thus did I drag on a miserable existence. Far from growing familiar with my prison, I beheld it every moment with new horror. The cold seemed more piercing and bitter, the air more thick and pestilential. My frame became weak, feverish, and emaciated. I was unable to rise from the bed of Straw, and exercise my limbs in the narrow limits, to which the length of my chain permitted me to move. Though exhausted, faint, and weary, I trembled to profit by the approach of Sleep: My slumbers were constantly interrupted by some obnoxious Insect crawling over me. Sometimes I felt the bloated Toad, hideous and pampered with the poisonous vapours of the dungeon, dragging his loathsome length along my bosom: Sometimes the quick cold Lizard rouzed me leaving his slimy track upon my face, and entangling itself in the tresses of my wild and matted hair: Often have I at waking found my fingers ringed with the long worms, which bred in the corrupted flesh of my Infant. At such times I shrieked with terror and disgust, and while I shook off the reptile, trembled with all a Woman's weakness.

Such was my situation, when Camilla was suddenly taken ill. A dangerous fever, supposed to be infectious, confined her to her bed. Every one except the Lay-Sister appointed to nurse her, avoided her with caution, and feared to catch the disease. She was perfectly delirious, and by no means capable of attending to me. The Domina and the Nuns admitted to the mystery, had latterly given me over entirely to Camilla's care: In consequence, they busied themselves no more about me; and occupied by preparing for the approaching Festival, it is more than probable, that I never once entered into their thoughts. Of the reason of Camilla's negligence, I have been informed since my release by the Mother St.

Ursula; At that time I was very far from suspecting its
cause. On the contrary, I waited for my Gaoler's appearance at first with impatience, and afterwards with despair. One day passed away; Another followed it; The
Third arrived. Still no Camilla! Still no food! I knew the
lapse of time by the wasting of my Lamp, to supply
which fortunately a week's supply of Oil had been left
me. I supposed, either that the Nuns had forgotten me,
or that the Domina had ordered them to let me perish.
The latter idea seemed the most probable; Yet so natural
is the love of life, that I trembled to find it true. Though
embittered by every species of misery, my existence was
still dear to me, and I dreaded to lose it. Every succeeding
minute proved to me, that I must abandon all hopes of
relief. I was become an absolute skeleton: My eyes already failed me, and my limbs were beginning to stiffen.
I could only express my anguish, and the pangs of that
hunger which gnawed my heart-strings, by frequent
groans, whose melancholy sound the vaulted roof of the
dungeon re-echoed. I resigned myself to my fate: I
already expected the moment of dissolution, when my
Guardian Angel, when my beloved Brother arrived in
time to save me. My sight grown dim and feeble at first
refused to recognize him; and when I did distinguish his
features, the sudden burst of rapture was too much for
me to bear. I was overpowered by the swell of joy at once
more beholding a Friend, and that a Friend so dear to me.
Nature could not support my emotions, and took her
refuge in insensibility.

You already know, what are my obligations to the
Family of Villa-Franca: But what you cannot know is
the extent of my gratitude, boundless as the excellence
of my Benefactors. Lorenzo! Raymond! Names so dear
to me! Teach me to bear with fortitude this sudden transition from misery to bliss. So lately a Captive, opprest
with chains, perishing with hunger, suffering every in-

convenience of cold and want, hidden from the light, excluded from society, hopeless, neglected, and as I feared, forgotten; Now restored to life and liberty, enjoying all the comforts of affluence and ease, surrounded by those who are most loved by me, and on the point of becoming his Bride who has long been wedded to my heart, my happiness is so exquisite, so perfect, that scarcely can my brain sustain the weight. One only wish remains ungratified: It is to see my Brother in his former health, and to know that Antonia's memory is buried in her grave. Granted this prayer, I have nothing more to desire. I trust, that my past sufferings have purchased from heaven the pardon of my momentary weakness. That I have offended, offended greatly and grievously, I am fully conscious; But let not my Husband, because He once conquered my virtue, doubt the propriety of my future conduct. I have been frail and full of error: But I yielded not to the the warmth of constitution; Raymond, affection for you betrayed me. I was too confident of my strength; But I depended no less on your honour than my own. I had vowed never to see you more: Had it not been for the consequences of that unguarded moment, my resolution had been kept. Fate willed it otherwise, and I cannot but rejoice at its decree. Still my conduct has been highly blameable, and while I attempt to justify myself, I blush at recollecting my imprudence. Let me then dismiss the ungrateful subject; First assuring you, Raymond, that you shall have no cause to repent our union, and that the more culpable have been the errors of your Mistress, the more exemplary shall be the conduct of your Wife.

Here Agnes ceased, and the Marquis replied to her address in terms equally sincere and affectionate. Lorenzo expressed his satisfaction at the prospect of being so closely connected with a Man, for whom He had ever entertained the highest esteem. The Pope's Bull had fully and effectually released Agnes from her religious engagements: The marriage was therefore celebrated as soon as the needful preparations had been made, for the Marquis wished to have the ceremony performed with all possible splendour and publicity. This being over, and the Bride having received the compliments of Madrid, She departed with Don Raymond for his Castle in Andalusia: Lorenzo accompanied them, as did also the Marchioness de Villa-Franca and her lovely Daughter. It is needless to say, that Theodore was of the party, and would be impossible to describe his joy at his Master's marriage. Previous to his departure, the Marquis to atone in some measure for his past neglect, made some enquiries relative to Elvira. Finding that She as well as her Daughter had received many services from Leonella and Jacintha, He showed his respect to the memory of his Sister-in-law by making the two Women handsome presents. Lorenzo followed his example—Leonella was highly flattered by the attentions of Noblemen so distinguished, and Jacintha blessed the hour on which her House was bewitched.

On her side, Agnes failed not to reward her Convent-Friends. The worthy Mother St. Ursula, to whom She owed her liberty, was named at her request Superintendent of 'The Ladies of Charity:' This was one of the best and most opulent Societies throughout Spain. Bertha and Cornelia not chusing to quit their Friend, were appointed to principal charges in the same establishment. As to the Nuns who had aided the Domina in persecuting Agnes, Camilla being confined by illness to her bed, had perished in the flames which consumed St. Clare's Convent. Mariana, Alix, and Violante, as well as two more, had fallen victims to the popular rage. The three Others who in Council had supported the Domina's sentence, were severely reprimanded, and banished to religious Houses in obscure and distant Provinces: Here they languished away a few years, ashamed of their former weakness, and shunned by their Companions with aversion and contempt.

Nor was the fidelity of Flora permitted to go unrewarded. Her wishes being consulted, She declared herself impatient to revisit her native land. In consequence, a passage was procured for her to Cuba, where She arrived in safety, loaded with the presents of Raymond and Lorenzo.

The debts of gratitude discharged, Agnes was at liberty to pursue her favourite plan. Lodged in the same House, Lorenzo and Virginia were eternally together. The more He saw of her, the more was He convinced of her merit. On her part, She laid herself out to please, and not to succeed was for her impossible. Lorenzo witnessed with admiration her beautiful person, elegant manners, innumerable talents, and sweet disposition: He was also much flattered by her prejudice in his favour, which She had not sufficient art to conceal. However, his sentiments partook not of that ardent character, which had marked his affection for Antonia. The image of that lovely and unfortunate Girl still lived in his heart, and baffled all Virginia's efforts to displace it. Still when the Duke proposed to him the match, which He wished to earnestly to take place, his Nephew did not reject the offer. The urgent supplications of his Friends, and the Lady's merit conquered his repugnance to entering into new engagements. He proposed himself to the Marquis de Villa-Franca, and was accepted with joy and gratitude. Virginia became his Wife, nor did She ever give him cause to repent his choice. His esteem increased for her daily. Her unremitted endeavours to please him could not but succeed. His affection assumed stronger and warmer colours. Antonia's image was gradually effaced from his bosom; and Virginia became sole Mistress of that heart, which She well deserved to possess without a Partner.

The remaining years of Raymond and Agnes, of Lorenzo and Virginia, were happy as can be those allotted to Mortals, born to be the prey of grief, and sport of disappointment. The exquisite sorrows with which they had been afflicted, made them think lightly of every succeeding woe. They had felt the sharpest darts in misfortune's quiver; Those which remained appeared blunt in comparison. Having weathered Fate's heaviest Storms, they looked calmly upon its terrors: or if ever they felt Affliction's casual gales, they seemed to them gentle as Zephyrs, which breathe over summer-seas.

CHAPTER V

——He was a fell despightful Fiend:
Hell holds none worse in baleful bower below:
By pride, and wit, and rage, and rancor keened;
Of Man alike, if good or bad the Foe.

                                    Thomson.*

ON THE DAY following Antonia's death, all Madrid was a scene of consternation and amazement. An Archer who had witnessed the adventure in the Sepulchre, had indiscreetly related the circumstances of the murder: He had also named the Perpetrator. The confusion was without example, which this intelligence raised among the Devotees. Most of them disbelieved it, and went themselves to the Abbey to ascertain the fact. Anxious to

avoid the shame to which their Superior's ill-conduct
exposed the whole Brotherhood, the Monks assured the
Visitors, that Ambrosio was prevented from receiving
them as usual by nothing but illness. This attempt was
unsuccessful: The same excuse being repeated day after
day, the Archer's story gradually obtained confidence.
His Partizans abandoned him: No one entertained a
doubt of his guilt; and they who before had been the
warmest in his praise, were now the most vociferous in
his condemnation.

While his innocence or guilt was debated in Madrid
with the utmost acrimony, Ambrosio was a prey to the
pangs of conscious villainy, and the terrors of punishment
impending over him. When He looked back to the
eminence on which He had lately stood, universally
honoured and respected, at peace with the world and with
himself, scarcely could He believe that He was indeed the
culprit, whose crimes and whose fate He trembled to
envisage. But a few weeks had elapsed, since He was pure
and virtuous, courted by the wisest and noblest in
Madrid, and regarded by the People with a reverence that
approached idolatry: He now saw himself stained with
the most loathed and monstrous sins, the object of universal execration, a Prisoner of the Holy Office, and
probably doomed to perish in tortures the most severe.
He could not hope to deceive his Judges: The proofs of
his guilt were too strong. His being in the Sepulchre at so
late an hour, his confusion at the discovery, the dagger
which in his first alarm He owned ·had been concealed
by him, and the blood which had spirted upon his habit
from Antonia's wound, sufficiently marked him out for
the Assassin. He waited with agony for the day of
examination: He had no resource to comfort him in his
distress. Religion could not inspire him with fortitude:
If He read the Books of morality which were put into his
hands, He saw in them nothing but the enormity of his

offences; If he attempted to pray, He recollected that He deserved not heaven's protection, and believed his crimes so monstrous, as to baffle even God's infinite goodness. For every other Sinner, He thought there might be hope, but for him there could be none. Shuddering at the past, anguished by the present, and dreading the future, thus passed He the few days preceding that which was marked for his Trial.

That day arrived. At nine in the morning his prison door was unlocked, and his Gaoler entering, commanded him to follow him. He obeyed with trembling. He was conducted into a spacious Hall, hung with black cloth. At the Table sat three grave stern-looking Men, also habited in black: One was the Grand Inquisitor,* whom the importance of this cause had induced to examine into it himself. At a smaller table at a little distance sat the Secretary, provided with all necessary implements for writing. Ambrosio was beckoned to advance, and take his station at the lower end of the Table. As his eye glanced downwards, He perceived various iron instruments lying scattered upon the floor. Their forms were unknown to him, but apprehension immediately guessed them to be engines of torture. He turned pale, and with difficulty prevented himself from sinking upon the ground.

Profound silence prevailed, except when the Inquisitors whispered a few words among themselves mysteriously. Near an hour past away, and with every second of it Ambrosio's fears grew more poignant. At length a small Door, opposite to that by which He had entered the Hall, grated heavily upon its hinges. An Officer appeared, and was immediately followed by the beautiful Matilda. Her hair hung about her face wildly; Her cheeks were pale, and her eyes sunk and hollow. She threw a melancholy look upon Ambrosio: He replied by one of aversion and reproach. She was placed

opposite to him. A Bell then sounded thrice. It was the
signal for opening the Court, and the Inquisitors entered
upon their office.

In these trials neither the accusation is mentioned, or
the name of the Accuser. The Prisoners are only asked,
whether they will confess: If they reply that having no
crime they can make no confession, they are put to the
torture without delay. This is repeated at intervals,
either till the suspected avow themselves culpable, or the
perseverance of the examinants is worn out and exhausted: But without a direct acknowledgment of their
guilt, the Inquisition never pronounces the final doom of
its Prisoners. In general much time is suffered to elapse
without their being questioned: But Ambrosio's trial had
been hastened, on account of a solemn Auto da Fé*which
would take place in a few days, and in which the
Inquisitors meant this distinguished Culprit to perform a
part, and give a striking testimony of their vigilance.

The Abbot was not merely accused of rape and
murder: The crime of Sorcery was laid to his charge, as
well as to Matilda's. She had been seized as an Accomplice in Antonia's assassination. On searching her Cell,
various suspicious books and instruments were found,
which justified the accusation brought against her. To
criminate the Monk, the constellated Mirror was produced, which Matilda had accidentally left in his chamber. The strange figures engraved upon it caught the
attention of Don Ramirez, while searching the Abbot's
Cell: In consequence, He carried it away with him. It
was shown to the Grand Inquisitor, who having considered it for some time, took off a small golden Cross
which hung at his girdle, and laid it upon the Mirror.
Instantly a loud noise was heard, resembling a clap of
thunder, and the steel shivered into a thousand pieces.
This circumstance confirmed the suspicion of the Monk's
having dealt in Magic: It was even supposed, that his

former influence over the minds of the People was entirely to be ascribed to witch-craft.

Determined to make him confess not only the crimes which He had committed, but those also of which He was innocent, the Inquisitors began their examination. Though dreading the tortures, as He dreaded death still more which would consign him to eternal torments, the Abbot asserted his purity in a voice bold and resolute. Matilda followed his example, but spoke with fear and trembling. Having in vain exhorted him to confess, the Inquisitors ordered the Monk to be put to the question. The Decree was immediately executed. Ambrosio suffered the most excruciating pangs, that ever were invented by human cruelty: Yet so dreadful is Death when guilt accompanies it, that He had sufficient fortitude to persist in his disavowal. His agonies were redoubled in consequence: Nor was He released till fainting from excess of pain, insensibility rescued him from the hands of his Tormentors.

Matilda was next ordered to the torture: But terrified by the sight of the Friar's sufferings, her courage totally deserted her. She sank upon her knees, acknowledged her corresponding with infernal Spirits, and that She had witnessed the Monk's assassination of Antonia: But as to the crime of Sorcery, She declared herself the sole criminal, and Ambrosio perfectly innocent. The latter assertion met with no credit. The Abbot had recovered his senses in time to hear the confession of his Accomplice: But He was too much enfeebled by what He had already undergone, to be capable at that time of sustaining new torments. He was commanded back to his Cell, but first informed, that as soon as He had gained strength sufficient, He must prepare himself for a second examination: The Inquisitors hoped, that He would then be less hardened and obstinate. To Matilda it was announced, that She must expiate her crime in fire on the approaching

Auto da Fé. All her tears and entreaties could procure no mitigation of her doom, and She was dragged by force from the Hall of Trial.

Returned to his dungeon, the sufferings of Ambrosio's body were far more supportable than those of his mind. His dislocated limbs, the nails torn from his hands and feet, and his fingers mashed and broken by the pressure of screws, were far surpassed in anguish by the agitation of his soul, and vehemence of his terrors. He saw, that guilty or innocent his Judges were bent upon condemning him: The remembrance of what his denial had already cost him, terrified him at the idea of being again applied to the question, and almost engaged him to confess his crimes. Then again the consequences of his confession flashed before him, and rendered him once more irresolute. His death would be inevitable, and that a death the most dreadful: He had listened to Matilda's doom, and doubted not that a similar was reserved for him. He shuddered at the approaching Auto da Fé, at the idea of perishing in flames, and only escaping from indurable torments to pass into others more subtile and ever-lasting! With affright did He bend his mind's eye on the space beyond the grave; nor could hide from himself, how justly he ought to dread Heaven's vengeance. In this Labyrinth of terrors, fain would He have taken his refuge in the gloom of Atheism: Fain would He have denied the soul's immortality; have persuaded himself that when his eyes once closed, they would never more open, and that the same moment would annihilate his soul and body. Even this resource was refused to him. To permit his being blind to the fallacy of this belief, his knowledge was too extensive, his understanding too solid and just. He could not help feeling the existence of a God. Those truths, once his comfort, now presented themselves before him in the clearest light; But they only served to drive him to distraction. They destroyed his ill-grounded hopes of escaping punishment; and dispelled by the irresistible brightness of Truth and convinction, Philosophy's deceitful vapours faded away like a dream.

In anguish almost too great for mortal frame to bear, He expected the time, when He was again to be examined. He busied himself in planning ineffectual schemes for escaping both present and future punishment. Of the first there was no possibility; Of the second Despair made him neglect the only means. While Reason forced him to acknowledge a God's existence, Conscience made him doubt the infinity of his goodness. He disbelieved, that a Sinner like him could find mercy. He had not been deceived into error: Ignorance could furnish him with no excuse. He had seen vice in her true colours; Before He committed his crimes, He had computed every scruple of their weight; and yet he had committed them.

'Pardon?' He would cry in an access of phrenzy; 'Oh! there can be none for me!'

Persuaded of this, instead of humbling himself in penitence, of deploring his guilt, and employing his few remaining hours in deprecating Heaven's wrath, He abandoned himself to the transports of desperate rage; He sorrowed for the punishment of his crimes, not their commission; and exhaled his bosom's anguish in idle sighs, in vain lamentations, in blasphemy and despair. As the few beams of day, which pierced through the bars of his prison-window, gradually disappeared, and their place was supplied by the pale and glimmering Lamp, He felt his terrors redouble, and his ideas become more gloomy, more solemn, more despondent. He dreaded the approach of sleep: No sooner did his eyes close, wearied with tears and watching, than the dreadful visions seemed to be realised, on which his mind had dwelt during the day. He found himself in sulphurous realms and burning Caverns, surrounded by Fiends appointed his Tormentors, and who drove him through a variety of tortures, each of which was more dreadful than the former. Amidst these dismal scenes wandered the Ghosts of Elvira and her Daughter. They reproached him with their deaths, recounted his crimes to the Dæmons, and urged them to inflict torments of cruelty yet more refined. Such were the pictures, which floated before his eyes in sleep: They vanished not till his repose was disturbed by excess of agony. Then would He start from the ground on which He had stretched himself, his brows running down with cold sweat, his eyes wild and phrenzied; and He only exchanged the terrible certainty for surmizes scarcely more supportable. He paced his dungeon with disordered steps; He gazed with terror upon the surrounding darkness, and often did He cry,

'Oh! fearful is night to the Guilty!'

The day of his second examination was at hand. He had been compelled to swallow cordials, whose virtues were calculated to restore his bodily strength, and enable him to support the question longer. On the night preceding this dreaded day, his fears for the morrow permitted him not to sleep. His terrors were so violent, as nearly to annihilate his mental powers. He sat like one stupefied near the Table on which his Lamp was burning dimly. Despair chained up his faculties in Idiotism, and He remained for some hours, unable to speak or move, or indeed to think.

'Look up, Ambrosio!' said a Voice in accents well-known to him—

The Monk started, and raised his melancholy eyes. Matilda stood before him. She had quitted her religious habit. She now wore a female dress, at once elegant and splendid: A profusion of diamonds blazed upon her robes, and her hair was confined by a coronet of Roses. In her right hand She held a small Book: A lively expression of pleasure beamed upon her countenance; But still it was mingled with a wild imperious majesty, which inspired the Monk with awe, and represt in some measure his transports at seeing her.

'You here, Matilda?' He at length exclaimed; 'How have you gained entrance? Where are your Chains? What means this magnificence, and the joy which sparkles in your eyes? Have our Judges relented? Is there a chance of my escaping? Answer me for pity, and tell me, what I have to hope, or fear.'

'Ambrosio!' She replied with an air of commanding dignity; 'I have baffled the Inquisition's fury. I am free: A few moments will place kingdoms between these dungeons and me. Yet I purchase my liberty at a dear, at a dreadful price! Dare you pay the same, Ambrosio? Dare you spring without fear over the bounds, which separate Men from Angels?—You are silent.—You look upon me with eyes of suspicion and alarm—I read your thoughts and confess their justice. Yes, Ambrosio; I have sacrificed all for life and liberty. I am no longer a candidate for heaven! I have renounced God's service, and am enlisted beneath the banners of his Foes. The deed is past recall: Yet were it in my power to go back, I would not. Oh! my Friend, to expire in such torments! To die amidst curses and execrations! To bear the insults of an exasperated Mob! To be exposed to all the mortifications of shame and infamy! Who can reflect without horror on such a doom? Let me then exult in my exchange. I have sold distant and uncertain happiness for present and secure: I have preserved a life, which otherwise I had lost in torture; and I have obtained the power of procuring every bliss, which can make that life delicious! The Infernal Spirits obey me as their Sovereign: By their aid shall my days be past in every refinement of luxury and voluptuousness. I will enjoy unrestrained the gratification of my senses: Every passion shall be indulged, even to satiety; Then will I bid my Servants invent new pleasures, to revive and stimulate my glutted appetites!

I go impatient to exercise my newly-gained dominion.
I pant to be at liberty. Nothing should hold me one
moment longer in this abhorred abode, but the hope of
persuading you to follow my example. Ambrosio, I still
love you: Our mutual guilt and danger have rendered
you dearer to me, than ever and I would fain save
you from impending destruction. Summon then your
resolution to your aid; and renounce for immediate
and certain benefits the hopes of a salvation, difficult
to obtain, and perhaps altogether erroneous. Shake off
the prejudice of vulgar souls; Abandon a God, who has
abandoned you, and raise yourself to the level of superior
Beings!'

She paused for the Monk's reply: He shuddered, while
He gave it.

'Matilda!' He said after a long silence in a low and
unsteady voice; 'What price gave you for liberty?'

She answered him firm and dauntless.

'Ambrosio, it was my Soul!'

'Wretched Woman, what have you done? Pass but a
few years, and how dreadful will be your sufferings!'

'Weak Man, pass but this night, and how dreadful
will be your own! Do you remember what you have
already endured? To-morrow you must bear torments
doubly exquisite. Do you remember the horrors of a fiery
punishment? In two days you must be led a Victim to the
Stake! What then will become of you? Still dare you
hope for pardon? Still are you beguiled with visions of
salvation? Think upon your crimes! Think upon your
lust, your perjury, inhumanity, and hypocrisy! Think
upon the innocent blood, which cries to the Throne of
God for vengeance, and then hope for mercy! Then
dream of heaven, and sigh for worlds of light, and realms
of peace and pleasure! Absurd! Open your eyes, Ambrosio, and be prudent. Hell is your lot; You are doomed to
eternal perdition; Nought lies beyond your grave, but a

gulph of devouring flames. And will you then speed
towards that Hell? Will you clasp that perdition in your
arms, ere 'tis needful? Will you plunge into those flames,
while you still have the power to shun them? 'Tis a Mad-
man's action. No, no, Ambrosio: Let us for awhile fly
from divine vengeance. Be advised by me; Purchase by
one moment's courage the bliss of years; Enjoy the
present, and forget that a future lags behind.'

'Matilda, your counsels are dangerous: I dare not, I
will not follow them. I must not give up my claim to
salvation. Monstrous are my crimes; But God is merciful,
and I will not despair of pardon.'

'Is such your resolution? I have no more to say. I
speed to joy and liberty, and abandon you to death and
eternal torments.'

'Yet stay one moment, Matilda! You command the
infernal Dæmons: You can force open these prison-doors;
You can release me from these chains, which weigh me
down. Save me, I conjure you, and bear me from these
fearful abodes!'

'You ask the only boon beyond my power to bestow.
I am forbidden to assist a Churchman and a Partizan of
God: Renounce those titles, and command me.'

'I will not sell my soul to perdition.'

'Persist in your obstinacy, till you find yourself at the
Stake: Then will you repent your error, and sigh for
escape when the moment is gone by. I quit you.—Yet ere
the hour of death arrives should wisdom enlighten you,
listen to the means of repairing your present fault. I leave
with you this Book. Read the four first lines of the
seventh page backwards: The Spirit whom you have
already once beheld, will immediately appear to you. If
you are wise, we shall meet again: If not, farewell for
ever!'

She let the Book fall upon the ground. A cloud of blue
fire wrapped itself round her: She waved her hand to

Ambrosio, and disappeared. The momentary glare
which the flames poured through the dungeon, on dissi-
pating suddenly, seemed to have increased its natural
gloom. The solitary Lamp scarcely gave light sufficient
to guide the Monk to a Chair. He threw himself into his
seat, folded his arms, and leaning his head upon the
table, sank into reflections perplexing and unconnected.

He was still in this attitude, when the opening of the
prison-door rouzed him from his stupor. He was summoned to appear before the Grand Inquisitor. He rose, and
followed his Gaoler with painful steps. He was led into
the same Hall, placed before the same Examiners, and
was again interrogated, whether He would confess. He
replied as before, that having no crimes, He could acknowledge none: But when the Executioners prepared to
put him to the question, when He saw the engines of
torture, and remembered the pangs, which they had
already inflicted, his resolution failed him entirely. For-
getting the consequences, and only anxious to escape
the terrors of the present moment, He made an ample
confession. He disclosed every circumstance of his guilt,
and owned not merely the crimes with which He was
charged, but those of which He had never been suspected. Being interrogated as to Matilda's flight which had
created much confusion, He confessed that She had sold
herself to Satan, and that She was indebted to Sorcery
for her escape. He still assured his Judges, that for his own
part He had never entered into any compact with the
infernal Spirits; But the threat of being tortured made
him declare himself to be a Sorcerer, and Heretic, and
whatever other title the Inquisitors chose to fix upon him.
In consequence of this avowal, his sentence was immediately pronounced. He was ordered to prepare himself to perish in the Auto da Fé, which was to be solem-
nized at twelve o'clock that night. This hour was chosen
from the idea, that the horror of the flames being heigh-

tened by the gloom of midnight, the execution would have a greater effect upon the mind of the People.

Ambrosio rather dead than alive was left alone in his dungeon. The moment in which this terrible decree was pronounced, had nearly proved that of his dissolution. He looked forward to the morrow with despair, and his terrors increased with the approach of midnight. Sometimes He was buried in gloomy silence: At others He raved with delirious passion, wrung his hands, and cursed the hour, when He first beheld the light. In one of these moments his eye rested upon Matilda's mysterious gift. His transports of rage were instantly suspended. He looked earnestly at the Book; He took it up, but immediately threw it from him with horror. He walked rapidly up and down his dungeon: Then stopped, and again fixed his eyes on the spot where the Book had fallen. He reflected, that here at least was a resource from the fate which He dreaded. He stooped, and took it up a second time. He remained for some time trembling and irresolute: He longed to try the charm, yet feared its consequences. The recollection of his sentence at length fixed his indecision. He opened the Volume; but his agitation was so great, that He at first sought in vain for the page mentioned by Matilda. Ashamed of himself, He called all his courage to his aid. He turned to the seventh leaf. He began to read it aloud; But his eyes frequently wandered from the Book, while He anxiously cast them round in search of the Spirit, whom He wished, yet dreaded to behold. Still He persisted in his design; and with a voice unassured and frequent interruptions, He contrived to finish the four first lines of the page.

They were in a language, whose import was totally unknown to him. Scarce had He pronounced the last word, when the effects of the charm were evident. A loud burst of Thunder was heard; The prison shook to its very foundations; A blaze of lightning flashed through the Cell; and in the next moment, borne upon sulphurous whirl-winds, Lucifer stood before him a second time. But He came not, as when at Matilda's summons He borrowed the Seraph's form to deceive Ambrosio. He appeared in all that ugliness, which since his fall from heaven had been his portion: His blasted limbs still bore marks of the Almighty's thunder: A swarthy darkness spread itself over his gigantic form: His hands and feet were armed with long Talons: Fury glared in his eyes, which might have struck the bravest heart with terror: Over his huge shoulders waved two enormous sable wings; and his hair was supplied by living snakes, which twined themselves round his brows with frightful hissings. In one hand He held a roll of parchment, and in the other an iron pen. Still the lightning flashed around him, and the Thunder with repeated bursts, seemed to announce the dissolution of Nature.

Terrified at an Apparition so different from what He had expected, Ambrosio remained gazing upon the Fiend, deprived of the power of utterance. The Thunder had ceased to roll: Universal silence reigned through the dungeon.

'For what am I summoned hither?' said the Dæmon, in a voice which *sulphurous fogs had damped to hoarseness**—

At the sound Nature seemed to tremble: A violent earth-quake rocked the ground, accompanied by a fresh burst of Thunder, louder and more appalling than the first.

Ambrosio was long unable to answer the Dæmon's demand.

'I am condemned to die;' He said with a faint voice, his blood running cold, while He gazed upon his dreadful Visitor. 'Save me! Bear me from hence!'

'Shall the reward of my services be paid me? Dare you embrace my cause? Will you be mine, body and soul? Are you prepared to renounce him who made you, and

him who died for you? Answer but "Yes" and Lucifer is
your Slave.'

'Will no less price content you? Can nothing satisfy
you but my eternal ruin? Spirit, you ask too much. Yet
convey me from this dungeon: Be my Servant for one
hour, and I will be yours for a thousand years. Will not
this offer suffice?'

'It will not. I must have your soul; must have it mine,
and mine for ever.'

'Insatiate Dæmon, I will not doom myself to endless
torments. I will not give up my hopes of being one day
pardoned.'

'You will not? On what Chimæra rest then your hopes?
Short-sighted Mortal! Miserable Wretch! Are you not
guilty? Are you not infamous in the eyes of Men and
Angels. Can such enormous sins be forgiven? Hope you
to escape my power? Your fate is already pronounced.
The Eternal has abandoned you; Mine you are marked in
the book of destiny, and mine you must and shall be!'

'Fiend, 'tis false! Infinite is the Almighty's mercy, and
the Penitent shall meet his forgiveness. My crimes are
monstrous, but I will not despair of pardon: Haply,
when they have received due chastisement . . . .'

'Chastisement? Was Purgatory meant for guilt like
yours? Hope you that your offences shall be bought off
by prayers of superstitious dotards and droning Monks?
Ambrosio, be wise! Mine you must be: You are doomed
to flames, but may shun them for the present. Sign this
parchment: I will bear you from hence, and you may
pass your remaining years in bliss and liberty. Enjoy
your existence: Indulge in every pleasure to which
appetite may lead you: But from the moment that it quits
your body, remember that your soul belongs to me, and
that I will not be defrauded of my right.'

The Monk was silent; But his looks declared, that the
Tempter's words were not thrown away. He reflected

on the conditions proposed with horror: On the other hand, He believed himself doomed to perdition, and that, by refusing the Dæmon's succour, He only hastened tortures which He never could escape. The Fiend saw, that his resolution was shaken: He renewed his instances, and endeavoured to fix the Abbot's indecision. He described the agonies of death in the most terrific colours; and He worked so powerfully upon Ambrosio's despair and fears, that He prevailed upon him to receive the Parchment. He then struck the iron Pen which He held into a vein of the Monk's left-hand. It pierced deep, and was instantly filled with blood; Yet Ambrosio felt no pain from the wound. The Pen was put into his hand: It trembled. The Wretch placed the Parchment on the Table before him, and prepared to sign it. Suddenly He held his hand: He started away hastily, and threw the Pen upon the table.*

'What am I doing?' He cried—Then turning to the Fiend with a desperate air, 'Leave me! Begone! I will not sign the Parchment.'

'Fool!' exclaimed the disappointed Dæmon, darting looks so furious as penetrated the Friar's soul with horror; 'Thus am I trifled with? Go then! Rave in agony, expire in tortures, and then learn the extent of the Eternal's mercy! But beware how you make me again your mock! Call me no more, till resolved to accept my offers! Summon me a second time to dismiss me thus idly, and these Talons shall rend you into a thousand pieces! Speak yet again; Will you sign the Parchment?'

'I will not! Leave me! Away!'

Instantly the Thunder was heard to roll horribly: Once more the earth trembled with violence: The Dungeon resounded with loud shrieks, and the Dæmon fled with blasphemy and curses.

At first, the Monk rejoiced at having resisted the Seducer's arts, and obtained a triumph over Mankind's

Enemy: But as the hour of punishment drew near, his former terrors revived in his heart. Their momentary repose seemed to have given them fresh vigour. The nearer that the time approached, the more did He dread appearing before the Throne of God. He shuddered to think how soon He must be plunged into eternity; How soon meet the eyes of his Creator, whom He had so grievously offended. The Bell announced mid-night: It was the signal for being led to the Stake! As He listened to the first stroke, the blood ceased to circulate in the Abbot's veins: He heard death and torture murmured in each succeeding sound. He expected to see the Archers entering his prison; and as the Bell forbore to toll, he seized the magic volume in a fit of despair. He opened it, turned hastily to the seventh page, and as if fearing to allow himself a moment's thought ran over the fatal lines with rapidity. Accompanied by his former terrors, Lucifer again stood before the Trembler.

'You have summoned me,' said the Fiend; 'Are you determined to be wise? Will you accept my conditions? You know them already. Renounce your claim to salvation, make over to me your soul, and I bear you from this dungeon instantly. Yet is it time. Resolve, or it will be too late. Will you sign the Parchment?'

'I must!—Fate urges me!—I accept your conditions.'

'Sign the Parchment!' replied the Dæmon in an exulting tone.

The Contract and the bloody Pen still lay upon the Table. Ambrosio drew near it. He prepared to sign his name. A moment's reflection made him hesitate.

'Hark!' cried the Tempter; 'They come! Be quick! Sign the Parchment, and I bear you from hence this moment.'

In effect, the Archers were heard approaching, appointed to lead Ambrosio to the Stake. The sound encouraged the Monk in his resolution.

'What is the import of this writing?' said He.

'It makes your soul over to me for ever, and without reserve.'

'What am I to receive in exchange?'

'My protection, and release from this dungeon. Sign it, and this instant I bear you away.'

Ambrosio took up the Pen; He set it to the Parchment. Again his courage failed him: He felt a pang of terror at his heart, and once more threw the Pen upon the Table.

'Weak and Puerile!' cried the exasperated Fiend: 'Away with this folly! Sign the writing this instant, or I sacrifice you to my rage!'

At this moment the bolt of the outward Door was drawn back. The Prisoner heard the rattling of Chains; The heavy Bar fell; The Archers were on the point of entering. Worked up to phrenzy by the urgent danger, shrinking from the approach of death, terrified by the Dæmon's threats, and seeing no other means to escape destruction, the wretched Monk complied. He signed the fatal contract, and gave it hastily into the evil Spirit's hands, whose eyes, as He received the gift, glared with malicious rapture.

'Take it!' said the God-abandoned; 'Now then save me! Snatch me from hence!'

'Hold! Do you freely and absolutely renounce your Creator and his Son?'

'I do! I do!'

'Do you make over your soul to me for ever?'

'For ever!'

'Without reserve or subterfuge? Without future appeal to the divine mercy?'

The last Chain fell from the door of the prison: The key was heard turning in the Lock: Already the iron door grated heavily upon its rusty hinges.

'I am yours for ever and irrevocably!' cried the Monk wild with terror: 'I abandon all claim to salvation! I own

no power but yours! Hark! Hark! They come! Oh! save
me! Bear me away!'

'I have triumphed! You are mine past reprieve, and I
fulfil my promise.'

While He spoke, the Door unclosed. Instantly the
Dæmon grasped one of Ambrosio's arms, spread his
broad pinions, and sprang with him into the air. The
roof opened as they soared upwards, and closed again
when they had quitted the Dungeon.

In the mean while, the Gaoler was thrown into the
utmost surprize by the disappearance of his Prisoner.
Though neither He nor the Archers were in time to witness the Monk's escape, a sulphurous smell prevailing
through the prison sufficiently informed them by whose
aid He had been liberated. They hastened to make their
report to the Grand Inquisitor. The story, how a
Sorcerer had been carried away by the Devil, was soon
noised about Madrid; and for some days the whole City
was employed in discussing the subject. Gradually it
ceased to be the topic of conversation: Other adventures
arose whose novelty engaged universal attention; and
Ambrosio was soon forgotten as totally, as if He never had
existed. While this was passing, the Monk supported by
his infernal guide, traversed the air with the rapidity of an
arrow, and a few moments placed him upon a Precipice's
brink, the steepest in Sierra Morena.

Though rescued from the Inquisition, Ambrosio as yet
was insensible of the blessings of liberty. The damning
contract weighed heavy upon his mind; and the scenes in
which He had been a principal actor, had left behind
them such impressions, as rendered his heart the seat of
anarchy and confusion. The Objects now before his
eyes, and which the full Moon sailing through clouds
permitted him to examine, were ill-calculated to inspire
that calm, of which He stood so much in need. The disorder of his imagination was increased by the wildness of

the surrounding scenery; By the gloomy Caverns and steep rocks, rising above each other, and dividing the passing clouds; solitary clusters of Trees scattered here and there, among whose thick-twined branches the wind of night sighed hoarsely and mournfully; the shrill cry of mountain Eagles, who had built their nests among these lonely Desarts; the stunning roar of torrents, as swelled by late rains they rushed violently down tremendous precipices; and the dark waters of a silent sluggish stream which faintly reflected the moon-beams, and bathed the Rock's base on which Ambrosio stood. The Abbot cast round him a look of terror. His infernal Conductor was still by his side, and eyed him with a look of mingled malice, exultation, and contempt.

'Whither have you brought me?' said the Monk at length in an hollow trembling voice: 'Why am I placed in this melancholy scene? Bear me from it quickly! Carry me to Matilda!'

The Fiend replied not, but continued to gaze upon him in silence. Ambrosio could not sustain his glance; He turned away his eyes, while thus spoke the Dæmon:

'I have him then in my power! This model of piety! This being without reproach! This Mortal who placed his puny virtues on a level with those of Angels. He is mine! Irrevocably, eternally mine! Companions of my sufferings! Denizens of hell! How grateful will be my present!'

He paused; then addressed himself to the Monk——

'Carry you to Matilda?' He continued, repeating Ambrosio's words: 'Wretch! you shall soon be with her! You well deserve a place near her, for hell boasts no miscreant more guilty than yourself. Hark, Ambrosio, while I unveil your crimes! You have shed the blood of two innocents; Antonia and Elvira perished by your hand. That Antonia whom you violated, was your Sister! That Elvira whom you murdered, gave you birth!

Tremble, abandoned Hypocrite! Inhuman Parricide!
Incestuous Ravisher! Tremble at the extent of your
offences! And you it was who thought yourself proof
against temptation, absolved from human frailties, and
free from error and vice! Is pride then a virtue? Is
inhumanity no fault? Know, vain Man! That I long
have marked you for my prey: I watched the movements
of your heart; I saw that you were virtuous from vanity,
not principle, and I seized the fit moment of seduction. I
observed your blind idolatry of the Madona's picture. I
bad a subordinate but crafty spirit assume a similar
form, and you eagerly yielded to the blandishments of
Matilda. Your pride was gratified by her flattery; Your
lust only needed an opportunity to break forth; You ran
into the snare blindly, and scrupled not to commit a
crime, which you blamed in another with unfeeling
severity. It was I who threw Matilda in your way; It was
I who gave you entrance to Antonia's chamber; It was I
who caused the dagger to be given you which pierced
your Sister's bosom; and it was I who warned Elvira in
dreams of your designs upon her Daughter, and thus, by
preventing your profiting by her sleep, compelled you to
add rape as well as incest to the catalogue of your crimes.
Hear, hear, Ambrosio! Had you resisted me one minute
longer, you had saved your body and soul. The guards
whom you heard at your prison-door, came to signify
your pardon. But I had already triumphed: My plots
had already succeeded. Scarcely could I propose crimes
so quick as you performed them. You are mine, and
Heaven itself cannot rescue you from my power. Hope
not that your penitence will make void our contract.
Here is your bond signed with your blood; You have
given up your claim to mercy, and nothing can restore
to you the rights which you have foolishly resigned.
Believe you, that your secret thoughts escaped me? No,
no, I read them all! You trusted that you should still

have time for repentance. I saw your artifice, knew its falsity, and rejoiced in deceiving the deceiver! You are mine beyond reprieve: I burn to possess my right, and alive you quit not these mountains.'

During the Dæmon's speech, Ambrosio had been stupefied by terror and surprize. This last declaration rouzed him.

'Not quit these mountains alive?' He exclaimed: 'Perfidious, what mean you? Have you forgotten our contract?'

The Fiend answered by a malicious laugh:

'Our contract? Have I not performed my part? What more did I promise than to save you from your prison? Have I not done so? Are you not safe from the Inquisition—safe from all but from me? Fool that you were to confide yourself to a Devil! Why did you not stipulate for life, and power, and pleasure? Then all would have been granted: Now, your reflections come too late. Miscreant, prepare for death; You have not many hours to live!'

On hearing this sentence, dreadful were the feelings of the devoted Wretch! He sank upon his knees, and raised his hands towards heaven. The Fiend read his intention and prevented it—

'What?' He cried, darting at him a look of fury: 'Dare you still implore the Eternal's mercy? Would you feign penitence, and again act an Hypocrite's part? Villain, resign your hopes of pardon. Thus I secure my prey!'

As He said this, darting his talons into the Monk's shaven crown, He sprang with him from the rock. The Caves and mountains rang with Ambrosio's shrieks. The Dæmon continued to soar aloft, till reaching a dreadful height, He released the sufferer. Headlong fell the Monk through the airy waste; The sharp point of a rock received him; and He rolled from precipice to precipice, till bruised and mangled He rested on the river's banks. Life still existed in his miserable frame: He attempted in vain to raise himself; His broken and dislocated limbs refused to perform their office, nor was He able to quit the spot where He had first fallen. The Sun now rose above the horizon; Its scorching beams darted full upon the head of the expiring Sinner. Myriads of insects were called forth by the warmth; They drank the blood which trickled from Ambrosio's wounds; He had no power to drive them from him, and they fastened upon his sores, darted their stings into his body, covered him with their multitudes, and inflicted on him tortures the most exquisite and insupportable. The Eagles of the rock tore his flesh piecemeal, and dug out his eye-balls with their crooked beaks. A burning thirst tormented him; He heard the river's murmur as it rolled beside him, but strove in vain to drag himself towards the sound. Blind, maimed, helpless, and despairing, venting his rage in blasphemy and curses, execrating his existence, yet dreading the arrival of death destined to yield him up to greater torments, six miserable days did the Villain languish. On the Seventh a violent storm arose: The winds in fury rent up rocks and forests: The sky was now black with clouds, now sheeted with fire: The rain fell in torrents; It swelled the stream; The waves overflowed their banks; They reached the spot where Ambrosio lay, and when they abated carried with them into the river the Corse of the despairing Monk.

EXPLANATORY NOTES

1 (Title-page) *Somnia . . . portentaque*: Horace, *Epistles*, II. ii. 208–9. Horace (Quintus Horatius Flaccus) 65–8 BC was a Latin poet, much admired in the eighteenth century, and extremely influential in the English satirical tradition.

3 (Preface) *In famous row called Paternoster*: Paternoster Row is located just north of St Paul's churchyard, London. It is a long, narrow street, which, in the second half of the eighteenth century, was filled with booksellers' shops.

Of Stockdale, Hookham, or Debrett: John Stockdale was a publisher and bookseller, whose premises were opposite Burlington House in Piccadilly. John Debrett, publisher, had a bookshop neighbouring Stockdale's. Thomas Hookham, bookseller, stationer, and bookbinder, ran a famous circulating library, with private reading-room, in 15 Old Bond Street.

4 *Of graceless form and dwarfish stature*: though not very complimentary, this description of Lewis tallies well with contemporary accounts of him, as does the line about being 'Extreme in hating and in loving': apparently he loved to pick a quarrel.

6 (Advertisement) *Santon Barsisa*: the 'History of Santon Barsisa' which, though Turkish, had an 'entirely Christian moral', according to Richard Steele in the *Guardian*, 148, of Monday, 31 August 1713. It tells of a holy man who stays praying in his grotto for 100 years. When the king's daughter is sick she is sent to him to be cured, whereupon a devil whispers in Barsisa's ear that he should rape her. So Barsisa 'approached the princess, took her into his arms, and in a moment cancelled out a virtue of an hundred years duration'. When he complains to the devil of his guilt, the devil lets him know that the princess is pregnant, and suggests murdering her. This he does, but her body is found. When the Santon is on the gallows, the devil appears, promising rescue if Barsisa will adore him. However, when he does this, the devil spits

in his face, and Barsisa is still hanged. The *Guardian* was reprinted many times throughout the eighteenth century. It was a well-known work, admired for its purity of tone and its moral rectitude. By citing the *Guardian* as an influence, Lewis gives his story an air of respectability.

6 *Lauenstein*: town in Saxony, east central Germany, near the Czech border. It does have an old castle.

Thuringia: a sovereignty in central Germany. It became part of the German Empire in 1871.

7 (Epigraph) *Lord Angelo . . . stone*: taken from Shakespeare's *Measure for Measure*, I. iii. 50–3.

Church of the Capuchins: the Capuchins were Franciscan friars of the reform of 1528, and were one of four mendicant orders. They were distinguished by their long, pointed, hooded cloaks.

9 *Medicean Venus*: statue of Venus. A Roman copy after original, *c*.150–100 BC, from the collection of the Medici family who ruled Florence in the fifteenth century. She is depicted with one hand covering her genitalia.

Hamadryad: wood nymph associated with the spirit of a particular tree, with which she comes into existence and dies.

11 *Murcia*: province in south-east Spain.

Holy St. Barbara: first mentioned in the tenth century, but suppressed in 1969, on the grounds that she never existed. She was supposed to have been killed for being a Christian by her father, who was then struck by lightning.

12 *mauvaise honte*: French, literal translation 'ill shame'; according to the *OED*, 'false shame; painful diffidence'.

13 *Cordova*: city in Andalucía in southern Spain, traversed by the Sierra Morena.

Condé: Spanish rank roughly equivalent to count or earl.

16 *Ambrosio, Abbot of this Monastery*: here Lewis displays a typically Gothic lack of concern for accuracy about Catholicism. If Ambrosio is the head of a group of Capuchins, who are friars, he cannot be an abbot, who is the head of a group of monks. Ambrosio would be the Guardian of a Capuchin

house. Note that Lewis indiscriminately refers to the Capuchins as both monks and friars all the way through the work. Still, maybe *The Friar* wouldn't have worked so well as a title. As a friar, Ambrosio is also able to be a practising priest, as witnessed by his administering of the final sacrament to Elvira.

19 *enthusiastic silence*: the concept of 'enthusiasm' at the end of the eighteenth century came to express, in the words of the *OED*, 'ill-regulated religious emotion or speculation'.

20 *a sacred relique*: this is a reference to the Catholic habit of venerating the physical remains of saints. The supposedly grossly material and misplaced nature of the practice is stressed by its application to Ambrosio.

Chaplet: small rosary, one-third of the size of a full rosary.

St. Francis himself: 1181–1226, of Assisi. Founded the Franciscan Order in 1208. They were renowed for their rules of extreme poverty.

25 *Casuist*: applies to one who studies and resolves cases of conscience, but is most often used in a derogatory sense for someone whose arguments are sophisticated and dishonest.

ten thousand pistoles: 'pistole' was the French name given to a Spanish gold coin in use from 1537.

St. Jago: or Santiago are both names for St James the Greater, St James of Compostela. According to a legend which started in the ninth century, James was the Apostle of Spain, and is enshrined at Compostela, which resulted in it becoming the third largest place of Christian pilgrimage.

26 *Knight of Mount Ætna*: unable to find.

29 *Vespers*: the sixth canonical hour, the time for prayer at evening.

30 *Prioress of St. Clare*: a prioress is head of a nunnery. The Order of St Clare is most likely the Poor Clares, who are associated with the Franciscans, as St Clare (1193–1252/3) and St Francis were young saints together in Assisi. They are noted for their rigorous poverty. They are also an enclosed order, which makes the passage at the end where they take part in a lavish procession impossible.

31 *the Domina*: the head of a nunnery, another term for the abbess.

Diavolo!: Italian for 'Devil'. Lewis does not seem to mind his Spanish characters talking Italian.

32 *Segnor Bravo*: a bravo is a daring villain, often hired.

the consequences of shedding blood on consecrated ground: if either of the combatants were killed, then the church would have to be reconsecrated, and the murderer might well be excommunicated.

33 *the Hotel de las Cisternas*: a hotel is a detached residence. In this case it is a palace as well.

35 *Philtre*: magic charm, usually a love-potion, but here a mender of virginity.

39 (Epigraph) *Fòrse ... spènde*: from Torquato Tasso's (1544–95) pastoral play *L'Aminta*, I. i. 26–31.

41 *Novice*: newcomer to a religious house who is still under probation.

42 *magnificent equipage*: carriage with attendant servants.

43 *my intercession*: prayers on someone else's behalf.

50 *the Abbey-Garden*: the garden of the 'Abbey' is not the secluded formal garden that might be expected, but instead is laid out in late eighteenth-century taste. Lewis's locale signifies beauty, languor, and the passions. The 'artificial wilderness' is a piece of ground planted with trees in picturesque disorder. Its 'rustic Grotto, formed in imitation of an Hermitage' is a structure built to look like a rocky cave in which a hermit might live. Grottoes were a common feature of large eighteenth-century gardens, and some owners even employed mock hermits.

Jessamine: jasmine.

51 *Desart*: desert. Somewhere uncultivated, wild, and barren.

53 *Ennui*: 'Mental weariness and dissatisfaction arising from want of occupation, or lack of interest' (*OED*).

56 *'You had a Sister?'*: c.f. Viola's speeches in *Twelfth Night*, II. iv. 106–19.

60 *sciences . . . lying under censure from the blindness of superstition*: such usage would usually suggest alchemy, though it could refer to blacker arts.

70 *Estramadura*: region of western Spain bordering on Portugal.

71 *A Serpent*: a crude allusion to the snake in the garden of Eden, Genesis 3: 1–7.

75 *the famous battle of Roncevalles [sic]*: in 777 Charlemagne marched against the Spanish Moors. The exact date of the battle of Roncesvalles is unknown. There is a sixteenth-century adventure ballad of Durandarte. It is interesting to note that the name 'Durandarte' is also that of the sword of the courageous knight Roland.

81 *Martin Galuppi*: there seems to be no modern reference to this painter.

83 *St. Anthony had withstood all seductions to lust*: St Anthony was a monk who lived from 251 to 356, and is considered to be the father of monasticism. He is often pictured as a hermit in the desert, renowned for being able to withstand all the temptations the devil sent him, even those in the form of seductive women.

91 (Epigraph) *These are the Villains . . . awful Men*: misquoted from Shakespeare's *Two Gentlemen of Verona*, IV. i. 44–6.

94 *Hispaniola*: the island in the West Indies now comprising Haiti and the Dominican Republic.

95 *Salamanca*: city in eastern Spain with a famous and ancient university.

the Duke of Villa Hermosa: Villa Hermosa translates as beautiful or splendid villa.

96 *an eye-witness of the sufferings of the People*: the Grand Tour of Europe was considered to be an essential part of a gentleman's education. However, Raymond's is a tour with a difference as he is to consider the social injustices wrought in barbarous foreign lands.

97 *I turned from the Inhabitants of Paris with disgust*: Parisians had, for the English, a reputation for debauchery.

Strasbourg: capital of Alsace in France, near the German border.

Luneville: Now 97 Lunéville; city about 60 miles from Strasbourg, in the Meurthe-et-Moselle province, France.

Longueville: town in north central France in the department of Seine-et-Marne.

98 *St. Denis*: died c.250. An Italian who became the first Bishop of Paris, but was beheaded. The Abbey of St Denis, where his tomb is, became the burial place for the kings of France.

107 *Banditti*: bandits.

128 *Bavaria*: formerly a kingdom in southern Germany bounded in the south by the Alps. Now part of Germany.

129 (Epigraph) *Avaunt! . . . Unreal mockery hence!*: from Shakespeare's *Macbeth*, III. iv. 93–6 and 106–7.

Lindenberg: town in the Lindau district of south-west Bavaria, ten miles north-east of Lindau, near the Austrian border.

132 *Cunegonda*: is named after St Cunegonda, a German empress who married Henry II of Bavaria in 1040. The name is also associated with the character Cunégonde in Voltaire's *Candide*.

134 *'Perceforest,' 'Tirante the White,' 'Palmerin of England,' and 'the Knight of the Sun' . . . 'the Loves of Tristan and the Queen Iseult'*: Names of romances. Some of them are original fourteenth- and fifteenth-century romances, some are 'learned romances', deliberately archaic imitations of the earlier works, written in the sixteenth century. *Tirant lo Blanch* is of the former kind, and is a fifteenth-century Catalan romance. *Palmerin de Inglaterra*, c.1544, is of the latter kind. Tristan and Iseult were a famous romance subject; there are two surviving fourteenth-century fragments, and there are also sixteenth-century imitations.

140 *Paternoster*: the Lord's prayer, beginning 'Our Father'.

De Profundis: meaning 'out of the depths', the first words of Psalm 130.

142 *Duenna*: governess or chaperon.

156 *Agnes! . . . Thine my soul!*: Lewis claims he heard the story of the Bleeding Nun in Germany, but this poem bears many similarities to a poem in a story on the same theme by

Musäus, which, however, Lewis claimed not to have read till years later. Maybe the refrain was taken from folk-tradition, or it was Musäus's version that Lewis heard by word of mouth. The passage from Musäus runs: 'He rushed towards her from his hiding place, took her lovingly in his arms and said: "I have you, I hold you, never to let you go, | Sweet love you are mine | Sweet love I am thine | You mine, I thine | With body and soul." ' (Johann August Musäus, 'Die Entführung', in *Die Volksmärchen der Deutschen* (1782–6), trans. Karen Tiedtke.)

158 *Ratisbon*: now called Regensburg, in east Bavaria, a port on the Danube 65 miles north-north-east of Munich.

   Rosenwald: there are two villages of Rosenwald, both in the east of former Prussia, one near Heinrichswald, and one near Königsberg (now Kaliningrad). Whichever one is referred to here, it is over 400 miles from Ratisbon, hence the disbelief of the villagers.

160 *the property of the Rattle-snake's*: that is, of entrancing its victim.

167 *the Great Mogul*: name give by the Portuguese to the emperors of Delhi. Hence a reference to the exotic appearance of the character.

   a Travelling Mountebank: one who 'dances and leaps', a travelling entertainer who might juggle or tell stories or sell quack remedies.

   Doctor Faustus: Faust was a magician of the sixteenth century, famous in legend and in literature. He was believed by many to be in league with the devil, to whom he had sold his soul. He was at first representative of the over-ambitious human, defying the limits to knowledge imposed by God. Lewis could have been familiar with his story through the play by Marlowe, and he certainly knew an early version of Goethe's *Faust* (which was not wholly completed until 1832), to which *The Monk* bears some similarities.

168 *He was a Man of majestic presence*: compare this passage with the following descriptions of 'the Armenian' in Schiller's *Der Geisterseher* (1789), which was one of Lewis's sources. 'Never in my life have I seen so many features and so little

character, such attractive goodwill with such repulsive cold-ness reside together in a person's face. All the passions seem to have done their work and then abandoned it again. There was nothing left except the quietly piercing look of an accom-plished judge of human nature.' (Trans. Karen Tiedtke.)

169 *Fate obliges me to be constantly in movement*: this speech is derived substantially from a poem by Christian Friedrich Daniel Schubart entitled 'Der Ewige Jude' (1787). Compare the following extract: 'From towering cliffs engulfed in cloud I threw myself into the Ocean, but foaming waves rolled me back to the shore ... I went amongst the slaughterers of mankind, but arrow and spear broke on me, and on my skull splintered the raised swords of the Saracen ... The tiger's tooth was blunted on me.' Compare also these lines from Schiller's *Der Geisterseher*: 'No sword's point can pierce him, no poison harm him, no fire scorches him, no ship which he is on will sink. Time itself seems not to wither him, and age cannot bleach his hair. There is no one who has seen him take food; never has a woman been touched by him. Sleep does not visit his eyes, and of all the hours of the day only one is known when he is not here, when no one has seen him, and he has not performed some earthly task!' (Trans. Karen Tiedtke.)

172 *Curiosity would not suffer me to keep my eyes off his face*: compare this detail from *Der Geisterseher*: 'I often tried to avert my eyes from this dreadful figure, but always they were drawn back.' (Trans. Karen Tiedtke.)

173 *Cleopatra*: 69–30 BC. Famous and fascinating Queen of Egypt. She was ousted from a shared throne but replaced by Caesar in 47 BC. She had a son, Caesarion, by Caesar, and three children by Mark Anthony. On losing her rule to Augustus, she is supposed to have committed suicide by causing an asp to bite her breast.

177 *the wandering Jew*: the legend of the Wandering Jew appears in many forms. He is first mentioned in 1228 by a monk of St Albans, Roger of Wendover, in *Flores Historiarum*, who tells how a visiting Armenian archbishop recounted how he entertained the Wandering Jew. The Wandering Jew is

supposed to have taunted Christ as he carried his cross, and for this unkindness he is doomed to wander the earth through time. In Schiller's version he is compelled to do good constantly, but visits the underworld for one hour a day—between twelve and one—a detail that Lewis seems to have adapted for the Bleeding Nun's visitation of Raymond.

181   *a dispensation from her vows*: Agnes would need a dispensation from the Pope to release her from her vows as a nun.

185   *the Cardinal-Duke of Lerma's influence*: Lerma is a town in northern Spain just south of the city of Burgos. It did have a Cardinal-Duke in the early seventeenth-century, who built a splendid palace there.

190   *the necessary Bull*: A papal Bull would seem to be a bit excessive: Agnes needs only a dispensation. Papal Bulls usually relate to affairs of state.

192   (Epigraph) *O You! . . . and a breath o'er-throws*: from Pope's *The First Epistle of the Second Book of Horace Imitated*, lines 296–301.

194   *Anacreon*: born *c.*570 BC. Greek lyrical poet famous for his love of poetry and for his longevity.

198   *Phœbus or the blue-eyed Maid*: Phoebus is another name for Apollo, the Greek god associated with the sun, and with archery, medicine, prophecy, and, most relevant here, with music and poetry. The rest of the names in this poem are conventional pastoral names. The phrase 'the blue-eyed Maid' refers to Athene, or Minerva, goddess of Wisdom, also associated with arts and crafts.

199   *Lope de Vega and Calderona*: Lope Felix de Vega Carpio (1562–1635), Spanish dramatist and poet. Pedro Calderón de la Barca (1600–81), Spanish dramatist.

203   *Montemayor's Diana*: Jorge de Montemayor (1515–61), Spanish novelist and poet. He wrote an unfinished pastoral romance, *Diana*, which influenced Philip Sidney and Shakespeare. It is evidently not supposed to be the kind of reading material that Leonella is capable of appreciating.

223   (Epigraph) *While in each other's arms . . . curst the coming day*: from Nathaniel Lee's (1653?–92) *Sophonisba; or Hannibal's Overthrow*, I. i. 240–1. Adapted.

224 *the Syren's luxurious Couch*: in Greek mythology a siren was a beast, half-bird, half-woman, who, by her beautiful singing, lured sailors to their doom. Here the word signifies a temptress.

225 *the burying-ground common to us and the Sister-hood of St. Clare*: the fact that the two institutions are separated only by a burial-ground and garden, which they share, seems very unlikely. The close proximity of monks and nuns features in many Gothic novels, though usually this is an allusion to their supposed mutual licentiousness.

234 *Matins*: the first canonical hour, the time for morning prayer.

That Men were fond, He smiled, and wondered how!: adapted from *Measure for Measure*, II. ii. 186–7.

238 *the constitutions of the Spanish Ladies*: notoriously hot and sensual, in the opinions of the more phlegmatic English.

246 *of lonely haunts ... which pale Passion loves!*: from William Strode's *Melancholy*, ll. 12–13: 'Fountains heads, and path-lesse groves, Places which pale Passion loves.' The authorship of this lyric is disputed. Traditionally it has been assigned to John Fletcher since it appears in *The Nice Valour* (III. i), a play by Fletcher and an unknown co-author. Bertram Dobell, however, points out that it first appeared in a book entitled *A Description of the King and Queene of Fayries, their habit, fare, their abode, pompe and state ... London. 1635*, and goes on to make a strong case in favour of Strode's authorship (*The Poetical Works of William Strode* (1907), pp. xxxvii–xxxix)— Howard Anderson, *The Monk* (Oxford: Oxford University Press, 1973).

251 *He fell from heaven*: this hints at an affinity between Ambrosio and Lucifer.

253 *St. Rosolia*: died 1160. Italian anchoress who lived in a cave. Patron saint of Palermo.

256 (Epigraph) *Ah! ... irksome*: Blair, *The Grave*, ll. 11–20.

'Amadis de Gaul' ... 'Damsel Plazer di mi vida': Amadis de Gaula was one of the most famous 'Libros de Caballeria' or 'Romances of Chivalry'. It dates from the mid-fourteenth century. In *The Gothic Quest* (London: Fortune Press, 1938),

Montague Summers notes that 'Lewis had the names from Don Quixote's library, *Don Quixote*, Part I, chapters i and vi. Don Galaor is the brother of Amadis de Gaul. Plazirdemavida is a maid of honour to the Princess Carmesina in *Tirante the White*' (299 n. 49).

267 *natural philosophy*: alchemy.

276 *an Agnus Dei*: Latin: literally 'Lamb of God'. In this instance a round cake of wax blessed by the Pope and stamped with a figure of a lamb as emblematic of Christ.

277 *Myrtle*: evergreen shrub or tree. It has a long connection with physical love. It is supposed to symbolize the eyes, and acts as atonement for the lust of the eyes in Judaic tradition. In Greek medicine, it was sacred to Aphrodite, goddess of love.

281 (Epigraph) *The crickets sing . . . sheets!*: from Shakespeare's *Cymbeline*, II. ii. 11–16.

283 *his Master's Chimœras*: the word is derived from the Greek meaning 'she-goat', but came to mean a mythical monster, with the head of a lion, the body of a goat, and the tail of a snake. In this context it refers to unfounded and fantastic whims.

Proteus: sea-god who was able to assume different shapes.

286 *By Anthropophagi . . . .shoulders*: from Shakespeare's *Othello*, I. iii. 144–5.

was born in Terra Incognita . . . Americans of Silesia: a series of joke references by Theodore. 'Terra Incognita' is Latin for 'unknown land'. Hottentots were natives of the Cape of Good Hope, in South Africa. The name derives from the fact that the Dutch settlers thought that their language comprised mainly of the words 'hot' and 'tot'. Thus, they are used here as a byword for savagery. Silesia is an area of eastern central Europe, part of which now falls in south-west Poland and part in the Czech Republic.

Loretto: Loreto is in the Ancona province of Italy. It has an episcopal see and was a well-known resort for pilgrims.

289 *the Water-King*: Lewis found a version of this poem, 'Der Wassermann', in a collection of poetry by Johann Gottfried

Herder, *Volkslieder* (1778–9). The first two stanzas are Lewis's own; the rest lies somewhere between translation and adaptation. For every two lines of the German, Lewis has spun out four lines of English. The German version does not have the gradual encroaching of the water up the maid's body reminiscent of the folk-song 'In Amsterdam there lived a Maid'.

291 *Blondel*: in 1194 Richard I (the Lionheart) was taken hostage by Henry VI of Austria. A large fine had to paid for his ransom. However, in folk tradition, he was helped to escape by his minstrel, Blondel, who sang under his window, and thus discovered his whereabouts.

292 *St. Genevieve*: *c.* 422–500. Born near Paris, took the veil at 15, and encouraged the defence of the city. She is pictured as a shepherdess holding a candle, which the devil is trying to blow out.

295 *Inquisition*: the Inquisition was established by the Catholic orthodoxy for the detection and punishment of heretics. Suspected heretics were imprisoned. Confession ensured reconciliation with the Church.

305 (Epigraph) *Tell us, ye Dead . . . give the alarum*: from Robert Blair's *The Grave*, ll. 431–7.

311 *her Caro Sposo*: 'dear husband'.

313 *Alonzo the Brave, and fair Imogine*: one of the inspirations for this poem was Bürger's (1747–94) 'Lenore', though the theme of the ghost-lover is found in folk-song more generally, and Bürger declared that he was inspired by the English ballad 'Sweet William'. The theme of the sepulchre turned bower of love, and vice versa, resonates through *The Monk*.

316 (end of poem): Lewis's fourth and fifth editions included the following footnote: 'After this raw-head and bloody-bones history, perhaps it may be agreeable to some readers to peruse the following parody. I must observe, that the lines in Italics, and the original idea of making a Brewer of the Baron, and a Physician of the Knight, are borrowed from another parody which appeared in the newspapers under the title of "Pil-Garlic the Brave and Brown Celestine." '

321 *St. James of Compostella*: see note on St Jago for p. 25.

Cain's punishment: see Genesis 4: 11–13. For killing his brother, Abel, Cain is doomed to be a fugitive and wanderer. His fate has been suggested as one of the sources for the tale of the Wandering Jew.

323 *a little Gallician*: Galicia used to be a kingdom, but is now a province of north-west Spain. The delicious chicken comes from this region.

342 *absolution*: the absolving, or remission, of sins through the Last Sacrament.

343 (Epigraph) *Oh! could I worship ... summer air* : from William Cowper's (1731–1800) *Charity*, ll. 254–9.

347 *St. Lucia*: St Lucy of Syracuse (d. 304) is one of the most famous Western virgin martyrs. When a judge ordered that she be violated in a brothel, she remained immovable; neither, later, could she be burnt. When her eyes were put out, she put them back in again. Finally she was put to death by sword. She is often depicted carrying a sword and palm, with her eyes on a platter, and a gash on her neck.

St. Catherine: Catherine of Alexandria, a virgin martyr who died *c.*307.

355 *venial*: from the Latin word for 'pardon'. Thus a pardonable sin, as opposed to a mortal sin.

377 (Epigraph) *Great Heaven! ... the lessening lands retreat*: from Matthew Prior's (1664–1721) *Solomon*, ll. 525–8, 531–2, 539–44.

379 *lay the sleeping Beauty*: compare *Romeo and Juliet*, v. iii.

399 *Men have died, and worms have eat them; but not for Love!*: misquoted from Shakespeare's *As You Like It*, IV. i. 106–8.

413 *it now reposes in consecrated ground*: though according to Anglican theology Agnes's unbaptized baby could have gone to heaven and been buried in consecrated ground, in Catholic teaching the baby would go to limbo, and could not be buried in consecrated ground.

420 (Epigraph) *He was a fell despightful Fiend ... the Foe* : from James Thomson's (1700–48) *Castle of Indolence*, II. lxxviii. 1–4.

422 *the Grand Inquisitor*: the official who presided at the Inquisition.

423 *Auto da Fé*: Spanish, translates as 'Act of Faith'. In Spain and Portugal, this was the public declaration of judgements passed on heretics, followed by their punishments.

433 *sulphurous fogs had damped to hoarseness*: compare Dryden's *King Arthur; or, The British Worthy*, II. i. The original lines run 'I had a voice in Heav'n, ere Sulph'rous Steams | Had damp'd it to a hoarseness.'

435 *threw the Pen upon the table*: compare Marlowe's *Dr Faustus*, where Faustus stabs himself in the arm to sign his soul away whilst a devil threatens him. Faustus, in his terror, later thinks he sees the words 'homo, fuge', 'flee, man', on his arm.

438 *Sierra Morena*: mountain range in Andalucía. The devil drops Ambrosio in the province that his mother came from.

442 *Myriads of insects were called forth by the warmth*: compare this to a passage in the story 'Die Teufelsbeschwörung' (1791) by Veit Weber, where the villain falls to his death over a cliff. 'His raw-skinned face attracted flies, wasps, and hornets; weakly shaking his head, he could not drive them away; they fastened themselves to him with barbed feet, sucked deeply into his naked flesh, and sated themselves with his blood.' (Trans. Karen Tiedtke.)